Amen Again in 2012

Pelon On the Lam

Antonio Solis Gomez

Cover Illustration by Miguel Molina

Special thanks to Rebecca Olson for editing and design,
and to Arturo Flores for his suggestions on plot.

Printed by CreateSpace, Charleston, SC
Available from Amazon.com and other online stores.

ISBN 978-0-9913548-0-1 (pbk.)

*This book is dedicated
to my wife, Margaret*

CONTENTS

PROLOGUE

It is difficult to imagine Mayans looking forward some five thousand years and foreseeing that 2012 was to be a turning point for humanity, that this date would in fact usher in a new era. It was a phenomenal accomplishment, yet when it came, few people knew what 2012 was and those that purported to know, really didn't know and they fabricated stories that sprang from their fears or from delusions of grandeur or from their need to claim leadership and gain control over those gullible enough to believe them. There was plenty of press though, media folks needing to sensationalize stories regardless of their ignorance on the matter. Well the thing is, they didn't know that they were ignorant and about all they could do was to report on those who purported to know, or write about those who pooh poohed any significance.

And the general population couldn't be blamed for not knowing. After all, it was an unheralded event, one that had no precedent, one that didn't even have good descriptive language attached. Some language did develop but it was not very useful to the uninitiated: a shift in consciousness, a renaissance of love, the ascension, the end of history, the fifth world, the bridge to infinity, the gateway, a paradigm shift, etc. And I was among those who were unaware, who would attach no importance or great or even little significance. It was just not on my personal radar of meaningful events. Although I didn't know it then, this was to change and I was to tumble headlong into a tunnel of events and experiences that at the time seemed not of my own doing.

This story begins — for the most part, because there are some flashbacks to an earlier time — in the year 2008, a tumultuous time in many aspects, perhaps in all aspects, for nothing seemed to be in place for very long. Everything seemed to be in flux, or to be changing, unbecoming, poised for a makeover, or even earmarked for destruction. Most people thought that the world was ending or unraveling and many were aching for the good old days, times when nuclear families were built around mothers and fathers, when corporations were beloved and acknowledged as the foundation of our economy, when the activities of the Government were synonymous with all things patriotic and churches reached deep into the pearly gates of heaven to give us the answers that were needed. Yes, everyone knew that great changes were in the making and most thought that unfortunately more was to come. And they were right; more was to come.

And it was not only the cultural environment that was undergoing change; so was the physical world, and we were experiencing earthquakes, volcanoes, tsunamis, tornadoes, severe and unfamiliar weather and even a shift in the position of the magnetic poles.

This was our world at the time, in 2008, and some of us thought that it was merely an anomaly, while others thought it spelled eventual doom. I was in the camp that attributed no significance to these physical or cultural happenings beyond that of change, for if anything, the intellectual environment of higher education and professional life, of which I was a part, had drilled into our heads that change was inevitable, and the ability to adapt to change characterized the successful person, and that, I thought, was going to be me.

Amen Again

in 2012

Pelon on the Lam

CHAPTER I

I begin my story in 2008 when I was a naïve young man, full of misconceptions about the world and struggling to find a niche where I could expend the creative energies that I knew existed within me. I graduated from the University of Arizona School of Law and passed the bar on my first try. Confident that I could make a difference, which was every young person's aspiration, I became a volunteer in the campaign of Congressman James R. Kelley running for re-election, hoping that once re-elected, he would ask me to join his Washington staff.

Congressman James R. Kelley was in reality a Latino, born and raised in the oldest barrio in Tucson, Barrio Viejo, made famous in a song by the same name, sung by Lalo Guerrero, who also grew up in Barrio Viejo and was lamenting its partial destruction, when much of it was razed under the guise of urban renewal. The Congressman's father had changed his name to Kelley at a time when it was an immense disadvantage to have a Hispanic surname—if one wanted to gain access to a middleclass lifestyle, which he did. But although his change of name pegged him as an Anglo, he remained true to his roots by living in the ancestral home, speaking Spanish and carrying on all of the customs of the Mexican people. Congressman James, or Jimmy as he was known by his friends and relatives, was honest and hardworking and attached to Barrio Viejo and his cultural roots much as was his father, but unlike his dad he preferred to call himself a Chicano.

Congressman Jimmy had amassed a large and loyal base of support from the disenfranchised people of Mexican ancestry and from ordinary middle class Democrats as well, who saw him as a bastion of liberal values and one who was unlikely to succumb to the large moneyed interests because his base of support consisted largely of small donors. And Congressman Jimmy often spoke of this large body of support in his campaign speeches and literature, thereby gaining much credibility among people that were beginning to understand the perils of big money interests in government.

Tucson, where I lived and went to school, was an oasis of liberalism in a desert of conservative and racist behaviors. There was every indication that the state was headed for even more restrictive policies regarding immigrants from Mexico and funding for schools and other social services. But the fact that Obama had drawn such a huge base of support gave all of us hope that the damage done by Bush and his administration might be corrected with the election of the first African American President.

But going into that 2008 election many of us were still smarting over the shameful manner in which the president was re-elected in 2004 and we had a foreboding of what the future might hold, for it was evident to us that a great travesty of our democracy had been perpetrated in the State of Florida and we could not discount the possibility of that happening once again. We knew that most people in 2004 were blinded by complacency and sidetracked by denial of what they were experiencing. They meekly accepted what they were told and made it fit their paradigm of the political process. No one believed that a power grab could occur in the United States—maybe in African nations or countries in Latin America but not in the USA. We thought we were beyond that. We had built a stable society with democratic processes and checks and balances. No other nation had what we had, we thought. Could this take place again in 2008? Most certainly, was the answer we gave.

That's not to say that there weren't plenty of observers and social critics pointing out the injustices that had been perpetrated. There were many of those, most of them self-styled or would-be journalists, publishing on the Internet, hoping that Machiavellian politics would never take place again. The regular media was self-censoring, cowed by the powers that be from publishing the truth. Of course nobody foresaw that those responsible for this blatant hijacking of our democratic principles would eventually create a truly totalitarian infrastructure that even Obama was wont to disassemble, and that would lead to the war on dissidents years hence. It was like a seed that germinated underground for a long time, finally sprouting and seeing the light of day to grow faster and stronger. When it finally happened, it seemed instantaneous but of course it wasn't and looking back I can see the signs that were clearly leading up to it. But the events were isolated and neither I nor anyone else was able to stand back far enough to connect the dots and decipher meaning.

But I'm getting ahead of the story and in 2008 my colleagues and I, along with liberal thinking people across the country, were jubilant that Obama was indeed elected and that our fears lingering from the 2004 election did not come to pass.

CHAPTER II

I was born in Los Angeles but I had moved to Tucson as a young man. Our home was actually in South Tucson, a small one-square-mile incorporated town, smack in the center of Tucson proper, that Chicanos have refused to relinquish to the large metropolis that completely surrounds them. It's a place where one might think that one's in Mexico and not in the USA, where the homes are modest, some even shabby and run down. It's poor by any standards and as is often the case with poor barrios, gang life is an important element. I was a homeboy in Los Angeles until a fight with a rival gang left several with gunshot wounds, and I was incarcerated in a youth camp for delinquent boys. Those events stripped the glamour of gang life and nothing could induce me to return. Now the only thing that might give me away as a homeboy is my nickname, Pelon, still used by old friends. In Spanish it means baldy.

Going from South Tucson to DC in January of 2009 to work for Congressman Jimmy required some major changes for me. It wasn't just that DC was covered in snow at that time of year or that it was much busier than Tucson or that I saw very few brown faces and I really felt like a minority. It was all of that plus having a fulltime job, living in my own place for the first time and not waking up to the smell of tortillas and my grandmother spoiling me. In Tucson, she did everything for me—cook my meals, wash and iron my clothes, change my bedding. She took care of me and now I had to learn to do all that for myself. I was really homesick but I would tuck it all in when I called home.

"Como estas, mijito?" My grandmother would ask how I was and I would answer that I was just fine.

There were a few of us from Tucson, young people I had worked with on the campaign and they became my surrogate family during those first couple of months. Well, with the exception of two of them—Esperanza and Naomi —who were doing everything possible to make my life miserable.

Naomi was really sharp, very articulate and well educated, having attended the prestigious Claremont Colleges in California. She was quite attractive and in any other circumstances I would have eagerly sought her friendship. Perhaps it was my fault that we got off to a bad start as on my first day at the office I had assumed that she was a clerical worker.

"Say girlfriend," I said, "Would you mind photo-copying some of these papers for me?"

"What the hell are you talking about? Copy them yourself." As she walked away from my outstretched hand, I heard her mutter under her breath, *What an asshole.*

"Hey I'm sorry if I said something that was out of place. I just assumed that clerical staff helped out in that way," I said.

The next day when Congressman Jimmy held his weekly staff meeting and everyone was introduced I realized what a big mistake I had made. I looked over at Naomi and threw up my hands in a gesture of *I'm sorry I didn't know*, but she just looked away.

Esperanza was Naomi's sidekick and a wiz with technology, setting up and maintaining all of the congressman's communication systems including telephone and Internet, blog, twitter and website, stuff that was over my head. She was an average-looking young woman, maybe in her early thirties, a smart dresser and when I first saw her I immediately thought of party invitations from the barrio that asked one to 'dress to impress.' Initially I wanted to get to know her, hoping to get a first-hand understanding of new technology.

"Esperanza," I said one day. "When can we hook up for a tutorial on Twitter and telegram?"

"Excuse me!" she said. "What's this about hooking up? You don't ever say hello to me and then all of a sudden you want to hook up? That's messed up dude. And by the way, it's not telegram, it's Instagram, you *tonto*."

"*U yu yui*," I said mockingly, letting her know that I thought she was being smug and rude.

One day, I asked Naomi, who seemed to be the leader of the two, "Hey Naomi, what's up girl, why are you always dissing me?"

"I'm not always dissing you," she said, looking at me with a look of contempt. "I'd have to be constantly thinking of you to always be dissing you and I'm certainly not doing that," she said and walked away.

But she was. At our morning briefings or whenever all of us got together after work, she would deride my comments or suggestions. And if she didn't then Esperanza would. At first I thought that it was just their personalities, people who relate to others by messing with them. But after awhile I noticed that most often they only directed their biting comments at me. I was puzzled because I hardly knew them and they seemed to have an intense dislike for me. I tried thinking of anything that I had done or said that might have brought this on. I couldn't.

The work for the Congressman was really challenging and we all had research assignments so that we could brief him and get him up to speed on the issues. My assignment was to gather information on the environmental and social impact of opening up Federal lands to mining and forestry. A lot of this area was totally new to me and I admit that I was naïve about many things. It's one thing to have some exposure to a topic in the classroom but quite another to dig around for information so that you can recommend to a Congressman how to vote on an issue or how to draft a piece of legislation. I was even a newbie at the political process and probably the youngest person on the Congressman's staff. Many of those on staff had worked for him when he was an Arizona State Senator and I was one of two that was a new hire. I had a lot to learn but I was eager and maybe a bit too enthusiastic. I didn't realize this until I went out with one of the other aides.

Lorraine had been with the Congressman since his first election and she was a few years older than I was, but we had hit it off nicely since my first day. She was a Tohono O'Odham and had grown up in the reservation just south of Tucson. But as with so many bright Native Americans, college had taken her off the reservation, in her case to Phoenix.

"Tell me, Lorraine," I asked. "Would I be out of line if I asked you to go with me to a movie or a concert or even for a walk? I would like to know you better."

She gave me a surprised expression with a half smile. "Are you sure you want to go out with me?" she asked.

"Yeah, I really want to get to know you."

"Okay," she said, still showing surprise.

"Where shall we go?" I asked.

"Any one of those choices is good for me. You choose."

"Well, I tell you what, tomorrow's Friday. Why don't we have dinner someplace after work and then we can decide where else to go."

"Okay," she said, still looking at me as if she was not quite sure what was going on in my head.

Lorraine and I had a great time that night. We had dinner at a Thai place in Georgetown and then we walked around the Mall.

"Do you get back to the reservation often?" I asked.

"When I was in Phoenix I'd go every couple of weeks. I'm very close to my family and this separation has been hard for me," she answered.

"Really. I'd never have known that. You always seem so together and upbeat," I said. "But I can understand because it's been hard for me too."

"No way!" she said. "Everybody thinks you own D.C. The way you strut around, your self-assurance, your over-the-top enthusiasm. You got it all, dude."

Naturally I had to ask her what over-the-top enthusiasm meant.

"Do I come across as overly enthusiastic?"

"Yeah, sort of. Some of the staff thinks you're too wired or implementing some sort of 'winning friends and influencing people' scheme."

"Really?" I was incredulous. "I'm just trying to be positive and outgoing. You know, breaking down the barrio aloofness syndrome."

"Well I have to tell you that the office gossip is that you're trying to be white and the fact that you got the juiciest assignment didn't sit well with the congressional aides that have been around much longer."

"You mean Esperanza and Naomi?"

"Yeah, them."

I was stunned. I guess I had never taken the time to see myself the way other people saw me. The surprise of what Lorraine had told me wore off quickly and I began to feel some resentment. Not at Lorraine though, she was totally honest and without guile. But thinking about my other colleagues pissed me off. I began to understand why Esperanza and Naomi had a burr up their ass. I tried to put those thoughts aside and enjoy myself with Lorraine but in the remaining time with her, my mind kept ruminating over the information she had supplied and I was only partially in the moment. By the time we parted she sensed that something was up with me and we ended the evening on a sour note. I hated the way I had been taken hostage by my feelings and unable to break their hold. I went home and had a fitful night.

The next few days at work I was confused by not knowing how I should act, and somewhat angry because of the secret feelings that my coworkers had about me. After awhile I knew that I was like a person lost in a forest and circling over the same ground. In desperation I asked Lorraine if I could talk to her after work.

We sat in front of the mall and I ran down the thoughts I was having.

"I'm really pissed with the people at the office, Lorraine, especially with Esperanza and Naomi. Why couldn't they just nudge me a little and let me know directly, instead of the end-around backbiting?"

"Maybe they don't know how to confront directly. Or, and maybe this is the real reason, they didn't like you enough to bother. Maybe you haven't made enough effort to develop friendships. Why's that?"

"If I'm honest I have to say that I'm not one to make friends or do stuff for someone just for the hell of it. I'm interested in getting ahead and I'm interested in people that can help me achieve my goals. Short of that, I stay pretty much to myself," I said.

"That sounds pretty damn selfish and if that's the message you are giving to staff, then they are reacting most appropriately," she said.

We talked for hours that evening. She was a great listener and every once in awhile she would ask a probing question or make a comment. In this way I began giving her an account in some detail of my early life and how I had carved out an identity that was separate and alienated from my past. By evening's end I realized that I had become this yuppie fellow in my professional life and inside was someone else entirely. Lorraine didn't seem fazed by my discoveries. She said that she too had felt some of these same tensions and that it was a price that minorities paid when they decided to jump into the Anglo world.

"So how did you handle those tensions and conflicts?" I asked.

"Through the power of medicine," she said laughing, "...my grandfather's medicine. "

"Yeah right," I said. "Hook me up with your grandfather."

"Well you might try the white man's medicine," she said.

"You mean a shrink? No way," I said.

"No just a group," she answered.

The next day I followed up on Lorraine's suggestion that I hook up with a facilitated group where I could discuss these feelings. Using the yellow pages I came across a bunch of names and I resorted to the tried and true methodology of selecting, *"eenie meenie miney mo"* and came up with the name of George Maier. I called him right away.

"Hello Dr. Maier, my name is Macias and I'm calling to see if perhaps I could join one of your group sessions?"

"Hello Mr. Macias. How did you get my name? Were you referred by someone?"

"Not really. I found you in the Yellow Pages."

"My my, the Yellow Pages. Tell me Mr. Macias, why do you think it appropriate to join a group?"

"A friend of mine thought it would be a good idea."

"Why does your friend think it would be a good idea?"

"I guess because I'm going through some identity issues."

"Are those your words or your friend's words?"

"They're mine. I'm feeling a bit confused about how I can integrate the person I grew up being and the person I have become more recently. I'm a Latino, grew up in a barrio but then I went to school and now I'm a lawyer and work for a Congressman."

Once I opened up in this way Dr. Maier and I talked a long while on the telephone, after which he invited me to a session that he thought would be appropriate. The rest of the day I began to feel better than I had all week. I even said something pleasant to Naomi, which left her scowling in bewilderment, probably wondering what I was up to.

I went to my first session at Dr. Maier's Georgetown home, an elegant two story Greek Revival, built in red brick with tall white columns in front supporting a tiny upstairs balcony. I could see that the good doctor was not hurting for money by the dark mahogany tables and chairs, plush leather couches and Persian carpets. He also had an eye for art and under soft light some original oil paintings and sculptured pieces were displayed. I was the first one to arrive and he allowed me to look at my leisure while we waited. Soon others arrived and I was introduced. The last to arrive was a stunningly attractive woman named Helga, who spoke with an accent that I assumed was European. Using clothing and demeanor as an indication of social status, I noted that everyone in the group was well to do and worked in a professional capacity, probably related in some manner to the Washington scene. I felt a twinge of discomfort, looked over my shirt and tie, thought that my shoes were too casual for my attire in the present company and worried about what I would say when the time came. The Doctor started us off by introducing me and asking me to say something about why I was there.

"I told you last week that I was bringing a new person into the fold and I would like you to make him feel welcome. I have asked him to say a few words about himself, as is our custom, and then we can carry on as we usually do. Mr. Macias please give us your first name as that's how we do it here in the group."

16

"Hello everyone, my name is Herculano Macias and I am here because of some confusion that I am having integrating my early life, which was spent in a barrio of East Los Angeles, and my more recent life as a lawyer and a Congressional Aide. I'm not here because of a crisis or anything like that but because someone at work has pointed out something they see in my personality that is not really the way I want to be."

"Go ahead and tell the group what that is specifically, Herculano," Dr. Maier interjected.

"This is kind of embarrassing but they think I'm acting as if I want to be White. What they are really saying is that I want to forget who I really am and that is not my intent at all."

As I spoke I looked around at the group. It was smaller than I had anticipated, just eight of us, and they were attentive, nodding and smiling appropriately. I answered a couple of questions and said a little about my gang life that the group found of great interest.

When I finished and took a seat the doctor asked if anyone was particularly keen on sharing and they looked at each other, not in embarrassment or shyness but more as a way of assessing who needed the time to talk. Helga started talking. She had a great throaty voice that sounded like Marlene Dietrich and I caught myself hearing only the sound and not what she was saying, so I missed the first few sentences.

"...then Andre returned late the other night and I'm sure that I could smell an unfamiliar perfume on him but when I confronted him, he brushed aside my concerns, actually becoming quite belligerent, by saying that he had merely hugged a few women that were at the meeting and not to be acting out my insecurities."

"It seems Helga that we're covering familiar ground here," a man said. "You have had these suspicions for awhile now, yet you merely forget them until the next time."

"That's because his explanations always seem logical and I begin to doubt what I sense and begin thinking that maybe I am acting out of my insecurities," she answered.

"Maybe your insecurities are involved," another person said, "but perhaps not in the way your husband points out but rather in the fact that they prevent you from making a break and being alone?"

"I think George makes a good point Helga. Being alone is not an easy proposition for many of us and it's difficult to let go of a relationship even if it is unhealthy. It can be damn scary." This was said by the woman next to me, whom I later learned was a pediatrician.

I was taken aback by the honesty that was being shown, something that I found both exhilarating and frightening. I wondered if I could be up front in that way, as others chimed in on what Helga had related.

Suddenly I heard Dr. Maier say, "Herculano, one of the group's protocols is to have a new member jump in feet first and share an observation. So please..."

"Gee... I don't feel prepared to comment..."

"Come now Herculano, nobody prepares for these sessions. One merely speaks his or her mind."

"Well I don't have that much experience with women but where I grew up it is all about respect. Somehow, and this relates directly to me and my situation, in immersing myself in the world beyond the barrio I have lost that understanding. I forgot that I need to respect others and not focus just on myself and on my path to success. So I would ask Helga if her husband respects her, if he shows respect in the way he talks with her, in the way he relates physically to her and in the choices that she makes about all sorts of things like her choices in clothing, in her choices in friends, in the way she chooses to spend her time. I think answers to these questions will tell her where she stands."

Over the next few months I began to feel more comfortable with the group process and I began to share in a way that I would have thought impossible. This translated well into my work and one day I decided to dress as I did when I was a teenage gang member in Los Angeles. I slipped on some shades, some baggy pants, cut a few inches below the knees and worn high on my waist, tall socks, white tennis shoes, and a white T shirt. I went early to work and stood by the entrance.

No one recognized me as they filed into the office. Hell no one looked at me, either because I was invisible or they feared me. When I went into the office and started rapping my shit everybody turned and stared open mouthed.

"Orale, Que Onda? I comes to see the boss man, yous knows the jefe, the mero mero, the dude that sits in the big chair in the big office. I hears he's on the up and up and that he's firme, a vato que no se dobla for the heavyweights with feria, who's not a winnie when the going gets tough and someone that gots your back."

"I'm sorry but the Congressman is not here right now. Is there someone else that can help you?" asked one of the clerical staff, a woman that actually ran the office and took charge of everything she could get her hands on.

"Chale, it's only the jefe that I wants to have a man to man platica with. Manana I be here, maybees then he listen to my gripe about the jura messing wit me right in front of my homies, acting all bad like their shit don't smell, like they be better cause they live uptown wit the gringos."

"I am not certain that the Congressman will be here tomorrow. Perhaps you can leave a telephone number where we can reach you and let you know when he can see you?"

"No way Jose," I said and then gradually I eased into my professional speak voice and took off my shades. "Clearly I see that you are merely trying to ease me out of the office with the least possible disruption to your activities and with the least possible inconvenience to all concerned."

"Macias is that you?" someone asked.

Then the staff came over to where I was standing and began firing questions. Someone asked if I was in a guerilla theater group, another thought I was testifying on gangs before some congressional committee. After I explained everyone had a good laugh. All accept you know who, Esperanza and Naomi. If they didn't like me before when I was coming across as Mr. Dale Carnegie incarnated, toothy smile and death grip handshake included, they liked me less as a homeboy and as the genuine homegrown barrio version of Mr. Smith goes to Washington. I didn't give a damn what they thought. By then I was finding comfort in the complete person that I was.

Lorraine thought it was great. "I gotta tell you homeboy, that was outta sight, way way over the top dude. Did you see the expression on some of those faces when you were into the whole barrio bit? Wow. There are no words to describe that scene."

"Were you frightened?"

"Hell no. I was getting ready to punch you if you became violent. I know how to take care of homies like you. I've dealt with them all my life."

"I figured as much. How about we grab lunch later?" I asked.

"I can do it after one. I have meetings all morning," she answered.

"That works for me. See you here at one."

We had gone on several dates by then and we had become supportive of each other in a way that only good friends can be. Twice I had even kissed her goodnight. Those kisses were soft and lingering and the passion they hinted at might have taken us further along but both times we pulled away, neither one of us was sure what we wanted and so it became nothing more than a friendship and I didn't kiss her any more. We did continue dating or more like what young people think of as 'hooking up'. On one of those hook ups she told me to meet her at the Library of Congress to hear a lecture.

"Aw Lorraine, I don't want to hear some boring bookworm," I complained.

"He won't be boring I promise. Besides it's really important that I hear what he has to say. He seems to be confirming something my grandfather has been telling me for some time."

"And what's that?" I asked.

"You'll see. And don't be late."

That evening we met at the appointed time.

"Let's take a seat near the aisle so I can exit if the speaker is putting me to sleep," I told her.

"Don't be so negative. You're about to expand your world view."

"Yeah right," I said

The speaker was a climatologist and I must admit that he was pretty entertaining, constantly pacing in front of the audience, constantly pulling at his necktie, talking in a quick almost confronting manner, as if someone was about to stand up and dispute what he was saying. He placed in front of us chart after chart with climatological data, with solar activity statistics and with simulations of what the U.S. might look like with most of the Great Lakes and the Eastern Seaboard covered in ice.

"The most important factor to take into consideration when looking at Earth's climate, in the past or now and into the future, is the amount of solar energy that we receive from the sun. All other factors are negligible and even insignificant in comparison," he said.

"Does this mean that all those scientists throughout the world, in the most prestigious Universities or working at government scientific agencies are wrong when they speak about global warming?" someone asked.

"Yes that is exactly what this means and there are many reputations at stake and fear when someone, such as I, dispute their faulty premises and baseless conclusions. Look, it's not the first time that the established scientific community has gotten it wrong. Of course everyone knows about Galileo but even more recently and closer to home is the work of the Cuban doctor Carlos Finlay, who for years was telling everyone that mosquitoes were the culprit in causing yellow fever. This seemed preposterous to the established scientific community where germ theory was the prevailing answer to every disease. It took years and thousands of deaths before anyone looked seriously at mosquitoes."

"Still the evidence for global warming seems overwhelming," someone said.

"It seems overwhelming only when one has a preconceived notion, that notion being that burning fossil fuels is wrong and damaging to the environment. I don't like the burning of fossil fuels either and I think that there is a degradation of the environment to do so, but I don't have to jump to the conclusion that it is permanently altering the planet's weather."

And he did indeed expand my worldview but not in the way Lorraine had expected.

"Well what did you think?" she asked on our walk back to the office, where we had left our car.

"What else can I think but that some corporate sponsor is paying him big bucks to make up some loony evidence that refutes global warming," I said. "These fossil fuel proponents will go to hell and back because their bottom line is threatened. We're entering a mini ice age in 2014—really!! Come on Lorraine. It's a crazy idea."

"You mean to say that you're discounting the evidence he presented about the decrease in sun activity as being the real factor in earth's climate."

"Yes I am and I'm also saying that the continued burning of fossil fuels at the present rate is the greatest threat to life on this planet."

"My grandfather has been saying for the last two years that we will have very cold weather because father sun is about to enter a period of rest."

"And has your grandfather always been right in what he says?"

"I've never known him to be wrong," she said.

One thing I had learned about Lorraine is that not only did she straddle two worlds, the Anglo world and her own Tohono O'Odham, but that when there was a choice to be made, she always chose her Native American culture. I didn't want to press the issue of climate change with her, as I knew trying to debate with her was a wasted effort.

"I guess we'll just have to see who's right," I said.

"Yes we will."

"Is your grandfather a prophet?"

"More of a keeper of our tribe's knowledge and at times a medicine man and a seer. He's wise too and gentle as a soft winter rain."

"He sounds like a very special person. Maybe I can meet him someday."

"Yes maybe you will."

That was our last hook up, supposedly because we were both extremely busy working late hours and sometimes even on weekends. My research on opening up Federal lands was exciting and full of unanticipated surprises. I rewrote my report several times before turning it in and Naomi was pissier than usual the day the Congressman congratulated me on a job well done. I was feeling great and maybe overly cocky because I went over to her desk and tried to wrangle a truce.

"Come on Naomi give me a break. I didn't choose this assignment. It was given to me."

"Fuck off," she said, not looking up from her work.

For the first time I saw something vulnerable in her. Beneath that iron will that had forged an impenetrable fortress of discipline was a woman not entirely sure of herself, a woman looking for something she couldn't find. I left her there. A few months earlier I couldn't have even approached her. I attributed my newly found courage to the interactions I was having in the group therapy, where confrontations were the basis of growth.

I had been both right and wrong in my initial assessment of the group. Yes I was right that they were all well off. But no they weren't all connected to politics. There were two lawyers, an executive at some large charity who was an asshole, Helga who was filthy rich because of an inheritance, a consultant to the Republican party that, surprisingly, I really liked. His name was Robert. And we had a pediatrician, and a lobbyist for a major construction firm. Besides Helga there were two other women, the pediatrician and one of the lawyers. I often wondered why Dr. Maier allowed me to join the group. I was the most junior and the one with the least wealth. At first I suspected that he wanted a token minority person but later with experience I knew that race hardly ever entered the mix directly. I guess he thought the group would profit from my perspective but this I never found out for sure. Much later, long after I had left the group, when Robert and Helga were close friends, I began to see that sometimes unseen forces are at work. Call it destiny or fate or even the work of Guardian Angels that led me there. But then I wasn't thinking of that and I was just enjoying the experience.

Dr. Maier dedicated an entire session to a biographical piece that I had written as a 17 year old. I had shared it with him and he felt it was important to share it with the entire group. Although I was nervous about revealing myself I went ahead and read.

* * *

It's easy to get off to a wrong start in life. It happened to me. But I'm not blaming anyone but myself. I'm a lot of things but I'm not a whiner and I like to face up to my responsibilities. I wasn't always that clear about what it was that was my own doing, like when my stepfather threw me out of the house and for a long time I felt that he was the reason I got into so much trouble. I was only fifteen at the time and in a way you can't blame me entirely for thinking that way. But I probably stayed with that excuse longer than I should have.

Those first few days when I was on my own I was pretty miserable. I fought constantly with myself as if I were two different people. One part of me wanted to go back home with my tail between my legs but another part of me was angry and that part finally won out and kept me on the streets for the next two years. Being homeless wasn't the easiest thing I have ever done, but it wasn't the hardest either. There are a lot of people who live in the streets. They eat from the fast food dumpsters, steal clothes from the Goodwill bins, sleep under bridges or in unlocked cars, wash up in public restrooms. Learning those tricks just took common sense. What took me longer to learn was who I could trust. There are a lot of sicko people on the streets who would like to rape you or cut you with their blade just for the heck of it. And then there are some who think they can be tall only if they can cut off your head. I had to learn to stay away from those types of people and to develop antennas to help me identify people with a good heart.

On my second week on the streets, still pretty green as they say, I thought I met a goodhearted person but really he was just a clever person pretending to be nice. I had found what I thought was the perfect sleeping place, a dumpster outside of a print shop, filled only with paper and cardboard. It was pretty clean trash. Once in awhile some ink would rub off on me but generally it was just like sleeping at home. One day as I was getting out of the dumpster and trying to hurry because I had been holding my piss for hours it seemed, I felt someone's hand giving my foot a little support. I turned and saw this young guy wearing a faded army field jacket, the kind you see Viet Nam veterans wear, and I say hey thanks. No problem he says and he turned and walked away. My bladder was near the bursting point, so I got off to the side of the dumpster and began to relieve myself. You know what a great feeling that is after holding it for so long. You just let it flow out and you stare up at the sky giving thanks that your bladder is emptying, thinking that nothing short of a bomb explosion could make you stop pissing. Well that's what I thought too until I finally noticed that the guy in the jacket had returned and was kneeling besides me, staring at my dick. Hey what the hell I yelled out in shocked surprise and he reached over and touched me before I could put it away. I admit that I have a hot temper and it didn't take me long to react to that pervert, pushing him forward as I backed away so that his head landed in *my pool of piss. I ran the hell out of there and I never slept in that dumpster again.*

That incident made me realize that I needed to partner up with someone or else one day I was going to get into a situation where I could get hurt. So I began to look around for someone that I could hang out with, someone that could watch my back and I his. That's how I met Rebecca. I wasn't looking for a girl, especially a girl like Rebecca, but sometimes it seems that life has a plan and you just have to go along with it. I only met her because the day the pervert was checking me out, was the day a pretty large storm came in and dumped the most rain the city had seen in a long time. It rained the entire afternoon and looked like it was going to rain the whole night. I started to worry about where I was going to find a dry place to sleep. Ordinarily after waking up I would look for some food in a dumpster or steal something at the supermarket and then I would just hang out the rest of the day at the skateboard park or go downtown and hang out at the stores. A few times I even went to the library and just read for a few hours. I had never really taken the time to read and I surprised myself because I actually enjoyed it. But as I was saying, that day was different in that I needed to find a place to crash when it got dark. One thing I had already learned was that you don't want to be out all night if you are underage because the cops will haul you away. So I walked around trying, to find maybe an abandoned house or building or even a doorway that would be protected from the rain. Even though it was a light rain I was getting good and soaked. I had cut a hole on a large plastic bag and slipped it over my head so that it covered my jacket, but my pants and my shoes were sponging up the rain and every step I took made a squishy sound. I was walking with my head down and when I reached the corner I didn't see that someone was crossing in front of me, someone also walking with their head down, and we crashed into each other.

After we recovered from the initial impact we looked at each other and I think we both smiled and then laughed when she said I see we both shop at the same clothing store, referring to the fact that she also had one of those plastic trash bags around her upper body. We stood on that corner kind of staring at each other, I guess both of us wanted to say something and really it was my turn but I was never very good at conversation with girls so I just stood there like an idiot until I became aware that we were blocking the way for people as they jumped the large puddle that had formed on the street near the curb. Well maybe I should say that I heard a woman call me a menso, *when she almost fell as she bumped into me, and that's when I became aware of where we were standing.*

I should stop here and tell you a little bit about where this is taking place so that you can picture it in your mind. Of course you already know that this is in the United States. That you probably guessed. What you couldn't have guessed is that this is taking place in LA. But LA is a huge place and so I should tell you that I was on the streets of Boyle Heights, a small community not far from downtown, and in the heart of East Los Angeles. At one time Boyle Heights was home to a lot of Jewish families and one can still find a few places that make this very clear, like the Jewish Retirement Home on 4th Avenue, or the Synagogue in what used to be Brooklyn Avenue but now has been

28

renamed Cesar Chavez Blvd. Some of the Jewish community in Los Angeles were upset when it was proposed that Brooklyn Avenue be renamed, this even though they no longer lived in the area and 95% of the population was Hispanic. I guess all people find change hard to accept.

Now you know a lot more than you first did, especially that I live in a Hispanic neighborhood and probably you can guess that I too am Hispanic and that I speak Spanish as do most of the people who live here. In fact some people live all their life speaking only Spanish as did my great grandmother. She died when she was ninety-eight, and lived and worked in Los Angeles most of her life and never learned English. I don't say that it's good or bad that she and thousands of others never learn English but as I said before, people don't like change and in East Los Angeles where Spanish is the spoken language there is no urgency to learn English. Like my great grandmother and the rest of my family, Spanish was my first language and I learned English at school and by watching television. Although you couldn't know that by reading this, if you were hearing me speak you would know immediately that English was my second language because of my heavy accent. This accent used to bother me a lot, especially when I would mispronounce a word, like at school when I wanted to say a sheet of paper and I would say a shit of paper and the class would burst out laughing. I guess it's funny but it wasn't funny to me because I wanted to be just a regular American and to blend in with everyone else. The other thing that bothered me was my nickname, Pelon, which means 'baldy.' My mother told me that I was called Pelon because when I was born I had very little hair. Mexican babies usually have a ton of hair, just like my brothers and sisters but I was unfortunately bald. By the time I started school I had hair like everyone else but the name followed me. Truthfully I could have insisted that people call me by my real name but that was even worse than Pelon. It was Herculano, which is Hercules.

I don't know why Hispanic people pick such weird and strange names. In my case it was my grandmother who suggested the name to my mother, or rather she demanded my mother name me Herculano. You see my mother had me out of wedlock and this was way too much for my grandmother to understand, she being a widow who lost her husband when she was still a young woman, but would never allow herself the thought of being with another man. Marriage was a big deal to her and my mother bearing a child and not having a husband really flipped her. So my mother gave in and named me Herculano, which was my grandmother's father's name. So I was stuck with Pelon and even the teachers agreed to call me that when they learned my real name.

When I bumped into Rebecca, I thought about introducing myself, but not wanting to say that my name was Pelon and certainly not wanting her to know that my name was Herculano, I was unable to say anything. Until the woman who jumped the puddle called me menso, which means stupid. Then I was suddenly released from my paralysis and I told Rebecca that maybe we should move and we started to walk the way she had been headed before our encounter. She asked me where I was going and I told her that I was just looking for a place to get out of the rain. She said that she was going to the boat house at *the park for the same reason and she invited me to go with her. I stopped dead in my tracks when she mentioned the boathouse.*

There's something that I should have mentioned earlier when I was telling you about the area where this story takes place. Boyle Heights and just about any place in East Los Angeles was carved out by different gangs. Each gang through tradition of living in an area or through conquest has made certain places their turf. The boathouse happened to belong to Segunda, a gang formed by immigrant teens to protect themselves against other gangs in the area. At first they were nobodies, just a bunch of boys fighting for survival. But over the years they grew in size and in determination until they became one of the most feared. Rebecca asked me why I was stopping and I told her that I didn't want to get my ass kicked by Segunda. Oh don't be silly she said. I belong to Segunda and nobody's going to hurt you. I wasn't entirely convinced but I had always daydreamed about having some chance meeting with a girl that would force me past my shyness because as I told you before, talking with girls wasn't my strong point. I decided that perhaps this was life answering my daydream and I said okay, I'll go with you. That's when Rebecca told me her name and I told her that my name was Pelon. Only much later would I reveal my real name to her.

The redbrick boathouse with its arched portico providing a panoramic view of the park's lake, a narrow twisting lake spanned by a green footbridge, was closed during weekdays and it was taken over by Segunda as their semiofficial headquarters. Several tough-looking young men were sitting on the ledge of the portico rubbing pennies on the cement and they stared at me as I walked in with Rebecca. Rebecca led me by the hand past them and towards the front of the portico where some others were gathered, including a few girls. Why are they rubbing those pennies? I asked Rebecca in a whisper. She told me that they were making them into the size of dimes and later they would use them in the vending machines. Wow, I thought, what a waste of time. I didn't know that one day I would be doing the same thing just to pass the time when I got bored.

Rebecca's homegirls greeted her in Spanish and they asked her who I was, as if I was not there, saying things like 'esta muy chulo, tiene buenas nalgas,' commenting on my good looks and nice buns. One of the girls even came over to me and rubbed my wet hair seductively when Rebecca introduced me as Pelon. Finally Rebecca told the girls to cut it out and leave us alone and she led me off to the side where we could be alone. Out of the corner of my eye I had seen that the homeboys were glaring at me during the entire time.

Another thing I noticed was that Rebecca had a lot of respect and as soon as she told her friends to stop teasing there were no further comments. I was a little in awe of just being there anyway, and having Rebecca sitting next to me gave me quite a high. Still I was a bit uneasy, maybe even scared by the whole scene. It was like the feeling I get when coming down the steep part of a roller coaster, thrilling because it was frightening. Rebecca was nice though. She sensed that I was not completely comfortable and she tried to put me at ease by telling me about her friends. 'That's Loli,' she said pointing out one of the girls. 'Last year she got pregnant by her boyfriend but she lost the baby *and now every time she gets high she cries like the* llorona.'

For those of you who don't know, the llorona *is the Mexican mother who killed her children and cries at night for them. At least that's the story I was told. There were four girls there and Rebecca talked about each one, giving me little details that helped me remember them. She didn't talk about the boys and I asked her to tell me about them. Before Rebecca could reply one of the homeboys swaggered over and stood right in front of me and asked Rebecca why she had brought me. He referred to me as an asshole, a* culero *in Spanish and I thought for sure that I would soon be fighting for my life. In that instant I regretted having come. The other homeboys kept their seats but were watching intently. Now as I told you before I have a temper but seeing Rebecca go off on that dude, I saw that I was a pussycat compared to her. I won't repeat everything that she said, some of it was even too much for me. It's not that I don't cuss but she was a damn champion, stringing words together that sounded like a heavy rain on a metal roof. What she told him was that she answered to no one and that just as she doesn't ask who he brings around neither should he. She was in fact speaking for all of the homegirls and it was then that I understood why her girl homies gave her respect.*

As thankful as I was to Rebecca she had also complicated my life and maybe put me in danger. The homeboy that she had embarrassed was now angry as hell and he would be out for my ass. I wouldn't ever be safe in Boyle Heights. Also I couldn't very well hide behind a homegirl. In the barrio this is a big no no. So either way my ass was cooked and I knew that my only play was to stand up for myself right then and there. As I look back in my life I can see that some decisions that I made in my life brought me a lot of changes but I didn't know that at the time I made the decision, like when I left my house. This decision was different because I knew that my life was about to change forever. I was really scared. My legs were shaking like I was doing an Elvis impression and my throat was so dry that I thought I was not going to be able to speak. Somehow the words came out and I said 'Orale si quieres pedo aqui estoy.' It was a challenge. The kind of challenge that I think men have used since men first walked this earth. "Hey, you want a piece of me?" As soon as I spoke everyone's eyes were riveted on me and then on him when he said 'Vamos,' let's go.

Because I was with Rebecca the upcoming fight would be guided by the rules that apply to fights that take place between homeboys. Otherwise all of them would have jumped me and beat me to a bloody pulp as might have happened if I had not challenged and later they caught me on the street. At least this way it would be one on one and I would have a chance to defend myself.

The homeboy I was to fight was called Puma. He was big boned and muscular and one could see that he still had plenty of growing to do. He was about the same age as I was but he outweighed me by thirty pounds. I was given the chance to decide if we would use knives, sticks or fists. His hands were huge like the hands of a heavyweight prizefighter. With one punch he might crack my head open, I thought. And I had no experience with blades and didn't want to risk getting stabbed. I chose sticks, stout, like the ones Robin

Hood and Little John used for their fight on the log crossing the stream. I used to play with such sticks with some of the neighborhood boys and therefore I had some experience.

We would fight out on the grass and as I was leaving the portico Rebecca gave me a weak smile and said a soft good luck. The sky was still a dark gray and a light drizzle was making patterns on the puddles as our band walked onto the grass and formed a circle around us. The ground was thoroughly soaked and I realized that a slip on the wet grass would be a fatal error. Puma and I begin circling each other, giving each other's stick a light tap, trying to see a weakness, an opening where we could strike. Suddenly with a swiftness that took me by surprise, Puma struck hard towards my left leg, a blow that I partially deflected but which nevertheless reached its target and send a sharp pain all along the lower left side of my body. All the anxiety and fear that I had been feeling left me and pure adrenaline seemed to be flowing through my veins, energizing my emotions.

Puma spoke to me for the first time, telling me that he hoped I had enjoyed that blow because he was going to give me some more in a minute. He was cocky now, fortified by the shouts of encouragement that the homeboys gave him. I kept quiet and continued to circle. He struck again, this time toward my head. But I was ready and I ducked his blow and stepped into a batter's stance, delivering a blow to his ribs. The power of the blow was evident immediately, a dull heavy thud followed by him sprawling backwards unto the ground. I was on top of him ready to strike again when he raised his hand and said 'hay muere' literally it dies here but meaning it's over.

We extended hands and I helped him to his feet. Luckily his jacket had absorbed some of the blow and his ribs were bruised but not broken. The initial disappointment that the homeboys felt when their hero was struck down was soon forgotten and I was welcomed back to the portico. Rebecca was smiling when I returned to her side. "You did good," she said. "Thanks," I answered.

The night of the fight Rebecca stayed with me. We slept on the cement floor of the portico on a bed of cardboard. We didn't make love, or anything even close to it. Mostly we talked, telling each other things about ourselves, about our families, about what we thought about school and about our friends. It was hard for me to fall asleep. I was excited about Rebecca and about being there with members of Segunda. Later I found out that only a couple of the members were homeless. The rest were like Rebecca. They had families of one sort or another. Some had loving parents who worried about their lifestyle and the friends they kept. They worried about their school attendance and didn't know that they missed school as often as they did. Others lived with parents or with relatives who didn't concern themselves too much about them, allowing them to come and go as they pleased. Rebecca was in the last group. She lived with an aunt who took her in when Rebecca's mother died. But she had her own kids and a demanding husband who wasn't thrilled about having to support another person. As Rebecca grew older she stayed home less and less. Sometimes she slept at the home of one of the other homegirls. Sometimes, like that night she stayed with me, she slept at the boathouse with some of the gang members.

I have to admit that I wasn't entirely sure that I wanted to become involved with her. It scared me that she could be carried away by such anger, blinding her to everything around her. I wondered if she could get angry like that with me and try to hurt me somehow. On the other hand she could be very gentle and sweet and that part of her was very attractive.

The next day and for weeks after that, I hung out with Rebecca and with members of Segunda. I got to know each of them better than I had ever known anyone else, better than I knew my own family. Several of them formed the core group and others just came by every so often. Naturally the homeless ones like myself were always around. At first my day was spent just horsing around with them, doing some of the things that I had done by myself except now I always had 3 or more friends with me. Rebecca was attending school and I didn't see her until the afternoon and then she and I would hang out. If she were going to school the next day, in the evening she would go home or stay with one of the girls. One day she said that I should go back to school and I got a weird feeling all over my body and the hair on my arms and in the back of my neck stood up. You can't understand my reaction unless you know that dropping out of school was what got me thrown out of my house. My stepfather had given me a choice, school or the streets. I hated school so much that it wasn't much of a choice. I couldn't look at Rebecca after her comment about school and I just shook my head and said no way. You already know that Rebecca is no pushover and she wasn't about to give up on the idea of school. She didn't say anything right away though. She just let it slide for the time being. A few days later she had one of her schoolbooks and she was trying to do some homework. At first I was just sitting next to her while she worked but then she started to get agitated and I moved away to give her some space. A little later I heard her cursing and she sent the book flying across the boathouse.

"You know anything about math?" she asked me.

I answered that I knew some and before I knew what was happening there I was doing math problems with her. I can't pretend that it wasn't fun though because it was. Only later did I realize that she had conned me into it. Hell she knew more math than I ever will. But that became our special thing, doing math problems and eventually reading her school assignments.

I know that I probably should say why I disliked school. Actually I've been avoiding it because it's an embarrassment. The thing is there are really two reasons. One of them I have already mentioned but I did it in such a way that you wouldn't think that it was such a big deal. But it is. Ever since elementary school I have dreaded whenever I had to read in front of the class because of my heavy accent. It got so bad that one day I even peed in my pants. Lucky for me most of those early classmates eventually went on to different schools and those who stayed with me just forgot about my accident. But things only got worse as I moved up into the higher grades because now I had to give reports, comment on current events and participate in class discussions. I could hear my classmates snicker under their breath whenever I got up. I had a lot of fights over that, but you can't fight the whole world and so I began to miss classes and began to fall behind.

The second reason is even more embarrassing but I suppose I should mention it because it's part of the story. The thing is when I started going to middle school and having to take gang showers I saw that my wiener was way thicker than the ones of the other kids. Kids started to look at me and point me out to their friends. I was like a freak show to them and they started calling me all sorts of weird things. Hell I stopped taking showers altogether and I failed P.E. By the time I started high school however, I figured that I would be no different than the rest of the guys so I signed up for football and hoped that I was right in thinking I was going to be just a regular guy. After that first practice I began to undress and in order to reassure myself I checked out a couple of the guys. Someone saw me looking at his cock and that was the end of that. They thought I was a homosexual and began teasing the hell out of me and I quit football and stopped going to classes. And that's why I hated school and why I was not going back, not even for Rebecca. And she didn't push me either or ask me why I had quit. And I certainly wasn't going to volunteer that information. So that's the way it stayed and in many ways it was the ideal situation. The only thing that would have made it better would have been if I could have gotten a job but that required a work permit which I couldn't get until I was sixteen and that would not be until the following year in March.

During those first weeks I was naïve about a couple of things. One of them was that hanging out with the Segunda homeboys was a free ride. That changed one Friday night when some of the homeboys from Aliso saw me and some of my new Segunda friends at a party in the Housing Project, which the Aliso boys controlled. They came at us with chains and baseball bats and we tried to defend ourselves but there were too many of them and they gave us a good beating before the cops arrived and everyone raced off into the darkness. Most of us were just severely bruised but a couple had knife wounds and we had to take them to the LA General Hospital. I realized that evening that even if I was not an official Segunda member, everyone else thought I was just because I hung out with them. They had asked me to join several times during the previous weeks but I had resisted the idea. After our beating I was asked to help them retaliate against Aliso or else to take a hike. It was a code that even Rebecca supported. Again I felt that I really didn't have a choice. If I were to leave, the guys from Aliso would continue to think that I belonged to Segunda and they would attack me wherever they found me. And I would be alone and defenseless. So I went back with Segunda to the housing project the next day and beat up a few of the homeboys from Aliso. This state of war was the nature of a gang member's life and there were times, such as when guns were used, that it became a matter of life and death.

My other blind spot was about drugs. The streets of the barrio were like a giant swap meet for drugs. You could get just about anything you wanted in a matter of minutes. Heroin, cocaine, weed, uppers and downers or the newer drugs like ecstasy. The younger members of Segunda that I was running with didn't usually have the cash for that kind of a high. We were more traditional and we got high on wine and beer and hard liquor when it was available. I had never actually gotten drunk before I met them but I had tasted beer, a taste that I didn't really like. But I got

40

used to it and especially on weekends we would all drink, even Rebecca would drink. Or maybe I should say especially Rebecca because she liked getting drunk. She was a quiet drunk and would usually go off by herself and want to be alone.

The other means of getting high was to sniff paint, which was cheap and available at any hardware store. Not all of the homeboys sniffed, but some did and I was not prepared for the weirdness. The first time I saw somebody high on it, I couldn't figure out why his face and hands were full of gold paint. And why he was acting so strange. At one point we had to restrain him because he wanted to run onto the Golden State Freeway that passed nearby. Afterwards, when he had come down from his high, I asked him about it and he said that it took him far away, far from Boyle Heights to a world filled with pretty lights and colors. He looked awful though. He was dirty from having rolled around on the ground and he was smeared with paint from head to foot. His body parts he could wash but there was no way to take off the paint that he had gotten on his clothing and shoes.

The other aspect of drugs was the involvement of the older Segunda members in the sale of drugs. Segunda had been around about thirty years, and some of the original members were still around. The older members were called veteranos and quite a few of them had served time in the joint and had become involved with the Chicano prison gang system. One day one of these hardcore guys showed up at the boathouse when Puma and someone named Lechero and I were the only ones around. Puma and Lechero knew him and introduced us. He was called Indio and later I found out that he was sort of the big enchilada *around there. I could see why. He was a big menacing looking dude, with muscles made big from pumping iron and a large scar along the side of his mouth that made him look like he was always sneering. As he talked to Puma and Lechero, I was having a hard time not staring at him and I knew that he would give me hell if he caught me doing it. Still he had so many unusual tattoos that I couldn't help myself. He had two lines on each side of his nose that looked like war paint and on his forehead some sort of Indian symbol, like a shield with feathers. On each side of his neck, running from his ear down to his shoulder was a large spear with a feather and around the back of his neck the word Segunda in large fancy letters. I was studying the face of a woman on his forearm when he said "Y tu cabron crees que soy show?" saying to me and you fucker do you think I'm some sort of show?*

Well the thing is that although I was almost ready to piss in my pants like I did when I was a little boy, I remembered a conversation with Rebecca after the fight with Puma, when she told me that I had done right in confronting him and not showing fear. Fear among homeboys, she had said, was like blood in the water for a shark and if you showed fear or any weakness, you were as good as dead. So instead of offering a weak apology I answered him in Spanish and said something like 'you ought to be in the movies dude.' I think he was surprised by what I said and maybe he took it as a compliment because he just turned away from me and continued talking to the others. He had just returned from the joint and he started coming around almost everyday along with some of the other veteranos. Truthfully I was not very at ease when these older homeboys were around. They gave off a whole different feel, like they had a lot of anger and a short fuse. Unlike the rest of us who laughed and joked most of the day these guys were often serious or high on heroin. They customarily stayed off in the corner by themselves and did their thing. I had seen Indio looking towards me and Rebecca a few times and although he was old enough to be her father I thought that he was checking her out.

Lechero, who had become one of my best friends and someone I could trust, told me what I had suspected, that Indio was interested in Rebecca and had already asked her to share some heroin with him. She had said no but when Rebecca didn't tell me about Indio, I began to feel jealous and angry. Finally I asked her about the incident and she said that it was nothing to her but the nice easy relationship that we had, began to unravel from then on. I was feeling really frustrated because I could see that Indio was not the type of person to easily give up on something that he wanted and knowing that Rebecca liked nothing better than to get high, it seemed that he would eventually get her to fix. And that's what happened.

It was the night of Halloween and some of us had gotten dressed as punk rockers and gone to get candy in the neighborhood. Rebecca was already drinking and didn't want to go with us. I had never been able to figure out what it was with Rebecca and the drinking. Whatever it was, it was her deep secret and nothing she ever wanted to share with me. She was already off in the corner when we left and although we were out only a couple of hours, she was gone when we returned with our bags full of candy. A couple of her home girls, who had stayed with her, reluctantly confirmed what I already suspected and I felt a deep sadness mixed with loneliness.

Lechero tried to cheer me up. He was dressed in his familiar fingertip length Air Force dress jacket that he had found, refusing to change his way of dressing even for Halloween. He was a natural clown and especially funny when he was talking about girls and sex, a topic about which he obsessed, masturbating frequently when he thought others weren't looking. The others kidded him because he was still a virgin but he never let them tear down his confidence that one day some girl would find him attractive. Everyone assumed that Rebecca and I were making it but the thing was that Rebecca would never let me touch her. One time I did and she went off on me and for days after wouldn't talk to me. So I was also a virgin but I wasn't about to let Lechero or the guys from Segunda know that.

There was no cheering me up though as the thought of Rebecca being high with Indio was the deepest sadness I had ever experienced. Lechero finally gave up and joined the others who were looking at their Halloween loot. I thought about going home that night. It was the first time since that first week that I had thoughts of returning home. I had passed by the house late at night a few times, just to check things out. But Rebecca and the others had given me a sense of belonging and I had gone just out of curiosity. Tonight if I had passed by the house I would have gone in. Instead I stayed under the portico deep in thought until I fell asleep.

For a few days nobody saw or heard anything about Rebecca. I was keeping to myself most of the time, trying to figure out what I could do in such a situation. Everyone respected my need to be alone and *only when news of Rebecca began to be received did they interrupt my thoughts. We learned that Indio was keeping her strung out all the time, never giving her time to clear her mind. They were moving around a lot but often ending up at an abandoned private school on Fourth Avenue. The boarded up school had a full time caretaker but Indio and his friends had either paid him off or had threatened to harm him, unless he gave them use of some of the rooms. Two weeks later Rebecca showed up with Indio.*

She was looking much older than when I last saw her. It was obvious from her manner that she was high. Indio was trying to sell the homies some weed, telling them that they were getting a deal because he needed some cash. Indio knew that the homies didn't have any money and so I knew that he had just come to show off Rebecca. He held her by the waist and occasionally looked over my way, his mouth sneering even more than usual with a look of satisfaction. Rebecca made no attempt to look at me. She did go off to the side with her girlfriends for a bit but Indio went and got her and then they left.

I didn't know what to think. Seeing Rebecca that way made me feel that she had changed forever, that her real self died somewhere that Halloween night. I was thinking that when I saw Pee Wee, one of the homegirls, approach me and secretly hand me a paper that had been folded so that it was no bigger than a small coin. She made some comment about how sorry she was, placed her hand on my shoulder and then walked away. I waited awhile with that little bundle held tightly in my sweaty hand before I walked to the men's restroom, where I could be alone. Seated inside a stall I saw that on the front of the paper Pelon was written on it in tiny writing. I carefully unfolded it. In Rebecca's handwriting it said, "Dear Pelon, forgive me for what has happened. I wasn't thinking when I went off with Indio that night. I thought that it would be fun to get so high that I could forget my problems completely. I didn't realize the consequences. Indio has me so addicted to the Heroin that now I'm asking him for it. I don't know if I'll ever have a chance to get this to you but I'm writing it while I still have some sense of shame and a memory of the good times we shared. Love Rebecca."

I could have stayed in that stall the rest of the day. It felt good to be in a small confined space. Inside I was a mix of emotions, but mostly it was anger. I was thinking about ways of killing Indio when I was awakened from this daydream by yelling and the sound of gunshots, coming from the direction of the lake. I ran outside and saw that the Aliso homeboys were raiding the boathouse. Without stopping to think I ran full speed at the first Aliso homeboy that I saw and ran into him like a football player, hitting him hard and sending him to the ground. He was the shooter and he dropped his gun with the force of my body. I picked up his gun and began shooting at the Aliso boys who panicked and began to run off. I saw two of them go down. The shooter was still sprawled on the ground and when he saw me with the gun he pleaded with me not to shoot him. And then, as I was telling him that I wasn't going to shoot his ass, an undercover narcotics policeman was behind me telling me to put the gun down.

I did as I was told and the policeman got me on the ground and cuffed me. It didn't take long before other policemen swarmed the park and ambulances came

46

for the victims. Luckily the two I shot had minor wounds. The Aliso shooter had managed to shoot three of the Segunda homeboys, the most serious of which was a boy nicknamed Gordo, who had been shot in the shoulder and required long term therapy. The other two had wounds that required hospital stay but were not life threatening.

At my trial my lawyer was able to prove that I was acting in self defense and I was only given two years in a youth camp. Naturally among my Segunda friends I was a hero and some of them came to court to see me and to personally thank me for saving their butts. But I didn't pay much attention to what they said. Something had changed me as I had sat around at Juvi waiting for my trial. I knew then that I would not be returning to the boathouse. And it wasn't because both my mother and my stepfather had come and asked me to return home. No, something else had gone from me and that thought began to grow and to get defined at the camp.

Some of that was started by Rebecca when she encouraged me to help with her homework. I realized that I liked learning. I always knew that I wasn't stupid but before Rebecca I had not known that I liked to learn new things. The other thing that happened in camp was that I became more confident and I didn't much care what people thought about my accent or about my dick. Actually there were other guys in there whose cock was even bigger.

From what I have just said you probably have guessed that I'm writing this from camp. It's for my English class, just one of several classes that I have taken so that I can get my High school Diploma by the time that I get cut loose from here. It's by far my favorite class although I also have really enjoyed the mixed martial arts class and I have become the best all around fighter and now hold a black belt in a Kung Foo style.

This brings me to the end and to something that I guess you want to know and I don't want to tell you. But my teacher says that to grow one has to face life as it really is. So here it is. After I got busted I lost all contact with the guys from Segunda until one day, in my second year at camp, one of the new guys had his girl friend visit him and was I surprised to see that it was Pee Wee. Man I can't tell you what a rush it was to see her and from where I was sitting with my mother and stepfather on one of the benches in the visiting area, I yelled out "Hey Pee Wee."

She too was glad to see me and she and her boyfriend came over and sat with us. Her boyfriend, by the way, is an okay guy from Fresno and he didn't get all bothered by the fact that I knew her, especially when she began to catch me up on all the happenings. When I asked her about Rebecca her eyes moistened and her throat didn't allow her to talk for a minute or so and everyone stared at their hands and moved uncomfortably in their portion of the bench. Pee Wee began to tell me how Indio began hustling Rebecca, using her as a prostitute for drug money and how finally one day she over dosed. It happened last year and Pee Wee moved to Fresno with her family right after that. Right then I wished that Pee Wee had not appeared, that I might have gone on pretending that Rebecca had managed by some miracle to escape. I was glad when Pee Wee and her boyfriend went back to their own bench and more glad when visiting hours were over and my mother and her husband left the *camp. Then I could be alone with my own thoughts and mourn Rebecca in my own way.*

I have asked a couple of my teachers about destiny and fate, looking for answers to what Rebecca and I experienced together and separately. I can't say that their explanations have satisfied me and so I'll have to continue searching. For now all I can understand is that her life had great meaning to me.

* * *

"That is quite a story Pelon," Helga said when I finished reading. "It's sad but also uplifting. Rebecca died so that you could live to be who you are."

"Yes, I think I see it like that also," I said.

The rest of the group also made appreciative comments and I felt really good for having unburdened myself in that way. I wanted to invite everyone out for a drink when our session ended but the doctor preferred that we didn't socialize together, thinking that the group might lose its honesty if friendships were involved. He did say that we could socialize on very special occasions. One such occasion was a Summer Solstice masquerade party hosted by Helga. She allowed us to bring guests and I invited Lorraine but she had another commitment and I ended up hanging out with Robert most of the night and getting stinking drunk.

Before we were both too stoned to talk intelligibly, we had some rather good moments, discussing our respective political points of view and general outlook on life. He was older, from a family that played a prominent role in the American Revolution and was much better at articulating his views. But what I lacked in vocabulary I made up in fervor, or at least that was the way I saw it that evening. Later I thought I sounded like a damn freshman.

"Tell me Robert, why does a nice guy like you work with a bunch of uptight assholes?"

"I can assure you that not all of us are uptight assholes," Robert said, giving me a knowing look.

"Touché my friend," I retorted.

"But seriously Pelon, there is as wide a range of personalities and points of view among conservatives as there are among liberals. At least that's been my experience. Certainly there are some conservatives that I wouldn't or couldn't associate with. Andre is a good case in point. And I'm sure it's true about some liberals that you can't associate with."

"Sure that's true," I said. "There are two women in my office like that. But what I'm trying to figure out is what drives conservatives. What is your world view that prompts you to vote against the President's health care program, for example?"

"I think that all conservatives think and feel that every person needs to make their own way in life and that the government has taken on too much responsibility in trying to take care of its citizenry. There are people that have taken unfair advantage of government programs, such as welfare, or disability benefits."

"Dude, people fall on hard times. It's the responsibility of the group to lend a hand."

"That's true but some people have turned a helping hand into a lifestyle and now they feel it's their God-given right. We are inadvertently converting a large portion of our population into unproductive freeloaders."

"I see your point Robert and I agree that some people abuse some government programs. But hell, corporate abuse of government tax breaks and lax oversight of their business practices drains tons of money from the country's coffers and I don't see conservatives jumping on them. I think that if someone is making money, conservatives are okay with whatever practices are used because it falls within the definition of work. But if a person is just getting a handout you guys get all hot and bothered."

"Conservatives are also about the rule of law, Pelon. We don't condone illegal acts…"

"Yeah, when they are committed by Joe Sixpack," I said. "But if it's a large corporation, some bank too big to fail, or some rich guy who's well connected, you'll likely look the other way. Just look at bailout of banks and the slaps on the hand of the mortgage companies responsible for almost destroying our economic system."

"Well I can't in good conscious defend those actions," Robert said. "I was as appalled by what took place as you, Pelon."

"Let me tell you my theory," I said, already beginning to slur words. "First, conservatives don't like to pay taxes for anything but the basics like roads and police. Liberals don't mind paying taxes. Me, I feel paying taxes is like paying for the privilege of living in this country. Second, conservatives are all about the individual and the individual doing whatever the hell he pleases, Ayn Rand style. Liberals are all about the group and taking care of the group and they get mad as hell whenever they see someone taking more then their fair share. Conservatives feel it's their right to get more than the next guy. Third, conservatives make their arguments by appealing to a person's feelings, like love of country, family ties, heroic behavior etc. Liberals like to appeal to the intellect and support their arguments with facts and statistics."

"What you say is interesting, Pelon, but much too broad to apply to the behavior of specific individuals that I know."

I felt like I was on a roll and ready to say more but unfortunately by then I was too damn drunk to spit straight and Helga ambled over with her husband.

"Hey Helga, who the hell are you dressed as?" I asked in my best effort to sound sober.

"Why I'm Persephone. And this is my husband Hades who stole me for himself."

"Why you no good bastard," I said, "stealing beautiful Helga all for yourself."

Robert who was equally drunk also chimed in. "My my, the stench of sulfur is rather overwhelming."

Helga who had had a few cups herself, joined us in laughter but her husband was not amused and he stepped away leaving Helga with us.

"*U yu yui*," I said.

"What's that mean?" Helga asked enthusiastically.

"It's an old barrio expression akin to saying, 'my my what a party pooper'," I answered.

And then both Robert and Helga began saying "*U yu yui*," and the three of us were bursting with laughter.

I was having fun in Washington in spite of the fact that the conservatives were kicking our liberal butts in Congress. According to the polls the country was still evenly divided between Democrats and Republicans, but the more telling division was between liberals and conservatives. This was especially true on the Hill, where Obama's efforts were being repeatedly thwarted by the Republican opposition. The birth of the Tea Party Movement in the following year gave rise to yet another faction that opposed the President. There were issues such as abortion, prayer, privacy, and funding for social programs that caused irreconcilable differences between people and within families. On the liberal conservative dimension, the country had become more conservative. And almost always a conservative legislator was a Republican and a supporter of the wealthy and the privileged, of legislation that favored large corporations and of special interest groups such as the National Rifle Association, the American Medical Association, and the Pharmaceutical Industry.

These Republicans were clever in the way they presented the issues to ordinary folks, fabricating lies that made it seem that ordinary folks were benefiting from their policies, most often relating them to the conservative issues that ordinary folks supported. And the only reason that they didn't always overrun us was that sometimes we liberals could promote the issue in a way that made it clear what truly was at stake.

Back home in Arizona in the spring of 2010 the conservative governor and legislature were thumping on the issue of 'illegal immigration' and had drafted a bill that came to be known as SB1070, a horrendous travesty of justice that would require police to stop individuals that they suspected of being in the USA without proper documentation. It was evident that they were going to profile Latinos and hassle them. Again the conservatives gave it a spin that made the public think that support of SB1070 was to support apprehension of drug smugglers. And much of the public did indeed fall for that nonsense.

Our congressman, as outraged as many of us were, supported a national boycott of Arizona, hoping that the cancellation of meetings, conventions, concerts and vacations of ordinary citizens would exert an economic impact that would force the state to abandon SB 1070. National support from liberal thinking people was strong but so was the backlash from conservative groups and soon other states began to consider and pass similar legislation to curb what they termed illegal immigration.

I was constantly angry about the spin that Republicans gave to issues to mask the true beneficiaries of their actions. One day Lorraine told me, "Listen up homeboy, you have to tone it down. People are beginning to think that you're some sort of radical wacko."

Of course she was right. I was totally out of balance. Maybe I needed something else to believe in. Lorraine had started dating some guy and I missed talking to her. I was thankful for the group, there at least once a week I could blow off some steam. But the rest of the week I kept it all inside.

If truth be told I was also angry that when Congressman Jimmy drafted his bill, it didn't include much of my report. I was really puzzled and feeling low. I read and reread his proposed legislation and decided to investigate specific language and issues that he was addressing in his bill.

On one afternoon that I was spending at the Library of Congress, I ran into a fellow law student that I had known briefly during my first year at the university. He was an African American and participated in a club that I belonged to, organized by minority law students. Although he was a senior and ready to graduate, he took an interest in me that at first made me uncomfortable as he had many effeminate characteristics. But I learned to put aside whatever misgivings I had about his motivation, and frankly that year at school he helped me quite a bit with information about classes and professors.

"Hey Farley, Farley Abrams, is it you?" I asked.

"Hello Macias. Imagine running into you."

"Yeah. How about that? Are you visiting D.C. or working here?"

"Working for NRDC. Do you know it?"

"Truthfully I have never heard of it. But I am a rookie, just arrived after the election."

"It's the Natural Resources Defense Council, a coalition of environmental groups. And you?" he asked.

"I'm working for a Congressman and came here to do some research."

"Did you pass the bar?"

"First try," I answered. "I guess you did too."

"Yes, but not on my first try," he said smiling. "What are you researching?"

"Stuff on public lands. What brings you to the library?"

"Really? What Congressman do you work for?"

"James Kelley. Why do you ask? Do you know something I don't?"

"Maybe. There's a lot of money at stake whenever a new administration begins to put their mark on public lands."

"So I'm finding out. Are you also on a public lands expedition?"

"Sort of. But I really can't say much about it here. If you want we can meet somewhere else."

"Let's do that. Where's a good place?"

"There's a small café on First Street. Just go south past the metro station. I'll meet you there around five."

"I'll be there," I said.

I arrived at the designated cafe a few minutes late as I still had a bit of trouble figuring out what streets went where. We greeted each other and I sat across from Farley and after a short session of small talk Farley began telling me things that shook me to my very core.

"As I told you earlier there's a lot of money riding on the outcome of this administration's plan for public lands. There will be winners and losers and everyone that has a stake in how it turns out is pouring money into the coffers of the key players. Your man is no exception."

"No way, Farley. Kelley is not into that sort of money politics."

"I'm not saying that he has taken money but there is immense pressure being exerted to choose a particular path. Whatever recommendations you make to your Congressman based on your research is but a formality and in some ways a smokescreen for how he will participate and vote when the time comes."

"But if he doesn't take money what sort of pressure could possibly work on him?" I asked.

"I didn't say that he didn't take money. I don't know whether he did or not. But there are many ways that pressure is applied, rewards on or off the floor that are made available."

"If what you say is true, then my research assignment is not the plum job I and everyone else thought it was. It's just a fucking sham."

"You are a rookie. Didn't you wonder why such a high profile assignment was given to you?"

"Maybe my ego was blinding me."

The rest of the afternoon Farley talked to me about environmental issues and about bills and riders that are attached to bills and how every stakeholder produces tons of information that hopes to convince readers of the advantages of their position and how this information gets to Congressmen and Senators and to their legislative aides. And that at times the lobbyists even write the proposed legislation. When I finally left I was drained and depressed and totally disheartened about the legislative process.

Over the next several days I moped around and pretended that I cared. I went to the Library of Congress several more times that week and began to follow the tips that Farley Abrams had given me, researching not only voting records and proceedings as reported in the Congressional Record but also registered lobbyists and their concerns. I made copious notes and read them a dozen times until a picture began to emerge of Congressman James R. Kelley that showed that he often spoke on behalf of issues that were of vital concern to a certain lobbyist that represented companies with huge investments in public lands. It didn't point to any wrongdoing per se, as I could not find any sort of under-the-table payments or other inducements, but to his loyal supporters it would seem traitorous.

Stumped by not finding what Congressman Jimmy was getting in return for his support I called Robert to see if he could shed some light on the matter.

"Hola Robert. It's Pelon. Do you have a minute?"

"Pelon. What gives, amigo? Yeah I can talk for a minute, longer if it's urgent."

"I really need to sit down with you and go over some things. Any chance of having dinner with you?"

"Sure, tonight if you want."

"Great. Can I meet you at the Carlyle Suites in Dupont Circle after work, say 6:00 pm?"

"Okay, but let me pick you up there and I'll drive you to a small restaurant that I like. You know my car."

"Thanks, Robert."

That evening after work I walked to the Carlyle Suites and Robert picked me up right on time.

"What's on your mind Pelon? You sound rather on edge."

"Lots of stuff. I feel like my world is crashing around me right now."

"The food is fabulous at this place we're going to. It'll help erase some of your troubles. That and a good bottle of wine."

During the drive to the restaurant I told Robert about my meeting with Farley and how I felt manipulated into thinking that I was some young hotshot on a meteoric trajectory and all I was serving was as a smoke screen to the real machinations that were going on.

"You wouldn't be the first to serve such a purpose," Robert commented. "It happens on both sides of the aisle."

"It's been so well orchestrated, even to the point of having co-workers jealous of my assignment. Are they in on it too?"

"I doubt it. They are probably genuinely jealous. Human nature is sometimes very predictable."

We arrived at the small restaurant and Robert was right, the food was delicious and the wine he selected (Charbono, a heavy smoky red) made me forget some of the slight that I felt. Still I was curious and eager to get to the heart of the matter, and I laid out the question to Robert.

"So Robert, what pressures or inducements can be brought to bear on someone like Congressman Kelley?"

"Well there are the obvious ones such as campaign contributions and all-expenses-paid trips. Then there are the more subtle ones such as untraceable valuable gifts, a diamond necklace, a Rolex and so on. And then there are the truly subtle ones such as scholarship money for children at a prestigious university, money placed in an offshore account, the financial services of someone that invests for wealthy clients. There are some very clever and creative people in this business, Pelon."

"That last one that you mention doesn't sound too subtle. Investments are reported."

"Yes but if someone places money into an IRA, only the money given is reported. The growth of that money doesn't become known until it is time to get distributions. And wealthy clients get a return of at least 20% compounded yearly interest. We're talking big money in 20 years of yearly contributions."

"Wow! That's the way I would go if I wanted to be secretive about my money," I said.

"Yes it's all perfectly legal and nearly impossible to verify."

"Well, perfectly legal is stretching it a bit. Kelley needs to be speaking and voting on their behalf, that's not kosher. But you said it would be nearly impossible to verify. Is there some way to bring this out into the open?"

"If you had access to his calendar you could determine if he met with someone from an investment firm that deals exclusively with wealthy clients. That's a start. Then you would have to verify that he is indeed a client. That part wouldn't be easy."

"I could pull a Watergate-like robbery," I ventured, "or hack their computer system."

"Take it one step at a time," Robert advised, "Get a hold of his calendar and see if he's met with someone that arouses suspicions and go from there."

"All right. I'll try that."

That's the way the conversation about my problem ended that evening. The rest of the time we talked about other topics, not the least about the real state of the union with Republicans and Democrats at each other's throats.

Helga invited Robert and me for Thanksgiving Dinner that year. We had been trying to honor the doctor's request that we not see one another socially but we had such a strong affinity for one another that unintentionally we had become an item in Dr. Maier's group, frequently sharing quips and insights as if no one else was present.

After our Thanksgiving meal the three of us were hanging out in her sumptuous library away from the rest of the guests and Robert excused himself to go use the bathroom.

Helga as I said was a total knockout and I was surprised and pleased that she liked me, because I was just an average looking guy and ordinarily I didn't meet someone of her beauty and social standing. I know this sounds like I was pretty shallow, I mean feeling pride because a beautiful woman enjoyed my friendship.

"Tell me Helga, why the hell do you hang out with me?" I asked her when we were alone.

"I suppose I think you're interesting in an exotic sort of way. And you're authentic and confident. You don't try to be somebody else."

"Seriously?" I asked with all sorts of doubts bouncing inside my head. "I can't figure you out, Helga. You're so beautiful and cosmopolitan. I'm just a barrio kid that's hoping to make a difference."

"And I'm just a woman who is trying to make a positive contribution. We're not that different, Pelon."

"Ha hah," I laughed. "Of course we're different," I claimed. "Hell, you travel in circles that I have only seen in movies. You know politicians and actors and artists by their first name. People of importance respect you and respect what you do."

"That's all true, but I have feelings that I'm sure are not that different from yours. At night I question whether or not I have behaved the way I should. Sometimes I cry at some slight I have suffered or feel unworthy because I have not done my very best. And I like the attention that men pay me because they think I'm beautiful and I wonder if I'm beginning to age when I don't get compliments."

I knew that what she was saying was really how she felt. She said about the same things in group. I knew that she lacked confidence, that she felt unsure about herself. And yet I couldn't understand her lack of self-esteem with so much money and good looks. But I was young and this was a very new experience. When Robert rejoined us we smoothly shifted the conversation.

Robert was a gay man, living with a partner, an older man with whom he had been for a long time. I was shocked when I found out because I had grown up thinking that gays were effeminate and he wasn't. He was very debonair and handsome. Helga used to laugh because women were always drooling over him at her parties. Robert was totally opposite me on the political and social dimension, but he was at the same time someone I had learned to trust completely. Helga, whom I also trusted, was difficult to peg, sometimes siding with me, sometimes with Robert. Together, the three of us made for lively conversations and when the conversation turned to politics and social conditions I tried to follow Lorraine's advice to tone myself down a few notches, but I was unable and I was soon popping my neck veins.

The country had been in an economic depression since the stock market crash of 2005 and the truth was that the economy hadn't been very strong since the end of the roaring nineties. Throughout the new century the disparity between poor and wealthy had been increasing and many from the middle class had fallen into poverty as the country lost its manufacturing base. We became a service economy with correspondingly lower wages. But what had exacerbated conditions were the trillions of dollars of debt that families accumulated as they attempted to maintain their lifestyle while their income eroded. The pollyannas kept telling people that the economy was improving, encouraging them to continue spending. But it was all smoke and mirrors and made even worse by the huge debt that the Federal government had, which led to the crash of the dollar on the world market.

"People are frustrated," I said in answer to Robert's comment about some unemployed workers storming a state employment office and burning it to the ground.

"I think that we are only beginning to see the tip of the proverbial iceberg," I continued.

"I hope you are not condoning the actions of that rabble," Robert said.

"No I'm not," I answered, "but neither am I condemning them. I grew up poor, but even I can't understand completely what those people must be feeling. There are people who have lost everything—their job, their home, their retirement, their self worth. And if this country doesn't address their needs I think all hell is going to break loose."

"Oh don't be so dramatic, Pelon," Robert said. "There's a little bit of an actor in you, my friend. I don't think that much will come of this. People have moved back and forth in social standing since time immemorial. Society will stand firm. We who comprise the leadership of this country will make sure of that."

"My my, who appointed you a leader Robert?" Helga offered. "Besides I think Pelon has a good point. I see that people are getting desperate. Just the other day a fellow ran up to my car and started berating me for oppressing him. Saying it was rich people like me that are responsible for his impoverishment. Hell, I'd be in the same boat as he, if my papa hadn't followed his own good common sense and converted his holdings into gold, while everyone else was heading for the stock market."

"It's not that someone has appointed me a leader, dear Helga. It's just that it falls on some of us to lead and on others to follow. The survival of the fittest isn't just for the lower species. We too are subject to those same evolutionary forces. I'm sure your father knew this, why else would he have ignored what the masses were doing to follow his own mind?"

"No my papa was never aware that he was different from anyone else," she answered. "All his life he worked his business and saved his money. He was a simple man."

"I think you misjudge your papa," Robert answered.

"Sometimes you are so damn arrogant Robert, it's a wonder someone doesn't knock you on your ass," Helga answered scornfully.

"Yes he is full of himself, isn't he," I said. "But I think that you uncovered the most important point, Robert, even though you may not have intended to."

"And what is that?" he asked.

"Well it's obvious that there are strains of elitism in many conservatives today. You are a prime example. We all know that people aren't created equal, really. Some people are cut out for leadership and others aren't. But when leadership becomes irresponsible because of arrogance and greed and social mobility is curtailed, then society becomes unstable. The people with talent who are born poor have to believe that they too will one day be rich. Or they become the agitators for change."

Helga spoke up. "There are other reasons that people agitate for change. It's not only because talented people want to be rich. People not having their basic needs met will also revolt. As will people who want to institute new values or re-establish old values that have eroded."

I agreed with Helga and added that maybe all of those reasons were coming into focus. Robert listened quietly and remained quiet as Helga and I awaited a response.

Robert finally gathered his thoughts and spoke. "I can't argue against the reasons given that lead to social change. My God there are more than ample historical examples that one easily can recall, but there's no reason to suppose that any of those conditions of which you speak are being met."

"Hey, you gotta be kidding," I said to him. "Hell, don't you read the damn newspaper? Everyday there are incidents that are the manifestation of those conditions. What is the burning of the employment office but a manifestation of one of those conditions?"

I guess I was close to shouting because Helga's husband Andre came over and asked if everything was all right.

Andre was a real sleaze ball. I didn't understand why Helga married him but it was obvious why he had married her. He reveled in the rich lifestyle that Helga's inheritance afforded him, wearing outrageously expensive clothing, partying and gambling, and carrying on with other women. Helga kept hinting in the group sessions that she was getting ready to dump him but so far she had not made a move to actualize any separation. It was difficult to hide my feelings about him and I purposely avoided looking at him as he slung his arm over Helga's shoulder.

"Yes, we're just talking politics," Helga answered her husband.

"Well it must be a hot debate," Andre said. "We could hear your young friend all the way into the living room."

Andre didn't like me either and that was his way of putting me down. Before marrying Helga he had been a demographer at a local university and a minor figure in the Republican Party apparatus. Now he was on first names with all of the Republican Party leaders, especially those who were proponents of greater social control measures. As with all would-be demagogues and tyrants, they disguised their real agenda with platitudes about issues that mattered to Joe Public, like global preeminence, national security and the creation of jobs.

"Yes it is a heated discussion," Robert answered Andre's question. "Perhaps you would like to add your opinion. We were talking about elitism within the Republican Party. That fellow Leo Strauss that you seem so fond of, was he not of that persuasion?"

Robert liked Andre even less than I did. He had known him a lot longer and suspected that Andre hated homosexuals as much as he hated poor people. He was baiting him, trying to engage him in a discussion where he would show his true colors. Robert was slick but Andre did not want any part of it.

"No no," Andre said, feigning an inadequate knowledge of what Strauss believed.

"Oh come now surely you must have your own opinion then," Robert proffered.

We all looked at Andre in that instant, Helga smiling encouragingly. Andre was trapped. He had to comment.

"Well there's all sorts of elitism," he said. "You find some in every group I suppose. I imagine that there are Republicans that feel superior in some sense."

"What about you, sir?" Robert asked him point blank. "Do you feel superior, to say someone like Pelon, or to a gay man such as myself?"

Andre's ears turned red and his voice became an octave deeper even as he tried smiling. He felt that he was being challenged and he was not going to back down.

"This country was founded and made great by men who had balls, Robert, like your ancestors—European white men, from the same stock that I come from. I think that's the answer you wanted. Now I think I better join my other guests."

Andre turned and left us looking at each other. Helga shook her head in disgust.

"Interesting," I said. "That was done very nicely, Robert. But you have to give Andre credit for deftly crafting a response that took care of you and me without compromising himself. It was beautifully done."

"Yes, he's a clever bastard," Robert said. "Whatever did you see in him anyway, Helga?"

"I was young and he was smooth and clever as you say," answered Helga.

"But tell me what's the difference between you and Andre?" I asked Robert.

"I hope you are joking, Pelon," he said. "We have so little in common I don't see how you can think we are alike."

"Come on Robert, be a good sport. It's an interesting question," Helga said.

"Well the thing is my good friends, that is a question that requires a bit of explanation. People such as Andre think they have a God-given right to rule and willfully manipulate circumstances favorable to themselves, regardless of what happens to others. I asked him about Leo Strauss because they have taken some of his teachings and distorted them, in order to justify all manner of devious and malevolent behavior.

"They first surfaced back in the Bush administration, when they convinced the nation that Iraq had weapons of mass destruction. When it was discovered that they had distorted the intelligence and there were no such weapons, they fell into disfavor. And there they sulked underground, sharpening their malefic skills, recruiting new members and then surfacing again with this new administration stronger than ever. In contrast to my own views on leadership, which are based on the concept of being a servant unto the people that one is leading, they have a disdain for people, not caring whether, nor how much, they suffer."

Robert's explanation was my introduction to Andre's group of elitist conservatives, mostly Republicans but also some Democrats. It was they, the conservatives, who were to become the enemy of the democracy that we had inherited, a democracy that had been a beacon to the world since its founding.

CHAPTER III

After that evening many changes took place. Some were quite dramatic, such as Helga's separation and annulment of her marriage to Andre. He took a special interest in Robert and me after that, blaming us for the demise of his cushy set-up. Unfortunately for him, a prenuptial agreement gave him little access to Helga's fortune. Still, he had wormed his way into a position of power with the conservative Republicans, and of course access to power frequently led to wealth. So Andre wasn't hurting for money, but his ego had been badly bruised and he was not about to forget our role in the way in which events had unfolded.

Andre was not my only concern that summer. I was still smarting from the manner in which Congressman Jimmy had ignored my report. If there was a silver lining in this, it was that he did not share my report with the staff. Thus nobody knew that all my work had been for naught. And I was so embarrassed that I didn't even share this with Lorraine.

And in order to follow up on the plan outlined with Robert I had to peruse the Congressman's calendar for a period of several months, maybe longer. After a couple of weeks of strategizing I came to the conclusion that there was really only one person that could help me in this situation and that was the computer wizard, Esperanza. But to take Esperanza into my confidence was to also take in Naomi, for the two seemed to be joined at the hip and there was no way that Esperanza would not share something this juicy with her. I finally concluded that

Naomi, being the leader of this duo, would not take well to learning about it second hand. I would have to tell her first and see if she would be amenable to my plan. But it could also blow up in my face for both Naomi and Esperanza were fiercely loyal to Congressman Jimmy and this thought kept me from acting.

I was also troubled by the fact that Dr. Maier also began to take issue with the friendship that had developed among Robert, Helga and me, saying, very correctly, that we had become a disruption to the group process. We didn't mean to be disruptive and so we voluntarily left the group. In some ways it was sad to leave Dr. Maier. During the two years that I was in the group I had made room for Pelon, my alter ego and barrio legacy. I liked who I was and liked even more who I was becoming. Months earlier during one of our regular meetings I had told Robert and Helga.

"This may sound like a strange request," I said, "but I'd like you to call me Pelon.

They didn't think it was strange at all to call me by my nickname. Of course it was strange hearing them say Pelon, especially Helga, whose father had insisted that German be spoken at home, lending her English a beautiful undertone of mysterious ancestry. She and I had been getting closer since her annulment, spending hours talking on the telephone whenever I had a free evening. Which weren't many, as I was often pulling in 14-hour days. And once in awhile we would get together for lunch or dinner without Robert. I really enjoyed those times with her but I kept hoping that she would drop the teacher role that somehow developed between us. It was a natural outgrowth as she was extremely well read and had been around intellectual people all her life. She was only 4 years older but I was just beginning my education and there was a lot that she could teach me. Still I found her very attractive and wished that she would reciprocate the feelings that I was developing for her.

One evening after Robert had left we were sitting on her sofa and out of nowhere Helga asked me about my love life.

"You do like women don't you?" she asked.

"Of course."

"So why don't you have one?"

"I imagine that I haven't met the right one," I answered, but then thought better and added, "That's not entirely true. I have met someone but I don't know if she feels the same way I do about her."

"You haven't asked?" She took my hand in hers.

"No. I haven't mustered the courage."

"Well you'll never get anywhere unless you make your feelings known."

Women are different from men. Here I had been agonizing about my feelings for Helga, trying not to overstep the boundary of friendship by revealing too much, and all along she knew. She had even talked to Robert about me, asking how she might prod me along.

We laughed after we made love on her sofa, when she told me that she had wanted me since I had read my essay and mentioned my penis. Our lovemaking had been wild and passionate. Helga was nothing like what I had fantasized. Because of her gentleness and soft soothing voice, I thought she would be quiet and reserved. I was wrong and startled when she began screaming and asking me to ram it into her. Actually Helga even surprised herself. Apparently our compatibility released her to new levels. My head swelled after she told me that.

My relationship with Helga made me feel complete. For the next several weeks I was euphoric. Still it was not something I was ready to share with my colleagues. Chicanos are no different from other ethnic groups in wanting to keep their men and women to themselves. Not only was Helga not a Latina, she was also wealthy. I didn't want to give Naomi and Esperanza more ammunition to use in their effort to discredit me.

One of the lessons that Helga taught me was that keeping one's money was just as difficult as acquiring it in the first place, and she had gone to Europe to attend to some business matters that would help safeguard her wealth.

Her trip coincided with the Congressman granting us a holiday the week of July Fourth. He sent me and several others back to Tucson to work on the possibility of bailing on the boycott of Arizona, and to figure out a way to help save the Mexican American Studies program that had been scrapped by Arizona.

My first day home, wanting to beat the desert heat, I was already running along the Santa Cruz River Trail when the sun came over the Catalina Mountains.

"Is that you, Pelon?" a boy's voice called out.

"Wow! Rodrigo," I said as I pulled to a stop. "You've grown, *ese*."

"Yeah a little." Rodrigo answered as he was getting off his mountain bike.

"You're up early bro," I commented.

"Yeah I'm staying in shape for baseball. When you come in, Pelon?"

"Just last night. I'll be here for a while. Wanna come by the house? We can have some breakfast and catch up."

"I guess so."

"What'd you mean I guess so? It's a yes or no question dude. Don't get into the habit of being wishy washy," I admonished him.

"Okay okay I'll go," he said.

"All right then. I'll finish my run and see you when I get home."

"Later Pelon."

Rodrigo's family was a neighbor of Grandma and I had known him since he was a small boy. He and I had always had a nice friendship and I always felt that we shared a special connection. I returned home and showered and told Grandma that Rodrigo would be having breakfast with us. He showed up just as I was shaving.

"Have a good workout?" I asked.

"I guess so."

"What?"

"Yes I did, Pelon."

"So what's going on with you?" I asked, as we dove into a chorizo and egg omelet that Grandma had set before us.

"Not much I guess.... I mean I've been really busy with school work and with all the cool technology that my school has," he added quickly when I had given him a cold stare.

"So you're liking all the techno gadgets. Just don't forget that you're there to learn other subjects too. Maybe you can give me a few pointers while I'm here. I know almost nothing of the newer stuff like Instagram and Twitter."

"Dude that's not new stuff," he said with a smile.

"Okay, so I'm a media dinosaur. Work with me will you," I said.

"Yeah whatever. Why'd you come back? Did they fire you?"

"Listen you smart ass, I'll have you know that I'm a rising star with the congressman's team. Media dinosaur or not."

Rodrigo gave me a thumbs-up.

"Are you taking a Chicano Studies class?" I asked him.

"Yeah. It's cool. They're going to close it down you know."

"Yeah I know. That's one of the reasons I'm here."

"Good luck with that."

"You don't think we can save it?"

71

Rodrigo shrugged. "I dunno. It seems like it's a done deal. It's all about the Benjamins. Que no? If Tucson keeps the classes they lose millions of dollars from the state. Isn't it always about the feria?"

"I wish it were that simple dude," I said. "Yeah money is involved, you're right about that, but it seems like the conservative bigots in Arizona want to eliminate as many Mexicans as they can and those they can't get rid of they want to brainwash with lies about USA history."

"Yeah, I've learned to distrust regular American History books. It's been good learning about Chicanos. It's given me more confidence," he said.

"Well that's good to hear, Rodrigo. And that's why we'd like to see the program continued." We finished breakfast and Rodrigo returned home, with a promise to come back some day soon.

Helga returned to D.C. the following week while I had to stay in Tucson and I missed her terribly. The long telephone conversations were not satisfying substitutes. I told her about everything that was happening in Tucson regarding the SB 1070 and the congressman joining the boycott that he was now considering a mistake. My assignment was to develop an opinion based on my investigation of how his plan to abandon the boycott would play out in the state's politics, and how that would affect his own personal career.

"God I wish you were with me." I said. "Is there any chance that you could come out here?"

"I have commitments for the rest of the month, Pelon. I wish I could."

"I want to have rough sex with you," I said softly.

"Me too," she answered.

"Better change the subject before I get all gushy and spoil my manly image," I said.

"I did want to tell you that I saw Andre the other day."

"Oh. Really," I said with apparent jealousy, because she had to calm me down.

"I didn't mean I had sex with him you silly man," she said. "What I wanted to tell you is that he's been put in charge of one of those new intelligence gathering agencies."

"Which one?" I asked.

"One called the National Geospatial..."

"Intelligence Agency," I finished her sentence. "I know it. They're gathering information to build a database of all major towns and cities, down to house level, for surveillance or military targets. They'll be able to watch the movements of people almost everywhere. God that's scary."

"What is more frightening is Andre being its head and being a key player in this New America. He didn't make explicit threats, he's too clever for that. But he did let me know that I should be careful with whom I associate. I assume that he was thinking of you, Pelon."

"Have you told Robert?"

"Yes. We talked earlier. Robert thinks that his days as a Republican Strategist are numbered."

"He's probably right. Robert has too damn much integrity for that bunch of assholes. When you see him, give him a big hug for me. I better get going. I'll call you back in a few days."

Not having Helga around left me with time on my hands, and much of my time away from work I was spending with Lorraine. I knew that I was lonely but I also knew that I liked spending time with Lorraine. She was in many ways like an older big sister yet when I had a vivid sexual dream involving her I began rethinking how I really felt.

"Hey Lorraine," I said when I saw her the next day.

"Hey yourself, homie," she answered. "Why are you looking like your dog just died?"

"Really. I don't even have a dog."

"You know what I mean you smart ass."

"I'm just feeling like I have too much idle time, that's all," I answered.

"Poor baby, he misses his girlfriend," Lorraine mocked. "Why don't you come over to the res this weekend? We're having a small celebration."

"Maybe," I said. "They won't string me up by my nipples, will they?"

"No but I was planning to handcuff you to my bed."

"Well then it's a date," I said.

It didn't make sense that here I was feeling guilty about Lorraine and yet I agreed to go to the Tohono O'Odham reservation with her. I didn't understand why I had said yes to her invitation. I guess I liked her. She was pretty and she had something that emanated from inside her that I was not sure was kindness or innocence. Maybe it was both. She was a little on the plump side, with heavy breasts and thick jet black hair that she wore long, past her shoulders.

The celebration was to be in the town of Sells, where her grandfather lived and that's where we hooked up. Lorraine was there with him, an elderly man with dark penetrating eyes and dark skin almost the color of ironwood. He was slender and wiry, with a thick head of black hair and his dark skin and dark hair made his eyes seem even more piercing then they might otherwise have been.

"This is my grandfather Otavio," she said. "And this is mighty Hercules, Grandpa."

"It's Herculano, sir," I corrected Lorraine. She was wearing a huge smile.

"Hello young man," the grandfather said. "My niece likes to fool with people."

"Yes, I know," I answered.

"We better get over to the plaza. They'll be starting the dance soon," Lorraine said.

"What's being celebrated?" I asked.

"It's a rainmaking ceremony," the grandfather said. "It's what brings us the monsoons."

I was transfixed by the ceremony but out of the corner of my eye I caught Lorraine looking at me a couple of times. After the ceremony ended we had a nice supper of beans and rice and a porridge made from acorns.

"Do you keep up with everything that's going on in Tucson?" I asked the grandfather as we sat around a small fire, the mountains in the background, now but dark outlines against a sky full of stars.

"A little," he said. "There are many evil forces at work right now. It will be difficult not to be involved, even for us who live on this beautiful land apart from everything." He reached out for my hands and clasped them in his. He murmured some unintelligible words and then said. "Difficult times lay ahead for you young man. Be guided by what your heart tells you and you will be safe from those that would harm you."

I sat there stunned, not sure if he was pulling my leg as Lorraine might or if he was some desert prophet who was able to see the future.

"Can you tell me more?" I asked finally.

"That is as much as I can tell you. I saw no more but that. Come next Friday for a purification sweat. There maybe you will receive some guidance."

"Really I can attend?"

"Yes. I have invited you. Be here at 6:00 in the evening."

"Thank you. I will be here."

Later when Lorraine and I were alone I asked about her grandfather.

"He's a strange one isn't he? But he does have the seer's gift," she answered.

"Well I can't say that this wasn't an interesting evening," I said. "Did you know that he invited me to a sweat next Friday?"

"He told me. He thought that you had special gifts."

"Yes and driving at night when I'm tired isn't one of them. I should be heading home."

"I'll walk you to your car," Lorraine said, placing her arm around mine.

We walked in step, her handclasp gentle and the warmth of her body penetrating through my shirt.

"Are you still dating that guy from the Native American Coalition?" I asked.

"Yes," she answered.

"I'm dating someone too," I said.

"I know," she answered. "You aren't as clever as you think."

"Does everyone in the office know?" I asked.

"You bet your ass we do, homeboy. Know all about her too."

"Dude. How the hell?" I said.

"We're the government, remember," she said laughing.

When we reached my car she asked if I wanted to stay the night. She said we could sleep outside under a ramada, a rustic square shelter made with the stout trunks of mesquites buried in the ground at each corner, the trunks serving as the principle support for the cross beams and the roof which was made from the ribs of the giant Sahuaro. I was torn between loyalty for Helga and sexual desire that was beginning to rage within me for Lorraine.

"I think I better go home," I said finally.

"Chicken." she said smiling.

The following week I kept busy and didn't have much contact with Lorraine. I spent time at the U of A campus researching the economic impact of the boycott and interviewing movers and shakers in the city regarding

Congressman Jimmy's chances for re-election. All the republicans were enraged that the congressman had taken such an extreme measure and were hell-bent on having him defeated at the polls. Yet the liberals that previously supported him in his district remained loyal but wanted him to quit supporting the boycott. I concluded that the congressman's chances for re-election looked quite good if he acted on his supporters' advice.

The congressman was happy with that report but miffed that I hadn't been able to give much attention to my other assignment, that of the Mexican American Studies program, especially since closing it seemed to be moving forward in spite of the negative national attention that the school district was receiving. I was instructed to spend all my time on it.

I finally spoke to Lorraine on the day of the sweat.

"Hey, homegirl. Are you going to the res?"

"I was thinking about it. Are you going?" she asked.

"I wouldn't miss it. I've always wanted to experience a sweat."

"It's intense, I gotta tell you."

"Well maybe if you gave me a little background and maybe some do's and don'ts, I can get through it," I said.

"I can do that. I can also give you a ride if you want."

"Am I compromising myself by accepting?"

"Maybe. Depends on how you feel after the sweat. I have to run an errand now but I'll be back by 3:00. We'll leave then. By the way, it is customary to offer some tobacco to my grandfather, so pick up a tin."

The drive to Sells through beautiful desert vegetation was enhanced by an intense thunderstorm that moved quickly through the area, leaving the moist air fragrant with the smell of wet earth and the oils from the creosote bush. We had driven in silence during the storm, with thunder and the heavy raindrops pounding on the car making hearing impossible. We continued in silence after the storm too, admiring the beauty of the rainbow that had formed near the mountains and taking in the various smells left in the storm's wake. Minutes after the rain stopped, tiny raindrops were still falling and entering through the car's open window and landing on my face. Finally she spoke.

"There is nothing in the whole world that is as beautiful as the desert after a thunderstorm," she said with emotion. "Just look at the power in the water of that arroyo carrying away everything in its path."

"Pretty impressive," I said. "It's too bad the background scenery is marred by those damn mine tailings."

"Yeah the fucking mines and their destruction of the land. They just don't get it."

"There's money to be made. There's demand for copper and other minerals," I said.

"I know. That doesn't make it right. Native peoples in every continent know that it's Mother Earth that sustains us and that we have to honor and respect her. It's through her that we live, not because of some goddamn technology that's been developed."

"You should see the pressure that's being placed on the Congress to vote to expand mining and oil drilling on public lands and offshore too. They have a lot of money to spend."

"What is it with this country? We're supposed to have a democracy and representative government but it seems that corporations and rich folks can dictate whatever the hell they want. What the hell is wrong with that picture?"

"We're just going to have to change laws and rules and regulations that have made these practices possible," I said timidly.

"Yeah right and when is that going to happen, when there is another horrendous oil spill that kills half of the ocean population or a Fukushima-like disaster in the United States? Too many people with money are not interested in others and we have empowered them to keep on screwing us even more."

"Can't argue with that," I said.

"Let's change the subject, OK? No use getting all worked up. I'll tell you about the sweat."

"Fine with me."

"Rule number one is to relax in there. Give yourself up to the heat. You may feel like you're about to die. That's good. It won't happen but it's like a living metaphor. Surrender your life and when it's over it will be like you have been in the womb and are being reborn. The protocols—don't worry about those. Grandfather will tell you what to do."

"What about the tobacco?"

"Give it to him before you enter."

"Will you be in there?

"Yeah I'll be there."

"You don't sound too enthusiastic."

"No no, don't misunderstand. I love the sweat. It's just that sometimes I feel like I'm in that arroyo that we saw earlier, being carried to what is my destiny."

"And what is that?"

"To inherit Grandfather's role as a spiritual guide."

"Really. Interesting. Maybe even nice to know where you are going. I don't have that sense. So how do you feel about that role?"

"Sometimes I look forward to it. Sometimes like today I feel confined. Like I don't have a choice."

"Of course you have a choice. You can say no. You have another life already started."

"Yes I know that. But I struggle because I do really like what Grandfather does and I love my people."

"Are you also a seer?" I asked.

"That's why he taught me all he knows. And it's not only what you might imagine, being a seer I mean. It's also more like having a heightened intuitiveness and a strong connection with Mother Earth and all that lives here. And I don't mean just the animals and birds but everything... plants, minerals, water, rocks, everything. We are really one with the entire cosmos."

Wow! I thought. I had a greater appreciation for Lorraine after that conversation.

"What about you, Hercules, are you destined to save the world, like your namesake?"

"Hell, Lorraine. My life events have always been a big surprise. I have never known from one minute to the other where I was heading."

"We still have some time before we arrive. Wanna share?"

"Sure, you've told me about yourself. It's my turn."

I launched into my story, telling her about Rebecca and even giving details I left out of the story I read at Dr. Maier's group session, such as that I had fought several forest fires while serving my time at the fire camp and that I had won a mixed martial arts tournament against other detention camps. I told her about going to school and studying law and how I struggled to overcome deficits in my earlier education.

"Wow! You really are a homeboy. I thought you were just making it all up, dude."

"Naw, I told it like it is."

When we arrived in Sells we were laughing with funny stories about our faux pas with white society.

"One time," I said, "I went out to a fellow law student's house for a fancy sit down dinner, and after the meal a waiter brought me a little bowl with water and I proceeded to drink from it, thinking it was an after dinner soup. Then I saw that everyone was carefully dipping their fingertips into their bowl and drying them on their napkin, everyone pretended that they didn't see me. I must have turned a deep shade of red."

"Dude that's way too embarrassing. I don't think I have any that can match yours," she said.

"Aw go on, we all have them."

"Okay, this is really embarrassing but okay. So I go to my first school off the res, a middle school. I was about 13 and I get my period and spot my dress and the nurse gives me a tampon without any questions or comments. She just gives it to me. Hell I never seen a tampon so I go to the girls toilet and sit on the floor with the dress in my hands and try rubbing my dress thinking I've been given a blood eraser. In walks this white girl and looks at me as if her eyes are going to pop out of her head and she turns and runs out."

"Aw you're killing me," I tell her amidst bursts of laughter and the slapping of my leg. "That can't be a true story," I say.

"Hope to die if it's not."

Once in town we parked the car, still smiling at the recollection of each other's stories, and made our way to the sweat lodge behind one of the main buildings.

"By the way, at the sweat after you speak or say your prayers, you must end it by saying 'all my relations,' that acknowledges not only your ancestors but all the creatures that live with us," she advised.

I nodded and she left to change. I slipped into a pair of trunks and stood at the ready by the sweat lodge, a round squat structure about five feet high covered in what appeared to be old blankets of different patterns and colors. Near the front entrance burned a large bonfire. I gave the grandfather my offering of tobacco and he acknowledged it with an ordinary thank you.

There were about fifteen of us standing there, many of them not appearing to be Native American, and more than half of those attending were men dressed in swim trunks. The women wore shorts with loose tops, and some had swimsuits with a towel wrapped around them. I saw

Lorraine. She wore shorts and a top that couldn't hide the fact that her breasts were quite large. I averted my gaze after that, as I didn't want anyone to catch me looking at her. Slowly we began filing in, the grandfather pointing out a direction for each of us, some to his left and some to his right, and all having to duck under the canvas flap that served as a door. Inside there was a round pit dug in the center about 30 inches in diameter and we sat down on pieces of carpet around the pit, close to the walls that were constructed of willow saplings.

The grandfather came in and sat in the middle of the group, opposite the doorway. A fire keeper began bringing in the stones on a long handled pitchfork and gently placing them in the center pit. They were glowing red, some sparkling with the energy obtained from the burning mesquite logs. Once the fire keeper brought the seven rocks ordered by grandfather, he sat down in the circle and lowered the flap, completely covering the doorway and creating a pitch-black darkness. Grandfather then ladled some water onto the rocks creating an intensely hot steam that made me back away as far as possible.

Grandfather began beating rhythmically on a drum and began singing songs in his native language. They were sorrowful songs, I thought, but soothing and most appropriate to the mood in that dark enclosed space. When he stopped about twenty minutes later, that concluded the first round. More rocks were brought in and the flap closed once again. This round was given over to the participants to say a little about themselves and their intentions.

The third round was again a chance for the participants to speak, this time for offering prayers for loved ones or for strength in meeting a particular challenge in their own life. For the last round the fire keeper was asked to bring in all of the remaining rocks from the bonfire, and the heat in there was so intense that I thought of asking permission from the grandfather to leave. Fortunately I was overcome by the thought that if I was to die that it was okay. Once I gave in to the heat, a calmness overtook me. Colorful visions came to me. One was of the ocean, the water a deep blue and a gentle surf with tips of white washing ashore. This was followed by another vision, just as colorful, but the color was that of thin electrical wires in which I had become entangled and was struggling to free myself. Grandfather's voice and that of the fire keeper singing a song and beating respective drums brought me back. Several songs later we ended and filed out as we had come in. My swimming trunks were soaked and perspiration ran freely down my arms and chest and along my legs to my feet.

It was nighttime and the air was still moist with an earlier rain that we heard beating on the blanket-covered sweat lodge. The night air felt cool and I dried myself with my towel and looked for Lorraine. She was standing off to the side speaking with her grandfather and I waited until they parted before going to her.

"I made it," I said to her.

"Never thought you wouldn't."

"You were right though, it was intense. For awhile there I thought I was going to have to bail, but I remembered what you said about surrendering to the heat and I did."

"Want to say more?"

I told her what I had seen and elaborated on the last one that had left me feeling anxious.

"What do you think it means?" I asked her.

"I think it means that you better watch your back, homeboy."

"Really? Your grandfather said something similar to me. It's starting to freak me out."

"Who are you involved with that could be dangerous? Do you gamble or score drugs?"

"No way. I stay clear of shit like that."

"Well if ever you need a place to hang out, the res would be it.

"Thanks, but I hope I never have to take you up on that offer."

"There's some food for us at Grandfather's. You hungry?" she asked.

"I could eat something, but I think I would rather sit and talk. Unless of course you're hungry."

"A little. Let me grab something and we can sit outside."

I waited outside and soon she returned carrying a paper plate with food.

"Here I brought this corn for you," she said handing me the roasted corn still in its husk and warm. "We can sit on that bench outside the sweat lodge."

We ate in silence. I had not realized that I was hungry until I tore into my roasted ear of corn.

"I thought you weren't that hungry, homeboy. And don't even think of making a move for the food on my plate, either."

"Hey cut me some slack. I wasn't eyeing your food."

"Don't lie to me. You're a sneaky one. I saw you looking at my plate and I saw you earlier looking me over before we entered the sweat lodge."

"What? I wasn't looking you over," I said, all the while thinking that my face was turning red and giving me away.

"It's okay, homeboy. I checked you out too. You have nice buns and nice muscular legs. Before you told me that you were into mixed martial arts I thought you were some weak-kneed lawyer like all the rest of those Washingtonians."

"Okay okay, so we both checked each other out. It doesn't mean anything, does it?"

"I guess not," she said, "unless you want it to mean something. Come on, let's grab a blanket from my car and we can lie down and look at the lightning over the mountains."

We walked into the desert and found a spot free of trees with a good view of the mountains and spread the blanket. The lightning was spectacular. Sometimes the strikes were lone bolts that cracked audibly even at that distance. Others started out as a single bolt and then branched out intricately like an upside down tree. I cradled her head on my shoulder and we talked until I couldn't stand it anymore and kissed her.

I had never made love outdoors, but apparently Lorraine had as she quickly took to her feet and slipped out of her clothes and was soon standing over me completely naked.

"Come on you big sissy. Get undressed."

I stood up and undressed as commanded. We hugged and then kissed again, her breasts tight against my body.

"I have a thing for big boobies," I said placing my hands on her breasts and squeezing her nipples. Yours are really big."

"You seem to be really big too but soft. What's wrong? Do you need encouragement? I can suck you."

"I don't think it would help. Some part of me is saying yes go for it. And another is throwing up all sorts of moral barriers. My penis is paralyzed with conflicting signals."

"Damn Hercules, I could have used a good working over."

"I'm sorry, it never seems like the right time for us," I said, and added, "Who knows about the future though?"

"Yeah maybe, but I wouldn't lose sleep over it," she answered, leaving me totally puzzled about why she had said it.

Lorraine and I continued our friendship on a purely platonic level after that evening. We shared meals, went to the reservation to visit her grandfather, took long walks and shared very intimate thoughts. At work I spent my time exclusively on preventing the abolition of the Mexican American Studies program at the local high schools. In the end it proved to be futile and I was recalled to Washington. Lorraine on the other hand was not returning because the Congressman granted her request to run his Tucson office.

CHAPTER IV

A few days before I left for D.C., I decided that I needed to share my public lands report with Lorraine and ask her advice. After she read it and compared it with the congressman's bill, she was confused.

"What the hell's going on, Pelon? I heard Congressman Jimmy congratulate you on a job well done but it's not reflected in his bill."

"It's a rather long story but I really needed to tell you before I left, hoping that you could give me some advice as to how I should proceed."

"Let's have it, homie. This is important shit."

We sat down and I recounted in detail my conversation with Farley Abrams and my subsequent conversation with Robert. I also told her about my plan to involve Esperanza and Naomi.

"Damn Homeboy, what the hell's wrong with you? I thought we were friends, dude. You should have told me sooner."

"It hasn't been easy keeping this to myself. But I have no actual proof other than the discrepancy between my report and the Congressman's bill. I didn't want to get you involved solely on a suspicion."

"Well you should have told me anyway. Besides I know some things that may help you."

"Well that's what I began hoping for after you hinted that Naomi and Esperanza share an apartment," I said.

"I never hinted at that."

"Yeah you did. They are a couple aren't they?"

"Yes but you're just guessing. I didn't set you on that path."

"Why all the secrecy? It's really no big deal," I said.

"Congressman Jimmy has his faults. He's a bit homophobic, staunch Catholic that he is."

"But how can knowing this help me?" I asked.

"Let's talk a bit about what you suspect. First of all I have a lot of respect for Congressman Jimmy but I also have my priorities and protecting Indian Lands and Mother Earth is at the highest level. And I think that you should know that Naomi's dad was Apache. She grew up with her Mexican mother in South Tucson but she has some loyalties to her ancestral roots. That's one of the reasons she was pissed when you got that assignment."

"Makes sense," I said. "So you think she would help if she thought something was amiss and detrimental to indigenous people?"

"I think she would. But I think it would have to first come from me. She doesn't much like you and wouldn't listen to you."

"She's been unrelenting in her disdain. Is it because I'm such a stud?"

"Maybe, but once I tell her that you couldn't get it up I think she'll change her opinion."

"Whoa, you're cold, sister."

"You started it. But seriously I'll make a call and set it up for you to meet and talk. I think she'll help if you don't go messing things up with your macho notions."

"I'm not like that! I was just joking."

"So was I."

"I'll miss you Lorraine. Washington won't be the same without you."

"Yeah well you'll have your gringa friend to keep you company. Let me know how things go between you and Naomi."

"I will and I'll still miss you, gringa girlfriend or not."

I arrived in D.C. on a red eye and after calling Helga and arranging to see her later that day, I called Naomi at the office.

"Hey Naomi. It's Pelon."

"Hello Pelon. Lorraine warned me that you would be calling."

Warning! I thought and I was about to say something nasty but held back.

"I'm sorry if I have made a bad impression on you. I hope to change that," I said.

"I guess it's also been partly my fault," she said. "Lorraine said you wanted to meet."

"Yes most definitely. When's a good time?"

"After work would be a good for us. Can you go to our apartment?"

"Sure, just tell me how to get there."

I got her address and directions and then went to see Helga and all thoughts of Lorraine faded into the background.

"I missed you, Pelon. I hope never to be apart from you again for such a long period of time."

"I missed you too, Helga."

"Why don't you move in with me, Pelon. It's silly to have a separate place when we enjoy one another's company so much."

"It is true that I enjoy being with you."

"Just stay with me a few days and see how it feels and you can decide afterwards."

We had crazy uninhibited sex for most of the afternoon and although I dreaded the commitment that such a move entailed, this time I agreed that it was silly to live apart. I always knew that I loved her but maybe this time the guilt over Lorraine helped push me over the edge. In spite of all her wealth, Helga was a very simple person. Sure she had all the material things she wanted, fancy furniture, tons of clothes and dozens of shoes but she wasn't burdened by it.

Her stuff didn't own her. Or so it seemed but then again maybe she just took it for granted that she could buy anything she wanted and she did like what people would consider the finer things in life. We always ate at the best restaurants and on weekend trips stayed at luxurious resorts. To her credit though she did try to use her wealth wisely. She gave tons of money to charity and she served on several boards, mostly related to the arts. It was a world that was foreign until I began accompanying her to the openings of art shows and musical events. I admit that I was impressed by that sort of thing. It was fun to own a tuxedo and mingle with 'la crema' as we called those on top of the social ladder. And I even met some interesting people and had some good conversations. Besides, we often invited Robert and if everyone else were a bore, he and I would rescue each other.

"I have a meeting this evening," I said when we were lying in bed. "After my meeting I'll stop at my place and pick up a few things and come back here."

"What's your meeting about? Something I might be interested in?" she asked.

"Remember I told you about my report and how it was not used by the Congressman?"

"Vaguely."

"I'm meeting a couple of co-workers on that and it's not really appropriate for you to attend. You don't mind do you?"

"Heavens no. I'll give you a key to let yourself in."

"I shouldn't be too late."

I arrived at the apartment on time and Esperanza invited me inside. Their apartment was small and tastefully modern in its décor, probably more of a reflection of Esperanza, judging by the attention to detail that she gave to her attire.

"Come in, Pelon," Esperanza said without much enthusiasm.

"Hello, Pelon," Naomi greeted me from a sumptuous black leather couch. "You can sit on that chair," pointing to a generous-sized companion to the couch. "Let's get right down to business," she added. "Esperanza downloaded your report, and we've read it and compared it to Congressman Jimmy's bill and agree that something is not right. Actually we were both laughing at how much you strutted around in vain."

"And how so much jealousy was produced for naught," I said smiling.

"Touché," Naomi said with a half-hearted smile. "Nevertheless, putting that all aside, it does seem that we should find out what the hell is going on. I think that Lorraine told you my specific reasons for wanting to clear this up so don't go off thinking that we're trying to be best buds with you."

"Understood," I said and waited for Naomi to continue, as she seemed hell-bent on controlling the conversation.

"Lorraine said that you could provide other information that would be helpful. So take it away."

Esperanza served us a glass of wine and Naomi stretched out her hand and took Esperanza's hand in hers and had her sit close to her. I recapped my conversation with Farley Abrams and was surprised when Naomi said that she knew him.

"Is he still working at the NRDC?" she asked.

"Yeah. How do you know Farley?"

"The NRDC's work touches on a lot of the issues that I'm interested in and he's also involved with the LGBT."

"You must also know Robert Harrison."

"I do. Not very well but what I do know of him, I like. Frankly I'm surprised that you know these two gay men."

"What's really going to surprise you is that Robert is also part of this story." The mood of our meeting changed considerably after I revealed my close friendship with

Robert and I relaxed as I told them what he had said to me and outlined the plan that we had conceived.

Esperanza spoke for the first time. "I would have to download a copy of Congressman Jimmy's calendar."

"Is it possible?" I asked.

"It's possible but not without some risk. Is that really necessary?"

"We can't think of any other way," I said.

Naomi looked at Esperanza and reassured her. "You're a wiz love. It'll be fine."

By the time I left several hours later we were all smiling and actually sorry that it was ending, at least that was what I was feeling. We had created a timeline of when Esperanza would download two years of calendar and how I would return to their apartment to get assistance in identifying individuals that met with the Congressman.

I hurried over to my place and picked up a few items that I would need in my new digs. I felt queasy as I drove over to Helga's, knowing again that I had made a decision that was life changing. It was later than I had planned on arriving and she was already in bed. I changed into pajamas and I slid into bed as quietly as I could and immediately went to sleep.

The following day Helga had to attend an opening for an art gallery and we invited Robert. Helga busied herself with other guests and Robert and I shared a glass of wine and I debriefed him on my meeting with Naomi and Esperanza.

"I have to tell you Robert that having you as a friend has provided many benefits. The ice between those two women and me melted immediately when I told them about you. So thanks buddy."

"You're welcome I'm sure," he said. "It's probably a good idea for me to also look at those names on the Congressman's calendar. I might be of some help in identifying some of them."

"I think so too. I'll ask Naomi if it's possible for you to attend the meeting when we go over his appointments. How are things at your end?" I asked him when we finished talking about my mission.

"Do you mean at work?" Robert asked.

"Yes at work!" I answered somewhat arrogantly. "Sometimes you piss me off, Robert," I said. "You're so damn precise about everything you say. What the hell do I see in you?"

"I have asked myself the same question about you my friend," he said. "And I have concluded that there are some things best left unexplored and just accepted for what they are. In our case we like each other and that's enough."

"Yeah I suppose you're right but sometimes you are still an asshole or as you would probably say 'a rectum'."

"No heavens I would never correct the vernacular. It is so expressive. Especially when it so aptly describes someone such as Helga's husband whom I just spotted across the way."

Robert pointed with his head in the direction of where he had seen Andre, and I looked and saw him talking with Helga.

"But in answer to your question," Robert continued, "the situation at work is quickly deteriorating for me. I find myself more and more at odds with the people with whom I am working, clients as well as colleagues. I'm sure that I'll resign shortly or be asked to resign."

"Really," I said surprised. "What are you going to do if you have no job? Jobs aren't so easy to come by right now."

"Oh I'll be all right. Jake has plenty of money saved up. And I have a few dollars as well. Money isn't what has me worried."

"What is worrying you?"

"I worry about us and people like us," Robert answered, "Look how quickly we have become inured to the travesties of the fascists who are now running the country. Every day we see a new infringement on our privacy or a new curtailment on our freedom. And we accept it without even so much as a whimper. Yesterday they were installing video cameras on our block. I'm giving it the old one finger salute every time I pass by it, a futile effort I suppose, but at least I'm showing some resistance and it makes me feel better."

There was a din of talk making it impossible for anyone to overhear our conversation, nevertheless I lowered my voice when I told him.

"No wonder they're going to fire your ass, Robert. You are beginning to sound like a militiaman. You best be careful where you say stuff like that."

"But you do agree, do you not?" he asked.

"Of course I do. But who would have thought that I, a radical liberal would be agreeing with a conservative and both of us agreeing with the crazy militia people who for years have been opposed to too much government in their lives."

"Yes it is ironic," he said sadly.

At home I asked Helga about her conversation with Andre.

"He's still pouting about our annulment," she answered. "He wants me to reconsider and he tells me that you're just after my money."

"Damn," I said. "How did he find out so fast? What gave me away? Was it the new tuxedo?"

"No he was serious. He called you a gold digging spic and he promised that he was going to put your ass in a sling. I'm worried for you sweetie. Andre can be very mean and vindictive."

"He's just blowing smoke up his ass," I said. "Don't worry about me. I can take care of myself. If I can survive on the streets, I can survive this."

"He apparently has a lot of power in this new position," she said. "He isn't just some jealous husband making empty threats. You've seen how they can now incarcerate people without making any formal charges. I'm worried about you."

I didn't tell Helga what Lorraine's grandfather had told me. That would have really freaked her. But I thought about it.

A few days after our initial meeting, Esperanza obtained the Congressman's calendar and Naomi let me know as clandestinely as possible that we were ready to meet.

"I was thinking, Naomi, that Robert with his vast Washington experience could help us. How would you feel about extending an invitation to him for this meeting?"

"Agreed. I think he could provide some valuable input." And she added, "Maybe it would also be prudent to invite Farley Abrams."

"I'll call him," I said.

"Good but don't make the call from the office. Esperanza just found out that our telephones are being tapped."

"By whom?" I asked in alarm.

"Don't know. Just be careful with calls and emails too. There's a good chance someone is also looking at them."

"I think I know something about that. I'll tell you later," I said.

It took several phone calls to Farley and Robert and conversations with Naomi to arrange the meeting but finally we arrived at a mutually convenient date and time. I had thought of suggesting Helga's place but thought better of it as I didn't want to destroy my newly found rapport with Naomi and Esperanza with the glitz of Helga's home.

Thus we were again meeting at Naomi and Esperanza's apartment.

Robert and I went together and Farley arrived shortly after we did, just as Robert was serving a wine that he had brought.

"Come on Farley," I said. "Grab a glass and I'll introduce you after the toast."

As soon as Farley was served Robert launched into his toast.

"Here's to a successful venture of like minded people regardless of their political persuasion or sexual orientation."

"Hear, hear!" we acclaimed in unison and drank heartily.

"I think no introductions are in order, Macias. I think we all know one another," Farley said and everyone assented by nodding their head.

"Well let's get down to business," Naomi said, once again taking charge. "Esperanza made a CD of all the names found in the calendar and referenced them so that we know when and where the meeting took place. She'll project them on to the wall and that way we can all go over the names. It'll be tedious but I think necessary. There's some munchies in the kitchen and of course more wine if you'd like."

We began in good spirits and moved quickly through the list in less than two hours, with someone in the room supplying information that eliminated irrelevant names. Farley and Robert were of most value, supplying information on several of the names that were unknown to the rest of us. Most of those names belonged to lobbyists for large concerns with interests in public lands.

"Well we know for certain that our Congressman was being heavily lobbied by big money interests in public lands," Naomi summarized. "What he did is still unclear."

"The name Randolph Hamilton that no one seems to know," Robert said, "can we look him up on the web and see who he is?"

"I can do that," Esperanza offered and her fingers dashed quickly across the keyboard of her laptop.

"He's well known," Esperanza said. "Says that he manages a fund for extremely wealthy clients."

"That's our man," Robert said and we all agreed by voice or body language.

"The next step will be to verify that the Congressman is indeed a client of Randolph Hamilton," Naomi said. "I'm not quite sure just how we'll do that but if you have some suggestions we can entertain those now."

"I guess I could call and pretend that I'm the Congressman and ask for an appointment with Hamilton," I said.

"No good," Robert said. "They'll ask for your account number right off."

"Maybe I could hack into their system," Esperanza offered.

"You could do that?" I asked incredulously.

"I think so. That or hack the Congressman's computer," Esperanza said with a smile of satisfaction."

"High five," Farley said to Esperanza and their open hands met in mid air.

"Okay, I think for now we're done here," Naomi said, "except for one important item that I think involves everyone. Esperanza has discovered that our office telephones are being monitored and there is a good possibility that if the phones are compromised so are our emails. The three of us have to assume that our communications are not private and so do Farley and Robert when contacting us. Pelon, you said that maybe you knew something about this."

"Robert and I have a mutual acquaintance, one Andre Matthews, that has taken an unsavory interest in us and he happens to be in a position of great power as head of the National Geospatial Intelligence Agency. That agency has the capability of monitoring telephone calls and all Internet based communication and Andre has probably ordered them to target us."

Farley waved his outstretched hand frantically. "I think I can add something that I've come across," he said and continued when we all focused on him. "For sometime now, several of our member organizations have been providing anecdotal accounts of private conversations being made available to hostile concerns. Until last week all of us suspected that perhaps someone within a particular organization had been careless and allowed critical information to get into the wrong hands. But then an IT person at one organization got wind of an effort by the NSA to monitor Internet traffic on quite a large scale."

"You're sure it's more widespread than just Congressman Jimmy's office?"

"That's correct. All of us have to assume that safeguards on our privacy have been breached."

We ended our meeting not being sure if our efforts were being directed at the real enemy. At the office I slid back into my regular work routine – well, as regular as was possible under the new conditions that had been imposed – all of us knowing that our telephone conversations and email were monitored and possibly even office conversations could be heard and taped. It made working conditions very difficult and everyone was on edge.

Later I was to find out that this level of scrutiny wasn't yet found in offices and places of employment in other parts of the country. DC was the prototype of what was to come. The most ambitious project was the geospatial database that had satellite images working in tandem with street level video to provide information on individuals. They could track a person's movements around the city as one could track a mouse in a laboratory maze. And with long distance sound tracking they could hear a person's conversations. Andre, a demographer with expertise in census tract information and satellite imagery, was heading this project. I knew that Helga was right. He did have enormous power at his command, but I was in denial about my vulnerability. It can happen to others but not to me, I thought.

All my apprehensions about moving in with Helga had vanished over time and I was enjoying being a part of her life. I had always been a closed and private person and it was Dr. Maier's group that had helped me learn to open up to people. I probably could not have enjoyed the intimacy of sharing with Helga prior to that experience. In the early part of our friendship we had already swapped information about family and friends and some childhood memories, but living together gave us the opportunity to fill in gaps and to expand on the stories that we had only partially revealed. She knew for example that I lived with my grandmother prior to moving to DC but I had not told her much about my grandmother or why I ended up with her. And I had never said much about my real father. One Sunday afternoon when we were lounging around after she had returned from church, she mentioned that maybe next time I could accompany her. She was a devout Catholic by the way, while I, although baptized as a Catholic, had never been a churchgoer. I made a sour face at her invitation.

"You have never attended mass regularly?" she asked accusingly.

"No," I answered sheepishly, adding, "but I did attend a Christian church for awhile." I had hoped that telling her about the Christian church would at least give me a little respect in her eyes. She laughed at my feeble effort.

"Tell me about your Christian church," she asked.

"It's in something I wrote for my freshman English class," I said. "Can I read it to you?"

"Yes, I like your stories," she answered.

"Okay," I said. "Actually it's also a story about my father and about my grandmother, the one I lived with."

"Why are you so nervous?" she asked me in her gentlest voice.

"Hell I don't know," I said. "Maybe because it has a lot of personal feelings."

"All the more reason why you should share it with me sweetie," she said.

"You're right," I said and I started to read.

* * *

There was no one shorter in our barrio than Inez. If you saw him from far away or could only see his back you would swear that he was a kid. But his face was already old and wrinkled so it was easy to tell that he was a man if you were looking straight at him. Otherwise as I said before he had the body of a young boy, weighing less than a hundred pounds. He was a very quiet man and that also made him different from the other men that lived on our street. Inez lived next door to us with four other men in Grandma's garage. The other men, Roberto, Javier, Julio and Leonardo were all from Mexico and didn't have any papers. They were like the men that you see standing at a corner waiting for someone to hire them for the day. Mostly they worked in construction as laborers or cleaning and gardening in private homes. They were young and didn't have any families and all of them talked about returning to Mexico some day. Except for Leonardo, who wanted to become an American and wanted everyone to call him Lenny, but no matter how much he reminded people, everyone still called him Leonardo. In fact they laughed at him for wanting to become an American and teased him about going to night school to learn English, telling him that he was a huero *with a* cola prieta, *that is a gringo with a brown butt. Inez never teased him though. Inez was a really good man and he went out of his way to help other people. One Thanksgiving for example, Roberto got a turkey from his boss but the garage where they lived didn't have a stove to cook it in. It was just a big room with a toilet and shower and a tiny microwave oven. Roberto was just going to give it to one of the neighbors. He didn't even try asking Grandma to use her oven because he already knew she would say no. She was kinda weird sometimes. She was a tightwad and you would think that she was about to starve the way she was always trying to make money. Maybe if Roberto had offered to pay for using her oven she would have let him but I guess he didn't think of that. Anyway Inez had an idea, offering to ask his boss to let him put the turkey in one of the bakery ovens where he worked. They were big ovens and it would be easy to make room for a small turkey. Well the boss said yes and in the afternoon when Inez got off from work he came home with the cooked turkey. The men had a feast that Thanksgiving and they even gave me some. Inez didn't eat any type of meat so he did what he did only for Roberto and the others. That was just how he was. I was only about 10 when that happened but I have always remembered that day.*

Inez had lived in my grandma's garage for a long long time, way before I was born and even before my grandfather died and Grandma became a widow. When Inez first arrived from Mexico, my grandfather invited Inez to stay in the garage until he got on his feet. They met because Inez started to work at the same bakery where my grandfather was working. My grandfather was letting Inez stay in the garage for free but when he died then Grandma started charging Inez rent and she also began renting to other men. Inez was actually like a member of the family and he has been the one that has told me what I know about my father and about my mother when she was young. Inez met her when she was a teenager and my mother shared many of her secrets with him, things that even my grandma doesn't know, and that's unusual because Grandma knows about everything. It isn't easy to keep something from her. I know because many times I have tried.

When Inez met my mother she was already beginning to feel that Grandma was too strict and too stingy. My grandfather had died a year after Inez moved in and it seems like Grandma started to change then or maybe she had been hiding her real personality all the time. Whatever, the thing is that my mother felt like moving out and began doing things behind Grandma's back, things like having boyfriends and hanging out with girls who were doing drugs. I had to beg Inez many times before he told me some of this stuff and the only reason he did was to help me avoid some of her mistakes when I too was starting to skip school and get into trouble. I guess my mother's lessons didn't help me very much, at least not so far.

My mother finally began to settle down when she met the man who was my father. He was a man that rented one of the bunk beds in Grandma's garage and according to Inez a very good looking and intelligent man. He and my mother fell in love and for a while they met in secret, knowing that Grandma would freak if she knew. But then my mother got pregnant and when Grandma found out she went and called the police. My father had no choice but to run back to Mexico since my mother was only seventeen and he was almost thirty. I think that they call that statutory rape. What Grandma didn't count on was that my mother would follow my father back to his small village in Michoacan. Inez says that after my mother went to Mexico, Grandma was really angry and was even meaner than usual, making threats about calling the migra on the men that rented from her, and yelling at her sister Chelo for every little thing. Chelo had been blind since childhood and had lived with Grandma forever and she had always done the cooking and much of the housework. It was amazing to see her cooking and moving around the house just by touching and feeling. She had memorized where everything was and whenever I couldn't find something she would say 'look with your hands muchacho,' and she would go and find it for me just like that. Inez made excuses for the way Grandma acted during that time, saying that she was heartbroken and didn't realize what she was doing but I think I know my grandma well enough to know that she's that way. Something was taken from her and she didn't like it. I've seen her get angry when she feels someone has cheated her out of some money. I tell you, you don't want to be around her then.

Inez was the one that gave me the details about my mother getting sick while giving birth. In the small Mexican village where she was living, they didn't have any doctors, just a partera, a woman who knew about babies. The partera was not able to stop my mother's bleeding and my father sent a telegram letting Grandma know that I was born and that my mother was sick. Inez said Grandma sent some money and arranged for my mother to be seen by a real doctor.

Afterwards Grandma stayed awake all night crying and saying over and over that she had warned her daughter not to go and that God punished my mother for disobeying her. They took my mother to a town with a doctor and for a while she was pretty sick but eventually she got better.

I once asked Inez why he knew so much about all that happened to my mother and he said that some of the things he saw and heard. But other things he learned from Chelo. I was kind of surprised when he mentioned Chelo as I had never noticed that they spoke. I have always been somewhat nosey and out of curiosity I began to watch Inez whenever he was with Chelo. Like I said before he was a very kind man so I had never paid much attention to the things that he did for Chelo. They were ordinary things like helping her down the back steps when she wanted to get to the garden or helping her put her arms through the sleeves of her sweater. But when I really looked I was shocked. He seemed to light up whenever he had a chance to help her and he did it with such gentleness that you would have thought that Chelo was a small bird that might be hurt unless he was really careful. Actually Chelo was not like that at all. She had grown up with a lot of brothers and her speech was full of street slang and cuss words. She liked nothing better than to sit around with the men who rented the garage and drink cold beer and sing Mexican songs, the kind that men sing when they are feeling heartbroken and sad, letting out a yell now and then. Chelo would not hold back yelling as loud as they and as often. Really a more unlikely match was not possible. Inez, as I told you, was quiet and gentle but he was also really shy, a nondrinker, never cussed or used words that implied

*sex in any way. Hell he was practically a minister at
the holy roller church that he attended.*

*I don't know what Inez saw in Chelo but he
seemed to be in love. Chelo seemed to enjoy his
attention but she wasn't all mushy about it. But the
whole thing then made sense to me. Why Inez stayed
in the garage. He was still working at the bakery and
earning good money. He probably could have bought
himself a house even. And he had his green card too.
But if he had left then he couldn't be close to Chelo,
the woman he loved. Naturally he never told anyone
that he loved her, not even Chelo. Maybe he was just
afraid that Chelo wouldn't want him or maybe he was
afraid of my grandma, knowing that she would never
let Chelo get involved with someone. Whatever the
reason, he kept it to himself and it would have stayed
like that if life had not interfered.*

*Even though I'm still young I'm learning that all of
life is connected somehow and that everything that
one wants to hide from others eventually gets known.
In Spanish we say 'se le salio la cola al chango' when
we want to point out that someone pretending to be
somebody else eventually gets discovered, translated it
says 'the monkey's tail came out' (from inside his
pants, leaving no doubt that he was a monkey all
along).*

*After my mother was well enough to travel, an
ambulance brought her back to the US and she was
put in the hospital. Chelo and my grandma took care
of me until my mother came home about a month
later. During that time Grandma found out that my
dad already had a family in Mexico with a woman in
a neighboring village and when she told my mother she
took it really hard and almost ended up in the hospital*

again. Lots of men leave their families back in Mexico when they come to the US to work and some of them start other families here and never go back. It is not an unusual situation. So my mother never returned to my father's village and she never tried to get in touch with him. When I was four she married my stepfather, a man who was a butcher at the local supermarket.

I was in middle school when I began to suspect that Inez had a thing for Chelo. But something else happened that year: my father showed up one day at my grandma's house. He didn't know that my mother and stepfather had bought the house next door. Hell, he didn't even know that my mother had survived the delivery. Inez was the one who recognized him and he took him into the garage and explained the situation. Inez knew that my grandma would be mad as hell if she saw him there so he tried to keep the whole thing hush-hush and hoped that he could get him to leave quietly. But my father was anything but quiet. He began to raise all kinds of hell and rushed out of the garage and went straight into my grandma's house without even knocking. My mother and I heard the commotion and went outside to see who was doing all the yelling. Inez was outside the garage looking quite worried and when we realized that the yelling was coming from Grandma's house we ran over there. Inside, my father was cussing out my grandma, telling her that she was a fucking bitch and that even hell was too good for her. My mother ran over to him and started hitting him with her fists and yelling for him to get out of the house and telling me to call the police. Somehow my father managed to tell my mother that years ago, after my birth, Grandma had written him a letter telling him that Mother and I had died in the hospital and even sent a photograph showing Grandma dressed in black, placing flowers on our grave. My mother stopped hitting him, shocked and confused by what he said but still managed to say that what died was their love because he was pinchi mujeriego, *a fucking womanizer. I stole a glance at my grandma who was unusually quiet and white in the face with fright. She was beginning to back out of the room and I assumed that the whole scene had freaked her.*

My father told my mother that he was no womanizer, that she was the only woman that he had ever loved and that to this day he remained faithful to her memory. My mother laughed at his face and asked him if he mourned her together with his other family. My father was confused and he asked her what she was talking about. Things weren't making sense to me either and then Chelo, who had been standing quietly off to one side of the room, Inez next to her just as quiet, spoke up, suggesting that maybe her sister had lied to everyone. After my mother and father calmed down and examined what Grandma had told each of them, it became clear that Chelo was right, Grandma had lied to my father and to my mother, to keep them apart. Wow, I was stunned but so were my parents. My father just sat down with his head between his hands, unable to say anything but 'que puta vida,' what a fucked up life. He would say that again when he found out that my mother had married and had three other kids. My mother was mixed up. She didn't know what to think or if she should feel anger or sadness. She had another life, another man in her life. My father had just been a bad memory until then, a man who had done her wrong, a man she hated. And I was totally out of it. Here was a stranger who was my father and I didn't feel anything for him. I was sorry for him. Sorry for the way Grandma had helped create a memory that became like a prison for him.

We stayed quiet and apart for what seemed a long time. No one knew what could be said or what should be said. That's when my stepfather walked in and my mother had to explain the situation. He wasn't too happy either. Welcome to the club I thought. Actually he had the least to worry about but maybe he didn't know that right then. All he was seeing was the man who was my mother's first lover and he was jealous. Big deal I thought.

Chelo left to look in on Grandma, who was probably hiding in her room. I would have been if I were her. Inez asked my father to go to the garage and he led him away, finally ending the tension in the room. I stayed until my mother suggested that I should go and get acquainted with my father, and my father and I sort of talked. Roberto offered him a beer and that loosened him up a bit. He told me he had a small ranch with some cattle. His mother and a younger sister lived with him. His dad died a few years ago. After finishing a second beer he said that he had to get going and we said goodbye. I watched him go and make a parting gesture towards Grandma's house, the same as giving her the finger, only Mexicans bang the palm of one hand with the other formed into a fist, the index finger sticking out. But it means the same 'fuck you.'

Some things returned to normal, others were never the same. My stepfather was irritable for many days after my father's visit but eventually he seemed to forget. I caught my mother deep in thought several *times but she would never tell me what she was thinking. She tried to have it out with my grandma, but Grandma was not her old feisty self and mom left her alone.*

I think Inez was the one who woke up and took the most notice. He saw how a true love had been broken up by the selfish needs of an old woman and he decided that he wasn't going to let any more time pass between him and his true love. He proposed to Chelo and didn't even ask for Grandma's permission. Chelo was tickled by the offer and she accepted. It was a nice wedding. They bought a house in the neighborhood, a part of which Inez used as a church. Chelo told me that now that she was a minister's wife she couldn't cuss like before and she laughed.

* * *

Helga's grey blue eyes were moistened when I finished reading. "Your stories are always a mix of sadness and joy," she said. "Come over here and let me hug you."

I stayed wrapped in her embrace for a long time before she asked.

"I'm sorry to say this, but your grandmother was awful. She was like the witch from the west," she said. "Your poor father. Did you ever see him again?"

"Yeah. After I got out of the youth camp I went to stay with him in Mexico. I didn't want to live with my stepfather anymore so it was an opportune time to establish a friendship with my father. I stayed several months with him at his ranch and he taught me how to ride a horse and how to herd cattle. It was really cool. But I wanted to go to college and my grandmother, who had moved to Tucson, said I could live with her while I was in school. I keep in touch with him and every so often I'll go and spend some time with him. He's a good man. Simple, hard working and very devout, like you."

"And was the Christian church you attended, the one Inez and Chelo opened?"

"Yes, for several months. I always felt good with him and mostly I went because he invited me. I never really cared for all the loud preaching and singing. Frankly, I never had a serious belief in God. I was afraid of hell and the devil and I prayed when I was in trouble or wanted something badly enough. But I can't say that I thought of God as a Living Entity who created me and loved me. You must feel like that about God?"

"Yes, about God and Christ," she said. "They are such an integral part of my life that loving them is second nature, like breathing. I can't imagine living without belief in God. I would have to die."

"I don't ever spend much time thinking about God," I said. "In fact I purposely avoid thinking about God because it is so confusing to think about all the related concepts like infinity and life after death. My mind can't wrap itself around where God originated and what exists outside our universe. So I'd rather just put those questions aside and focus on what is here and now and try and be a good person. And if I were asked point blank if I believed in God I would say yes. But maybe I would say yes just because I don't have the courage to say no."

"I don't think it is lack of courage, my love," she said. "You simply don't have a mature understanding of God. Do you know who Piaget is?"

"Not really," I answered. "I remember the name from an education class, but it's just a name."

"Yes," she said, "he would be included in education classes because he conducted developmental studies with his own children. By observing them, he learned that young children, around preschool age, were not able to grasp certain concepts that adults take for granted. One of

110

his famous experiments was to show children two identical glasses filled with equal amounts of water. He would first ask the children which of the glasses contained the most water. All of the children would say that they contained equal amounts. Next he would take one of the original glasses and in front of the children pour its water into a tall and narrow glass. Then placing the narrow tall glass next to the remaining original glass he would ask the children which glass had the most water. Only some of the children could see that the glasses had equal amounts. The others thought that the tall, narrow glass had more water. Only as they matured could they see that the glasses, regardless of their shape, had an identical volume of water."

"Are you saying that my brain has not matured?" I asked, not sure if I should feel slighted.

"Perhaps, but before you get all in a huff let me finish, and suspend your judgment until then."

"Okay," I said, "but I don't think you'll pull it off."

"Just hold on. The truth is that although we are all on the same planet, we don't have a uniform view of the world. We come here with different capacities and talents, different life experiences and different challenges. These color and shade what we see. Some artists have played with these phenomena by hiding an image within a primary image. In one famous drawing, an artist depicts a young girl in which some people, by looking in just the right way, can also see an old woman. However there are some people who can only see the young woman. I think the world of Spirit is like that also. Behind the primary image of the daily activity we call life, is the world of Spirit, hidden and waiting to be discovered. When Christ said 'Those who are first will be last and those who are last will be first,' He meant that people who focus on the hidden world of Spirit, who acquire the spiritual virtues will eventually be more rewarded than those whose only focus is becoming materially successful."

"Does that mean that those who live by the motto, 'He who in the end has the most toys wins' are wrong?" I asked jokingly.

"Absolutely," she answered.

When Helga came out with stuff like that she blew me away and filled me with admiration for her intellect and humanity. And I sort of understood what she was trying to tell me, but when I went to church with her the next Sunday, I felt nothing of the joy that she felt. All I could think of as I sat in the pew was the church's wealth and how much good it could do in the world if it were given to the poor.

"Don't worry about that," Helga advised. "You're doing the right thing by focusing on being a good person. Being good is living in the world of Spirit. If you struggle to understand, you will eventually be rewarded with understanding."

.^.^.^.

CHAPTER V

Four days after our secret meeting, Naomi let me know that Esperanza had been successful in determining that Congressman Jimmy was a client of Randolph Hamilton, having found his name and account number when she hacked into the database.

"But we have a problem, Pelon. Someone in Hamilton's office was able to discover the hack and traced it back to our office."

"That is a problem," I said. "Good thing Esperanza didn't do it from home."

"I guess," Naomi answered. "The other complication is that Hamilton has other elected officials as clients, Democrats and Republicans. Esperanza recognized them and had the foresight to download the entire database."

"Oh wow! What the hell do we do with that information? It's like having a tiger by the tail."

"It's bigger than a tiger; it's more like a Tyrannosaurus Rex," she said. "What Esperanza downloaded has not only names and account numbers, it also has net worth. Some of those clients have been with Hamilton for many years and their assets are worth millions. It's a mini who's who of Washington."

"Damn," I uttered. "I guess some things are best left alone. I'm sorry I got you and Esperanza involved, Naomi. Maybe it's best that I hold on to the list and say that it was I that downloaded the information. Do you have it on a flash drive?"

"Yes, but don't feel like you have to take on all of the responsibility. We all went in with our eyes wide open," she said and placed the drive into my hand. She allowed her hand to remain in mine momentarily, a gesture of friendship I assumed.

"I'll take it to Farley this evening. Maybe he has some ideas of what to do with it."

"Call me tonight and let me know what you and Farley decide," she said.

I was anxious the rest of the morning, and knowing that I needed to talk with someone, I went to a pay telephone and called Robert.

"Hola Robert. Sorry to bother you, but there's a big wrinkle in our plan. Can I meet you for lunch?"

"Not a bother, Pelon. Sure lunch is possible. I already had something set up, but I'm actually glad to have an excuse to get out of it. Want to go to the Carlyle? It's close to you."

"Yeah that's fine. Let's meet in a half-hour."

"OK."

During lunch I told Robert about my conversation with Naomi and I showed him the flash drive. I was not surprised that his reaction was one of astonishment.

"You have to get that flash drive to a safe place, Pelon. It's a ticking bomb."

"You don't think I should hand it over to Farley?"

"Eventually yes, but right now we have to determine if someone actually knows what you have."

"I guess you are right. Maybe I'm all paranoid for nothing."

"Nothing wrong with being cautious," Robert said.

"All right. I'll hide the flash drive but don't ask me where. The less you and anybody else know, the better. I will meet with Farley and let him know what's going on."

After my lunch with Robert I went to the post office and mailed the flash drive to Rodrigo, asking him to save it for me and not to go snooping around in its contents.

In my life, October 2, 2010 is the day that brought great changes. It was a Friday and a cold wind was whipping through the area. I left the office and was walking through Georgetown on my way to a meeting that I set up with Farley. It was already dark and I was wrapped in my heavy long coat with my collar up for added warmth.

Having lived in barrios where survival depends on being alert and always knowing or sensing who's around, I became aware of two large men in back of me who were keeping the same pace over the course of several blocks. I went into a small store that sells produce and specialty foods and I ordered some paté and grabbed a can of imported olives from the shelf. I asked the clerk to double bag my purchases. Outside I glanced around quickly and spotted the two men off to the side, waiting for me to come out.

I gave no sign of having spotted them and continued my walk home. Along a particular stretch where cars roared past and with no other pedestrians, they made their move. I swung the plastic bag at the one who reached me first and I caught him square on the side of his face, the can of olives making a dull thud as it landed. He went down but the other one shoved me from behind into the street, hoping to push me into the path of a car.

I stumbled, landing hard on my elbow and rolling over. Fortunately I came to a stop in the middle of the two lanes while cars whizzed by blaring their horns. I didn't wait to see what my attacker would do next and throwing caution to the wind I sprinted across to the other side of the busy street. I started running but a van pulled up and two other burly men jumped out in front of me. They came at me punching and kicking, joined by my two original attackers. I landed a roundhouse kick to the temple of one, who went crashing to the ground, punched one in the throat bringing him down to his knees and landed a few more blows on the third man before I felt my entire body convulsing when the fourth man used a taser on me. Once on the ground I was punched and kicked until I was senseless.

My left eye was nearly shut when I came to and I had to turn my whole body to look around a small windowless room. There was a small water basin, a toilet, a thin blanket on the floor next to me, and a bright ceiling light. It was a tall ceiling and on one of the corners a video camera was mounted. I didn't have to wait long to find out where I was. The metal door opened and Andre walked in.

"It's not as fancy as Helga's," he said "but here as there, you won't have to worry about the rent."

When I was about to tell him to go fuck himself, I felt a searing pain on my jaw as if it were broken.

"My guy didn't appreciate the can in his face. He's the one that did that to your jaw. Actually he would have killed you but they knew I wanted you alive so he was restrained. You might say that I saved your life."

It took all my strength but I lifted my arm and gave him the finger.

"You need to be more appreciative," Andre said, "otherwise I don't know how long I can hold him back. He's the vengeful type. You're supposed to have something that belongs to some of my associates. I need to get it back from you.

"I don't have anything of the sort," I answered.

"It wasn't on your person so you must have hid it somewhere."

"You seem to have all the answers."

"I do know quite a bit about it. I had a good conversation with Naomi who told me that she handed it to you. Not willingly of course. I had to apply some inducement. Seems she values Esperanza a lot more than she values you. Robert on the other hand told me that you did have the item in question when you had lunch with him. He's a very sensitive man and I do believe him when

116

he said that you didn't want him to know where you were going to hide the item. So again I ask you. Where is it?"

"Fuck you Andre."

Andre turned and opened the door to leave. "I'll tell Helga not to wait up for you," he said, turning to see me one more time. "Tomorrow my burly friend will visit you and maybe you'll be more cooperative."

It was easy to see that Andre had been ordered to retrieve the flash drive but that he also saw this as an opportunity to get Helga back. And knowing Helga, she would bargain herself for me. I remembered having the same feelings of rage towards Indio when he went to the boathouse to show off Rebecca. The similarities didn't escape me and then I thought about my father and I wondered if there was a curse on his family that I had inherited. But curse or no curse I decided then that I was not going to let Andre take Helga as I had let Indio take Rebecca. Nor was I about to let him take the flash drive.

"When can I have a shower?" I yelled out and Andre turned briefly and I knew he had heard me. I was reeking of sweat by then and there was nothing else that I wanted more at that time.

Shortly after a guard opened the door and told me that he was taking me to shower. He threw some handcuffs at me and told me to put them on. I did and he checked them before we walked down a long corridor with doors similar to that of my room, lining the sides. We passed by an elevator and a stairwell and finally came to the door leading to the showers. Once inside, the guard stood aside while I undressed. My shirt wouldn't slip by the cuffs and he came over and ripped my shirt down the back.

"Try it now," he said.

When I took off my shorts I caught him looking at my penis but he didn't look away.

"Nice cock," he said. "You're supposed to get only 3 minutes in the shower but you can have another five if you let me suck your cock," he said as I turned on the water.

That hot water felt terrific and I would have been tempted to say yes just because of that but I said yes for another reason. He turned my back towards the showerhead so he wouldn't get wet as he went down on me. I pretended it was Helga going down on me and once my cock swelled inside his mouth and he was beside himself with pleasure I quickly brought up my knee into his throat and then brought my handcuffed hands hard against the back of his neck. His head slumped forward and he was unconscious but not dead, and after I had freed myself and stripped him, I tied him up with my shirt. I was dressed in the guard's clothes and was wearing his sunglasses when I walked out of the shower and headed for the stairs. Andre, coming from some other place and also headed toward the stairwell, saw me. He raced toward me, intending to crash into me and knock me down with the impact. *He's quite fit,* I thought when I felt his muscular body slam into mine. I went down but adrenaline filled me with surprising strength and I was on my feet as he was shaking off the numbness in his brain. I gave him no time to gain clarity. A swift blow to his nose laid him out cold.

I hobbled down two flights and entered what appeared to be an ordinary government building. The receptionist and guards didn't give me a second look as I walked out the front door onto another cold and windy day.

I didn't know how much time I had before they discovered Andre and the guard and realized that I was missing. Probably not more than five or ten minutes. I still had my wallet and some money and I caught a taxi and had him drive me to work. There at least I would have some witnesses if Andre's men came for me

Seeing me dressed as a prison guard, Naomi didn't know what to think when she saw me enter.

"Pelon! I was so worried about you when you didn't call last night and this morning you didn't show up for work. Are you all right?"

"Yeah I'm OK. How's Esperanza?"

"She's scared naturally. That pig Andre frightened the hell out of both of us. I'm so sorry I gave you up."

"No, you did the right thing. He got to Robert too but it's going to be all right. Andre now knows that I have the drive and he'll leave all of you alone."

"You're hurt," Naomi said when she noticed that I winced when she touched my arm.

"Not badly," I answered. "Listen I have to leave town and hide out for awhile. I won't be able to call without making my whereabouts known to Andre so let Robert and Farley know what has happened. If and when there is no danger I'll get in touch. You and Esperanza take care."

"You too Pelon."

I quickly called Helga.

"Helga."

"Pelon! Where are you? Are you all right?"

"I'm okay. Andre kidnapped me but I managed to escape and I came to the office. I don't think they'll try and take me from here."

"I'll come and get you," she said.

Helga came for me right away and I got into her car and we drove around, trying to figure out what to do. We resolved to get out of DC knowing that there was little I could do to protect myself against the resources that Andre and his associates had available. Even the hiring of a bodyguard would be a futile gesture. I had to go underground or leave the country. Helga said we could stay with her crazy aunt who lived in an isolated area in Michigan.

"I don't think I can take any more crazy people right now," I said to her suggestion.

"She's not really crazy," Helga said. "She's eccentric. She likes to live the old fashioned life with few conveniences and no one to bother her. I have never told anyone about her. You might say that she's the black sheep of the family."

"Andre doesn't know about her?"

"No one does. I know she'll be glad to see me. I haven't been there for several years but we always got along well."

I agreed to Helga's plan and we went to her bank and withdrew a sizeable amount of money and bought some train tickets to Detroit. In Detroit we bought a used four-wheel-drive truck and drove towards the town of Cadillac, the closest town to her aunt's cabin.

.^.^.^.

CHAPTER VI

The fall colors were amazing at that time of year. We entered the aunt's property, completely canopied by yellow leaves. I felt as if I had been dropped into another world where everything was bright yellow.

As we drove up, a woman with a comely face came out with a two barrel shotgun at her side. She was slender, almost gaunt, but she moved with ease and assurance as she walked towards us to get a better look.

"Hello Aunt Marie," Helga called out. "It's Helga."

A bright smile broke out on the aunt's face.

"My goodness if it's not really you," Aunt Marie said. "I'm shocked to see you."

Helga jumped out of the truck and went and gave her aunt a hug. I was relieved to see how well Aunt Marie received Helga. It was a good sign that she wasn't crazy. It was late afternoon and I sat in the truck watching the beautiful colors while they chatted. Finally Helga motioned for me to join them and I was introduced. Aunt Marie had a firm handshake and it was evident that she knew her way around tools and hard work. As we walked to the cabin I saw a huge stack of firewood leaning up against the side of the cabin and I suspected she had chopped it all herself.

The cabin was small. It had a small bedroom, a kitchen and a third area that served as the dining and living room. But it also had an attic which the aunt offered us and insisted on showing to us right away. We had to climb a pull-down ladder and she led the way as if she was a schoolgirl and not a fifty-plus year old woman.

The attic was tidy and sparse. It had a double bed, a nightstand with a kerosene lamp, a worn easy chair and a small cast iron pot stove. Two windows at either end let in some muted light.

"If you're tired from your trip you can rest while I cook us some supper," Aunt Marie said to me.

"That would be great," I said, feeling tired from the driving and from the stress of recent events.

"I'll help you, Auntie," Helga said.

It was dark when I heard Helga calling me and I had a hard time waking up, at first not knowing where I was and only slowly remembering that we were at the aunt's cabin. The kitchen was dimly lit with a kerosene lamp sitting in the center of the table. It was simple fare that the aunt had put before us. She had made a delicious vegetable soup with lentils and freshly baked bread that filled the small cabin with its aroma. I ate greedily and much too quickly, it being the first decent food that I had eaten since before my abduction.

After eating and cleaning up, we sat and talked. The aunt had no electricity or running water and I was most curious about this woman and her austere existence in this out of the way place. She was completely integrated with her surroundings and by the end of our meal I felt that it was most natural for her to live in that manner.

"That was a great meal, Aunt Marie," I said. "I've always had lentils with bacon, that's the way my grandmother makes them, but your soup was truly delicious."

"Why thank you Pelon. It's always good when someone else enjoys my vegetarian meals."

"Are you a vegetarian?"

"Yes, for about thirty years."

"Wow! That's a long time to go without a burger."

"I have never missed meat."

"I could never be a vegetarian," Helga said. "There are too many meat dishes that I could never foreswear... paté, caviar, Kobe steaks."

"And what about tamales, cocido, and chile verde? Yum," I said. "But why a vegetarian, Aunt Marie?" I asked.

"It's just easier on my body. It's not for everyone. I have never been one to extol the virtues of a vegetarian diet. Some people need meat protein and I just happen to be one that doesn't."

"Really, that's it? I asked. "There are no great philosophical underpinnings to your diet?"

"Sure there are," Helga said. "Tell him about the time you spent in India with your guru, Aunt Marie," Helga encouraged.

"I'm sure that he doesn't want to hear about that."

"You bet I do. I've never met anyone who had a guru."

"Well the word guru has been so loosely used," she said. "The media uses the word guru interchangeably with expert or mentor but a real guru is not that at all. A real guru is a person that has found God and who takes on disciples to help each one of them to also know God directly."

"Was Christ then a guru to his disciples?" I asked.

"Exactly so," she answered emphatically. "I know that Helga's Christian beliefs don't acknowledge other Masters, individuals who have taken on disciples that were ready for release from the wheel of reincarnation."

"There have been other great teachers or gurus if you will," Helga said, "but certainly no one else on the same level as Christ."

"Let it be as you say niece. Nevertheless I was with my guru for ten glorious years in his ashram in India and it completely changed my life."

"Wow! And what about that wheel of reincarnation, what's that all about?"

"At one time reincarnation was a basic understanding in the early Catholic Church. I guess it was removed because they didn't want people believing that there is no death and that we are souls that come to earth to remember that we are a part of God. One lifetime is not enough time to learn this and so after what we know as death we return time and time again, hundreds or maybe thousands of times. With every incarnation we learn more and more and eventually come to understand that our only purpose here is to know God."

"So when a person develops to the point of knowing God then that person no longer has to incarnate. That's what getting off the wheel means?" I asked.

"That's exactly right, Pelon," Aunt Marie said.

"Will you be getting off the wheel, Aunt Marie?" I asked.

"Well that's not for me to say, Pelon. It's something that only God knows."

We continued similar conversations after supper from then on, as most of her days were spent either in meditation or taking long walks in the woods. Helga and I adjusted to a pace of life that was slow with a capital S. We took long walks, had great sex in the forest on a blanket that we spread out under the trees, ate whole grains and vegetables and slept better than we had ever slept. I quickly gained back the weight I had lost and the walking put some muscles in my legs. The beautiful fall colors quickly gave way to the first snowfalls and we started cross-country skiing, and my arms and chest also filled in. I was really content and happy. Helga wasn't as enthusiastic.

"What is it Helga? You seem a little out of sorts today." I asked one day.

"It's nothing."

"Come on, Helga, I know you better than that. I can see that it's something."

"It's hard living out here, Pelon."

"What do you mean? It's a great life."

"I knew you would say that. You're not cooking all our meals on the wood stove, hauling water from the well, washing clothes by hand, tending the fireplace. This is like a great vacation for you."

"I chop wood and take it inside," I answered sheepishly.

"Yes and that's about all you do. I'm not used to all this work and I'm missing some of the things I most enjoyed, like going shopping in New York, going to nice parties, getting my hair done. Just look at my hair, it's atrocious."

"Your hair looks great Helga as does the rest of you. Really."

Helga gave me a look of resignation and it prompted me to resolve to change.

"I'm sorry, Helga. I've been really selfish and I'll start helping with the chores. I promise."

And so I did and found out that Helga was right. It was a lot of work. But I rather enjoyed it. Helga seemed happier for a few days after I started helping but still there remained a cloud over her.

"Want to talk about what's bothering you?" I asked one day after we had finished breakfast and were sitting at the table.

"I feel depressed, Pelon. Maybe it's this cold weather and gray skies, or maybe it's being stuck out here with very little to do. Maybe it's all of it. I don't want to feel this way. I want to enjoy it as much as you and Aunt Marie do."

"I'm sorry I got you in this mess, Helga."

One day while Helga was taking a bath I confided in Aunt Marie. "I'm worried about Helga, Aunt Marie. I don't know how much longer she can take the rigors of living out here. She's been trying to be a good sport but more recently she's been really cranky.

"Yes I've noticed the change in her. The illusory world of Maya is very difficult to transcend."

"What does that mean, Aunt Marie, this world of Maya?" I asked.

"Maya is the material world that we identify with and think of as reality. We identify with our body and think that we are the body. We also seek out the comforts of the body and begin to think that we can't be without those comforts, they become part of our identity."

"I can't imagine myself being anything else but me, this face and this body that I see every morning," I said. "That's who I am."

"Well, that's the illusion of Maya. It gets us to think that our immortal soul is one and the same as our temporal body," she said.

"So we should understand that our body is only a temporary vessel that ages and eventually turns to dust, but our soul never dies and reincarnates in another body?"

"You remembered what I said about reincarnation Pelon, that's good. So Maya, the material world, is like the background in a painting and the foreground is the soul, experiencing life, learning about and loving God and loving and enjoying the entire creation."

"Kinda hard to forget that the material world is not real," I said. "It's always in our face as they say. It's what everyone believes."

"That's true. It is difficult not to mistake the background for the foreground. And the larger world will bully and condemn those that see it differently. Those that don't buy into their defined reality, those that don't affirm their biases and prejudices about gender, race, religion, economic and political system, dress code, et cetera, they will ostracize, or perhaps even kill."

"You just ran down the history of the world, Aunt Marie. It seems that conflict has always centered on the intolerance that groups develop toward others."

"I'm afraid that what you say is true, Pelon. And I think that my niece, though she is not intolerant, is caught up in the web of Maya, and she believes that she must have what she is used to and that to not have them is cause for sadness and unhappiness."

"Yes I think you are right, and I'm thinking that maybe it is time that Helga and I go separate ways. It's really me that Andre is after and I don't think he would harm her if she were to return to Washington."

"Have you spoken to her about this?"

"I've tried to bring up the subject but she refuses to hear me out."

"Well for now it's a moot point as the road from here to the main highway is pretty much impassable by car," she said.

"Really?"

"I'm afraid it'll be that way until spring."

"What about food?"

"Oh I have plenty of food for us. The cellar is well stocked."

I tried having lively conversations with Helga in the hope of cheering her up (as did Aunt Marie) but Helga's spirit continued to decline. She tried to keep busy by reading and every now and again I was able to convince her to don the cross country skis, but generally she would spend hours staring into space and cursing the snow, the bone chilling cold, and the isolation.

I, had it not been for Helga's state of mind, could not have been more tranquil and at peace. Frankly in contrast to Helga, I loved the winter weather. Being able to ski the vast forest that adjoined Aunt Marie's property was the most fun I had ever experienced. My positive moods began to irritate Helga and I sensed a growing resentment that gradually diminished physical pleasures with her.

"Would you like to learn to meditate?" Aunt Marie asked me one day after supper.

"Okay," I answered in a voice filled more with curiosity than enthusiasm.

"Sit over here in this chair and don't let your spine touch the back of the chair. The Kundalini energy has to be able to travel freely up and down the spine."

"Shall I cross my legs?" I asked.

"No, you don't have to do that. Just place your feet flat on the floor. Unless of course it feels more comfortable to cross your legs."

"What about my arms?"

"Just place your hands on your legs in a comfortable position. Try not to worry too much about your body. The important thing is your mind and what goes on in there."

"What'd you mean?"

"Meditation is a process of quieting the mind and being able to commune with Spirit. Ordinarily the mind keeps very busy entertaining a vast array of thoughts and memories."

"So I'll be trying not to think about anything. That seems impossible."

"No it's not that at all. You'll be selecting a mantra that you'll repeat silently and that will help you keep other thoughts at bay. Also you'll need to close your eyes and gently lift your gaze to a spot just above the bridge of your nose. That's where your third eye is positioned."

"Aunt Marie. What's a mantra?"

"Sorry, Pelon. I'll slow down. Let's just say that your mantra will be a string of words that have some spiritual significance to you. Traditionally a mantra has sounds and symbolism that is specifically selected by a person's guru. Because I'm not a guru, that's not going to happen. If you are Catholic you could select something like the Hail Mary or the Our Father."

"I'm not a Catholic," I blurted.

"Well then maybe just the Om sound. Or something like Peace on Earth or…"

"I have always liked, Love is All, All is Love," I said.

"Yes that's a good choice, Pelon. Now about that third eye, the one that's also called the spiritual eye."

"Is it a metaphor?"

"Not really a metaphor, more like something you can't ordinarily see."

"Like a person's aura?" I suggested.

"Yes something like that, and when you lift your gaze to that spot it puts your attention on the superconscious aspect of mind. Now if you allow your gaze to drop down as far as it can go, that is the realm of the unconscious and you'll fall asleep. If your gaze is kept straight ahead, that is the conscious mind. In meditation you always want to keep your gaze lifted to the third eye."

"Wow. I never knew that but it makes perfect sense."

"Now you just have to find a place, and some time, and try what I've told you. Don't get discouraged, as it'll be difficult to keep thoughts from entering your mind. You'll find that one thought soon leads to another and then another. Eventually, when you realize that thoughts have taken over, you'll have to get back to your mantra. You just have to keep at it."

I found that I liked the cellar best for those initial efforts. It was warm enough and quiet with little chance of being disturbed. But Aunt Marie was right. It was difficult work not losing my focus, for then thoughts would flood in or my gaze would drop and I would doze off.. But for some unknown reason I had a lot of determination to master that meditation technique and I kept at it. Maybe it was that there was very little else to do with my time, especially with Helga being so withdrawn. It's not that we never talked anymore because we did. We even laughed occasionally and sometimes we made love in our upstairs bedroom. But it was not like it was before. There was a strain to our friendship that wouldn't go away.

Time passed fairly quickly for me that winter as I had acquired a routine that suited me perfectly. I'd get up early and go downstairs to the cellar and try meditating. At first all I could take was fifteen minutes, then twenty and fairly soon I was up to a half hour. I wasn't in any deep trance though. It was just a peaceful kind of feeling, some days better than others, and a couple of times leaving me with a profound sense of love. Wow, I thought.

After meditation, Helga was usually awake and I would make tea for us. After a couple of cups I would go outside and work up a sweat sawing logs for the fireplace or splitting them for the woodstove. Then Helga and I would have breakfast, usually some hot cereal and homemade bread with a piece of cheese or some stew left over from the previous night's dinner. Household chores would follow and then weather permitting some cross-country skiing through the forest.

Aunt Marie had a nice library and I would usually read until it was time to prepare and eat supper. Some nights after we cleaned the kitchen we sat around and talked until bedtime, while other nights I would continue reading by the light of the fireplace. Aunt Marie had majored in Literature and she had kept all the books that she used for her classes. My favorites were the Russian writers and I read stories by Turgenev, Tolstoy and Dostoevsky. She also had some modern writers that she would trade or buy when she went into town. That's how I ended up reading a book about a German forester who contended that water was a living entity, whose vitality depended on water being able to flow freely, without impediments such as dams or without mankind straightening its riverbed and lining it with concrete. I felt a tremendous affinity with the forester Viktor Schauberger as I skied the Michigan forest, for it was the forest that had taught him lessons that he could not have learned at a university. Never had I felt so strong and alive for it was then that I realized that I had been totally wrong in assuming that because I had a college and law degree, that there was little left for me to know. I had acquired the best of what a university based in the USA provided, but now I knew that there was so much more that apparently was outside the parameters of what it considered worthy of knowing. The desire to learn more was ablaze within me.

The month of March continued cold and gray, and Helga's spirits sank lower when she heard Aunt Marie say, "We have had more snow this winter than in any of the 20 years that I have lived here."

"Really?" I asked, remembering the lecture by the climatologist who contended that in 2014 we would be entering a mini ice age. But it was only 2011, I reminded myself.

April finally brought better news when we saw some beautiful purple flowers poking through the snow near the cabin.

"Oh my, the crocuses are blooming. Spring is upon us, my friends," said Aunt Marie.

And indeed we began to experience warmer days and the snow cover in the forest began to thin and finally disappear altogether. Helga's spirit began to elevate and she seemed to regain the bounce in her step at the thought of finally being able to leave our sanctuary.

"I think a few more warm days and the road will be passable," Aunt Marie contended. "You'll have to travel in the early morning though, when the road is frozen, otherwise later in the day the snow will melt and the road will become muddy and you'll get stuck."

One day coming back from one of our excursions to inspect the road we saw a truck parked next to ours. Aunt Marie was in conversation with a large bearded man in blue overalls and heavy boots. She knew everything about my situation and we trusted her not to reveal anything incriminating, nevertheless I was quite anxious when I saw him, and only relaxed when she introduced us to her old friend Henry and I saw that his truck was covered with bumper stickers that extolled the rights of Americans and the perils of a meddling government.

"What brings you folks to this beautiful country?" Henry asked us. "

"Couldn't be that you're fleeing the big city. You folks live in Detroit? Left there myself some thirty years ago. It was awful then, must be worse now. Only thing I miss is going to hear me some good blues. Yes sir, nothin' better to cheer you up like a night of hearing the blues. You folks like the blues?" Finally Henry paused and looked at us expectantly.

Helga and I both smiled, not knowing which of his questions he wanted answered. I ventured, "The only thing better than Detroit blues, is a good Mexican ranchera, the kind that when you hear it you need to let out a yell with so much passion you think your heart is going to jump out your throat."

Henry laughed heartily. "I like this fellow," Henry said to Aunt Marie. "Me and him will have to have us a few beers. How about you, miss? Will you join us in a few beers one day? No use inviting Marie, here. She's a straight and narrow teetotaler."

"Why certainly. And I do like the blues as well," Helga answered.

"Henry comes around in the spring as soon as his four wheel truck can get through to bring me some supplies from town. I pay him for his troubles with a home cooked meal," Aunt Marie said. "You are staying, Henry?"

"You bet," he said and he turned to me and under his breath said jokingly, "I come every time I need to clean myself out with the roughage."

"I heard that Henry," Aunt Marie said and smiled.

Henry and I hung out by the trucks while Helga and Aunt Marie rustled up some food.

"How are things going in the world?" I asked.

Henry gave me a deep penetrating look, sizing me up. "To hell in a hand basket," he said. "That's where this world is going."

"I saw your bumper stickers," I said. "I agree with most of it."

"No sane American wouldn't agree. Freedom is the foundation of this country. Without Freedom there's nothing. And, pardon my French, fuck anyone who denies it or who tries to take those freedoms away. Especially those power hungry yellow bellies in Washington who keep chipping away at those freedoms in the name of fucking national security."

"Amen," I said.

"Actually I've come for another reason," Henry said in a low voice, when Helga and her aunt were busy preparing food in the kitchen area.

"Really?" I whispered

"There's a group of men come into my store this morning to do some ice fishing in the lake they said, but they seemed more interested in knowing if there were any 'local characters,' the kind that adds ambience to a town like ours they said. Hell I told them that we're all characters of that sort. They laughed but they pressed me, with one of them saying that they would be most appreciative if I could give them some names of old pioneer type women and he flashed me his wallet. By nature I'm a suspicious fellow and I told them straight off, that out here we don't go around telling tales about our neighbors and I chased them off. I came over here as soon as I saw them drive off as I figured that maybe it was Marie they were trying to locate. As soon as I saw you I knew that my hunch was correct."

My heart sank. Andre had sent his henchmen to check out Helga's aunt. It was common knowledge among Washington insiders that the government had access to the content of every form of public communication, or so we had learned from Robert. Although we had taken precautions not to reveal our plans to anyone, still Andre must have found something about Helga's aunt, given his position and access to that ocean of information.

"What are you two whispering about?" asked Helga from the kitchen.

"Come over here," I answered. "You need to hear this."

Henry proceeded to tell Helga everything he had told me and then Helga and I also filled him in on what had brought us to Cadillac and why those men were looking for us. Henry was livid, his face flushed and the veins in his forehead protruding.

"So that's what this country has come to," he said. "Well I'm not going to stand for it, no sir I'm not."

Aunt Marie who had ambled over and was listening intently to the conversation and putting her hand on his shoulder said, "Now Henry calm down. No use getting all worked up about this."

"Come on Marie," Henry said. "This is no time for peace making. These assholes are destroying our country and they have to be stopped, goddammit!"

"We better make plans to leave," I ventured, in the hope of keeping the focus on us. *No use involving other people,* I thought. "They must not know who Helga's aunt is, just that she has an aunt but they'll continue looking and eventually they'll show up here."

"Pelon's right," Helga said. "I'll get my things."

"Nonsense," Aunt Marie said. "From what you've told me, it's clear that you haven't broken any laws."

"Right now Andre is a law unto himself and he's able to call all the shots," I said."

"If I were you kids I'd take the back road out of here, heading west toward Lake Michigan and not go back towards Detroit. I think you'll have a better chance of not running into those men if you do that," Henry said.

"What then?" I asked.

"Well, just before getting to the lake you'll hit Highway 31, that will take you south to Ludington. You can board the ferry there and it'll take you to the other side to Wisconsin or if you don't want to take the ferry, just continue south on that 31 till you run into the interstate highway that'll take you west into Chicago."

"Sounds like a good plan," I answered. "I'll get my things. Henry can you help me start our truck? The battery's probably run down in this cold."

"Sure thing. I'll get my cables."

Aunt Marie, Helga and I were teary when we said goodbye.

"I've learned many things in these few months we spent with you, Aunt Marie," I said. "I'll always treasure this time."

"Don't make it sound as if we'll never see one another, as I'm sure we will," she answered.

"Of course we will," Helga answered.

"You bet," I said, knowing full well that I would never come back this way again and already formulating plans to break away from Helga once we reached Ludington.

We drove mostly in silence over the frozen dirt road that led to the highway, which would take us west toward Lake Michigan.

"Helga, I think that we ought to split up at Ludington. I'll take the ferry across to Wisconsin, and you can continue driving south to the highway that will take you east and eventually back to Washington. I'm sure Andre won't bother you. He's not after you."

"How can you talk of splitting away from me, Pelon? After all we have endured."

"You're not cut out for the life of a fugitive that I'll have to lead until it is safe for me to resurface. I won't put you through another period like you have experienced at Aunt Marie's."

"My head tells me that you're right but my heart is breaking when I think that I won't be near you. I know that I haven't been the best companion lately, but once back in warmer weather I'll be fine," she said in a weak voice.

"No you won't, Helga. Besides, you'll slow me down, or maybe even expose me to greater danger."

When the time came for parting at Ludington she welled up with tears, but her protestations were shallow and we both knew that it was time, and that life was taking us in different directions.

.^.^.^.

CHAPTER VII

The ferry was a large steamboat, yet still the waves sent it up and down upsetting my stomach and making me upchuck over the side. I was surprised at how big the lake was, looking more like an ocean than a lake. Not until we had traveled nearly two hours did the Wisconsin shore come into view.

I caught a Greyhound bus to Milwaukee and from there to Chicago where I planned to take a train, preferably to someplace that was sunny and warm. Helga had offered me more than five thousand dollars when we parted, and I took it without hesitation, thinking of it more as a loan to be repaid. Once in Chicago I got directions to the neighborhood where the largest population of Chicanos, outside of Los Angeles, lived.

I bought a good knife at a pawn shop and began looking for places where I might meet someone who knew where I could get some fake identification papers. I was pretty rugged looking at that point, and more than likely I would raise few suspicions when I began asking. Yet by sunset I had gotten nowhere. I had asked men that stood next to me in line at taco shops, men working at car washes and I even entered a few bars and ordered beers that I never finished. In desperation I boarded a public bus and sat next to a middle-aged woman with all the features of a person from a village in Mexico.

"Perdon senora, disculpe la molestia pero tengo gran necesidad de comprar documentos de identificacion. No me podria ayudar?" I had in essence told her what I needed and she gave me a cold silent once over. Yet her eyes were kind behind the wrinkles and the sunburnt face she acquired from years spent outdoors in agricultural fields, I suspected.

"Como te llamas y de donde vienes?" She had asked for my name and where I was from.

Without hesitation I told her that I was from Tijuana, trusting that my time spent with the guys from Segunda learning the way they spoke would make me sound authentic, and that I was trying to buy a train ticket to Los Angeles.

She asked several more questions about where I had been working and if I was married and had kids, all questions to establish if I was for real. Fortunately I had seen the film about the men and women that went to pick cherries in and around the city of Traverse, Michigan (not far from Cadillac) and that became my story, told in good Spanish but with lots of slang learned from my gang days. I even told her about Helga, with appropriate omissions of course, and soon we were chatting as if we were old friends.

"Soy de Oaxaca," she answered when I asked where she was from.

"Deberas? Me gustan los animales tallados que vienen de por alla," I answered, telling her that I like the carved animals that came from there.

"Los conoces?" she asked, surprised that I knew of them.

"Claro, son famosos," I answered.

"Mi papa los hacia y muy buen dinero que recibia," she said telling me that her father made a good living making and selling them.

When we came to her stop she told me to follow behind her, and when we passed a particular house she would change her purse from one shoulder to the other.

"Tocas alli la puerta y diles que te mando Ofelia. Que te vaya bien muchacho," she said wishing me good luck.

138

I knocked on the door as told and informed the man that answered that I had been sent by Ofelia. He looked me over for what seemed a long time and finally asked me to go in. The dilapidated exterior of the house belied the inside, a nicely decorated home with wall hangings from somewhere in Latin America, my guess was Peru, a big leather couch and love seat, and bookshelves against two walls. I had to suppress my impulse to check out the books, knowing that I was supposed to be an indigent from Tijuana.

"Que es lo que necesitas?" he asked what I needed.

"Una licencia," I said to him.

"Treceintos dollars," he said.

Ofelia had told me that it would cost me three hundred for a license so I had come prepared with crumpled twenties and ones so as not to arouse suspicion. I placed the money in his outstretched hand and he led me to a back room where he asked me my name, date of birth, and for an address I gave him one on the street where I had boarded the bus. He took my picture and laminated it onto a card that looked totally official. He didn't say as much as a goodbye as he escorted me out the front door.

So far so good I thought, and I headed off to the train station where I bought a ticket on the Southwest Chief that left at 9:05 for Albuquerque and then on to Los Angeles. I had a few hours before my train's departure and I bought a burn phone and called Naomi.

"Hello, Naomi. It's Pelon."

"Pelon! Oh my God we all thought you were dead! Why haven't you called?"

"I'm sorry Naomi. It just wasn't safe to call from where I was staying."

"Are you all right?"

"Yes I'm fine. How are you and Esperanza? Have you had any trouble?"

"Not since that day with that creep Andre. Things aren't the same around the office though. I think that Congressman Jimmy must have been told that his lie was uncovered and he's been acting strange. He probably hasn't fired us because he thinks that we'll blow his cover. Do you still have the flash drive?"

"Not with me but it's in a safe place."

"Have you decided what you'll do with it?"

"I'm not quite sure. I guess I could give it to Andre and put an end to this drama or I could send it to some journalist and let him expose those on the list. What do you think?"

"Actually the four of us talked about it at some length."

"You've seen Robert and Farley?"

"Quite a lot actually. Thanks to you, we bonded after that meeting and we get together for dinner or at LGBT functions. Anyway I think we've come to the conclusion that it would be a great embarrassment to those on the list and maybe even hurt their chance at re-election. But really there are no laws being broken, maybe some ethical violations at best."

"Yet Andre wants it back and is still chasing me," I said.

"Are you sure? He's left all of us alone."

"Pretty sure. He sent some men to the place where I was staying. It's the only reason I'm on the move again."

"I imagine you don't want to tell me where you are right now or where you're going," she said.

"No, and I'm talking on a burn phone and I have to say goodbye for now. It makes me really glad that the four of you have become friends. Please give them all my best. I'll call when it's possible. Bye Naomi. Take care."

After my conversation with Naomi, I went to the Art Institute where I saw that it being Thursday it was open until 8:00 and free to residents. '*Wow, my chance to see a free show,*' I thought.

As I went through the various galleries I couldn't help but think of Helga and the many times that we had gone together to attend openings of various contemporary artists. I missed her terribly at that moment and I had a strong urge to make a quick telephone call to her home, thinking that she was probably there by now. Fortunately my attention was diverted just then by the announcement that the Institute was closing and I left.

The train ride was boring that first day, hot in the day and cold at night, noisy with kids running up and down aisles and through doors leading to other cars. It was a forty-hour trip and by the time we reached Albuquerque I felt like jumping off and hitchhiking.

A Mexican man came and sat next to me when we left Albuquerque and we greeted one another with a simple nod of the head.

"Soy Inez," I said after a few minutes.

"Miguel," he answered. "You go Los Angeles?" he asked.

"Si. Vengo desde Chicago," I said.

"Oh gez, Chicago big city. I knows Chicago. Many Mexican peoples."

"Yes many. Los Angeles also," I said.

"Gez. Too many peoples. I no likes too many peoples. I lives farm. Encinitas. You knows Encinitas?"

"Near San Diego?" I asked.

"Little bit near," he answered and with one hand showed me Los Angeles on the tip of his index finger and Encinitas nearly touching San Diego near his thumb. "Thirty miles San Diego. You liked baseball? Padres play San Diego."

"Yes, I like Baseball. The Washington Nationals is my team."

"No Dogers?"

"No."

"Ha good, I no like Dogers," Miguel said. "You no lives Los Angeles?"

"Not any more. I used to live there."

"Where yous live now?"

"No place now. I'm trying to find me a place."

"Los Angeles place?"

"Maybe," I said.

"Encinitas very pritty. Ocean, flowers, how you say *aire limpio*?

"Clean air."

"Gez, clean air from ocean. You work farm with me little bit. Much hard work now," Miguel said with a big smile.

"Really?"

"Gez. Yous stays farm. Small room, clean. Money little bit."

"What kind of farm, Miguel?"

"Avocados, vegetables. "

"Is it a big farm?"

"No no, little bit farm. Ten acres."

"I like," I said, falling into Miguel's manner of speaking. "But I have to see my mother first, here in Los Angeles."

"So k. You come tomorrow, next day. So k."

We spent the next several hours talking about ourselves, I, maybe revealing too much. But Miguel was totally open and trustworthy, I felt. He was from Zamora, a town south of Guadalajara, but had been in the USA for ten years. He had a green card and was studying to become a citizen. The offer to work with him was to also give him a chance to practice his English. He was no dummy.

We finally reached Union Station in Los Angeles on a late Saturday afternoon, and Miguel gave me the number to his cell.

"Yus takes Metro link Oceanside. Oceanside yus takes Coaster. Get off Encinitas. Yu call. I come."

142

Miguel and I parted and I began walking to the corner where I wanted to catch the public bus. On the train I had developed a sort of plan, to go to the boathouse in the hope of seeing someone from Segunda that could put me up and help me settle in with my new identity. I had chosen the name Inez Segura, my grandmother's old tenant, the man that married Chelo. It was a stupid plan really, one that wasn't very well thought out and purely reactive. Meeting up with Miguel was an undisguised blessing and I felt much better about going to see my mother and not only reassure her that I was well, but also to learn if someone had come around looking for me.

My mother is obsessive about schedules and she went to great lengths to be on time and to do things in accord with her planned agenda. She worked as a maid at a fancy hotel on Wilshire, and everyday took the same buses to and from home. She always caught the 2:10 bus in front of the hotel to get home and I planned to catch it a few blocks from where she would board, and thus be on it when she got on.

I boarded the bus and kept looking out the window from where I was standing. Finally I saw her waiting on the corner, ready to board the bus, which as always was packed tightly with workers making their way home from the Westside to Latino barrios in the center of town or to East Los Angeles.

"Hello Mother," I whispered when she finally reached the spot where she always stood. I noticed that her hand, holding the overhead ring for support, was looking older, as was her face, than when I last saw her.

"Mijo," she gasped, momentarily calling attention to herself and forcing me to put my finger to my lips, asking her not to make any further noise, but the passengers hardly took notice as they stared out the window or spoke noisily with a companion.

"Que haces aqui?" She demanded to know why I was on the bus.

"I wanted to surprise you as soon as I came into town," I answered.

"Don't you lie to me, Herculano," she answered in her heavily accented English. "I know that something is going on with you."

"I'm fine. Can't you tell by looking at me?"

"I can see that you did put on some weight but you are pale as a ghost. Is there no sun where you have been living? And if you are fine why did those men come to the house looking for you?"

"When was that?" I asked with tremor in my voice that she noticed right off.

"Herculano, what have you gotten into? Hay mijo!"

"It's okay mom really. It's just a misunderstanding. Let's not talk about it now. I'll tell you all about it when we get off this bus."

Once reaching what used to be the center of Los Angeles, we got off and went to a taqueria to have a taco while we talked. And for the next half hour we eagerly asked for news from one another. I was especially interested in knowing about my grandmother, and she was more interesting in knowing about those men who were looking for me.

I told her all about Helga and about Andre blaming me for the break-up of his marriage and seeking vengeance. I purposefully left out where I had been the last few months and said nothing about Miguel and Encinitas. The less she knew the better off she would be, I thought.

"What are you going to do, Mijo?" she asked. "That Andre sounds like a real cabron."

"I was thinking of visiting my father in Mexico," I said. "I'd be safe there until this all goes away."

"That's a good idea Mijo. A very good idea."

144

Telling her I was planning to visit my father in Mexico wasn't a complete lie. I had considered it and as a matter of fact I continued to entertain that possibility, just not right away.

We caught the bus that would take her home, a bus even more crowded as we had spent more than an hour talking at the taqueria and it was now quitting time for thousands more. I knew she was enjoying talking with me yet I could see that she was also anxious to get home.

"I'll try to see you again tomorrow, mom," I said just before she got off at her stop."

"OK mijito. Que dios te bendiga." She blessed me and left.

I stayed on the bus and got off two stops later so that I could walk to the boathouse and see if any of the Segunda members were around. I wanted to pay my respects and also to ask for a favor.

Lechero was there, no longer wearing his Air Force jacket but looking much the same. He was in conversation with Piteco, who back in the old days was one of the younger members and now a full-grown man. Others hanging out at the boathouse I didn't recognize and when they saw me walking towards them, they stiffened and I knew they were about to challenge me. I flashed them the Segunda hand sign, fingers contorted in such a way that it had taken me days to learn when I first began hanging out with Segunda. The boys relaxed a bit but I could see they were still wary. Lechero never bothered to turn, knowing that his boys had his back.

"Orale Lechero," I called out. Lechero turned slowly and when he saw me smiled.

"Pinche Guey, que onda?" Hey dude what's up is what he said. He came over and gave me a big hug.

"This is the famous Pelon," he announced in his still imperfect English. "The vato that saved my fucking life."

145

By then Piteco had also come over and he too gave me a big hug.

I nodded to the rest of the twenty or so young men standing around us, young men not looking too much different than the boys that I hung out with ten years ago.

"Chingao Pelon I can't believe it's really you ese. You look a toda madre Guey. Come sit down and tell me donde chingaos has estado."

Lechero, Piteco and I moved over to the side and sat down to talk. I was moved by old memories and old feelings that came rushing at me from somewhere deep within. Wow! I had not expected that, I told myself, shaking my head in disbelief.

"Hey man. I can't believe I'm standing here in this spot with you and Piteco. It's been ten years."

"Ten years?" Lechero asked with doubt in his voice.

"Yeah. Pelon's right. I was 12," Piteco said.

"You're twenty two?" I asked him and he nodded in the old style, head and shoulders bobbing. "Any of my old friends still around?"

"Simon," Lechero affirmed. "Chicago comes around, tambien Jorge and Manuelito, Gordo. Hay un chingo.

"There's a bunch huh? What about Puma?" I asked.

"El pinche Puma es jura," Lechero said.

"He's a cop?" I asked incredulously. "No way. Puma hated cops."

"Tell me about it," Lechero said.

"He's been a cop about five years," Piteco said.

"Wow," was all I could say.

"Yeah and he thinks he's an Americano and doesn't even want to speak Spanish. He works with gangs and comes around to hassle us. He was here last week asking about you vato."

"Asking about me?"

"Yeah. Weird ese, him asking and you showing up ese. Que tranza?"

"I don't know why he was asking for me. Maybe he needs a lawyer," I said, to change the subject.

"You a lawyer now dude?" Piteco asked in surprise.

I smiled and said, "Yeah, I'm a pinchi lawyer."

"Hijole a lawyer! Wow vato, you must be making the feria."

"I do alright. I could make more but I'm working for a Congressman so the money actually sucks. And you Lechero. Did you ever get married?"

"O yeah. Married una Mexicanita. Have three moritos running around. Things are good for me ese. I drive a truck up and down the coast."

"What about you Piteco? What are you doing?"

"I work at an upholstery shop."

"Did you hear about Rebecca?" Lechero asked before I could say anything else to Piteco.

I nodded and told him that I had and then I recounted meeting up with Pee Wee at the fire camp and even told them that I had cried all night like a little baby. They nodded in understanding, the gang code allowing us to cry when our heart was breaking over a woman.

"What happened to Chief? Is he still around?" I asked.

"He's a fucking wino now. He comes around asking for money every once in awhile," Piteco offered.

"No shit," I said, not really that surprised.

"So what brings you back after all these years, Pelon?" Lechero asked.

"I was passing through and just thought I would stop by to see you vatos." Right away I could see that neither of them believed me. They knew I was running from something.

"We got your back homie," Piteco said.

"Simon que si Pelon. You're still in Segunda vato," Lechero added.

"Naw, Puma coming around asking for me is not good. He'll make life hard for you if he knows you've...." I never finished.

One of the younger men whistled loud and shrill, the Segunda signal for danger, and we all looked towards the street and saw a large man in a suit exit a police car and head towards the boathouse.

"A la madre!" Lechero exclaimed. "Es el Puma."

I recognized him also even though he was a good four inches taller and heavier by at least fifty pounds. He was trotting now, ambling smoothly for such a big dude. No use trying to escape from the boathouse now, I thought.

I walked from the portico of the boathouse and went toward the grass and was there by the time Puma arrived, puffing hard. He took off his suit jacket, tossed it casually on the grass and began loosening his tie.

"Orale Puma, que onda," I said.

"Pelon," he answered with a nod of his head. "Gotta take you in dude. You're a wanted man."

"Chale ese, not going to happen," I said. "Unless you can take me down."

There I had said it, even though my stomach was dancing with butterflies, I had challenged him and with all the guys from Segunda looking on, even he couldn't turn it down, for in his heart he was still Segunda, he still abided by the code.

Or perhaps he had come with that expectation. The members of Segunda knew that I had defeated him once and as his reputation for cruelty increased so did my fame. He needed that story to have a different ending. Whatever the reason we were once again facing one another. I was in the best shape I thought. The cross-country skiing and hauling and chopping wood had left me fit and seeing him puffing after that short trot told me that he could be beat. Still he was heavier and taller and with a longer reach. It wasn't going to be easy.

148

We got ready, our closed fists held at head level, we began dancing around one another. He obviously wanted to land one of his huge fists in my face and end it, as he quickly threw a right left combination that I moved away from and countered with one that landed in his soft gut.

We continued pawing at each other, every so often throwing an actual punch. He caught me on the side of the head with one punch and I tried not to let him see that he had rung my bell. Then I got another lucky punch to his chest and felt him reel back just ever so slightly. He angered then and became wilder with his punches, especially hearing the guys from Segunda shouting Pelon! Pelon! I wanted him angry. I wanted him to tire out by throwing wild punches. He threw a punch that left him momentarily off balance and then I saw my opportunity and sprang up in the air, turned head down into a flip while wrapping my legs around his neck. My leg strength coupled with my momentum brought him crashing down in a heap. He was out. A momentary silence followed by whistles and shouting of Pelon! Pelon!

I got up as Lechero reached me to slap my back.

"Chingado ese that was a toda madre," he said.

"I have to leave de volada. Do you have wheels?"

"Simon it's in the parking lot."

"Can I come?" Piteco asked.

"Orale, let's go."

We made our way through the Segunda members that had thronged around us, patting me on the back shouting "way to go dude" and other similar forms of congratulations. We got into Lechero's car, an older model SUV, and drove off.

"Where to ese?"

"Drop me off where the Mariachis hang out."

"Porque alli? I can take you wherever ese."

"That's where I need to go."

Lechero continued to protest to no avail. I didn't want them to know where I was going. There were a handful of musicians already gathered at the spot where potential customers went to hire them, as I got out of the car. I quickly said goodbye to my homies and they drove away.

There was a bus stop nearby and I didn't have to wait long before I was on board and once again headed towards downtown, this time to Union Station.

.^.^.^.

CHAPTER VIII

The train station is an older beautiful building, one of the few historical buildings not razed to make room for the ugly monstrosities that have been erected in downtown and used often by Hollywood for their films. I went and bought my Metrolink ticket to Oceanside and found out that I had an hour wait, so I walked to Philippe's and had one of their pastrami sandwiches.

It was dark when the Metrolink pulled out, and not being able to see anything out the window, I fell asleep. I woke up as we pulled into Oceanside and I heard the conductor yell, "End of the line, everyone off."

The Coaster was already taking on passengers, and I bought my ticket and boarded. It was a half-hour trip to Encinitas and I paid attention to the stops and got off as instructed by Miguel.

I called him and I went and sat on a bench, enjoying the smells of the ocean air as it breezed through the area. Miguel arrived shortly after I had sat down.

"Hello Miguel. Thanks for coming so quickly."

"No problem. I not expecting you today. Tomorrow maybe."

"Yeah, I finished my business early."

"You sees jefita?"

"Yeah, I saw her."

"She good. No problems?"

"Yes, she's great."

We drove into the bluffs not far from the ocean, an area of residential homes, some of which had ocean views and some had no views whatsoever. Quite soon we came to a small house with large trees in front, in a fairly flat area.

"We here," Miguel said enthusiastically. "Come I show you room you sleeps. Me introduce wife, you."

Miguel led me inside the modest but clean home.

"Here we sleeps. Sara me there," he said, pointing east, "and you sleeps there," showing me a door off to the side.

"This wife Sara," Miguel said, introducing me to a petite, shy woman with a crooked smile that showed that she was missing a front tooth.

"Hola, me llamo Herculano pero me conocen como Pelon."

"Mucho gusto Herculano. Yo soy Sara," she said extending a small hand.

"Sara she makes dinner. Come eats Pelon," Miguel said.

"Thank you, Miguel," I said, not realizing until then that I was still hungry. I was reminded of the homes in Mexico as we sat down at a small table on one side to eat a very good meal of squash, beans, rice and of course corn tortillas.

After dinner Miguel took me to my small room that had a single bed, an easy chair, and a small chest of drawers. A freestanding lamp provided light.

"We up 6:00, so k? Much work tomorrow."

As promised at 6:00 a.m. the next morning I walked out of my room and I could smell the breakfast that Sara had prepared.

"Buenos dias, Sara.

"Buenos dias, Herculano. Toma café?"

I nodded a yes. Sara made coffee in the old Mexican way, in a saucepan, producing a strong heavy liquid much like espresso. She served a small amount into a cup and topped it off with boiled milk.

"Azucar?" she asked.

"Si por favor," I answered as she heaped a tablespoon of sugar into my cup.

"Cuantos anos con Miguel, Sara?"

"Casados cinco, pero nos conocemos desde chicos. Somos del mismo pueblo," she answered letting me know that she and Miguel had been married five years but had grown up together.

"Y tu Herculano, eres casado?"

I shook my head and Helga flashed before me when she asked if I was married.

"No todavia no. Quizas algun dia," I answered.

"Pues mas vale que te apures. No es bueno estar solo en este mundo," she said advising me to hurry as it was not good to be alone.

Sara was serving me some muffin-like breads that she had baked, when Miguel walked in the front door.

"Good morning Pelon."

"Good morning, Miguel. Were you already working?"

"Gez. Little bit. I show you farm. We eat, drink coffee."

Miguel and Sara followed the traditional Mexican continental style breakfast of coffee and sweet rolls. A substantial meal would not be until noon.

After our breakfast, Miguel and I walked around the ten acre farm, situated smack in the middle of a residential area and overlooking the ocean, which as the crow flies was but a quarter mile from where we stood.

"What is that building down there Miguel? The one with the gold dome."

"That monks place. They owns farm."

"Really? I am going to work for monks?"

"No no, yous work me. I has arreglo. How yous say?"

"Arrangement."

"Gez I has arrangement monks. They pays me, I pays yous. Good, no?"

Little by little as we walked around the farm I learned that Miguel grew fresh produce for the monks, and in July

153

sold the avocados to a large grocery chain. He was given a monthly salary that included money to hire a helper. Plus when he sold the avocados, he could keep 20% of the money. And he had free housing. Not a bad deal, I thought.

"Today plant lettuce. Come I show."

Miguel led me to a metal frame structure covered in plastic that served as a greenhouse. Supported by sawhorses, plywood sheets served as tables that ran the length of the green house and held dozens of black plastic trays that contained various seedlings.

"Lettuce here," Miguel said, pointing to a set of trays that contained a varied array of lettuce. "Four kind lettuce. Romaine, Red leaves, Butterhead, Icyberg? Come I show how."

And thus my farm worker career started. Miguel took me to the outdoor field that was prepared for the lettuce seedlings, dozens of rows with plastic tubing that would drip water to each lettuce plant. Miguel stooped down and quickly and expertly dug a hole with one hand and with the other took out the seedling from the tray and placed it in the ground. If his work was quick and smooth my first efforts were labored and clumsy. But he left me alone while he went over to the avocado grove to begin pruning and by the time he came back for me to have lunch, I had finished five rows and Miguel thought I was doing good.

Sara made chicken soup with zucchini, celery and rice for our lunch and fresh corn tortillas. I was glad she served generous portions as I was used to always having breakfast and I was very hungry by the time noon rolled around.

"Delicioso, Sara," I said. "Muchisimas gracias."

"De nada," she answered. "Me agrada que te halla gustado."

I had noticed that in our previous meals Sara always took time to pray before she partook of any food. I assumed that she had a religious life that Miguel didn't share as he dove into his food without ceremony. I didn't say anything then but I made a mental note to ask her when Miguel wasn't around. After the noon meal the next day, Miguel had to drive into town to pick up some supplies and I was left alone with her.

"Sara, a cual iglesia asistes?"

"Voy a una iglesia cristiana aqui cercas," she said pointing toward the beach where the Christian church she attended was located, not far from where the gold domed structure of the monks was.

"Eres cristiano, Herculano?"

"Me bautizaron Catolico pero realmente no voy a ninguna iglesia," I said, telling her that I was baptized Catholic but didn't attend church.

"Y eso por que? Yo sin la iglesia no estaria contenta," asking me why I didn't attend, as she without church could not be happy.

She went on to explain that she had also been raised Catholic and had found the small Christian church quite by accident when she was waiting for Miguel, while he met with the monks. She was so well received by the members that she began attending regularly. Miguel on the other hand was not interested and reluctant to support her conversion to the extent that he refused to drive her and she had to resort to walking down the hill and across the railroad tracks. I never asked her more questions but observed that she was a good kind woman, never judgmental and always cheerful.

By the end of the first week I knew that I would stay on for a while. The work was tiring and exactly why it felt gratifying I didn't know. It just felt good that I was helping food to grow. But perhaps I was feeling great because while I worked I could look at the beautiful Pacific Ocean and feel the ocean breezes wash over my perspiring body.

In addition to the lettuce and other leafy salad greens, we grew a variety of garden crops such as eggplant, artichokes, broccoli, zucchini, cabbage, green beans, carrots and tomatoes. We also had some apple and fig trees, and of course avocados. Because we didn't use pesticides, every Saturday volunteers from the ashram would arrive to wash the green leafy salad greens to rid them of bugs such as aphids and worms.

One of the volunteers was a woman named Ima, who immediately took an interest in me.

"Tell me about yourself, Pelon. You seem like a bright fellow, why are you working here?" We were working side by side at the large outdoor basins.

"Wow, you're kidding right?" I asked. "Just look around at all the beauty, blue skies all the time, the ocean, the growing plants."

"Yes, but you could live in Encinitas and have all this beauty without working at the farm."

"I want to live a simple life and feel like I'm doing a good thing," I said. "I help grow food for monks and nuns. Could it get any better elsewhere? I don't think so." I wanted her to stop pestering me with questions about my personal life and changed the subject.

"Tell me about the Ashram," I said to Ima.

"I could tell you lots of things," she said, "but you would still have to go to the temple to experience it for yourself."

"Yes that's true, but can't you just tell me some basic stuff?"

"I suppose I could," she said somewhat reluctantly. "The teachings were given by a guru from India that came to show the similarities between original Christianity as seen in the New Testament and the Hindu classic, the Bhagavad Gita. They teach Kriya Yoga, a form of meditation that is capable of accelerating a person's spiritual evolution. If what I said is of interest, you should attend the Sunday service."

"Wow, I don't think anyone could be more basic than that," I said and thought to myself that she was a weirdo.

"I thought I gave you what you needed to know."

"Yeah you did, and maybe I'll go to the temple some day."

And since the next day was Sunday and my day off, I really didn't want to stay at the farm and I decided that I would go to the temple. I left early, not knowing the hours of the service and hoping to go to the beach either before or after. As I was leaving, I spotted Sara at the back gate.

"Buenos dias Sara. Vas a la iglesia?" I asked if she was going to church.

"Buenos dias Herculano. Si voy a la iglesia. Gustas acompanarme?"

"No, muchas gracias, voy a visitar el temple de los monjes.

I had asked if she was going to church and she was and she asked if I wanted to go with her. I declined, telling her that I was going to the temple. But we walked down the hill together and talked about life in her Mexican village and how it compared to the life she now led.

"No, pues es muy diferente. Claro que aqui se encuentran mas conveniencias pero la vida en Mexico es mas tranquila y saludable," she said, telling me that even though the USA had more conveniences, life in Mexico was more peaceful and healthier.

"Pero lo importante es alabar a dios," she continued, "y eso, uno lo puede hacer donde quiera," telling me that what was really important in life was to praise God and that one could do so anywhere.

We crossed the railroad tracks right below our hill, learning later that it was against the law not to cross at the street intersection, which was a quarter mile away. I left Sara in front of her church, she as usual asking God to bless me, "Dios te bendiga," and I continued to the temple.

157

Sara reminded me so much of Inez from my childhood whose name I had on my fake Illinois drivers license. Both were simple good persons, completely trustworthy and totally immersed in their Christian faith. For them there was no distinction between Christ and God. A distinction that I was to learn was a fundamental tenet of the temple I was about to visit.

The service was already underway when I walked in, the congregation singing a song about keeping the door of their heart wide open. A monk, dressed in an orange colored robe playing a box instrument that sounded like a small organ, led the singing. A prayer followed invoking Christ and Krishna and others, whose names I didn't recognize. The monk also gave a sermon about the woman at the well citing the New Testament and followed by a parallel comment from the Bhagavad Gita. After a short meditation period we concluded with another prayer.

As I exited, I picked up some handouts and a small booklet of chants, both of which I looked over while standing off to the side of the entrance.

"What did you think?"

I turned to see who was asking. It was Ima. I just can't get rid of this woman, I thought.

"Hello Ima. I thought it was interesting," I said, hoping that would satisfy her and she would leave me alone.

"Interesting doesn't tell me anything. Give me something that you have given some thought to."

"Ima why are you always so abrasive?"

"Abrasive, that's not a farm worker's vocabulary. Who are you really Pelon, or whatever your name is?"

"Just leave me alone will you," I said and walked away.

I was really enjoying the work at the farm. Being outdoors the entire day and getting my hands into the dirt was an experience I had not had since childhood. And seeing the energy contained in those tiny seeds that allowed them to grow and knowing that I was playing a part by watering and weeding, gave me a special feeling, a connectedness to Earth that I had never before experienced, especially when I shed my shoes and worked barefoot.

Throughout the day I worked alone. Because the work entailed mostly repetitive manual tasks my mind was free to think. I thought often about Helga, wondering how she was and hoping that she was settled and happy. I visualized her amazing body and thought about making love with her. I happily relived my fight with Puma and wondered how the guys from Segunda were coping. And I often wondered if I would ever be able to return to my former life. But what I thought about most was what I had been learning at the temple on Sunday and on Thursday evening when they gave a more formal talk. It was all so new and strange, frightening even, yet all the while alluring and drawing me in with mind, body and soul.

There was a public library not far from the farm, a fifteen-minute walk that I took on the evenings when I was not otherwise engaged with work or at the temple. This was my time to read newspapers and magazines and stay abreast of current events. I was amazed at all that was happening in the world, especially all that was taking place in the middle east in what was being called the Arab Spring, and of course the killing of Osama Bin Laden.

"Farm workers don't usually go to libraries," I heard someone say as I sat in an easy chair reading. I looked up. It was Ima.

"Hello Ima. Are you stalking me?" I asked in jest.

"I could say the same about you."

"Yeah right."

"Chance meetings are not by chance at all, I hear," Ima said.

"Our meetings are not by chance? What are they then?"

"Synchronicity. The word describes what seems to be a coincidence but is actually related in a very meaningful way. You and I must have some sort of connection that is not readily apparent in our three dimensional reality."

"Sounds like hocus pocus new age jargon to me," I said.

"No, the concept is actually older than new age. Jung talked and wrote about it. He said that synchronicities are moments when there is a tear in the fabric in what is our agreed upon reality and we get a glimpse of a higher dimension."

"Like I said, hocus pocus."

"You think that we live in the one and only dimension?"

"Actually I haven't given it much thought," I said, finally putting down my reading material.

"Well you should. You can't understand all that you're trying to learn at the temple without believing in other dimensions. What do you think heaven is but a place in another dimension? And the acts of saints and avatars when they perform so called miracles are nothing less than actions that conform to the laws of another dimension."

"Okay you've convinced me. I'll think about it. Now can I get back to my reading?"

"Maybe if you allow me to buy you a cup of tea?"

"You're joking right?"

"I seldom joke."

"Why me? There are lots of men in Encinitas that I'm sure would love to spend some time with you. You're not bad looking."

"What about my personality. You didn't mention that I was charming and fun to be with."

I had to smile and actually almost laughed.

"Okay so you have a knack for driving people away," I said.

"You haven't skipped town."

"You haven't given me a chance. Everywhere I turn, there you are."

"Synchronicity."

"Okay. I'll have tea with you. I was getting tired of reading anyway. Lead the way."

Since neither of us owned a car and we walked down the hill to Highway 101 that was also the main street in Encinitas and where most of the retail stores were located, including the Tea Cove. It was a small one-room shop, fragrant with the oils emanating from a large assortment of teas lined against two walls.

"I recommend a nice Oolong or a Pu'erh."

"I'll have what you have. I don't know much about teas."

"We'll have to do this more often then, so you can learn. Tea is one of the true gifts bestowed on humanity."

"Bestowed by whom?"

"By the Creator of course. Everything comes from the Creator. Everything is alive with the Creator's essence."

"Everything?"

"Yes. Everything. There is no such thing as an inanimate object. The plants, the rocks, the planets, minerals, water."

"Water? You think water is a living entity?"

"Naturally. There is an Austrian…"

"Viktor Schauberger?" I asked proudly.

"My my, I'm impressed that you know him."

"Why, because I'm just a farm worker?"

"I know you're not just a farm worker."

"How can you know that I'm not?"

"I can see the spark in your eyes and there's intelligence and integrity oozing out of you like from some primeval well. With me you can drop the pretensions, I'm not interested in revealing anything about you."

Actually it was good to hang around with someone with whom I didn't have to pretend even if she was somewhat confrontational and brutally honest. I knew that there was much that I could learn from her and I even suggested that we could have tea at least once a week, an idea that she found acceptable. She was not unattractive but there was never a physical attraction. She was as tall as I and very lean with breasts that were but small protrusions. She had a pleasant freckled face and deep penetrating eyes that she habitually shielded from the sun with her hand.

I came to look forward to our tea sessions almost as much as I did to the Thursday talks given at the temple by one of the monks or at times by one of the nuns. Although our conversations were initially about spiritual matters, after awhile our talks had few boundaries.

"Do you support Occupy Wall Street?" I asked one evening over a cup of a blend of black tea and rose petals.

"Absolutely. It's a manifestation of the new energies that we are receiving that will assist humanity in bringing about a more equitable world."

"Seriously? It's not just about people getting sick and tired of getting screwed?"

"We're saying the same thing."

"We are? I thought I was talking about gut feelings assisted by social media technology… you about some hifalutin metaphysical concepts."

"Same thing."

"And from where do these bursts of energy come?"

"Earth is passing through the Galactic Center and it is from whence they come."

"What!! I know that you are somewhat geeky but even for you this sounds pretty far out."

"Just look around. Why do you think that the Middle East is experiencing what is being called the Arab Spring? This is the beginning of a new and more just world. People that have been oppressed are beginning to awaken to the fact that they have great power."

"That's pretty hard to believe Ima. It's been a dog eat dog world since humans walked the earth. Big dogs have always ruled."

"How do you know that?"

"Because it's that way now. I assume it was so back then and that it'll be so in the future."

"Your assumptions are wrong. And if I know you at all, I think that your heart tells you that it should not be that way. It's our heart that will create this new world."

"And is this new world imminent?"

"Of course not. It's an evolutionary process. It'll take generations. This is but the beginning. I came up with a good metaphor. Want to hear it?"

"Can I prevent you from telling it?"

"I guess not. Think of an ecosystem such as a forest. It is supported by the amount of rainwater, by year around temperature, by the insects and animal populations etc. Lets say that those factors begin to change. Rainfall diminishes or a mini ice age ensues, or all the termites die off etc. Slowly over time a new ecosystem will develop. Right?"

"I'm with you so far."

"The earth too has had energies that have supported certain types of human behavior. A dog-eat-dog world as you said or a good-guys-finish-last world. The energies that we have been receiving have changed and now those old behaviors will begin to slowly die off, sometimes because people will change, sometimes because people who are greedy, violent, exclusive, et cetera, will die and new souls will incarnate here that are more suited to the new Earth."

"Interesting outlook but it all seems to hinge on whether or not it's true that new energies are to be the norm and that our hearts will be the foundation of this new earth."

"Keep looking around… you'll continue to see new evidence of what I've said."

"By the way, was there a specific reason for mentioning a mini ice age?"

"Winter is coming. Did you read the Game of Thrones books?" she asked.

"I saw the HBO movie."

"In the book they keep repeating that winter is coming. I think that the author tapped into some collective fear because at some deep level, we all know that a mini ice age starts in 2014 or so.

"Interesting," I said and thought more seriously about the talk that Lorraine and I heard that she said confirmed what her grandfather had been telling her. This opened another avenue of discussion with Ima and it was late when we finally parted and went our separate ways.

I continued to like the work on the farm. I even enjoyed mundane tasks such as weeding as they gave me an opportunity to practice the presence of God as taught at the temple. Silently I would repeat the mantra I had used in meditation: love is all, all is love. Such practice gave me great joy as well as helping me to strengthen my mind to stay focused during my morning and evening meditations.

Sometime in late spring I had begun modeling correct English to Miguel.

"I wants yous to helps me cut avocado… how you say ramas?"

"You want me to help you prune the avocado trees?" I would ask showing him the correct structure and then have him say it correctly.

"Gez I want you to help me prune the avocado trees."

By the end of summer he had learned quite a bit and both of us were gaining from the relationship.

"Thank you, Pelon," he said one day during supper. "I have learned very much from you."

"And I have learned much from you, Miguel," I answered.

"Next week Pelon," Miguel said, "we need to pick the pumpkins. The monks will come and help us."

"They are big and heavy," I affirmed. And they were indeed, some weighing probably as much as 200 lbs.

Seldom would Miguel revert to Spanish as difficult as it was at times to express himself. Sara on the other hand only spoke Spanish and was not making any effort to learn English, even though I offered to help her.

"No para que?" What for, she said. "Mi mundo es pequeno, aqui con Miguel y halla en la iglesia no necesito ingles." Saying that in her small world consisting of Miguel and her church, she didn't need English.

The monks came as promised to help with the harvest of the pumpkins, bringing a good size stake truck that we used to haul them out of the fields.

"What do you do with the pumpkins?" I asked a monk called Brother Ananda.

"We decorate them for the Halloween celebration. You must come by and enjoy the festivities. It's a lot of fun."

The Halloween celebration was a big deal in Encinitas. It was held in the large vacant area where one day they hoped to build housing for the monks. The free event was a long standing tradition and hundreds, if not thousands attended.

"Let's go down, Miguel. It will be fun."

"No, I will stay home with Sara. She tell me that Halloween is a devil celebration."

"She said that it is a celebration for the devil?"

"Gez, she said it is a celebration for the devil."

"I don't think so Miguel and I am going. I will see you in the morning."

Lately Miguel had begun to attend church with Sara and to espouse some of her Christian beliefs. Now we had to pray openly before our meals and every parting was an occasion for a Dios te bendiga. I was fine with all the changes as I too was changing and incorporating new habits because of the teachings from the temple. Meditation was also bringing about changes in my outlook and in my behavior. I gave up cussing and drinking alcohol and I cut down on meat but was not ready to be a vegetarian. I also tried to stop masturbating when I heard at the temple that it drained away some of our vital life force. However since I was not having sex, masturbation had been providing some release. This led to a complication when one early morning as I was going at it, I let out a moan and Sara walked into my room to see if I was okay. She saw me holding my boner and for what seemed like several minutes, but probably wasn't, she stood at the open door and stared. Finally she closed the door and nothing was ever said but from then on I tried to refrain.

I walked down the hill that Halloween evening and was amazed at the transformation that had taken place in the vacant lot. On one corner of the land was the golden dome structure and the rest miraculously became a fantasyland of ghouls, monsters, ghosts as well as fairy princesses, magical unicorns and mermaids. The monks and nuns had put up a puppet stage, booths for a variety of carnival games, a mock cemetery full of ghosts and vampires, a haunted castle, a stage for folk music with a Halloween theme and the good fairy's castle where they gave out candy. Rivaling what the ashram had put together were the people that came to the celebration in every imaginable costume and then some that were beyond my imagination.

I walked around, played a few games and took in a child's puppet show where I stood next to a person dressed as a Hindu deity with several arms flapping around, some of which occasionally slapped at me. When it was over and I began shuffling away from the stage I noticed that it was Ima that had been standing next to me.

"Who are you supposed to be?" I asked.

"Who do you want me to be?" She countered without looking at who was speaking to her.

"Just be yourself."

She turned and saw me. "Well well my stalker. And to answer your question I'm the Goddess protector of the righteous from all the evils of the world."

"Good to know."

"Yes and good to stay on my good side too. By the way I had a feeling I would see you here."

"Me too," I answered. "This is quite a show. I didn't expect such an elaborate affair."

"It is great isn't it?"

I nodded a yes. "I was surprised that I didn't see you at the farm this morning."

"Why, did you miss me?"

"Did I miss you?" I asked myself more than her. "Yes I guess I did," I answered in surprise, for I did miss her, strange as that seemed at the moment. We did spend a lot of time together. One evening a week we met at the teahouse. After the Sunday service we usually strolled the Temple garden and sat looking at the ocean from the bluff where the garden was located. Friday morning we washed the salad greens and other crops. I had planned to ask her to meet me at the Halloween event but she had never showed that Friday morning.

"I don't even know where you live or how to get in touch with you." I said.

"You have never asked."

"Okay, how do I get in touch with you? Do you have a phone? I assume you live close by."

"No telephone. I do live close by. I'll show you where later."

"I was just about to go home when I saw you. I had a tiring day."

"We can go now. I live up the hill too."

"Are you walking home like that?" I asked.

"Why not? I came down like this. Are you embarrassed to be seen with a Goddess?"

"If I didn't know better I would have thought that you just made an attempt at humor."

"Maybe I did."

Up the hill we went, with me trying to stay clear of her wailing arms and she hitting me on purpose and actually laughing at my feeble attempts. I was in shock. I had seldom seen her smile much less actually laugh. We stopped at the top and looked at one another and I pulled her to me and kissed her ever so gently on the mouth, thinking that any moment she would reach out with her real arm and slap me. But she didn't. She kissed me right back.

We sat down on the hill and stared out at the ocean. A moon partially obscured by thin clouds cast its light on the water. We didn't speak for a while, both of us lost somewhere in our thoughts about the kiss and what it meant or if it meant anything at all. Finally she spoke.

"I have never kissed anyone."

"Are you kidding?" I asked, incredulous.

"No. I'm dead serious."

"You're still a virgin!!?"

"Well duh as they say."

"I know it's not polite but how old are you?"

"How old are you?"

"I'm 26 in May. The 11th of May," I said.

"I will be 27 on October 1st."

"I have never kissed a virgin," I said. "So it's a first for me too."

"Have you made love to a virgin?"

"Nope, that has never happened."

"Do you want to?"

"Do I want to make love with you?" I said. "I don't know. I had never thought of you in this way until tonight. It's been a complete surprise for me to realize how much I care for you. I haven't even begun to digest the thoughts and feelings that I am having."

"Yes it's been quite a night. But unlike you, I have thought about you in that way and although I have never felt that way about another person, I'm certain of my feelings."

"Nevertheless," I said, "I am not ready to make love to a multi-armed pretend Goddess."

"No problem there," she said and began pulling off her costume.

We found a clearing on the hill, a spot that was hardly sloping, and proceeded to make love. She was a quiet lover, her moans barely audible. And she was quick to come and to laugh with pleasure when it was over. It had been intense for me, partly because I had not made love to a woman for several months. But also because surprisingly this woman aroused feelings from deep inside of me. When I was walking home after seeing her to the studio that she rented on a property not far from the farm, I was deep in thought, pondering the night's events. It was a mystery, was all I came to decide.

.^.^.^.

CHAPTER IX

The next day Miguel let me know that he was driving to Los Angeles and wanted to know if I wanted to go along.

"I was going to plant tomatoes today," I said. "Can they wait?"

"Gez sure they can wait," Miguel answered.

"Is Sara coming?"

"Gez she is coming." Please you get her, *mientras* I go to the greenhouse."

"Of course I will get her while you go to the greenhouse."

"While is *mientras*?"

I nodded to Miguel and I went inside to tell Sara that we were ready. "Sara ya estamos listos."

"Ya mero estoy, por favor ven ayudame," she answered from inside her room that she was almost ready and to go and help her, with what I didn't know.

I opened the door to their room and she was standing stark naked and about to slip a dress over her head. She had large breasts with the biggest nipples I had ever seen and a small slender brown body partially covered by long thick black hair that went down as far as her buttocks.

My eyes opened wide and I quickly closed the door. I thought I saw her smile but I quickly suppressed that possibility.

"Ahora si," I heard Sara say, asking me to go in and telling me that we were taking a large steamer trunk, "Esa petaca va con nosotros." She said nothing about the incident and showed no noticeable embarrassment. Of course I didn't say anything either.

On the way we made plans for them to leave me downtown and to rendezvous at the same place at 7:00 that evening. I wanted to see my mother once again and find out if there was any new information.

My plan was the same as before, but we arrived at noon in Los Angeles and it would be a couple of hours before my mother would be on the bus. I decided to visit the new downtown Catholic Cathedral, whose radical design had aroused an avalanche of controversy. While sitting in one of the pews and actually admiring the open architectural design, a priest came and sat beside me.

"It is beautiful, regardless of the criticism about its high cost and its modernistic design. Don't you agree?" he asked.

"I do think it's beautiful. I especially like the tapestries and those massive front doors. I don't know what it cost and really it's not important to me. At one time I did think that church money was better spent on poor people."

"What made you change your mind?"

"The story about Martha buying the oil to use on Christ. Poor people will always be with us."

"That's so true. Do you attend this church?"

"No. I was raised in Los Angeles but now I live near San Diego."

"I love that area. Where exactly do you live?"

Should I tell him...? I thought. Oh what the hell. Why not?

"I live in Encinitas."

"Really, by the ashram?"

"Yes, as a matter of fact I do. I'm surprised that a Catholic priest would know about the ashram."

"I guess I'm not an ordinary priest in that regard. I'm curious by nature and always trying to experience what other people find of interest. I've gone to a few services at the temple in Hollywood."

"I'm impressed Father, that you keep an open mind about such things."

"It's not all that impressive son, God's works are impressive. The Grand Canyon, the Giant Redwoods, Niagara Falls, those are impressive. The actions of men and women seldom are."

"Point taken Father. Tell me did you ever try any of the temple's meditation techniques?"

"As a matter of fact I have, and secretly continue to employ one of them. I don't go around telling anyone but I feel the presence of God very acutely during those meditative sessions when I do."

"Me too, Father."

"Well that's what's important, so you keep at it. I must run now. I have confessions in a little while."

It was 1:30 and I hurried out of the Cathedral and headed for the bus that would take me to the hotel where my mother worked.

At exactly 2:10 my mother boarded. She saw me and managed to work her way past other passengers to stand beside me. I gave her a one-arm hug and said hello.

"Hay Herculano. You have put me through hell, Mijito."

"Why mom. Didn't Lechero stop by to tell you that I was okay?"

"Yes but that only made me worry more. Lechero said he didn't know where you had gone. Only that you were fine. And then those men showed up again and so did that Puma fellow that you were friends with. He said that he's a cop now. Is that true?"

"Yeah it's true. He's gone from gang banger to cop."

"Maybe he can help you, Mijito?"

"No mom. He can't be trusted. Never, never tell him anything. Please."

Hay mijito it's all so confusing. He promised me that he would help you but that he had to first take you in for your own protection. He asked me how and when I had last seen you.

"And you told him?"

"Yes and he gave me this phone and said to press this button if ever you came to see me on the bus again."

"Did you press it already?"

"Yes, when I first saw you."

"Gotta go mom. Love you."

I got off as soon as the bus stopped and I ran down the first side street that I came upon. I heard police sirens and kept running. When I saw a group of young men putting a game of basketball together at a local playground, I stopped and asked if they needed another player. Fortunately they did and they asked me to take off my shirt and play with the skins team. A couple of hours later the game ended and I asked one of the players if he could give me a ride.

"Where to bro?"

"About ten blocks from here. I'll give you five for gas."

"Solid bro."

I arrived at the designated pick up point an hour early and tried to blend in with the throng of workers going and coming on the city buses. It wasn't difficult. Miguel arrived right on time and I got in and we drove away.

"Did you see your Mother?" Miguel asked.

"Yes she's fine. We had a good visit. Did you complete your business at the consulate?"

"Yes, but very difficult to brings my mother from Mexico."

"Why is it difficult to bring your mother, Miguel?"

"They think she go work when she get here. I tells them she old lady."

"They think she will go to work when she gets here?"

"Gez. Is bullshit. She old lady."

As we drove south on the Santa Ana Freeway, all four lanes bumper to bumper even at this late hour, I finally started to relax and feel safe. The basketball game had been a good cover and a good way to allow my mind to forget the fact that I was being chased. I thought by now Andre would have forgotten about me and dropped his silly pursuit. Apparently he hadn't.

We arrived at the farm after nine and there was a note pinned to the door. Miguel handed it to me to read. It was from Ima.

"Sorry I missed you. Please come to my place when you return. I'll be up late. Ima"

"It's for me, Miguel," was all I said.

I was already sleepy and tired but my interest in seeing her and in seeing where she lived won me over. The previous night when we were about to make love I suggested that we go to her place but she said no that she wanted her first time to be out in the open, under the stars and overlooking the ocean. When I walked her home she didn't invite me inside, saying that she was tired. My interest was piqued. Fortunately the ocean air revived me on my walk to her place and I arrived wide awake.

"Where were you today?' she asked when she greeted me with a strong hug. "I went by the farm three times looking for you. I finally left that note hoping you would see it and come over."

"I went to Los Angeles with Miguel."

"I was worried. Do you realize that I still know nothing about you? I thought that maybe the immigration patrol had whisked all of you away to Mexico. Are you here illegally?"

"No! I was born here just like you. Are you going to invite me in?"

"Of course. I'm just a little distracted. Sorry. Make yourself at home."

Eager to document everything that I was about to see, I walked into the middle of a cozy carpeted room with a futon on the floor on my left and a rectangular table along the wall at the other end with so much computer hardware that it looked like a display at a store. The wall directly in front of where I was standing had a door that I assumed was the bathroom. Fragrant incense was burning at her altar on the same wall as the entrance. Everything was clean and tidy as I suspected it would be.

"Nice," I said. "I like those paintings on the wall. They are so vibrant with color."

"You like them. Really?

"Yes they offset the starkness of all that computer hardware and make the room come alive."

She was holding onto my arm and she gave me an appreciative squeeze.

"Some day I'll paint one especially for you," she said.

"You painted them!!? Damn Ima, there's so much I don't know about you."

"Ditto my friend. We can sit on the futon and talk."

"Do you want me to take my shoes off?" I asked after seeing shoes at the entrance.

"Yes please. Hope you don't mind."

"No of course not. Can I kiss you before we sit?"

"Yes but I don't know if I can make love. I'm pretty sore from last night."

"Just a kiss will be fine," I said.

The kiss was long and pleasurable, eliciting a fiery passion in both of us and soon she was aggressively biting my nipples and touching my penis.

"Are you sure about this?" I asked.

"Quite sure."

She slept in my arms that night. We had stayed up late telling one another factual bits and pieces about our lives that we hadn't revealed previously. I learned that she was an only child raised by her dad after her mother died when she was ten. Her dad, a doctor in Santa Barbara, allowed her great freedom to be who she wanted to be. She was a smart, precocious child, always very much a geek who went on to graduate from Stanford with a double master's in Computer Science and Fine Arts.

"I always thought you were a geek," I said.

"And I always thought you were an illegal alien."

"I was right and you were wrong."

"Why are you in hiding?"

"Who said I was in hiding?"

"It's pretty obvious that you're off the grid and want to keep it that way. You get paid in cash and use cash for all your expenditures. You don't have an ATM card. You don't have a phone. You don't drive. You don't have a computer. You don't use any social media that I can see. You have no friends other than me."

"Okay okay. Are you sure you want to know my story? There's another woman."

"Now I really want to know."

I started my story in Washington, about my job as a Congressional Aide, about Dr. Maier's group session, about Robert and about Helga.

"I know it's Helga. She's the other woman isn't she?"

I nodded. "Yes she is. Shall I go on?"

"I trust your feelings for me Pelon, and I trust the friendship that we have. Nothing can dissuade me from that which I have experienced with you. So yes, please go on. I already have a ton of questions."

I bopped, my body language affirming that I would continue.

"What is that body bopping that you do Pelon? Where does that come from?"

"That's a whole different story. I'll have to tell you some other day," I answered and continued telling her about my work for Congressman Jimmy and about my report and his legislation. I described Farley, Robert, Naomi and Esperanza and the roles they played in helping me obtain proof about Congressman Jimmy's true alliances.

"Wow. Naomi and Esperanza changed their minds about you. That's incredible," Ima said.

"You changed your mind about me, what's so incredible about it?"

"Oh just finish your story and stop gloating. You still have that flash drive?" she asked.

"I mailed it to a friend in Tucson, just before Andre abducted me."

"Are you making this up? It sounds too bizarre to actually have taken place."

"I wish I was making it up or that it was a bad dream. But it's the truth and even more bizarre is that he's still after me."

I wanted to jump ahead and tell her about the trip to Los Angeles but showed restraint and continued in a chronological fashion.

"I like Aunt Marie," she said when I was describing where and how she lived in that remote area outside of Cadillac.

"I think you two would get along," I said.

"What about your trophy girlfriend Helga, did she take to that lifestyle?"

"Ima! She wasn't a trophy girlfriend," I protested. "And no she didn't. She wasn't raised that way and got really depressed."

"Is that why you're here and not there?"

"Partly," I said. "But who can tell why things turn out the way they do. If she and I had stayed in Washington, in her milieu, I might still be with her. But that's not what happened. There seemed to be a force that intervened, something beyond my control. Was it fate? Was it my guardian angel? Was it a random accident? I don't know."

"Did she bail on you?"

I answered that she hadn't and proceeded to tell Ima about the men that had come looking for me, and how I

178

decided that there was no reason that Helga should go with me to my next hideout.

"I think that both of us came to realize that we were from different worlds and that we needed to separate for our own highest good. It was a sad parting," I said.

"And that's how you came to me?" Ima asked.

"Yes and no. There were some intervening events, but it's late and I need to get some sleep. Monday will be a busy day at the farm."

"Stay with me then. It'll be nice to sleep next to you."

"Really. I'd love to sleep with you.... And I will continue the story some other day."

"Promise?"

"Yeah I promise."

CHAPTER X

Mondays were our busiest days. It was then that we readied the crates with the produce that was being sent to the local ashram and to the three other ashrams in Los Angeles. A large truck came around noon and we took our crates from the large walk-in cooler and loaded them for the trip.

"Where did you sleep last night?" Miguel asked after we had finished loading the crates.

"I slept at the house of a friend."

"A girlfriend?"

"Just a friend."

"It be a sin to sleep with woman not your wife."

"Who said that it is a sin to sleep with a woman that is not my wife?"

"The Bible says it is a sin."

I shrugged and said that I didn't think the Bible said that.

"Sara said it does say."

I wasn't surprised that Sara would say something like that, as my experience with born again Christians was that they had a proclivity to pick and choose from the Bible to fit whatever moral stand they supported. When I went to Ima's that evening I told her what Miguel said. She laughed.

"I read someplace that the world's major religions rely heavily on printed texts; the Koran, Bible, Torah, Bhagavad Gita or Upanishads. They were established and grew in the era of print culture."

"Clearly that's true but how is that connected to a born again Christian or a radical Islamist?"

"In that authority is removed from direct personal experience. Someone outside the practitioner is able to dictate what Truth is," she added. "Someone like Sara relies on others telling her what she needs to believe."

"But the scriptures are there for everyone to read. Maybe this wasn't so originally, but now everyone has access to those religious texts."

"That's true, but all those religions have something like a priestly class, some person that mediates and interprets what to believe and what is correct behavior," she countered.

"While at the temple, a person is asked to go *within* during meditation to perceive Truth directly?" I asked.

"Exactly," she answered.

"But there too is a priestly class and also some do's and don'ts that get passed along, are there not, such as no masturbating, that seem very prescribed?"

"It's funny that you should mention that one. Now I have a different struggle," she said and winked knowingly at me. "Anyway what you are telling me is true and I am questioning some things."

"Really? That comes as a big surprise. I have always seen you as the perfect disciple."

"I still am but I've been reading more articles about 2012 that are undermining some of what I have learned."

"Like?"

"I've already told you that the earth is passing through the galactic center and that it heralds a major shift in human consciousness, and yet no one at the temple is even talking about it. Or the importance of the messages that Archangels are giving to various individuals about this shift, and the physiological changes that our bodies are undergoing, or the shift into a higher dimension that…."

"Whoa!"

"Too much too fast?"

"Yeah. Where are you getting all this?"

"It's from the Internet. I admit that much that is found on the Internet about 2012 is farfetched and ludicrous. The world is ending! The Earth is going to split apart! Vapors from a comet are going to poison everyone! One has to be discerning."

"What about the messages from the Archangels, that sounds like a stretch?"

"That's what I thought at first and I was excluding anything that purported to be channeled. Then I realized that humanity has always received messages from the other side of the veil."

"That's the second time you used that veil expression."

"It's a common expression with this material. It means that it is being communicated by a spiritual entity from beyond our world."

"From what we call heaven or from the astral world," I said, hoping that I was understanding what she said.

"Yeah, from a higher dimension. We live in the 3rd dimension," when she saw a puzzled look on my face she added, "these spiritual entities are in higher dimensions. I know this is confusing and I'm new at it so I don't have it all straight in my mind either. But what I have read and understood so far makes sense. It rings true in my heart."

"I won't press you because I know it's getting late, but just explain what you said about humanity always getting these kinds of messages."

"Yes, it is getting late isn't it? We don't want to spend the entire evening in our heads," she said as she leaned over to my side of the futon and kissed me tenderly.

That's as far as we got that evening with the discussion, the kiss erasing all thought of further conversation.

The next morning I woke up early and moved carefully away from Ima so as not to awaken her from a sound sleep. I dressed and was opening the door when she sat up.

"Trying to sneak off?"

"Yeah. Nothing left to conquer here," I joked.

"You're right about that. My surrender was total and unconditional. Can't you stay awhile? I can make some tea."

"Sure. Do you have anything to eat? I'm starving."

"There's some good cheese and some bread in the refrigerator," she said as she uncovered herself and got up from the futon. Her back was contoured, her stomach flat, her breasts tiny, her shoulders and arms had good definition and her long legs muscular. Her great physique attributed to biking the Encinitas hills.

"What are you doing today?" I asked as I retrieved what was to be my breakfast.

"I have a couple of appointments at the fire house. Not until ten though, did you have something in mind?" she asked and quickly jumped to her feet and tried to wrestle me down to the futon.

"Watch out for my sandwich, Ima," I said laughing at her antics.

"You're a dud. I thought all Latino men were oversexed," she said when she finally released me.

"That's pretty harsh even for you Ima."

"I is calling 'em as I see 'em. I'll make us some tea maybe that'll warm you up."

"What's with the fire station?"

"It's a new consulting job. They want me to create software that will interface with the other fire departments in the area and with the police too. It's all about integration nowadays."

"Maybe down the road you can see if I'm on some sort of database."

"Sure I could do that. But it'll cost you big."

"Are you talking about a sexual favor?"

"Maybe. Or it could be all about money."

I quickly ate my breakfast and hustled over to the farm.

Miguel and I worked together that day, hauling branches and limbs he had pruned from the avocado trees as well as from the other fruit trees, mostly figs and oranges. It was a bone-tiring day and I made no effort to walk to Ima's house after dinner and instead went straight to bed. I was awakened from sleep by movement in my bed and when I turned, my arm landed on a soft body. It was Sara.

"Sara que haces aqui?" What are you doing here? I asked her.

"Quiero que me embaraces."

"Estas loquita? Claro que no!" I was indignant that she would ask me to impregnate her.

"Quiero ser madre y Miguel no puede porque lo tiene muy chiquito."

Oh God I thought. She thinks Miguel's penis is too small to impregnate her.

"Si Miguel te encuentra aqui, nos mata a los dos," I warned her that if Miguel were to find her with me he'd kill both of us.

"No viene. Fue con su compadre a la cantina," she said, telling me that Miguel went drinking with a friend and would not show up.

"De todos modos yo no quiero hacer eso contigo. Salte." I told her I would not make love to her, and to leave.

"Por favor. Tu estas como toro, se que me puedes embarazar." You are like a bull she said, please I know I'll get pregnant.

I had to push her out and quickly shut the door, placing a chair under the doorknob. I gathered my clothing and stuffed them into a small knapsack and walked out without saying anything more to Sara. I went straight to Ima's and told her what had happened.

"Hell hath no fury like a woman scorned," she said smiling.

"This is no time for jokes, Ima. I have a bad feeling about this."

"Loosen up, Pelon. It's going to be fine. She may try to seduce you again though."

"That's what I'm afraid of."

"You can stay with me if you like."

"I thought about asking you if I could. It's a small space though. Have you ever had a roommate?"

"Nope. Couldn't stand the thought of a roommate."

"That's not giving me any assurances that this will work."

"You can't consider yourself a roommate."

I didn't have much choice really and I consented to move in. It was still early and she made some tea and we sat on the futon and talked.

"How was your meeting with the fire chief?" I asked her.

"It went fine. I think it'll be a challenging fun project. He's been a member of the temple for many years. We had a conversation about spiritual matters and I asked him what he thought of 2012."

"What did he say?"

"He discounted its importance. It's threatening to accept as true what is being said about 2012."

"In what way?"

"In all sorts of ways, but starting with the idea that for the first time humanity will have the capacity to ascend to a higher dimension while maintaining the physical body. This is such a radical notion because heretofore only the most advanced avatars have been able to achieve this state. And now humanity as a whole is being offered this possibility."

"You're right, it is a far out idea. How can you be so sure it's true?"

"I've been reading the messages from the Archangels such as Metatron and from the Pleiadian Council. They all say it."

"I know messages from the other side of the veil. The other night you didn't finish your thought about humanity always receiving them."

"Well, just in recent history we have verifiable accounts of messages from the Virgin Mary given to individuals at places like Fatima or Lourdes and even more recently at Medjugorje. In the history of Mexico there's the apparition of the Virgin de Guadalupe. This is not a new phenomenon."

"I've never thought about the Virgen de Guadalupe in that way, but I guess you're right. Juan Diego did get messages from her. But getting back to what you said about ascension to a higher dimension, will it just happen one day like on December 21, 2012?"

"No. It's an individual choice. Each and everyone has to want it and the consciousness has to expand before it can happen. And our physical bodies also have to incorporate big changes to handle the potency of the new energies."

"Are we getting beamed up to the mother ship for some surgical procedure? Is that why aliens have been abducting people?"

"No. It's way better and stranger than any science fiction I've ever read."

"So how will it happen?"

"You do know that the temple teaches an advanced form of meditation that changes the physiology of a person?" she asked.

"Yeah, I remember reading something about that."

"Well, the physiological changes are necessary to be able to absorb a greater, more intense amount of energy. The human body is already equipped to have an upgrade that allows this to happen. One of the changes entails activating more strands of DNA. Right now we operate with two strands and we have ten more that are dormant, that scientists have found but that they tagged as junk. These dormant ten strands are being activated and we'll have use of all twelve."

I started humming the tune from Rod Serling's Twilight Zone to show that this conversation was getting very weird.

"I know, I know. But aren't you feeling strangely fatigued and isn't your bed feeling like the best place in the whole world, not wanting to leave it in the morning and eager to return to it at night and sometimes even in the middle of the day for a short nap? These are some of the symptoms that are manifesting in the body as it incorporates the new energies and accommodates the changes in the body. And also they are present when a person is clearing stuff that is impeding his or her progress."

"Can't say that I haven't felt some of that. But I think it's just that I'm doing some very physical work that my body is not used to doing. It needs more rest."

"What about other symptoms like heart burn and neck pain. Have you experienced them? Or waking up at two or three in the morning and seldom sleeping straight through until morning?"

"Again I think it's normal to have neck pain and heart burn."

"What about waking up at 2 or 3 in the morning?"

"I admit that is a little puzzling. I have always been a sleep through everything kind of guy. Still your explanation is too incredible for me to accept without more evidence."

"Fair enough. But not tonight, Ima answered. "I'm tired and need some sleep."

I was surprised at how well we both adjusted to living together in such a small space. During the day when she worked at her computer I was at the farm, and at night we had dinner there or walked to one of several restaurants in downtown Encinitas. A few times we even took the Coaster to Old Town San Diego. Hanging out with Ima was really fun, as I never knew what she would bring up for conversation. Her interests were varied and wide ranging. Some days it was about science, some days literature, some days technology and of course often it was about 2012.

"What are we doing for Thanksgiving?" I asked her. "We can't cook a turkey here."

"Some friends invited me for dinner. I have permission to bring a guest. Or we can visit my father in Santa Barbara, he always cooks a big meal for friends."

"You want to take me to meet your dad? Uh oh, this is a big step. Have you ever invited someone to his house before?"

"No. He'll be surprised."

"Will he freak out because I'm a Chicano?"

"Oh no. He's an old commie from the sixties. He'll love the fact that he's finally getting a chance to prove that he walks the talk."

"Does he know that I live with you?"

"No, but he's always hinting about grandchildren."

"Whoa. Grandchildren?"

"All parents are like that. They want another chance to put into practice all they've learned about parenting since the time they were parents."

.^.^.^.

CHAPTER XI

Wednesday we took the train to Santa Barbara and the dad met us at the depot.

"Dad this is my boyfriend, Herculano."

"Well this is a surprise, you having a real boyfriend. Hi Herculano, you may call me Geoffrey, spelled with a G like the Brits."

"How do you do sir? It's a pleasure to meet you," I said and I extended my hand for his handshake.

Ima's dad was in his early seventies but his grip was strong and he looked as if he was only in his fifties. He had a full head of graying hair and he was taller than either Ima or I and stocky in build. He wore shorts and a colorful Hawaiian shirt and a pair of worn leather sandals.

"My look at you, Ima. You're much prettier than the last time I saw you. Life must be good. Come give us a hug."

Geoffrey loaded us into his late model Peugot and drove us to his home in the upscale Montecito neighborhood where large homes on large plots of land vied with one another for grandeur and beauty. Although his home was also on a large parcel, it was modest and simple in a Spanish style with red clay tiles for a roof.

"Nice place, Geoffrey."

"Thanks Herculano. I bought this place when it was more affordable than it is now. Frankly I couldn't afford it now and when I'm with some of my old friends, I'm embarrassed to say I live here."

"Well it's a very nice place and for sure you don't have to be embarrassed with me. And please call me Pelon, Geoffrey. It means...."

"Baldy, I know. I had a good friend named Pelon. He was from the Big Hazard barrio."

"How did you come to know someone from Big Hazard?" I asked in total surprise.

"Not now Dad, let us get settled in before you launch into one of your stories," Ima said.

"You're right, my girl. Come I'll show you to your room. You do sleep together?"

"Yes Dad, we do sleep together, and no we have no plans to get married and have children."

"Well okay then. Come out when you're ready and we can have some food. You are hungry, no?"

"Starved," Ima said, "but I want to shower first. You can show Pelon around."

"Come on Pelon, she's giving us some time for man to man talk."

We went outside and walked around the grounds.

"This is really nice, Geoffrey. So what about Pelon from Big Hazard?"

"I met him when I interned at the LA County General Hospital in the early 60's." Do you know that area?"

"Yeah I grew up in Boyle Heights."

"You a homeboy from Flats?"

"No, from Segunda."

"I see," he said with some trepidation in his voice.

"That was a long time ago. You needn't worry."

"I'm not worried Pelon. Ima is a good judge of character. At least she's always been. But you are her first boyfriend and I guess I do worry a little that no one take advantage of her."

"Actually I think you should worry more about me. Ima is a very strong woman."

"Yes she is," he said with a large smile. "Anyway back to Pelon from Big Hazard. I did my intern at the General Hospital and I rented a room from Pelon's family. It was within walking distance of the hospital and the rent was cheap because it was in gang turf. I lived with them for two years and I got to know all of the Big Hazard members because I treated their wounds from their gang fights, even some of the homeboys from Little Hazard."

"That's a pretty interesting experience. You speak Spanish, Geoffrey?"

"Claro que si and my placa is el docta."

"Did you stay in touch?"

"With some of them, especially those that became active in the Movimiento, the fight for civil rights that erupted in the later part of the 60's. By then I was a doctor right there at the General and every so often one of them would come by to talk or I would see them by chance at a rally or demonstration."

"No kidding. You were attending those events?"

"It was the sixties, Pelon. Man was it exhilarating! There was unity in barrios and ghettos and in hippie enclaves like never before. And I think that we're seeing that unity return."

"You think we're going back to a time like the 1960's?"

"Better than the 60's, Pelon. We had the right ideas in the 60's but we got bogged down with drugs and sex, and that turned out to be very counterproductive. It ruined our good intentions. You young people today are blessed not only with the desire for unity, but with social media that is facilitating your efforts, and drugs are not part of the lifestyle. Yours is a fascinating group—idealistic, altruistic and it's all about the group, all about being inclusive and wanting everyone to get a rightful piece of the pie."

"Let's eat," Ima's voice rang out from the backdoor. "Did you tell him stories from your time in the barrio, Dad?" she asked as we went inside.

193

"Yes and he seemed far more appreciative then you've ever been."

"That's because he's still a homeboy at heart. Oh he says he's not but he still has all the mannerisms, like bopping when he wants to affirm something, or tilting his head back when greeting someone."

"Yeah and don't mess with me. I could be dangerous."

"Ooooh I'm scared," she mocked.

"What now, Geoffrey? You still practice medicine?" I asked.

"Mostly I'm retired but I do work at the free clinic two or three days a week. And you Pelon, what do you do?"

I looked over at Ima. "You can trust Dad, Pelon," she said.

"I'm really a lawyer and a Congressional Aide but I got into some trouble and right now I'm working at an organic farm, there in Encinitas."

"What sort of trouble?"

"It's a long complicated story, Geoffrey. You sure you want the sordid details?"

"I've heard plenty in my line of work. Go ahead. Don't think you can shock me."

"Okay then."

I recounted the story of working in Washington and meeting Helga in a counseling group and hooking up with her when she ended her marriage and how her ex-husband got it into his head that I was the reason she had ended it with him.

"And were you responsible?"

"No way. He was a jerk. He had been running around with other women and she finally told him to get lost."

"And how is it that he is the reason for you having to go into hiding? You are hiding are you not?"

"Yeah. I'm like the Fugitive and Andre, the ex-husband, is after me. But it's not only because he lost everything with Helga because of a pre-nup. When he became head of one of the data-gathering agencies in Washington, he was asked by some unknown people in power to retrieve some information that I got a hold of, containing embarrassing information on some elected officials, including the Congressman that employed me."

"Why are you so sure he's after you?"

"He had me abducted once."

I went on to tell Geoffrey about my abduction in Washington and how I escaped to Michigan and about Aunt Marie and my parting company with Helga. I told him about Los Angeles and my fight with Puma and how I ended up in Encinitas. By the time I was finished, Geoffrey was shaking his head in disgust.

"If what you say is true, and really I have no reason to doubt what you've told me, then this country is going to be in the grip of men like Andre, men with access to information on each and every one of us that will kill our freedoms once and for all."

"If one looks at the big picture, you're right," I said. "My situation can germinate into every abuse of freedom imaginable. And right now I seem to have no recourse against such a powerful enemy."

"That was true until I came along," Ima said. "Digital data can be a double-edged sword. If I can gain access to information about Andre's solo vendetta against you, then we can cook his goose."

"Yes but how can you perform this deed, dear?" Geoffrey asked. "You're not a government agent, at least I don't think you are."

"I don't have to be an agent of any sort, Dad. I can gain access through the network that I'm helping build for the Fire Department."

"Really you can do that?" I asked.

"Yes, but not right away. I have a few weeks of work to get to that point but once I do, I can get in."

"It would be nice to get my life back. Not that I don't enjoy farm work but it feels odd to live under an assumed name. I don't even like to see movies where the good guy goes under cover under a false identity to infiltrate the bad guys' organization. It just seems treacherous and unhealthy to try being someone else."

"Are you saying that I'm just part of your cover?" Ima asked with eyes raised.

I gave her a wink and a crooked smile and went and gave her a bear hug and she squealed with laughter.

"I'm not very good with this new technology," Geoffrey said. "Networks and databases in the clouds, it's all meaningless. Maybe you can give me a few pointers, Pelon. Ima doesn't seem to have much patience with me."

"I think you've asked the wrong person, Geoffrey. I know little about it myself. Ima is really the one."

"Normally I'm a patient person but with dad, well he seems to have fallen into a technology crevasse from which there is no rescue."

We had a light meal, *very bohemian* Geoffrey said. It consisted of several kinds of cheese, freshly baked bread, marinated olives and fruit. Geoffrey drank wine while Ima and I stuck to a nice orange blossom tea. After our meal we drove to Stearn's Wharf and had an ice cream cone.

"Santa Barbara's very nice, Geoffrey. It suits you well too," I said.

"Why do you say that, Pelon?"

"I don't know, maybe because it has a pretty laid back feel to it in spite of being sophisticated and obviously wealthy."

"It's also conservative as hell, Pelon. That's not me, for sure. I have always thought of myself as being united with the common man, the 99% that tried to bring down Wall Street. Hell I think that one day we will put an end to all the corruption and demagoguery found in Wall Street and along with that, strip all corporations of the many powers that have been granted to them by the goddamn courts."

"Take it easy Dad. Don't go tearing your aorta."

"I'm sorry if I offended you, Geoffrey," I said. "I didn't mean to say that you were with the 1%."

"Oh hell, I know I have all the trappings of the 1%– medical degree, money, my home in Montecito. My values however are with the people."

"That's what's important, Geoffrey. And I like what you said about Wall Street and corporations. When I was in Washington I learned that it's one of the issues where Tea Party members and liberals can agree."

"Isn't that a bitch," Geoffrey said, "that there can be common ground amidst all the negative hoopla."

"Well, conservative Democrats or Republicans don't like to admit it but they also have common ground when it comes to supporting the Patriot Act and any other activities falling under the guise of national security," I said.

"Really?" Ima asked. "Is that verifiable?"

"Absolutely. It's information obtained from voting records. Some of Obama's biggest supporters when it comes to those issues are conservative Republicans. But it's a topic that nobody wants publicized."

"That really pisses me off," Geoffrey said. "I never thought I would see the day that Obama would support erosion of our civil liberties. But that's what has happened."

That evening, ensconced in our bedroom, I asked Ima about her father.

"Did your dad ever remarry?"

"Hah. Are you kidding? He was devoted to mother before and after her death. And there were many women that pursued him but he turned all of them away."

"I can see why he was a great catch, smart, successful, good looking. So what did he do to avoid getting caught?" I asked.

"He threw himself into his work after Mom died. And into making sure I was getting what I needed, attention, love and freedom to explore. He was always a great dad."

"Do you remember your mother?"

"Of course I do. I was already halfway to womanhood when she died. She was a hell on wheels type, always involved in some project or another, or busy taking me to gymnastics or swimming or exploring tidal pools or hiking the back country around Lake Cachuma."

"And how did she die?"

"In a car accident. She had gone to Santa Maria for a conference and a drunk driver crossed the double line."

"I'm sorry Ima. I don't know what else to say that would be meaningful."

"It's okay Pelon. Don't feel badly for me. Until recently I did feel a great loss and I had a lot of anger because some idiot deprived me of a great part of my childhood, but I have since obtained a better understanding."

"Something that was channeled?"

"Not that difficult to guess that it was. Want to hear about it?"

"Of course," I said.

"Are you sure? It's a concept that is not easy to grasp and frankly a bit bizarre."

"I can handle it Ima."

"Okay then. What I found to be the most startling is the idea that we are angelic beings that volunteered to be here on this Earth so that we could push the envelope of creation. We wanted to experience what it would be like, living in a three dimensional world where we would forget our true identity and begin thinking that we were solely human beings. Nobody realized how dense this Earth was and how completely we would forget our Spiritual nature."

"Hard to believe that angelic beings would volunteer for this world," I said.

"Right. I know, huh. Yet that's exactly what took place. It's like an experiment. Could it be done? Could humans living in this world remember who they are and where they come from?"

"And the answer is?"

"Yes, it can be done. Look at Christ or Buddha or Krishna. They did it. And of course there have been others that have remembered that God dwells within."

"Let's say that what you told me is true and by the way I need some time to think about it, but for now let's assume it's true. How does knowing this help you deal with the death of your mother?" I asked.

"Because remembering our true nature cannot be accomplished in one lifetime. It takes hundreds maybe thousands of rebirths. Every time we die, we don't really die. We just go into the astral world, a world of a higher dimension where we do remember and it is there that we again choose to return to this world and to act out our next lifetime. We plan, based on probabilities and tendencies, for certain events that will provide the challenges and experiences that we need to evolve. My mother's death then was something she chose willingly to undergo. She was not a victim."

"Wow! There are no victims in this world? Can you even begin to understand the profound consequences of what you've said? It's flabbergasting. It's bizarre. It's unheard of," I almost shouted.

"I know that hearing what I've said for the first time comes as a shock to our perception of reality because it was just as shocking to me when I first read it."

"Our society is based to a large extent on the understanding that some people, through no fault of their own, become victims of poverty or of physical or mental handicaps, or of violence. That's always been the way it is. Now you're saying that we all willingly chose to incarnate on Earth to experience the conditions we are born into and experience events having a high degree of probability of occurring. I am more than shocked," I said.

"Wild huh? I think of what Christ is supposed to have said. 'You are gods.' Christ knew the same Truth that is today being revealed. Don't you think?"

"I don't know what to think. This is all too new to digest."

"I think that's enough head stuff for tonight. We should go to bed. We'll need to get up early to help dad prepare the dinner," she said as she stretched with obvious pleasure.

"It'll be hard getting to sleep tonight. I can't just stash away what you've told me. Maybe I'll sit in the garden for awhile."

"Ok if that's what you want," she said. "I do want a goodnight kiss before you go."

We kissed and she tugged gently at my hand as if to encourage me to go to bed with her. But I wasn't in the mood for lovemaking and I went to the back door and saw through the window that Geoffrey was already in one of the lawn chairs. One step out the door and I could smell the sweet smell of marijuana.

'Hey Geoffrey. I thought you had gone to bed."

"No. Too early for bed and I need some tokes. You want some?" he asked and extended the joint to me.

"No, I'm good. I will sit with you though."

"Been smoking here for thirty years, all homegrown, Pelon. I have a man that comes and cares for my plants, right over there against the tall Eugenia hedge."

Geoffrey smoked in silence for a short while and then he asked. "Tell me Pelon, are you with Ima just until you get your life back? I can tell that she really likes you. I guess I don't want to see her get hurt."

"No worries there, Geoffrey. I don't see a life without her in it."

"I'm glad to hear that Pelon, because I think you've been good for her."

Thanksgiving Dinners at Geoffrey's were a big deal, an event that he hosted for the group, Doctors Without Walls that practiced 'street medicine.' He went all out, hired a couple of local Mexican women to help cook and later to serve. Geoffrey orchestrated the entire affair, and he had Ima and me cutting and dicing and making iced teas for the afternoon gathering.

Doctors and guests began arriving and we all scurried around serving drinks and appetizers. They were a varied group in spite of having a well-defined common interest. I sat next to a woman who I would guess was at least seventy and her specialty had been neuromedicine.

"No I'm not a doctor, and frankly I have never heard of your group before this evening," I told her, when she asked if I was recently recruited as a volunteer doctor. "But I think it's a great service that you are providing."

"Oh," she said, "I just assumed…"

"No worries," I said. "At least you didn't think that I was the gardener."

"Why would I possibly think that? Do you think I'm racist? Well I'm not."

"Now it is I that is embarrassed. It was crude of me to say that. Please forgive me." I stammered.

"No worries," she said, smiling. "I was just pulling your leg, young man. I'm not so old that I don't enjoy a bit of fun at someone else's expense."

"Well, you had me pretty good there. My name is, well everyone calls me Pelon."

"How do you do, Pe-lon. My name is Henrietta but friends call me Mini. If you're not a doctor, how is it that you are here?"

"I'm a friend of Geoffrey's daughter."

"Oh yes, Ima uptight."

"She's not uptight," I said.

"Does Geoffrey have another daughter?"

"Are you messing with me Mini?"

"You catch on fast Pe-lon. Actually I don't really know Ima. Just by reputation. My stepson knows her from school. He tried dating her but she refused him."

"Perhaps she was waiting for me," I said.

"You believe in predestination?"

"Maybe. In some respect I would say that it seems highly probable that she and I were destined to meet. So maybe I would hedge predestination by saying, 'in all probability.'"

"That actually is not a bad response, Pe-lon. Scientists are not supposed to believe in predestination but we certainly do believe in probabilities, and probabilities are the basis for the new quantum physics that is all the rage in the scientific world and in the emerging metaphysical community."

"The metaphysical community?" I asked in surprise.

"Yes, the metaphysical community. Scientists originally thought that quantum activity was only found at the subatomic level, but now it is being theorized that a quantum state is the norm in higher dimensions. We here on Earth live in a three dimensional world where we seldom see quantum activity. However in new age thinking it is said that our planet Earth and humanity is moving into a higher dimension, ergo, quantum conditions will prevail."

"And how will this play out? If I remember correctly at the subatomic level particles can be observed at two places at the same time. Will people now have this capability?" I asked.

"Good question, Pe-lon. I don't know. I'm just telling you what I read. I think that the metaphysical community or the new age adherents would say yes to your question. And I think that they would say that saints and avatars have always been capable of manifesting such capabilities."

Mini and I were interrupted when her cell phone rang and she went outside to take the call. I finished my dinner and began helping clear the table for dessert. I cornered Ima when I saw her in the kitchen.

"I have to tell you about this really interesting conversation I had with my neighbor Henrietta," I said to her.

"Oh I know Mini, I can't ever tell when she's giving facts or making up stories. I have a couple of things I'd like to tell you too, but not about her."

"Maybe tonight we can swap stories," I said.

That evening after we had cleaned the kitchen and put the house back in order, we said goodnight to Geoffrey, and went to our bedroom and had a good hour of Tantric sex, an activity initiated by Ima.

"Can I come now Ima? I'm going crazy with desire."

"Hasn't it been fun though?"

"Yes it has but I can only take so much."

It was intense and the best sex I have ever had. And I told Ima that it was.

"I told you it would be good. I hope Dad didn't hear us. And what did good old Mini have to tell you?"

"Talk about suddenly changing gears," I said.

"I do like to be efficient. So what did she say?"

"We had a conversation about quantum states. She said that we are living in the third dimension and only experience quantum activity at the subatomic level but that scientists are theorizing that there are higher dimensions where quantumness is the norm. But that according to the metaphysical community Earth will soon move into a higher dimension. I thought of you and what you were telling me the other night."

"Did I say that Earth was moving into a higher dimension and humanity was as well? I don't remember getting that far into the conversation."

"No, I suppose you didn't. But it seems logical that is where you were going with it."

"Well, that's exactly what will happen come the Winter Solstice of 2012. But remember that we are not being transformed instantaneously. This is to be an evolutionary process with everyone needing to express intent to ascend to a higher dimension and thereby also raising his or her consciousness to a higher level."

"To a higher level means what?"

"It means that many different types of beliefs and practices based on greed, fear, aggression and ego are to be replaced by those based on compassion, unity and love. That we will no longer employ violence and war to solve problems, that unity and inclusiveness will be the norm as opposed to separateness and exclusivity, that we'll no longer seek just for ourselves but we'll always be conscious of others and their needs."

"I wish I had your optimism Ima. It sounds like something I would support but I just don't see it happening. Humanity is not built that way. We're built for competitiveness, for winning, for acquisition, for rubbing others' noses in the dirt."

"But you would want to live in the world whose attributes I just described and you would want your children to live there as well. Isn't that true?"

"Well yeah. Who wouldn't?"

"Who wouldn't, would be all those individuals that are built the way you described, competitive, looking out for themselves, prone towards violence, greedy and so on. But the new energies will no longer support them. Such individuals will find it harder and harder to employ those attitudes and behaviors after 2012 and either they will change or eventually they will die. The children being born today and henceforth will come wired with new templates of values and behaviors."

A knock on the door startled us until we heard Geoffrey say "I heard you talking, mind if I join you?"

"Give us a minute, Dad."

We quickly threw on PJ's and Ima invited him in.

"We're just catching up on conversations we had earlier."

"Really, your mother and I would do that. Anything interesting?"

"I was telling Ima about Henrietta. She's pretty sharp."

"She claims that staying in touch with her inner child keeps her mind young," Geoffrey told us. "What was she telling you?"

"Heady stuff about quantum conditions," I answered.

"Oh yeah, we've had some talks over that. She says she can't seem to decide if she's a scientist or a prophet."

"She does not, Dad," Ima protested.

"Well, maybe not a prophet but at least a shaman."

"Well it is being said that science and spirituality are beginning to merge, as in reality there is no division," Ima said.

"Of course there is a split, Ima," I said. "Science thinks that there is no God, and without God... "

"No, not really," she interjected. "There is a division between science and religious dogma, but scientists are now saying that the universe and life have intelligent design, that it could not have evolved randomly. Oh they don't say outright that God exists but that is the logical conclusion when they say that the universe was designed by Intelligence."

"I read something about that," Geoffrey said. "If pressed I would say I agree. Did you know that of all the primates, that only humans have twenty-three chromosomes? All the rest have twenty-four. How is that possible, if we all evolved from the same stock? Somebody must have tinkered with us."

"Ooooo. Aliens tinkered with us," I said mockingly.

"Supposedly the Pleidians upgraded our DNA, some two hundred thousand years ago," Ima said.

"Oh come on Ima! Now you've gone too far," I said.

"I'm only telling you what is being communicated."

"It does seem far fetched Ima," Geoffrey added. "And it is without evidence, I take it?"

"Without the sort of evidence that three dimensional scientists affirm. But there is evidence."

"You mean the channelings?" I asked.

"In a way. But everyone is always asked not to accept any channeling *a priori*, to test everything communicated with one's own experience and capacity for discerning truth. We all have the ability to test for truth with our heart."

"We know how that turns out for most people," Geoffrey said. "The heart leads most people astray."

"Astray from what? By whose yardstick would we measure? It's true that people are sometimes manipulated or cheated or taken advantage of, but if individuals follow their heart, they have done what is true for them. If another person acts badly, well that's for that person to deal with."

"That is so pollyanna, Ima," I said. "That goes against the most basic survival inkling a person has, not to get hurt."

"That may be and it may be for most people for some time to come, but eventually people will begin to live more through their heart, because we are moving into a quantum world and the heart if anything is quantum."

"I was with you for most of what you said, in fact it's all very existential and Buddhist to live for now and for yourself, it was the way we wanted to live in the 60's, but you definitely lost me with the heart being quantum," Geoffrey said.

"Most people that even know about quantum think it covers only the micro world, but in fact whatever is outside time-space limitations is quantum. Take dreams for example, where there can occur a juxtaposition of events and people that don't ordinarily co-exist in our three-dimensional world."

"And you're saying that the heart also is not limited by time-space constraints, that it can soar beyond and above everything that this world tries to impose on it? The heart wants what the heart wants. Is that it?" her dad asked.

"That's right, Dad. That's exactly what it is. And our mind is also quantum. What else can explain premonitions or insights or intuitive awareness?"

"You say quantum can explain those attributes? How so?" I asked.

"Everything is connected, everything exists now. We are part of everything. In the higher dimensions we exist here and there and everywhere. With the shift in consciousness in 2012, we will have support for living in that manner."

"'Be here now'– that was our mantra in the '60's," Geoffrey said.

"What you say, Ima, reminds me of a conversation I had with a friend of mine in Tucson, a member of the Tohono O'Odham. She said practically the same thing when she was talking about being connected to all living and nonliving things."

"You're right. We're fortunate that indigenous people have not forgotten their beliefs and practices and right now it's important that we reconnect with what everyone knew at one time. And we need to also re-establish ceremonies to help maintain balance and open up our spiritual nature."

"I used to go to a Chumash sweat lodge," Geoffrey said. "Back in the early 1970's I was trying to find myself in their ceremonial traditions. It doesn't work though."

"I agree with Geoffrey. I went to a sweat with the Tohono O'Odham and it was interesting but it wasn't me. I felt like a foreigner."

"It'll be a challenge to develop ceremonies that are connected to our lives and our experiences," Ima added.

We spent the next two days with Geoffrey, lazing around, talking and eating great food. On Saturday we drove North on Highway 101 to the beach at the UCSB campus. We took a long walk and got our feet full of the tar that washes up from the offshore oil drilling platforms that sit quietly in the middle of dark blue water.

"It's quite deep where those platforms sit," Geoffrey informed. "They have been a source of controversy for many years. I suppose we can't deny the need for oil, but I despise their presence."

"Drilling into Mother Earth is a travesty, according to my Tohono O'Odham friend," I said.

"And a bad idea when it's done offshore" Geoffrey said. "Hardly anyone remembers the Santa Barbara oil spill of 1969, but those of us that were here certainly do. It was for me my introduction to environmental activism. Hard to believe that such a hard lesson seems to have been forgotten by BP."

On the way back to the house I asked Geoffrey to stop at a store where I could buy a burn phone.

"I need to make a few telephone calls to see if I can find out anything about my situation," I said.

"Take him to the mall Dad. I want to buy a few things also."

We got to the mall and parked and agreed to rendezvous at a certain time, as each of us was going in a different direction. I went and bought the burn phone.

My first call was to my mother.

"Hello Mom."

"Mijito where are you? Are you okay?"

"I'm fine Mom. How are you and the family?"

"Your grandmother is the only one not doing well. She had a stroke and ended up in the hospital. She's home now and one of her nieces has moved in with her. But when I went to visit her I spoke to her doctor and he thinks she doesn't have very long to live."

"I'm sorry to hear that, Mom. I'll make plans to go visit her as soon as I can. Has there been anyone else looking for me?"

"No but your friend, the one they call Lechero, was here a few weeks ago asking for you."

"Did he say anything about my situation?"

"Just that your old friend Puma is having babies because he can't find you."

"And I hope to keep it that way, Mom. When I get a chance I'll go visit you too. I have to go now. God bless you, Mom."

My second call was to Robert.

"Robert this is Pelon."

"Pelon! Good God man. Where the hell are you? And are you all right?"

"I'm actually quite good. I can't give you any details or tell you where I am, you know that."

"Well I'm glad to hear that you're doing well. We've been wondering when you would call."

"You've seen the gang of four?"

"Yes and Helga too. Everyone's fine. Helga has a new beau and I don't see her as often, but once in a while we get together for lunch and I think she's happy."

"Robert, sorry to say that I don't have much time on this burn phone so I'll have to rush off. Before I do however, can you tell me what you know about my situation?"

"From what I can determine from some of my sleuthing, the flash drive contains not only the names of Randolph Hamilton's clients but perhaps some other critical and important financial data. Why else would Andre be so relentless in his pursuit? Sure you broke his nose and you put the guard's neck in a brace. That's an assault charge on a Federal Officer. And that's all that he's been able to charge you with. But he has tremendous resources working for him to capture you. You'll be better off if the police arrest you, because if Andre gets his hands on you, well you probably won't be around to write your memoirs."

"Thanks Robert. What you've told me makes good sense. Abrazos my friend."

My third call was to Lorraine's grandfather.

"Hello sir, this is Lorraine's friend, Herculano."

"Yes Herculano. Lorraine is not here. Can I help you?"

"Is Lorraine going to visit you anytime soon?"

"She always comes on Sunday so yes she will be here early tomorrow in the morning. Can you call back? I know she would like to talk with you."

"Yes, I'll call at nine o'clock your time. Thank you sir."

"Goodbye Herculano. I'll tell Lorraine to expect your call."

We spent our last evening with Geoffrey at home. Ima cooked a pasta dinner, Geoffrey made a salad and I got to select the dessert. We stayed up talking and laughing at family stories and then went to bed.

The next morning I took a long walk by myself and stopped at a small café to make my call to Lorraine's grandfather and she answered.

"Hello Lorraine."

"Hello yourself homeboy. This is a surprise, I thought you were history."

"It was close, I gotta tell you. But listen I don't have much time and I need a big favor."

"Name it homeboy."

I need to visit my grandmother and need a ride and a place to stay. I'll arrive on Tuesday by Greyhound at 8:00 pm. Can you pick me up?"

"No problem, I'll be there."

"Thanks, Lorraine. We'll talk then. Bye."

"Bye."

CHAPTER XII

We had to take three different trains to finally arrive in Encinitas and had one tense moment when the Immigration Service boarded and began checking for undocumented persons. They looked me over but moved on to the next car where they questioned two men and escorted them off the train.

"Damn I hate feeling tense every time I see someone in a uniform. It was bad enough when I was a kid and doing stupid things," I said.

"I'm sorry Pelon. Maybe you shouldn't visit your grandmother."

"No Ima, there's no way I cannot go see her. I'll be all right. I've dodged cops all my life."

Monday morning I went to the farm to pick up the rest of my clothing and to tell Miguel that I was leaving for a few days.

"Hola Sara. Donde esta Miguel?" I asked

"Se fue de compras al Safeway," she answered.

"Vengo por mi ropa y a decirle a Miguel que tengo que salir por una semana," I told her why I was there.

"Pasa," she said, and I walked in and went to my old bedroom where I quickly gathered my things, but not before Sara undressed and went to stand at the doorway, blocking my way.

"Sara, por favor."

"Tu eres mi unico recurso," she said.

I pushed my way past her, she standing her ground, rubbing her naked body against me and pleading for me to impregnate her. I headed for the door and she followed me. As I opened it, there was Miguel with a plastic grocery bag in each hand and with his mouth open. He looked at me and then at his wife fully undressed, as I flew out of there instinctively, not knowing what explanation would suffice under the circumstances.

When I told Ima what had happened, this time she didn't laugh or make light of the situation.

"What do think Miguel will do?"

"Hell I don't know. Maybe he'll shoot me next time he sees me."

"Then it's good that you leave in the morning. Maybe by the time you return next week he'll have cooled off. You sure I can't go with you?"

"It'll make it harder for me, having to worry about you. I will miss you."

"And I you."

The Greyhound ride into Tucson was long and uncomfortable. I sat next to a large woman who had two small children with her in the seat across the aisle. The children were even more bored than I, fighting with one another over every imaginable thing and asking the mother to referee. And she did, calmly and decisively, at times harshly with a hand to their rear.

"Children nowadays just don't know how to behave. My brothers and I would never have dared to act so spoiled," she said to me.

"Maybe you should separate them? You sit with one and I'll sit with the other."

"That's a good idea if you really will do that for me."

"Sure. No problem."

That's how we were all finally able to get some rest. In Yuma I offered to buy them some food, as it was quite obvious that she was short on cash, being perhaps a single mother on welfare.

214

"Okay Tony, what do you want, a hotdog or a hamburger?" I asked my seat partner, the older boy who was probably seven.

"Hamburger," Tony said without hesitation.

"And you Joey?" I asked Tony's brother, a boy of about five.

"Me too. Hamburger," he shouted.

Mari, the mother also wanted a hamburger.

"Four hamburgers and four milk shakes," I said.

We boarded the bus and continued our journey and to pass the time we conversed and I came to know quite a bit about Mari and her two boys. She was indeed a welfare mom, her husband having been incarcerated in Arizona, convicted of possession of drugs. He was a mule she said, carrying pot on his back and lugging it across the Sonoran Desert from Nogales Mexico into the USA. They were on their way to visit him in prison and were to stay with his parents in Tucson.

"Where do they live?" I asked Mari.

"In South Tucson, near the Greyhound Race Park."

"I know that area. My grandmother lives near there. How long will you be staying?"

"Until Christmas."

"What about school for Tony?"

"He'll miss a little. He gets good grades, so it'll be ok."

"It's a whole month, Mari. At least check out some books for him from the library so he won't fall behind."

"Yeah I guess I could do that."

"I have a friend that could tutor him while you're in Tucson if you want."

"Really. You've been so nice already."

"Just write down the address and I'll talk to my friend and set it up. His name is Rodrigo and he's a student at the high school."

We arrived at the bus station on time and I said goodbye to Mari and her kids. I spotted Lorraine's car in the parking lot and she stuck her hand out the window and waved at me. She was out of the car when I reached her and saw that she was very pregnant.

We hugged as best we could.

"Wow! You're so pregnant!"

"Tell me about it homeboy. This damn kid's going to be a soccer star, the way he kicks."

"It suits you though," I said. "Even makes me a little jealous."

"You had your chance."

"I know. It just wasn't in the stars. Who's the dad?"

"The same guy I was dating."

"Can we go? I'm a little nervous standing here in the open. We can catch up while we drive."

"Yeah if I can get back in the car. Why don't you drive? It'll be easier."

"Ok. Can we first stop at my grandmother's before anything else?"

"Sure. Is she ok?"

"She had a stroke. That's really why I came."

The soft neon glare of a television screen was visible through the sheer curtains on the front window when I drove past to see if it looked safe to stop and visit her.

"Looks ok," I said. "I'll stop across the street. Want to get off?"

"No not really. I'll wait in the car if that's ok."

"Absolutely. I wont be long."

"Take your time. I'll take a nap while you're gone."

I knocked softly on the door and a middle-aged woman went to the window and looked me over while I stood on the porch.

"Soy Herculano," I said in a soft voice.

"Hola Herculano," she said when she opened the door. "Soy Clara, la sobrina de tu abuela.

"Hi Clara. Where is Grandma?"

"She in her bedroom. Go see."

"Hello Grandma," I said when I saw that her eyes were open.

When I greeted her she managed a soft smile but nothing else. She was half sitting in her bed against pillows supported by the headboard. She looked terrible, her face gaunt and without much color.

"I came to see you hoping that you would get better so that we can attend posadas. And we can make tamales and champurado for Christmas too."

I didn't get much past Christmas, my eyes welling up with tears and my throat tight as a drum. I walked out of the room and tried to compose myself.

"She not good. Maybe you come again, she better."

"I will Clara. I'll come as soon as I can."

I walked back to the car and got in. Lorraine was reclined as far as the seat would let her.

"Are we staying at your grandfathers?"

"As of tonight, that's where I'll be staying until I deliver."

"When's that?"

"Sometime around Christmas. I can't wait, it's been one of the hardest things I've ever gone through."

We got in the car and I drove south to the reservation.

"How was your grandmother?" she asked.

"Not good. I need to see her again. Are you coming into town anytime this week?"

"I have a prenatal appointment at Tucson Medical on Thursday."

"Can I come with you?"

"Sure. I'll tell them you're the father."

"I take it you're not living with the father?"

"It's complicated. I'll tell you all about it later."

"It's cold in Tucson. I'm not used to cold after being in California."

"So that's where you've been. Hell Pelon. You just upped and disappeared. Not even a damn note to say you're okay. You gotta tell me what's up dude."

"I know, and I'm sorry. I thought it was best not to get you involved. It's like I'm contaminated right now and I don't want my loved ones being hassled. And I thought for sure that Naomi would have called you to let you know that I was okay."

"And she did, more than once, but it's not the same as hearing from you. Maybe you can fill in the details that she didn't provide."

"Fair enough," I said. For the next half hour I told her how it came about that Naomi and Esperanza warmed up to me, about the meetings and how Esperanza had used her skills to obtain the information on Congressman Jimmy.

"That is quite a story Pelon. Naomi did mention that your friends Robert and Farley played a part, but I see it more clearly the way you tell it."

"What's interesting is that the four of them have continued the friendship that started at that meeting."

"Okay, so what happened after they handed you the flash drive?"

I answered her question and I told her about Helga and how her ex-husband Andre was involved in this nightmarish adventure, how he had me abducted, how I managed to escape and his dogged hunt for me ever since. Lorraine said she had to comment.

"Homeboys have no business getting into bed with rich white women. It's bad medicine."

"Bad medicine? Seriously?"

"Okay so it's from Hollywood. But you get the point?"

I nodded and continued telling her my story. Lorraine listened and every once in awhile she would ask me something or make a comment.

"Dude, good riddance Helga!"

"You're the man homeboy. That Puma is a goddamn sellout. I'm glad you kicked his ass."

"No Dude, not another white girl. She does seem nice though. Do you really think she was a virgin? Girls say that you know."

"Wow, you just drive the girls crazy homeboy. That Sara is a piece of work, all Christian and horny."

"She's not horny, Lorraine. She just wants a kid."

"I think she's just horny," she said adamantly.

We drove in silence for a while after I finished my story. And then Lorraine said, "The only thing you've left out is the whereabouts of that flash drive. You do have it?"

"Yes but I'm not telling you where it is. You know too much already."

We came upon a stretch of road that was as dark as the others but also had uneven pavement and many ruts that demanded total concentration.

"It's so dark out here, Lorraine. Just look at all those stars – they completely cover the sky from one horizon to another. It's like we're inside an upside down bowl."

"It is beautiful out here. I hope my son gets to grow up here."

"Why is it a hope?"

"The father and I are of two minds on where we're going to live. He's from Michigan but as you know he works in Washington and really likes it there. I don't want my son growing up in a big city and getting cut off from his roots."

"So why did you get pregnant?"

"Stupidity. We got caught up in the moment when he came to visit and he didn't use a condom. It was really dumb, I know."

"Do you love him? What's his name anyway?"

"His name is James. I guess I love him but I have doubts at times. He's really good looking and quite a catch really. But I would be giving up so much."

"He wouldn't consider living here?"

"Oh hell no, James hated it here, said it was so dry and brown."

"He doesn't have an Indian name?"

"His name is White Elk but in the Anglo world, he's known as James. We're almost there. Slow down and take the dirt road on the right."

It was past eleven when we pulled into the parking area of Lorraine's grandfather's house. All the lights were turned off except for a small lamp towards the rear of the front room.

"You'll have to sleep with me tonight," she said softly so as not to wake her grandfather.

She led me by the hand to the small bedroom that she said was hers and tired as I was I didn't hesitate to fall into the queen size bed.

"Don't fall asleep like that," she whispered. "We have to get under the covers. It'll get even colder later on."

I fell asleep quickly after I undressed and put on pajamas but woke up sometime in the middle of the night, spooning Lorraine as if it was the most natural thing in the world to be doing. Her body heat felt good in the chilly room where we were and soon I went back to sleep with my arm around her waist. Next time I woke up, I was hearing Lorraine's voice.

"We're about to have breakfast Pelon, want to join us?"

"What time is it?"

"It's past eight."

"Give me a few minutes. I'll be right there."

The air was cold in the room and I had to slip into my jacket for warmth. I used the bathroom and joined Lorraine and her grandfather seated at a small kitchen table. They both had their hands around coffee mugs.

"Coffee?" she asked.

"No thanks. Got any tea?"

"Loose herbal that my aunt collects."

"OK. Something warm to drink will be good. Good morning sir."

"Good morning Herculano. Sleep good?"

"Very good, thanks," I replied, as I slipped out of my jacket, the kitchen's wood stove providing more than enough heat.

"Lorraine tells me that you're having some trouble."

"Yes sir that's right. It's trouble that came to me through no fault of my own. One day I'm living my dream life and the next day, it became a nightmare."

"Has it all been bad since then?"

"Well no, not really. I've had some good moments and I've met some great people. But I've been uprooted."

"Maybe you were not supposed to be planted where you were. Maybe you had to move on and have the experiences that you have had. Maybe life had to move you along, like a cow that has stayed too long in one part of the pasture gets moved by her owner."

"Git along little dogie," Lorraine sang.

"Very funny, Lorraine," I said while trying to hold back a smile, which in the end I couldn't.

"You can stay here as long us you want, Herculano. I don't think that anyone will bother you here," he said.

"Thank you sir. I really appreciate that."

"And call me Otavio."

We ate an American style breakfast with hot cereal and bread toasted on a comal, a thin flat skillet-like implement, used by Mexicans to make tortillas.

"Sorry there are no eggs in the house. I get sick just looking at them," Lorraine said. "And Grandfather doesn't like electric toasters."

"It's fine. My grandmother also uses a comal to toast her bread."

There wasn't much to do at the grandfather's and after our breakfast I went for a walk in the desert. Lorraine declined my invitation saying that she wanted to put up her feet and rest. The sun was almost at its apex and its warmth belied that it was winter.

I thought about what the grandfather told me earlier about life nudging me along the path I needed to take and saw how similar that idea was to what Ima had told me in Santa Barbara, about a soul deciding prior to incarnating, the life experiences and lessons that he or she needed to have. It was also true that I had been feeling like a victim, and I remember Ima saying that in reality there are no victims. That we all agree to experience what we experience. Umm! I thought.

When I returned, Lorraine was in the kitchen preparing lunch.

"Can I help? In fact, why don't you let me prepare lunch for us while you sit and give orders?"

"Don't offer something you can't do."

"Hey I know my way around a kitchen. Just tell me what you were planning."

"Our meals are simple homeboy, nothing like your white girlfriends prepared, I'm sure."

"Don't be catty, Lorraine. You'll make me think that you're jealous."

"I'm not jealous. I just don't understand why you are attracted to Anglo women. What's up with that homeboy? What's wrong with us brown women?"

"I don't know. I really haven't thought about it in that way. And I am attracted to you. The timing has never been in our favor. Remember our first kisses? We both pulled back. I wasn't the only one that wasn't sure if we should go for it."

"I'm sorry. I'm just feeling very hormonal and very fat too."

"I think you look beautiful Lorraine and I loved spooning you last night. Did you know I was up against you?"

"Yes, I felt you."

I prepared the zucchini like my grandmother prepared it, sautéed in olive oil with diced onion and slices of tomato. When cooked I cut thin slices of yellow cheese and placed them on top and covered the skillet with a cover, letting it sit until the cheese melted.

Beans were already cooked and I placed them in a skillet with some oil and mashed them, adding a pinch of cumin while they simmered. The three of us sat down for our meal.

"Not bad homeboy. Somebody has taught you well. Was it your grandmother?"

"Yep. And sometimes I worked in the kitchen when I was at Juvi."

"I almost forgot about your stint at the fire camp."

"Two years."

We finished our lunch and I also received compliments from Lorraine's grandfather.

"Better watch yourself. Lorraine will have you doing all the cooking," he said.

After lunch Otavio asked if I was interested in learning to work wood.

"Making mesquite furniture was my trade," he said. "Now I'm not strong enough to handle the big slabs so I stick to making small stuff."

"Yeah, I'd be interested in learning," I said.

"Come on then, I work in that garage in back of the house."

"I'm impressed," I said when I walked into the spacious garage, neat and well organized. All I see are hand tools though. Where are the power tools?"

"No power tools. I work everything by hand the way I was taught. It takes a little longer but it gets done.

"I'll teach you the same way I was taught. You start by learning to sharpen your tools. Here, take this chisel in your hand, put a few drops of this oil on the sharpening stone, and with the bevel flat against the stone make nice circles."

"Like this?" I asked.

"Yes. Try to keep the bevel flat at all times."

I spent the rest of the afternoon with Otavio, learning to sharpen chisels until my hand was numb from gripping the handles.

"Tomorrow you'll sharpen the blade from the hand planes," he said and I thought satirically, *'oh goody.'*

Actually it was a good afternoon, giving me time to think. I thought about Ima and wondered what she would think of me, sleeping with and spooning Lorraine. I also wondered if I should risk calling her to let her know how I was, but decided that it was too soon. Perhaps next week I'll call, I thought.

I also thought more about what Lorraine had said about me seeking out Anglo women. Was it true that I was attracted to them as a compensation for feelings of inadequacy, which is what Lorraine was implying? I didn't know. It was something that I should have explored with Dr. Maier's group.

And what was I feeling for Lorraine? Some was love I supposed, maybe some of my feelings were simply friendship, and maybe also empathy with her situation regarding the father of the child she was carrying. And was I to sleep with her again tonight? Nothing had been said but there were only two bedrooms and the grandfather had one and Lorraine the other. And there was only one bed in her room. *We shall see,* I said to myself.

Dinner at the grandfather's house was around eight o'clock. Lorraine fried some chicken and I prepared pasta and made a yummy salad. Dessert was ice cream. I helped clean the kitchen after our dinner and when I finished went with Otavio to the youth center, where I played a few games of pool with some teens.

I walked back alone, the grandfather having left earlier. Lorraine was already in the bedroom.

"Hey," I said. "Going to bed?"

"Pretty soon. I'm dog tired and my feet are killing me."

"Want a foot rub?"

"Really?"

"For sure."

"What's it going to cost me?"

"Nada, nothing at all. Think of it as payment for putting me up," I said.

"OK then. Get to it slave boy."

I had her recline on the bed and went to work. She had nicely shaped feet even if they were swollen at the time and she moaned appreciatively with every pressure point that I relieved.

"Slave boy you really do know your business. Just a bit more at the arch, oh yeah right there," she said.

She thanked me when I finished and said that she felt one hundred percent better.

"I'm glad I helped. By the way, what time is your appointment tomorrow?"

"At ten. We have to leave about 8:30."

"Are we sleeping together?"

"Unless you want to sleep on the couch."

"No, it was fine for me last night."

We both went to bed after 11:00 and I fell asleep almost as quickly as on the previous night. Again I awoke in the middle of the night, up against Lorraine's backside. I checked the time. It was 2:15. I went back to sleep, feeling safe and warm.

We both were up late that morning and we were rushing to leave the house as planned, for her prenatal visit.

"We'll have to get breakfast in Tucson," she said. "And I was hoping that you would stay with me at the prenatal clinic. There's to be a demo on massage that I want to attend."

"Sure, no problem. I do want to see my grandmother and one of her neighbors but that shouldn't take too long."

The prenatal massage session was primarily for the pregnant woman's partner, helping him or her to learn how to massage to help relieve discomfort on the lower back as a consequence of the growing fetus. It also provided techniques for massaging legs and feet.

"Lorraine, I feel as if I've been had," I said in jest after the session ended and we were walking to the car, "manipulated to learn massage for your benefit."

"Gotta take advantage of every resource available to me. Besides you're getting to spoon me every night. That should count for something."

"Yeah about that. I have a little bit of guilt and fear that it'll result in sex. Maybe I should sleep somewhere else."

"No problem while I'm pregnant homeboy. Sex is not at all appealing right now. But I can't lie on the same side all night, so when I nudge you, know that I have to turn."

"Good to know."

"I'll drop you off at your grandmother's, and while you visit and take care of your other business, I'll go to my place and pick up a few things. How much time do you need?"

"Is two hours too long?"

"No. I'll run a couple of errands also."

As she was about to drop me off, I decided to see Rodrigo first since he was more likely to leave than my grandmother. *It's all about probabilities*, I thought. *Am I thinking quantumly? Umm...* "Drop me off here instead, Lorraine. It's where my friend Rodrigo lives."

"I'll see you in two."

"Bye."

Rodrigo's house was a neighbor in name only, his house being a block removed. I knocked on the door and his mother answered.

"Hi Pelon, what a surprise. I guess I shouldn't really be surprised. Did you come see your grandmother?"

"Hi Isabel. Yes I came to see her. Not doing too well, I guess you know that."

"Yes, we're all praying for her. Did you want to see Rodrigo?"

"Yes I wanted to see if he wanted to earn a few dollars. Is he here?"

"He's in his room doing the usual. Video games! I don't see what he gets out of those things. Come in, I'll go get him."

"Hey Pelon," Rodrigo said when he entered the room.

"Hey Rodrigo. I was hoping you were still on break."

"Yeah my new quarter starts after the New Year. Wanna sit?"

"Sure. But I won't stay long. I have to go see Grandma."

"Yeah, I'm sorry about that."

Rodrigo's mom came into the room to tell us she was going to the store and promptly left.

"Anyway I came to ask if you received the package that I sent you and if you would be interested in tutoring a young boy that's staying a few blocks from here. I met him and his mom on the bus on the way here and they are visiting until after Christmas. He's missing a lot of school and I thought maybe you could help him. I'll pay you of course."

"I've never tutored anyone before. What do I have to do?"

"Basic stuff. He's seven. Probably some math and geography. Maybe you can walk him over to the library and get him some books to practice reading. What'd you think?"

"I guess so… I mean sure, why not. How many hours?"

"Just a couple, maybe three times a week. I'll pay you minimum, $8.00 an hour."

"Sounds good, Pelon."

"Ok then. I'll give you a hundred now and that should cover it. You'll need to call or go over there in person. The mother Mari is expecting you. Here's the number and address," I said and handed him the paper Mari had given me, and the money.

"I'll go over this afternoon," Rodrigo said.

"What about the package?" I asked. "Do you have it?"

"The flash drive? Yeah, it's in my room someplace."

"Rodrigo! The drive is important. Can you find it?"

"Dude, calm down."

"I'll help you look for it," I said.

"My room is a mess. You sure you want to see it?"

"No choice bro."

I sat down at the desk and hidden amongst an array of books, papers, socks and tee shirts, was the empty envelope. The rest of the bedroom where Rodrigo was searching was equally in disorder.

"I told you it was here," Rodrigo said triumphantly when I showed him the envelope.

"There's no drive in here, Rodrigo."

"There isn't?" he said, his face showing a bit of fear. "I know it's here, Pelon."

I placed my head in my hands and tried to quell the anger that seemed to be rising all on its own. I finally spoke in as calm a voice as I could muster when I concluded that I should not have placed such a heavy burden on a young boy without his knowledge.

"Try to find it, OK? It's very important. I'll call you tomorrow to see if the drive turns up. Don't worry too much if it doesn't. It won't be the end of the world." We walked out to the porch and I noticed that a dark blue sedan was parked across the street and a few doors down from my grandmother's house. "Hey Rodrigo, look over there," I said pointing towards the sedan. "Do you recognize that car?"

"No but it looks like narcs."

"Anybody selling on that block?"

"Nope."

"Do me a favor, walk over by the car and see who's in it. If it looks like cops, drop something on the ground, pick it up and walk around the block and come back here through the alley so that you're not seen. Can you do that?"

"Well yeah. I live in South Tucson remember. We're trained to spot cops and avoid suspicion."

Rodrigo left and went back into the house and partially closed the door so that I still had a good view of the sedan. When Rodrigo had passed the car, he dropped his baseball cap, casually picked it up and kept walking very naturally.

"Damn," I said and sat down to review my situation. I knew I had to call Lorraine and ask her to meet me elsewhere. And I had to call Ima, never doubting that there was no one that could connect me to her.

Rodrigo came in from the rear of the house into the front room where I was sitting.

"They're cops," he said. "And they seem to be looking at your grandmother's house, Pelon."

"Yeah I was afraid of that. Can you let me use your telephone, I need to make a call."

"Sure," he said and went to get me the telephone from the kitchen.

"Change of plans, Lorraine. Can you pick me up at the Greyhound Park?"

"Are you in trouble?"

"I think so."

"How soon?"

"Give me twenty minutes."

"Ok. See you in twenty. Be careful Pelon," she cautioned.

"Always," I said. "Hey Rodrigo, can I use your computer? I need to send a message to a friend."

"You'll have to go back to my room."

I smiled. "Call the paramedic if I don't come out," I said.

I sat at the computer and started typing. "Ima, hope I find you at the firehouse as I can't trust contacting you anywhere else. I'm fairly certain someone tipped off the police about my visit to my grandmother's. I think it was her niece as she is the only one that saw me there. I'm safe for now but I will be returning as there is little chance that I'll get to see my grandmother again on this trip. Please write back and let me know how you are. Love you."

"Tried to warn you about the mess," Rodrigo said as I typed.

"You have to clean your room dude. You probably have vermin in here," I said when I finished the message to Ima.

"No way. Not even the vermin could stand it in here."

A ping sound from Rodrigo's computer alerted me that a message had come in.

"I think it's for me Rodrigo."

"Go for it."

And it was a reply from Ima.

"I'm fine but I'm sorry to have to tell you that the police came to my house looking for you the day you left. I think your friend Miguel must be involved. No one else knew that you were spending time with me. It seems like the net is tightened around you my love. You can't return here. Can I join you?"

I replied. "I'd love for you to join me but hold off for a few days until I can determine if that is a possibility. I'll contact you as I did today. Love you."

After I finished sending the second message to Ima, I told Rodrigo to tell his mother not to mention my visit to anyone and I left the house through the back alley. It was a short walk to the Greyhound Race Park and I found Lorraine already waiting.

"What happened?" she asked as soon as I reached the drivers side window.

"I'll tell you on the way," I answered. "Want me to drive?"

"If I can get out you can," she said and then struggled to free herself from the confines of her seat. "I'm so huge," she added as she ambled over to the passenger's door and eased herself in.

"Ok, tell me," she said when we got underway.

"There were a couple of detectives in a car in front of my grandmother's house. I think her niece told them I had visited."

"That sucks."

"That's not all. I found out from Ima that the police went to her house looking for me."

"Shit Pelon. What are you going to do?"

"I can't do very much, right now. Are you apprehensive about me staying with you?"

"Hell no. I've run with fugitives all my life."

"Good to know."

"I have some news too, not bad news like yours though. At least right now it doesn't seem like bad news."

"What's that?"

"There was a phone message from James, you know White Elk."

"Oh yeah, the absent masseur."

"Very funny, ha hah," she said derisively. "You don't have to massage me you know. You'll probably get all hot and bothered anyway."

"Hee hee," I said. "If I wanted you I could have taken you last night. I felt you rubbing up against me."

"Oh please. You were probably having an erotic dream about me."

"I did have an erotic dream about you when we were working the Tucson office."

"I had a couple of you too. But that's neither here nor there, is it?"

"True. So what did James want?"

"He wants to come out for Christmas and be here when the baby is born."

"No kidding. And what then?"

"I don't know. He just wants to be here."

"Speaking of which, I meant to ask earlier, why are you going to Tucson for prenatal care? Are you going to deliver there?"

"No way. My boy is going to be a T.O., born and raised. There's an excellent midwife here on the res."

"And when James gets here where is he going to sleep, in the workshop?"

"What's with you Pelon, you're making all these funnies. Are you trying to release tension?"

"Maybe I am. But seriously, back to James' visit. Ima asked if she could join me. I told her to wait a few days before we decide if she can come."

"And where is she going to sleep? With James in the workshop?"

"My turn to laugh," I said. "I thought that I should see if there is a place I can rent."

"You could probably find something, a trailer if not a house. But that's not imminent is it?"

"I don't think so. We still have a few nights to spoon," I said and smiled wickedly.

We arrived in Sells in the early afternoon and I asked Lorraine if she wanted a practice massage now or later. She said later, maybe before bedtime. Right now she said, she needed a nap.

I went out to the workshop and began sharpening the cutting irons for Otavio's wood planes, under his direction.

"That's right Herculano. Make nice big circles and keep the bevel flat against the stone. Put a few more drops of oil on the stone so it's slippery."

I spent most of my time thinking about the flash drive as I sharpened, wondering how I could use it as leverage to get Andre to back off. I wondered also if Robert was correct in his speculation that the drive contained more information than we had assumed. And if Rodrigo ever found it, I would want to show it to Ima. Having Ima on my mind I remembered that I had to rent a place.

"Otavio, do you know if someone on the reservation has a house they want to rent?"

"Maybe a trailer. Why do you ask? Are you not comfortable here?"

"I'm very comfortable but the sleeping arrangements are awkward."

"Why are they awkward? Are you and Lorraine having problems?"

"No we're not having problems. But we're not a couple. We're just friends."

"Just friends? Are you not sleeping together?"

"Yes but we don't have sex."

"You sleep together but you don't have relations? That's very strange."

"I know it's hard to believe but it's true. We have a complicated friendship and it is about to get more complicated because the father of Lorraine's baby is coming for the birth and my girlfriend also wants to visit. Lorraine and I can't continue sleeping together."

Otavio couldn't help letting out a hoot and slapping his thigh. "This is like one of those Cary Grant movies," he said laughing.

I kept sharpening, letting my mind think about the absurdity of my friendship with Lorraine that other people saw.

"Didn't you ever love a woman that you couldn't have relations with?" I asked Otavio.

"Sure there were a few. But I never got to sleep with one of them and not have relations. A man and a woman share a bed to have relations. There is no other reason to sleep together. You and my granddaughter have much love for each other. That is clear to see. What you do about it is up to you. And yes, you must rent a trailer. I'll ask around."

Otavio called a halt to our work in the late afternoon and we went inside to help prepare dinner.

"It smells delicious," I said as I walked into the kitchen.

Lorraine was at the stove stirring a pot. "It's Pozole, beans, hominy and pork with a few other things," she said. "Come sit, it's ready."

"I'll just wash up," I said.

We ate mostly in silence, until Otavio spoke. "There's a special session of the elders tonight."

"What for, Grandfather?"

"What else? It's the Border Patrol. Last night they went into Lorreta's house. They said they were looking for the drugs her son is moving into the city from Mexico."

"They can do that?" I asked.

"They think they own this land," Lorraine said. "They forget that we are a sovereign nation. They spy on us, drive their vehicles anywhere they want and destroy the vegetation, stop T.O's when they are driving home late at night after a ceremony. The hysteria over drugs has allowed the Border Patrol to extend their numbers and their authority into areas where they shouldn't be."

"Granddaughter, have patience. One day we will correct this injustice."

"Not soon enough for me. I don't want my son growing up in what amounts to a police state. I caught an agent looking into my bedroom last month, Pelon."

"What a creep," I said.

"I know, right. Course he denied it. Be sure you tell them that story at the meeting tonight, Grandfather."

After I washed dishes and Otavio went to his meeting, Lorraine said she was ready for her massage.

"You're sure you're not too tired?" she asked.

"Naw, I feel fine. Where do you think we should do it?"

"We're not going to do it. I told you," she said jokingly. "But seriously, probably best in the bedroom. I have a yoga mat that I can lie on."

"OK."

She went into the bedroom and she sent me to get the mat from the linen closet. When I joined her, she was without clothing except for her panties. My eyes must have popped out.

"What's the matter, you never see a pregnant woman before?"

"Not a naked pregnant woman."

Her extended belly was enormous; her breasts were huge, way bigger than I remembered. And her nipples, the size of cherries, sat on areolas that were dark chocolate in color and large like small pancakes.

"How long are you going to stare? I'm getting cold standing here."

"I'm sorry. It's just that you're so big. That kid is not going to have any problem locating your breasts."

"I guess that's the positive spin on them. Right now all I can think of is that they weigh a ton and hurt like hell."

She eased down onto the mat and got on her side and I began to apply the techniques I was taught. I did her shoulders, her upper back and then her lower back. She shifted to the other side and I repeated the routine. She moaned with satisfaction and contentment. She then turned over on her back and after placing a pillow under her knees, I massaged her legs, starting at the upper thigh, working down to the calf and finishing at the feet. Next I worked on her neck, then her head and finally her face. The entire massage took almost two hours.

"Wow! That was so good Pelon. I know you've been massaging me for a long time already but can I ask you to do my breasts? Is it too much to ask?"

"I was hoping you'd forget. But yeah why not? I've already seen and touched most of you."

I did one breast at a tine, cupping the breast with both hands at first and lifting it off her chest. They were very heavy and I sympathized with her. Next with two fingers moving in a circular motion I went over the entire breast, including the nipple which she specifically asked me to massage. There was some leakage from the nipple but she said it was normal and I continued. I thoroughly enjoyed massaging her and I was sorry we had to end it. We went to bed soon after, said good night and she turned to her side and I slid my body next to hers.

Sometime during the night she nudged me and I automatically turned to my other side and she commenced to spoon me. This nudging and turning happened three times before we woke in the morning and got dressed for the day.

After breakfast I asked Lorraine if I could use the telephone to call a friend.

"Who you calling?" Lorraine asked, more as a habit than out of real curiosity.

"A young man that lives by my grandmother. I want to find out if his mother went to see my grandmother," I lied, not wanting Lorraine to get involved with knowledge of the flash drive.

"Rodrigo this is Pelon," I asked when I was finally alone and able to call him.

"I know it's you."

"Well?"

"Not yet. It's here someplace."

236

Momentarily I didn't know what to say but finally managed to ask him to keep looking and that I would call the next day.

I established a routine at the grandfather's house that included walks in the desert, going to the workshop to get tutored in woodworking techniques, helping Lorraine clean the house and prepare food, massaging her three or four times a week, accompanying her to the prenatal clinic and calling Rodrigo to see how my grandmother was doing and to ask about the still missing flash drive. Asking about the flash drive became like reading a script. I would say well and he would respond no. But I continued to call, more really because of what he had to say about my grandmother as in my gut I had already accepted the fact that the flash drive was lost. And my grandmother's condition had not changed other than she was no longer aware of her visitors. The only positive news was that the police were no longer parked in front of my grandmother's house.

My luck renting a place fared no better. I did locate a trailer not far from the grandfather's house and the owner Varelo was surprised that I wanted to rent it.

"It's dirty in there," he said. "Probably has mice, maybe snakes and a few ghosts even," He laughed. "You can have it for $100 a month if you do the cleaning."

"Can I see the inside?"

"Sure. It's open."

Varelo was right it was dirty, full of mice droppings and packed with an assortment of discarded furniture and clothing. *I think I'll pass on this one,* I said to myself.

"Too much work Varelo."

"Told you," he said.

It was now the week before Christmas and I had not contacted Ima, hoping to call her after I had secured a place for us. James, the father of Lorraine's baby was arriving on the twenty-third. That Monday we went into Tucson for a visit to the clinic.

"I need to contact Ima," I said. "She's probably thinking the worst right now."

"I wouldn't be worried if I were her. I'd be pissed."

"Well thanks a lot for that sentiment."

"Just saying, homeboy."

"You don't understand. I can't just call or send a message from anywhere. There would be consequences," I said. "It's not as if I'm avoiding her."

"Aren't you?

"Of course not," I protested. "And where would we stay anyway?"

"You could stay at my place in Tucson," she answered.

"You think it would be safe?"

"As safe as the res is right now with all those goddamn Border Patrol playing cowboys and interrogating everybody. I think you'll be fine. Use the computer at the Med Center to send her a message."

I did as Lorraine suggested and got a quick response from Ima.

"Darn you Pelon. I thought for sure you had been apprehended. Why didn't you contact me sooner? Sorry that I'm ranting. You must have had a good reason. And yes I'll take the train into Tucson. I'll arrive early Saturday morning."

Lorraine and I made a plan as we drove back to Sells.

"Can you pick up James at the airport on Friday and drive him to Sells? That way you can return to my Tucson apartment to sleep and pick up Ima on Saturday morning."

"We'll say that I have been staying in Tucson all along?"

"Hell no, just say that you've been sleeping on the couch."

"Will James be jealous?"

"Don't care if he is."

I was at the airport at noon on Friday, holding a placard with James written on it in big letters, as I had seen dozens of times when I happened to be in an airport.

A tall good-looking fellow in blue jeans and black cord jacket and a rather large turquoise bolo tie against his white shirt, made his way to where I was standing.

"How's it going?" he said. "I'm White Elk."

"Hi. I'm Pelon. You have other bags?"

"I checked in a couple."

We walked over to where the corresponding baggage conveyor was tumbling out bags, strollers and car seats and people were reaching in and getting what belonged to them.

"Lorraine tells me you were colleagues with the Congressman. Where are you now?" he asked as he straightened his ponytail and tugged at the silver band that held it.

"I'm trying to set up a practice but can't decide between here and California," I said.

"Between jobs huh?"

"I guess you could say that."

"There's one of my bags," James said. "Where the fuck is the other one. Goddamn podunk airport probably lost it."

He retrieved the large bag and waited anxiously for the other.

"Finally," he said as the twin to his bag tumbled out. He pulled it out and asked, "Will you take one?"

"Sure," I said taking the bag and setting up the handle and we wheeled our respective bags out of the airport.

"I keep telling Lorraine to buy herself a new car," he said as we began our trip to Sells. "This piece of shit just doesn't cut it. It's not as if she couldn't afford it, know what I mean."

"That's how she is," I said.

239

"Yeah. She still has that poverty mentality. Damn it's brown out here. Doesn't it ever rain?"

"We get most of our rain in late summer but we get a little during winter. It is a desert," I said.

"Lorraine wants me to live out here. No way in hell would I do that."

"Are you still working in Washington?"

"Still there. Been there 12 years. Some headhunter is after me to take an administrative position with a college but that's not where the action is. Know what I mean."

"You mean where big wheels make big decisions?"

"Nobody says big wheels Pelon. It's outdated. How long have you been out of the loop anyway? It's more accurate to think about it as the place where responsible men make decisions that create an energy that is quite intoxicating. Know what I mean."

A Tohono O'Odham police car began following me with lights flashing soon after I began exceeding the speed limit in my effort to get White Elk to Sells as quickly as possible.

"Oh shit," I said, "we're getting pulled over."

"Let me take care of this," White Elk said. "I know how to handle these cops on the res."

He got out of the car and through my side mirror I saw him talking to the policeman, at one point digging through his wallet and showing him some identification. Soon he had the cop smiling and he came back into the car.

"And that is the way it's done," he said proudly.

"I'm impressed. What did you tell him?"

"Some bullshit about me having to leave Washington to come here to see the birth of my kid and having to speed because she was going into labor. He knows Lorraine. It was a slam-dunk. Know what I mean."

"I sure do," I said.

We finally arrived and I helped him unload his bags and took one into the house. Lorraine was waiting for us in the front room.

"Good grief woman you're as big as a house," he said unsmiling.

"There's a big boy in there. What'd you expect?"

"Well I have to get back to Tucson," I said interrupting. "I have to attend to some business. I'll be back tomorrow so you can meet Ima. Nice meeting you White Elk."

"The pleasure is all mine," he said.

"You sure you have to go so soon?" Lorraine asked.

"Yeah. Sorry. It's rather pressing."

I left as quickly as I could but drove cautiously, mindful of the speed limits. *What an asshole*, I thought as I drove, and felt terrible for Lorraine.

I had a restless night in Lorraine's apartment and had honesty prevailed, I would have admitted that I missed sleeping next to Lorraine. Instead I attributed my interrupted sleep to noise from loud cars, sirens from emergency vehicles and at one point, musicians serenading someone nearby. And also to bad dreams of men chasing me and I unable to move my legs to run away.

I woke up tired and rushed to arrive at the train station on time. When I got there, Ima was already standing at the curb, her small suitcase next to her on the ground. She was wearing a puffy down jacket that made her seem larger than she really was and smart wool slacks. She looked radiant and I rushed to hug her.

"Darn Ima, you look great."

"I would like to say the same about you, but you look like you didn't sleep all night."

"That's because I didn't. Come, let's get out of here."

Lorraine's apartment was on the west side of Tucson, just off a busy main thoroughfare. It was new and clean and comfortable. And priced inexpensively compared to other areas for this also was an area populated by Latinos. It was but a ten-minute drive from the train depot and we held hands and kissed at every stop light.

Once in the apartment we wasted no time undressing and getting in bed where we hugged for several minutes without saying anything and without doing much else. She spoke first.

"It was hard being alone. I have never felt as alone as I was when you left and I didn't like feeling that way. I have always been fiercely independent and have never needed anyone. Did you miss me?" she asked.

"Of course I missed you. But I wasn't alone like you. I've been staying with Lorraine and her grandfather. We'll go there later so you can meet them. But right now I just want to make love to you."

"It's about time."

We stayed in bed until noon and only left it because we were both ravenous by then. We had exchanged pieces of information about what had taken place in our lives since I had left Encinitas. I told her about my train ride and meeting Mari and her family, and about my grandmother and her treacherous niece. And I told her everything about Lorraine including our sleeping arrangements, which she thought were odd but not a concern.

She in turn told me about her work with the fire department and about Miguel.

"I haven't gone to the farm since the police paid me a visit. I was really angry that Miguel had done what he did," she said.

"Don't hold it against him. It's really his wife that's behind it. I'm sure she made up a story about what took place."

"You're right. I'm trying not to be as judgmental, that's one of the big four behaviors that we are being asked to incorporate."

242

We had walked over to a nearby tortilleria that also made a terrific breakfast burrito. We each ordered one and sat down in the tiny eating area with other customers, most of them men that worked blue-collar jobs.

"And what are the other three? You said there were four behaviors."

"Not to be fearful, as fear inhibits our ability to love; to have compassion, as it opens our heart; and not to rely on others to affirm us, that is to have confidence that our heart and intuition are leading us on the right path."

"Those are good qualities to have," I said. "But why are they now more important?"

"We are living in a special time with horrendous natural disasters world wide, we are asked to keep our focus on the fact that Mother earth is making necessary adjustments, that at times lead to volcanoes or earthquakes and to bizarre weather. And there is an opportunity for us to be compassionate with those that experience disasters directly or with those that suffer at the hands of crazed individuals, such as those shot along with the congresswoman here in Tucson. There is a lot of negative energy that is bursting to the surface as the new energy comes in to clear it away."

"Most people won't be able to stop being fearful nor can they put an end to looking for the approval of others or stop judging people. That's just human nature," I said.

"I know but those that are able, must try. It will only take a very small percentage of us to create the conditions necessary for the whole of humanity to ascend to this higher dimension. It's like the story of the hundredth monkey, where a critical mass needs to be reached."

"I miss these conversations Ima. And I have missed making love to you."

We returned to the apartment and made love one last time before driving to Sells.

"This is beautiful country Pelon, different from the coast but equally beautiful," she said on our drive. "What is that tall mountain with the white structures?"

"That's the University's Observatory. They call it Kitt Peak but it's on a Tohono O'Odham sacred mountain that they call Baboquivari."

"What audacity to have built it there."

"Right in line with all the other acts of injustice that indigenous people have suffered."

"Fortunately in time there will be a greater appreciation for the contributions of indigenous people, including the stewardship of the land."

"I hope you're right Ima. And maybe the emergence of casinos is part of that renewal of indigenous people."

"Amen."

"Ima I hate to mention this but you may have to participate in a little white lie."

"Is it for a worthy cause?"

"Of course, it might help Lorraine with the father of her baby. Although, and I know we're not supposed to judge, he really is an asshole and how she hooked up with him, I'll never understand."

"What's the lie?"

"That I've been sleeping on the couch. It may not come up but if it does that's the story Lorraine and I cooked up."

"Not a problem," she said.

They were all in the kitchen when we arrived, eating green corn tamales that Lorraine had pulled out of the freezer and a bowl of freshly cooked beans. I introduced Ima and we were invited to sit and have some food.

"These are really good tamales, Lorraine," Ima said. "I've never had them before."

They're a specialty of this area, made from the green corn in summer. They just have cheese and butter and a bit of green chile," Lorraine informed.

"Speaking of which, where is the meat dish?" White Elk asked. "Some rabbit food is ok but you can't have a meal without some meat."

"The corn and the beans make complete protein," Ima volunteered. "One doesn't need meat when having such a meal."

"Maybe you don't cause you're so skinny but a big man like me needs animal protein."

Lorraine went out of her way to diffuse the tension that settled after White Elk's assertion by saying. "I have Pozole from last night that I can heat. Do you eat pork?" she asked White Elk.

"Hell yes. I love pork."

After we ate and were washing dishes, Lorraine said she was having strong contractions and she asked if Ima and I could finish while she went and sat down in the front room with White Elk and her grandfather.

A little later we heard Lorraine let out a healthy scream.

"Ahhh! This damn baby is coming right now," she screamed. "Go get the midwife, Pelon."

I ran the short distance to Otilia's, the local midwife and told her that Lorraine was about to give birth.

"Calm down young man. Your baby is going to be fine. Lorraine is a healthy woman. She won't have any problems," Otilia said.

She was an elderly woman, a bit overweight and her chubby face wrinkled and pock marked. I tried to walk fast hoping she would want to keep up with me but she didn't see the need and I had to slow down to her leisurely pace.

When we arrived at the house, the men were still in the front room and Ima and Lorraine were in the bedroom. Lorraine was on the bed, perspiring and at times yelling or cursing like a sailor.

"Goddamn, ohhh ahhh! Come out you little fucker hurry it up! It's about time Otilia. I'm dying here. Get this little son of a bitch out."

"Just calm down Lorraine. You're fine. Here let me look at you. Yes I can see his little head," the midwife said.

"Little head my ass. It's as big as a goddamn basketball. Ahhhh. Here's another of those fucking pains, aaahh."

"Ok Lorraine you're doing fine. Keep pushing girl. That's right one big push and he's out. Breathe now ok here he comes."

"Aaahh. Oh my god he's out, he's out. Oh it still hurts like hell."

Otilia held the baby high, expertly grabbed him by the ankles and turned him upside down, giving him a swift spank. The baby gasped momentarily and then let out a healthy cry.

Ima handed Otilia a clean towel and she wiped him down and swaddled him with the same towel while she cut the cord. Once that was done she cleaned him and placed him in his blanket and handed him to Lorraine who was still wet with perspiration.

"See if he will nurse," Otilia said.

I left the bedroom at that point and called Rodrigo. "Well?" I said.

"I told you it was here," he said.

"No way. You found it?"

"Yeah, yesterday one of my friends came over to play catch and when I put on my glove I found it inside. I had forgotten that I stashed it in my baseball glove so I wouldn't lose it. Smart huh?"

"Yeah real smart," I said. "You made me sweat bullets on this one Rodrigo. You owe me big time."

"You got this all wrong Pelon. "It's you who owes me big time. I kept it safe didn't I?"

"Yeah, if you say so smart ass," I said. "I need to pick that up from you tonight. You going to be home?"

"Course. It's Christmas Eve dude. Mom and her sisters are making tamales."

"See you later Rodrigo, and thanks for keeping the drive safe."

"No problem Pelon."

After my conversation with Rodrigo I joined White Elk and Otavio, who were still sitting in the front room.

"You're a father of a boy, White Elk. Lorraine is breastfeeding him. You can go in and to see them." I said.

"I'm not very good right now. It's a jolt to the system. Know what I mean? I'll wait until tomorrow. Does he look like me?"

"Looks like he'll have your nose."

"That's crazy," he said while shaking his head with satisfaction.

"I'll go see Lorraine and my new grandson." Otavio said as he got up from the sofa.

Ima joined White Elk and me in the front room.

"Ready to go, Ima? I asked.

"Yes. Lorraine looks exhausted, she'll need to rest."

"Congratulations, White Elk. You have a fine son," Ima said.

"Why thank you. I appreciate what you say," he answered.

"We'll be back tomorrow. Lorraine invited us for Christmas Dinner," I said.

"Good, I look forward to your visit," White Elk said.

Ima and I talked all the way back to Lorraine's apartment. "That was simply amazing," Ima said. "I've never witnessed a live birth before."

"It was," I agreed. "I felt a strong connection with that little person. Ima, I need to make a stop at a friend's before we go to the apartment," I said. "It shouldn't take long. Is that okay?"

Ima bopped her head and her body shook in mock imitation. "Ora-le," she said.

"Very funny, Ima," I said and tried to hold back a smile. "The thing is, I have much more finesse."

"Sure you do, Pelon. What's that other thing you do when you greet someone? You tilt you head up and say Ora-le. I think it's hilarious."

We arrived at Rodrigo's laughing.

"Come on in. Maybe we can score some of the tamales they're making," I said.

Rodrigo's mom answered the door and invited us in. As soon as the door opened, the distinctive smell of tamales being steamed wafted around us.

"Come in, Pelon," she said. "You're just in time to taste the tamales."

"Isabel, this is my friend Ima."

"Hello Ima. Come to the kitchen, we're all in there," Isabel said.

We walked into the kitchen and were introduced to Isabel's sisters and to their respective husbands, who took time to shake hands with me and quickly returned to their conversation about the NFL team from Phoenix. Three adolescent girls were huddled around a smart phone giggling at Rodrigo, who was at the kitchen table eating tamales and who waved when we walked in. On the stove sat two large pots, and Isabel went over to one of the pots and began pulling out some tamales with large metal tongs.

"Sit there by Rodrigo and I'll get you started," Isabel instructed.

"How's it going, Rod man," I said to Rodrigo. "This is my friend Ima."

"Hi Rodrigo," Ima said when Rodrigo stood up to shake her hand.

"Hi, Ima."

Ima and I sat down at the table with Rodrigo and began taking off the cornhusks and with hardly any conversation began eating.

"These are very good, Isabel," Ima said.

"I'm glad you like them. It's our grandmother's recipe."

"Well Rodrigo," I said when I saw that he had finished his last tamale. "The moment of truth has arrived."

"I got it Pelon. You don't have to worry," he said and reached into his pants pocket and pulled out the flash drive and handed it to me. "You see."

I gave him a smile and thanked him.

"Have you been tutoring Tony? I've been forgetting to ask you."

"Yeah I have. I saw him for the last time on Tuesday. They'll be going back to LA right after Christmas."

"Do I owe you any money?"

"Not really. Unless you want to play Santo Clos?"

"As a matter of fact I do," I said and pulled out my wallet and gave him a twenty.

We stayed another hour with the family. I went over to where the men were talking and drinking beer, and Ima helped clean up the kitchen. Isabel protested that she didn't need her help, but Ima helped anyway.

Ima was tired when we finally left and drove over to Lorraine's apartment, but I was anxious to look carefully at the flash drive to see if it contained other information than what we had seen at Naomi's. Naturally Ima was the one who actually found another file that was secretly imbedded in the drive.

"Wow!" Ima exclaimed. "There are some big names here. It looks like they all have received regular yearly deposits. I would guess they are secret deposits over and above what the government allows."

"So that's why Andre wants me so badly. I see why they would want to keep this sort of information from the public. It shows that almost the entire governing system is corrupt."

"What are you going to do with it?"

"Right now, nothing. We're going to bed and sleep on it."

Lying next to Ima was a welcome treat, and we both slept soundly.

"Merry Christmas, Pelon. Here's a small gift from Santa," Ima said as I was waking up the next morning. It was a smart phone with a red ribbon around it.

"A cell phone?"

"I know you can't use it now, but soon you will," Ima said. "It's putting the potential out there, like a prayer."

"Well thanks very much Ima. I'm sure I'll be using it soon. There's something for you also," I said. "It's under the bed."

"Is it this sandwich baggie?" she asked.

"Yes that's it."

"It's a ring? An engagement ring?"

"Yes. My grandmother gave it to me a long time ago. I picked it up when I went to visit her. Will you consider it?"

"I don't need to consider it. It's a big yes, Pelon. I'm in shock though, getting asked to marry. God, it's something I had never ever thought would happen to me. It is pretty clichéd though, asking me to marry on Christmas."

"Yeah I know. I thought you would appreciate the triteness."

"I do. Let's celebrate with a kiss."

We got dressed and I placed the flash drive in a padded manila envelope with a small note and addressed it to Farley at the NRDC. He was the one person that Andre did not know had been involved, and the ideal person to release the information, if that's what was needed. On the way to Sells we stopped at a mailbox and dropped the envelope inside.

.^.^.^.

CHAPTER XIII

Christmas Dinner was at the home of Otavio's son, there on the reservation. There were several other families, all relatives of theirs and they made us feel quite welcome. White Elk was enthralled with his son and he held and carried him around at every opportunity.

"He doesn't seem like the same man that I picked up at the airport," I told Lorraine who was bravely in attendance.

"Tell me about it. He's been like that since morning. I don't know, Pelon, maybe this can work for me."

"I hope it does, Lorraine."

"Ima showed me the engagement ring, you dog. Why didn't you tell me?"

"I wasn't sure until I saw her again and we spent time together."

"Boy this is some Christmas," she said and shook her head to express her disbelief.

We left the Christmas gathering late and we were on the road in total darkness except for the car lights.

"It's pitch black out here. Can you pull over somewhere so I can see the stars?" asked Ima.

"They are awesome, I said. "Up ahead there's a spot where I can pull off the road."

I reached the spot I had seen on other occasions and turned off the motor. We got off and were immediately surrounded by silence and a canopy of millions of stars.

"This is incredible," Ima said. "Look there's the Milky Way. I had never seen it in person. My god I want to cry it's so beautiful."

We got on the hood and leaned against the windshield and stared into the depths of the Universe.

"Do you know that scientists are now saying that there are many universes, not just the one we have been taught we inhabit?"

"Really. Scientists are saying this?"

"Yes it's really wild, because of course in the channeled communications they often make references to multiverse or omniverse. It's another instance where science and new age thinking are coming together."

If Ima was going to say more she never got a chance, for all of a sudden we were set upon by a large SUV with lights shining on us and a man's voice on a loudspeaker was telling us to get down from the hood with our hands behind our heads.

Ima began screaming in fright and I tried to calm her down at the same time as I was trying to follow the instruction we had been given. Then I felt someone roughly pushing me against the car and twisting my hands behind my back and putting a plastic tie on them. Ima was now also next to me with her hands tied behind her. Fortunately she had now stopped screaming.

My adrenaline was on high. In my mind I saw my opportunity to strike when the agent struggled while trying to tie my hands together. *I saw myself twisting my hands free and grabbing the agent by the shoulders and flipping him to the ground. Next I saw myself kicking the other agent with a flying spinning round house to the head. Then I would fall on top of the first agent and deliver a crushing blow to the head. I knew I could easily escape but then what? Where would I run?* I calmed down and stopped the violent imaginings. Besides now I had the flash drive as a bargaining chip.

"No need to get so rough," I said. "We're just admiring the night sky."

"Please," Ima added. "You saw us reclined on the hood looking up."

One of the men finally said, "This is a favorite pick up point for human smugglers." It was then that I realized that they were with the Border Patrol.

"We're not smugglers of any sort," Ima said. "We're coming from the home of a friend who just gave birth."

"What's your friend's name?"

"Lorraine Matus. She's staying with her grandfather Otavio Matus," I said.

"You have identification?" he asked looking at me, then at Ima.

"My purse is in the car," Ima said.

"And where's your identification?" he asked me directly.

"Listen, I'm a lawyer and know my rights," I said. "You can stop us and question us and ask for identification, but you can't mistreat us nor cuff us. And you can't go through our belongings without our permission. So free our hands and we'll show you our papers."

The agent said "Whatever," and felt my back pockets for my wallet and pulled it out when he found it. "Get her purse," he told the other agent.

Under his flashlight the agent looked through my wallet and pulled out my Arizona Driver's license, but he also found the fake one from Michigan.

"What do we have here?" he said it slowly, savoring the discovery, a sneer forming on his face. "So who are you Pancho, Inez Segura or Herculano Macias? Doesn't matter now what you say, I have probable cause to take you in for questioning. And your accomplice too."

They put both of us in the backseat of the SUV, and I suspected they were taking us to the checkpoint the Border Patrol had set up on the highway leading back to Tucson.

Ima was terrified. She had heard the agent discover that I had two driver's licenses. "What do you think is going to happen, Pelon?"

"They'll run my fingerprints and find out that there is an outstanding warrant for my arrest. Probably I'll end up tonight at the county detention center. After that I don't know. Maybe they'll send me back to D.C."

"God this is a nightmare. What about me? Will I be arrested too?"

"I'm sure they won't. They'll cut you loose. You haven't done anything wrong. I'll give you Lorraine's cell number. Memorize it and call her. She'll help you get back to California.

We arrived at the Border Patrol checkpoint on the highway, illuminated by so many large lights that one would have thought it was the inside of a building. They took us into a large bungalow that was their office and also a holding cell for undocumented persons and suspected smugglers. They separated us and I was fingerprinted and interrogated at length about my identity.

It did not take long before someone came into the interrogation room and whispered to the agent. Nevertheless I heard what he said.

"You're a wanted man, Mr. Herculano Macias," the agent said politely. "You won't be going anywhere tonight but in the morning you'll be transported to the Pima County Detention Center."

"What about my friend Ima? She was unaware that there was a warrant out for me."

"If she checks out clean, we'll release her. Meantime you'll be placed in the holding cell."

"Can I make a telephone call?"

"No sorry, we're not set up for telephone calls. Maybe at the county jail they'll let you make a call."

"Can I at least speak with my friend Ima?"

"Only if she is released. Then we'll give you a few minutes."

I was taken through a door into a room where the holding cell was located, a simple affair constructed with heavy gauged wire. The agent opened the wire cage's door and I was placed inside. Four young men were seated on the floor, their backs leaning against the bungalow's walls, talking quietly. We nodded to each other in greeting.

I sat down and put my head against the wall. I was tired and could have fallen asleep had not one of the young men asked me if I knew what was to happen to them. I told them that if they were wanted for a crime it would be jail, otherwise they would be returned voluntarily to their country.

"Depende. Si han cometido un crimen, los hechan a la carcel. Si solamente estan aqui sin documentos, los regresan a su pais. Son mexicanos?"

"Si, Somos del otro lado. Y no somos criminals. Venimos a trabajar. Y tu que onda?"

"Soy de aqui, pero tengo unos cargos falsos y me arrestaron," I said, when he asked why I was in there, telling him that I was from the USA but that I had been falsely accused of a crime.

He laughed at my claim of innocence saying I didn't have to lie to them.

"Carnal, entre nosotros no tienes que mentir."

"Es la neta," I claimed it was the truth.

Ima walked into the room accompanied by an agent.

"You have a few minutes," he said to her.

"Don't look so glum, Ima," I said smiling. "There are no victims, remember."

"God, what I said about there being no victims feels so false right now. All I can feel right now is pain, yours and mine."

"Naw, I feel fine. I'm ready, come what may. I've been in tough situations before and I have always been fine."

"They tell me that you'll be sent to the local jail in the morning."

"That's what I was told, too. If the car is not impounded, drive back to Lorraine's apartment and call her to let her know what happened. And you should go back to Encinitas, there's nothing more that you can do here."

"Shouldn't I get you a lawyer? You'll need one."

"I think that's premature right now. As soon as they send me back to D.C. I'll contact you. In the meantime, when you get back to Lorraine's apartment, find my address book and find Robert's telephone number and call him. He'll know what needs to be done."

"Time's up lady," the agent said.

"I'll see you, OK?" I said.

"Bye Pelon," she said and slid her finger through the cage to touch my finger.

"Tu esposa, carnal?" one of the men asked if she was my wife.

"No, mi prometida." My fiancée, I answered.

"Esta bonita," he said. "Yo soy Chava, Pelon."

We shook hands and he introduced me to his three friends and I sat down and got acquainted with them. They were young and innocent villagers from the interior of Mexico, eager to try bettering their lives by coming to work in the United States. Their guide had taken their money and abandoned them in the desert, where they would have probably frozen to death had they not been rescued by the Border Patrol. They were downcast at having lost all their savings and having to return to their homes without anything to show for it. One by one we fell asleep, in spite of the cold floor and the glare of the flickering fluorescent light.

At dawn an agent and his partner came into the room and woke us up and began getting my cellmates ready for transporting them back to Mexico.

"Levantense," he said in perfect Spanish and proceeded to unlock the cage.

"Ahorita mismo los regresamos a Mexico."

He marched them out the door and I wished them good luck.

An hour later it was my turn to be transported and I was handcuffed and driven to the county detention center, a concrete four story building on what used to be the outskirts of Tucson but was now among industrial buildings and housing.

I was processed and issued a bright orange jumpsuit and taken up the stairs to a large room with tables and chairs, a television and a pay telephone. Around the perimeter of this central room were cells on two floor levels. I was assigned one of those cells on the lower level and I went in and placed my bedding on the vacant bottom bunk. I sat down on my bunk and thought about my situation, and I wondered how Ima was coping with my incarceration. I hoped for the best.

My cellmate walked in, a short pudgy young man that paid no attention to me and went about his business as if I was not present. Surprisingly agile for his body type, he scrambled up to his bunk with ease, using the end frame of my bunk for support.

A little later lunch was announced and my cellmate came down and went out the door to the large common room where men were already beginning to sit at the tables with their tray of food. It was simple fare, a baloney sandwich, an apple and some fries. I was hungry and I got my food and sat at a table with some of the other men.

One of the men nodded and said. "Hey homes. Why you here?"

"A trumped up charge, what else," I said smiling.

"Right on, carnal. I'm here for the same thing," he said and laughed. "Name's Joker. What's yours?"

"Pelon."

"Okay Pelon, this here is Joey, that's Spider and over there is Tin Man," he said pointing out each of the men at our table.

"How long you gonna be wit us vato?"

"Don't know for sure. Somebody wants me in D.C."

"You ain't from here?"

"Used to live here. How about you Joker? How long are we having you over for lunch?"

"Hey that's funny Pelon. But you know what, Pelon. This here is a rough place and I think maybe you should get some protection."

"You mean protection from you," I said. "Tell you what Joker, I think maybe I should protect you. What do you think of that as a counter offer?"

"What are you, some smart ass college boy?"

"Just saying, vato. And just so you know what you're up against, I'll have you a little arm wrestle right here on the table. Let's see how much protection I should give you."

Joker was a tough looking dude with neck and arm tattoos and lots of muscle and I looked him straight in the eyes until he eventually averted my look.

"Tell you what Joker, let's forget this conversation ever took place and let's just eat our lunch and get on with our business. No harm, no foul, as they say. How's that sound to you?"

"Sounds good to me Pelon," and he bopped his head and his body shook ever so slightly.

I finished my lunch and went back into my cell to take a nap. My cellmate was already up in his bunk reading a book. Joker and the Tin Man walked in.

"Hey Pelon, my boys think I should've busted your balls for the smart ass way yous talked to me."

Tin Man lifted his leg to stomp my face but I moved back in time and his foot landed harmlessly on the thin mattress. Grabbing the bunk frame above my head I swung my legs up and extended them into the Tin man's stomach who went down doubled over. I left my bunk and faced Joker who had his fists up boxer style.

"You sure you want to do this, Joker?"

"I'm gonna to kick your ass college…."

A swift round house kick to Joker's temple ended that conversation. When he came to I was lying on my bunk reading. Tin Man had already roused himself and left.

"You okay, Joker?" I asked.

"Yeah I'm okay, asshole. That was some move yous put on me homes. Where'd you learn that?"

"Some ninja movie I saw in juvi. Are we good? "

"Yeah we're good. Nothing happened right?"

"I didn't see anything," I said.

"How's about yous fat boy. Yous see anything?" Joker asked my cellmate.

"No I didn't see anything," I heard him answer.

Joker left the cell rubbing the side of his head.

"That was some display of testosterone," my cellmate said. "Joker is one of the big kahunas around here."

"Had to be done roomie. Otherwise he'd be hounding me all the time. I actually feel sorry for him."

"To know all is to forgive all," my roommate quoted.

"Maybe that's what it is. I've known men like Joker all my life."

My roommate climbed down as gingerly as he climbed up and went and sat on the floor in front of our bunks.

"Sorry I snubbed you earlier. It's my way of steering clear of trouble."

"Not a problem," I said. "Whatever works for you is fine with me. Jails are not known for bringing nice people together."

"You got that right. This has been the scariest experience I've ever had. I heard Joker call you Pelon. My name is Robbie."

"Nice to meet you Robbie. You been here long?"

"Seems like forever but it's only three months. I'll get out next week. And you, how long will you be here?"

"Don't know for sure. I think I'll be extradited to D.C. sometime soon."

"D.C., the hub of all things nefarious. Who wants you back in the pit of evildoers?"

"I don't know if I would call it a pit, not everyone is bad. I met good friends there."

"I'm referring to all those that are hell bent on spying on us. We think we have privacy but everyday more and more of us are being spied upon. Do you think our telephone conversations and our emails are not compromised by the feds? Ever since 911 when Bush was in office, the government has been chipping away at our rights. Look what happened to Occupy, there's a good example of them fucking with our right to free speech and assembly."

"Yeah I agree with you on Occupy, but I think that the Internet is still relatively safe from prying eyes, at least for the general public."

"Don't believe that crap. How do you think they got onto me? They read my damn emails. There was no other way they could have known."

A loud buzzer resonated throughout the complex.

"What's that?" I asked.

"It's time to get back to our work assignments. I work the library. See you later."

When Robbie left I looked through the stack of books that he had on the floor under the bunks. One book caught my attention. It was a book about messages from Kryon. I remembered Ima mentioning that name and I leafed though the section on DNA, remembering what she said about our bodies getting use of the additional ten strands that science now considers junk.

.^.^.^.

260

CHAPTER XIV

A guard walked into the cell and said I was to be transported.

"Where to?" I asked, as the guard placed me in handcuffs.

"Sorry but I don't know. I'm to take you downstairs."

A couple of suits were in the office and they took charge of me, shackling me and marching me out to an awaiting car. We were driven to the nearby Davis Monthan airbase where the two suits and I boarded an air transport plane carrying military personnel, men and women in camouflaged fatigues.

Some of my fellow passengers stared as I was cuffed to my seat. Others never gave me a second thought, and simply continued reading or talking with their neighbors.

"Where are you taking me?" I asked one of my guards as I had on the way to the airbase but was never given an answer.

"You're headed for a dark place, asshole," he answered.

"Can you be more specific, dark place could be any number of jails or prisons?"

"Does it really matter?" he said.

"I suppose it doesn't in some respects but it does when I notify my family and friends of my whereabouts."

"There won't be any need for that I assure you. Now shut up and enjoy the ride. It may be the last one you take for a long time."

It was a long turbulent ride and we finally touched down after nightfall in some other airport. I caught one of the female soldiers looking at me and asked her, "Where are we?"

"Langley," she said.

"Don't talk to him," my guard ordered her.

After everyone else had disembarked, I was loosened from my seat and taken off the airplane. We were picked up by an electric cart and driven to a building some distance away. There I was taken to a cell with metal bars and finally unshackled.

I sat on the metal bunk and awaited my fate. In an hour Andre showed up. He had a wicked sneer and was obviously quite pleased to see me.

"You eluded me longer than I thought possible," he said. "You're going to live to regret breaking my nose."

"It adds character to your otherwise pretty looks Andre," I said. "You might even fool someone into thinking that you're some sort of tough guy."

"You can laugh all you want Pelon, but I get the last laugh."

"Have you also set your sights on Helga's new boyfriend, Andre? Or have you realized that she left you because you are an asshole and not because I took her from you?"

"You know that you caused this situation to get out of hand," Andre said. "I was just trying to scare you into giving back that flash drive. But you had to get all macho and break out and injure me, and that guard. Now there's an official assault charge and it's out of my hands."

"Really. You don't want the flash drive back?"

"I don't think you have it. If you did, by now you would have used it in some fashion."

"Maybe I was biding my time."

Andre stared at me as if he was trying to read my face and decide whether or not I was lying.

"Maybe something can be worked out," he finally said. "What is it you want?"

"I want to be released and my friends and I to be left alone."

"What about the information that belongs to my associates?" What assurances do we get that the information does not go public?"

"My word of honor," I said and smiled.

"Maybe I'll just have you shot and say that you were trying to escape. That would bring this to an end."

"Come on Andre. That would be really stupid. My friends would release the information."

Andre turned and started to walk away.

"Can you really afford a public trial Andre? Your real reason for locking me up will be revealed, that I know. So will the entire infrastructure for spying on ordinary people."

"Don't underestimate me Pelon, and don't underestimate the lengths to which the intelligence community has gone to carry out its vital work. You'll be up against a very formidable opponent."

"I realize that and therefore coming to some agreements that would be beneficial to both of us would be most prudent."

"What do you have in mind?"

"Release me and change the venue from here to Santa Barbara County and I will plead no contest to a misdemeanor assault charge. As a condition of this plea bargain the information on the flash drive cannot be released. Your name gets kept out of the eyes of your friends and colleagues and I serve my six months at the Lompoc prison near the home of my fiancée."

"You've given this some thought Pelon. I see no reason why this arrangement might not be a good way to save taxpayer money. I'll speak to someone connected to this case and see if what you outlined is possible. I'll get in touch with you."

Andre left and I felt quite positive that my fugitive status was finally coming to an end. I didn't relish the thought of spending six months in prison, but compared to that of a long expensive trial with the possibility of a felony conviction, it was the better choice.

The next day I was processed and moved to the main portion of the brig where other cells were occupied by airmen that had committed infractions of one sort or another such as fighting or insubordination, but nothing serious that required lengthy prison stays.

The days passed uneventfully and although the food was decent and I had reading material that kept my mind occupied, still I was quite sad that I had to be apart from Ima when the New Year of 2012 rolled in. I was certain that she was with her father in Santa Barbara and worried about me. And since I had no telephone privileges there was no way to get in touch with her.

Two weeks had passed when I was notified that I had visitors. I was led out of my cell to a larger room where Andre was seated and much to my surprise, so were Helga and Robert.

Unrestrained, I was able to greet both of my friends with a hug and a quick comment or two before Andre cleared his throat, indicating that he wanted to speak.

"I know that in the past we have had our differences but let us let bygones be bygones. And in that spirit I've come to tell Pelon that his proposal has been met with approval, and the paperwork to that end is being processed as we speak. When it's ready, in about a half hour, you'll be free to go. The court date will also be given to you. We'll be in touch, Pelon."

Andre left the room and momentarily there was silence.

I spoke first. "I'm speechless. After all these months, seeing you here is quite a shock. So much has happened, so much to tell you and so much I want to ask."

"I know. It's overwhelming," Helga said. "You do look good Pelon, in spite of what you must have gone through."

"You both look great," I said. "And I haven't had it so bad. I've had a few bad moments but overall my life has been good. How about you?"

Helga spoke. "I know that Robert told you that I met someone, and I'm glad I don't have to reveal that to you today of all days."

"And I'm still with John," Robert said. "But isn't this something, Andre getting us together. Do you suppose he has some ulterior motive? What would possess him to do this, I wonder?"

"He did tell us that you and he were able to reach some agreement but declined to explain, saying that he would leave that up to you Pelon," Helga added.

"It does seem out of character," I said in response to Robert's suspicions. "But right now I'm willing to take him at face value. This whole situation has been bizarre from the get go, and there's no reason to think that it'll be any different when it comes to an end."

"And what is the agreement?" Robert asked.

"The deal I struck up with Andre is that the venue would be changed from D.C. to Santa Barbara, where I would plead no contest to a misdemeanor assault charge and probably have to serve six months at the federal facility in Lompoc."

"That doesn't seem like a good deal for you Pelon. You only assaulted Andre and that guard because he unlawfully imprisoned you," Robert said shaking his head.

"Yeah, but in a court of law, the deck would be stacked against me. He'll claim that he had every right to bring me in for questioning, and that I was in the wrong in escaping. I couldn't prove otherwise."

"It is not fair to have put you through such hell, and walk away without even as much as a scratch," Helga said in dismay.

"I did break his nose," I said smiling.

"Yes you did my friend," Robert said. "I saw him at a republican function soon after, and he was wearing a bandage on what looked like a rather large nose."

"Seriously Pelon, spending six months in prison seems quite harsh, and why Lompoc? What's there?"

"I have someone else too. Actually she's my fiancée and her dad lives in Santa Barbara."

"Really I didn't know," Helga said, not able to hide her surprise. "It does seem rather sudden."

"I suppose in some ways it is," I said. "Life is funny in what it lays before us."

"Tell us more Pelon. Who is she?" Robert asked.

"Her name is Ima and she lives in Encinitas. I was working on a farm and met her there."

"She's a farm worker?"

"She's not a farm worker Helga, she volunteers there. The farm belongs to a religious group that she belongs to, or used to. I don't know if she still does."

"Is she in a cult?"

"No, she's not in a cult. It's a group started by a Guru from India. They have services in a temple and it's run by nuns and monks much like the Catholic Church."

"Unless they believe in Christ, it's nothing like the Catholic Church."

"They do in a way. They revere Christ but they also revere Krishna and other enlightened beings, avatars they call them."

"They may be enlightened but Christ is the only Son of God and I hope they don't claim that there are others."

"Didn't Christ affirm that we are all children of the most high?"

"Yes but he also said that he was the Son of God."

"Why would God offer salvation to just one group of people in one historical period? That doesn't make sense to me, Helga, not if God is perfect and all loving. I think I am more convinced that we are all angels that make a choice to be here, and we will all discover one day that we are all indeed children of the most high, just as Christ is."

"You don't even believe in God," Helga said.

"I don't believe in the God as described by religious groups, a god that is vengeful, that offers love conditionally, that has created a hell to punish wrongdoers. That's not a God I can believe in."

"Before the next religious war breaks out between you two, how about telling us where you have been, Pelon. Were you in Encinitas?"

"Until my grandmother had a stroke. Then I went to see her in Tucson and stayed there for over a month. I was on the Tohono O'Odham Reservation when the Border Patrol stopped me on a routine check."

"Did they profile you?"

"No, actually they saw that I had a fake driver's license and they ran my prints and found the warrant for my arrest."

"Didn't you work with a woman that was from the Tohono... whatever?" Helga asked.

"Yeah, Lorraine. I stayed with her and her grandfather. She just gave birth to a boy on Christmas eve."

"Not yours though?" Robert asked.

"No, of course not! The dad is a man that works for the Native American Alliance there in Washington. White Elk is his name."

"Oh I know him," Robert answered. "He's sort of a dandy and ladies man."

"He does like clothes. But I think he's going to be a good dad. You should have seen him the day after the birth. He was all puffed up with pride like he was about to burst."

"How about your new friend, Helga? Tell me about him."

"Rufus, Rufus McGuire. He's a bit older, has a couple of grown children. I met him at a fundraiser. He's a widower. He worked for an insurance company, has money and is good looking."

"Is he Catholic?"

"As a matter of fact he is, but that's not why I like him. He's kind and considerate and likes many of the things I like, art shows, concerts and family. We enjoy doing things with his kids."

"I'm happy for you Helga. I hope things work out for you. What about you Robert? What have you been doing? Are you working somewhere?"

"Most definitely. I'm with a public relations firm that does work for a host of concerns, most of them Republican related, as you might guess."

"So what's the hottest issue on the table right now, Robert?"

"It's an election year Pelon, what else? All the Republican presidential candidates are scrambling for the post position. We just had the Iowa Caucus and of course Romney looks like he'll be hard to beat. But you know that already."

"Yeah. I was hoping that you would give me the real scoop, you know, what's really at the heart of Republican thinking, right now."

"Off the record, I think that Republicans as well as Democrats are really worried about the mood of the country regarding reforms in various areas, such as elections, banking, the Federal Reserve, investments, even the status of corporations. It seems that the mood of the entire world really, is one of regular folks beginning to take notice that they are getting screwed and they want to put a stop to it. The Arab Spring in the Middle East is somewhat of a preview of what we in this country will be experiencing. It scares a lot of people and most people are not talking openly about their fears."

"And why is that?" Helga asked.

"Because Helga, to give voice to these fears indicates to everyone that they like the status quo. They know and understand the system that has evolved, that's in place. They are one with this system, hardwired for this system. A new system will have different values, different behaviors, and attitudes that are foreign, even distasteful to them."

"Ima told me something similar one day," I said. "She was telling me about the earth receiving new energies that will be supporting new values and new behaviors, that the world of dog-eat-dog was coming to an end."

"Doo dee doodooo," Helga said, a la Twilight zone theme song.

"It is stretching credibility Pelon," Robert said when I furrowed my eyebrows at Helga.

"I know it is, but I haven't seen anything else that tries to explain the phenomena of people trying to take power."

"But do you actually believe such nonsense?" Helga asked

"Let's say that I'm keeping score between it being right or it being wrong. Right now Ima's explanation is ahead."

"But how did she come up with such a scenario? Is it coming from that cult she belongs to? That would make perfect sense if it came from them."

"No it doesn't come from that group. On the contrary, Ima is becoming self-marginalized because they are not embracing this thinking."

"Don't tell me she's a psychic," Robert said.

"No she's not a psychic but she does get it from people that are, people that are channeling this information."

"This is going from bad to worse, Pelon. Who have you gotten mixed up with? Is she practicing witchcraft?"

"Hell no, she's not into any witchcraft. Just keep an open mind will you. Channeling is no different than any of the messages that were given to the children at Fatima or Lourdes. And you believe those, don't you Helga?"

"But those are different. That was Mary appearing. Those were miraculous apparitions."

"I saw the film on Fatima and it was entertaining, but I can't say that I believe that it really took place," Robert said, matter-of-fact.

"Millions do though and it's they that will begin to see that channelings have been with us for a long time."

"God Pelon, I can't believe how much you have changed in one year. You're like another person," Helga said.

"I think all of us have changed. We are all evolving," I added.

"Maybe so. I guess I have changed too. I think I know myself a lot better," Helga said.

A serviceman suddenly entered the room and handed me some papers and a bag with my clothing. "You're free to go," he said. "When you change into your clothes, go down the hall and take a left at the double doors. Show the guard your paperwork and you'll be escorted off the base."

"Thanks," I said. I looked at Helga and Robert. "Can you give me a ride out of here?"

"Can you Robert? I have to pick up Rufus," Helga said.

"It'll be my pleasure," Robert answered.

Helga and I hugged one last time and said goodbye with a wave of emotion sweeping over us that seemed sad and hopeful at the same time. We were both sporting tears when we broke away to go our respective ways.

"Do you want to stay at my place?" Robert asked when we were driving into D.C.

"Maybe for a couple of days. I want to see the gang of four before leaving. Can we arrange that?"

"Most certainly. I know that they want to see you too."

When we reached Robert's home, I used my new cell phone to call Ima.

"Hello Ima. It's me."

"Pelon! Are you ok? Where are you? I haven't been able to learn anything about you."

"And here I thought you were an expert at finding information with all that computer background that you have."

"Don't try to make light of this Pelon. I've been going crazy with worry."

"I'm sorry. I was just trying to let you know that I am well and that everything will work out. I'm here with my friend Robert in D.C."

"They freed you?" she asked with great surprise.

"Sort of. I cut a deal with Andre."

"What sort of deal, Pelon?"

"I'll have to plead no contest to a misdemeanor charge of assault, and probably have to serve six months in Lompoc."

"Six Months! Pelon you don't deserve six months in prison for something that was not your fault."

"Not in this life I don't, but maybe in some previous one," I said smiling.

"You don't know that. All we know is that some malevolent creep acting on behalf of equally malevolent persons is trying to cover up their evil deeds."

"I know but I couldn't risk getting found guilty on a felony charge of assault. That carries years in prison and disbarment. I had no other choice. I'll serve my time and get back to my life. But how about you, how are you?"

"I'm fine. In spite of all that's going on, I'm fine. I've kept busy with work and doing my usual at the temple. I am finding though that I need to go there less and less for meditation. Meditation at home by myself seems to work just fine for me."

"I missed celebrating the 2012 New Year with you," I said. "Did you spend it at your father's place?"

"No, he came down here and we went to the beach and lit candles and sent them out to sea. And you already know how he likes to conclude an evening."

"Yeah I do. Your dad is an original. Incidentally, speaking of 2012, have you noticed that time seems to be speeding up? I can't believe that we're in February already."

"It does seem that way, when we are in a dimension where there is no time, and where we just live in the present, in the now."

"Wouldn't you know it? My telephone battery has run out. Ironic, no?" I said.

"Oh Pelon there's so much I want to share with you. When can you call again? And when will you be home?"

"I'll call you tonight. And I'll book a flight later today."

"All right, take care Pelon."

By six that evening when Naomi and Esperanza came over to Robert's, I had booked a flight to San Diego for the next day. Robert's partner was out of town and we had the house to ourselves.

"Hello there. Welcome. You are both looking fabulous," I heard Robert say when he went to answer the front doorbell.

"Well what's the big surprise?" I heard Naomi ask and realized why Robert had asked me to sit away from the door. "Is Farley already here?" Naomi asked.

I heard coats rustling. "He'll be here momentarily. Here let me take your coats."

Esperanza and Naomi walked into the front room holding hands and they both stopped when they saw me and gasped.

Esperanza was the first to regain her voice and she screamed "Pelon!"

And she rushed over to hug me.

Naomi was still in shock but finally she went over to hug me and the three of us stood there embracing, until I began to feel uncomfortable and eased away.

"You both look great," I said.

"Thanks Pelon, but what I want to hear right now is, how is it that you're here." Naomi said. "What happened since we last spoke?"

"Why don't we all sit down," Robert said, "and have some wine until Farley gets here. That way Pelon doesn't have to repeat everything."

"Maybe you and Esperanza can tell me what's been going on at the office. That's something that Farley can miss," I said.

"That story might take all evening," Esperanza volunteered.

"The abbreviated version is that we're both disenchanted and are looking for a way to bail on Congressman Jimmy," Naomi said.

"It's amazing what a creep he's turned out to be," Esperanza added.

"He still has some good qualities. It's not as if he turned completely to the dark force like Darth Vader," Naomi explained. "He still supports lots of good legislation that will benefit Chicanos and the Tucson area he represents."

"It's only that now we know that he's beholden to some money interests and we can never be sure what he'll support," Esperanza said.

"Does anybody else in the office know?" I asked.

"That's the thing Pelon. We weren't about to jeopardize your chances of survival by letting this information out," Naomi said.

"We were watching your back like we said we would," Esperanza said. "But we were also concerned for our safety and Robert's."

The doorbell rang and Robert got up to answer it. "It's probably Farley," he said.

Naomi was describing the session with Andre when Robert's voice rang out. "You can't just barge in," followed by the noise of men's feet and the door being pushed open and slamming against the wall. Andre walked into the room followed by two large men in dark suits. Esperanza, Naomi and I sat with mouths agape.

"I'm glad to see that you're all here. It makes things much easier for me," Andre said. "So we're off to a good start and I hope that with your cooperation it can continue in that way."

Robert stood at the room's threshold with a bloody nose.

"You can go take care of that nose Robert, I wouldn't want your white carpet to get stained," Andre said and Robert hurried off.

"As I was saying," Andre continued, "I hope we can come to some understanding as your life may depend on it."

"Why are you doing this Andre? I thought we already had an agreement," I said.

"We do. We do. I just wanted to make sure that everyone involved has the same information and the proper emotion attached to it, an emotion which I'm sure is being impressed on you right now. So don't fuck with me and everything will be ok."

Robert had come back into the room with a small towel to his nose.

"I think you have seen and heard most of what I wanted to convey Robert, and unless you have questions we'll be on our way." Andre and his men withdrew and we heard them go out the door.

"You all right Robert?" Naomi asked.

"Yes I'm fine. I'm more perturbed by the invasion of my home. What an uncouth son of a bitch he is."

"Come sit, Robert. Can I get you some ice?"

"Yes thank you."

We all tried to get Robert comfortable while trying to fathom what we were feeling and trying to figure out what we could say to one another after the shock of tonight's drama. The doorbell rang again and momentarily we all held our breath until I volunteered to answer it. I returned with Farley in tow.

Most times Farley was able to modulate his naturally high-pitched voice but upon seeing Robert sitting on the couch with a bloodied towel he let out a piercing shriek. "Oh my God Robert have you been shot?"

"Calm down Farley. He just has a bloody nose," Esperanza told him.

"Sit down and have some wine and we'll tell you all about it," Naomi said.

We all sat down and we all drank a bit of wine and settled our nerves.

Naomi and Esperanza took turns describing to Farley what we had just lived through including how Robert's nose got bloodied. And when that was finished I was asked to tell them what I had experienced since our last gathering. I grew weary giving every detail that I could remember and still they had questions, which I dutifully answered. Robert ordered a couple of pizzas and brought out more wine and we continued way into the night, and everyone, except myself, got a little tipsy.

"So the quick and dirty version of what you're saying, Pelon," Naomi slurred, "and what Andre has so dramatically and nightmarishly made clear, is that we risked our jobs, we risked going to jail and we have even put our lives on the line for nothing, nada, mierda?"

"We are better people for it," I said smiling.

There was raucous laughter by Naomi, Esperanza and Farley. Robert merely smiled.

"It's true that what is on the flash drive, both what we saw that evening at Naomi and Esperanza's apartment and what Pelon and his fiancée Ima discovered later, is information that cannot be made public at the risk of getting killed. But I, working at the NRDC, can investigate individuals on that list and see what other dirt I can find on them. It'll be like reverse engineering a piece of technology since I know what individuals are corrupt and I try to work from there."

"That's true Farley," Naomi said.

"And quite possible," Robert added.

"It'll take time and patience, not nearly as fast or as efficient as releasing the list all at once," Esperanza said.

"And we'll all be better people," I said and Naomi threw a cushion at my head.

Naomi asked me to drive her and Esperanza home in their car and said I could sleep in the spare bedroom. She also volunteered to drive me to the airport the next day. They fell asleep on the way home and left me to ponder all that had transpired. The funny part was that I no longer felt any anger or animosity toward Andre. I saw him as just another actor playing out his part. I also marveled at how Esperanza had grown during the time I was away, and how well she and Naomi worked as a team. Life was amazing, I thought.

The next day they both went to the airport to drop me off.

"It's been fun, Pelon," Naomi said.

"And a great learning," Esperanza added.

"I expect you at the wedding," I said.

"Just let us know when and where. We'll be there. Bye Pelon. Call us when you arrive."

"Bye Naomi. And I will call," I said. "Bye Esperanza. Don't take any wooden Bitcoins."

"You know about Bitcoins?"

"Course. I'm not a technology dinosaur."

CHAPTER XV

I flew to Los Angeles and again took the two trains that brought me into Encinitas. Ima met me at the station and after a long hug we started walking up the hill to her studio apartment.

"When will you have to start serving that sentence, Pelon?"

"I have a court date in Santa Barbara next week and I'll be sentenced then. Did you find the warrant for my arrest on that database you worked on?"

"Yes it was there just as you said, assaulting an officer. Nothing else. I still think it's wrong to have taken that deal, Pelon."

"I know you do Ima, but after what I have experienced it'll be good to put this all behind me."

I then told her about Andre breaking into our meeting at Robert's home and the threats he made.

"He is a dangerous man," Ima said. "Maybe you are right in bringing this episode to a conclusion. I certainly would not want to have to be looking over our shoulder from now on."

"Don't you feel instinctively though, that the surveillance infrastructure will eventually come out into the open? I mean if what you have said is true, that transparency and the exposing of secrets is part and parcel of the 2012 energies?"

"Yes, I suppose that's true," she answered.

We reached the top of the hill and were walking on the paved road when Miguel passed by in his truck going in the opposite direction. He stopped and began backing up to where we were. I swallowed hard, not wanting to go through another confrontation.

"I sorry, Pelon," Miguel said as he leaned out the car's window.

Hearing Miguel apologize I felt compelled to hear what else he had to say and I told Ima that I wanted to have a private conversation with him.

"Absolutely," she said. "I'll just keep walking and see you at the house."

"Hello Miguel," I said when I walked over to his truck now parked on the shoulder of the road.

"Hello Pelon," he answered. "Sara and me want baby. We makes plan together. I come home too soon."

"You knew that Sara wanted me to have sex with her?" I said.

"Gez I knows! Sara Christian woman. She not puta! I no can have childrens, no money for doctor. This only way we thinks. "

"Well you could have asked me and saved us all this trouble," I said.

"You doos this for us?"

"No I can't."

"Why not? Sara good person, be good mother, me be good father."

"Don't ask me again Miguel. I can't do that," I said and walked away.

"You give me mecos, I put in Sara like horse," he yelled.

I continued walking and raised my hand and waved goodbye. Miguel started his truck and drove off.

Ima was halfway to the studio when I caught up to her and I recounted my conversation with Miguel.

"They sound so desperate to have a child. I would be okay with it, if you wanted to help them Pelon."

"Ima! That's not why I said no. I just don't like the idea of knowing that I fathered a child and then not being able to have any involvement."

"Maybe I'll ask my dad if he has any suggestions," Ima said. "I'm thinking of moving in with my dad while you're in Lompoc. It'll make it much easier to visit you on weekends."

"You'll give up the studio?"

"Yes, there's no good reason to keep it. I'm almost finished with my contract with the fire department, and if need be I can always take the train back here to Encinitas."

"That sounds good. Being able to see you every weekend will make the time go even faster."

We spent the next few days enjoying one another's company, taking long walks on the beach, visiting the teahouse, reading and having long conversations. We took the train to Santa Barbara the day before my court hearing, and that night stayed with Geoffrey.

The conversation with my court appointed lawyer as well as the actual court hearing, the next day, were perfunctory and I was sentenced to six months in Lompoc, making my release date in June of 2012 because of time already served. Ima and Geoffrey were present but I barely had time to signal them goodbye when they hauled me away.

"Are conjugal visits allowed?" was the first thing Ima asked when I was finally allowed to call her.

"No, they don't provide that as a privilege."

"Too bad. I'm dying to be with you."

"Me too. Soon my love. The time will pass quickly."

The following week I was able to have Ima visit. It was a cool foggy day when she drove up from Santa Barbara and we sat outside bundled in warm jackets.

"How is it in there?" she asked.

"Not bad but not great either. I'm assigned to the low security camp along with more than three hundred other inmates. It's a bit crowded. I sleep in one of the bungalows with bunks really close to one another. I can't even stretch out my arms without touching another inmate.

"That's horrid. You would think that such a large complex would have better sleeping arrangements."

"I just have four months left in my sentence. I can do this."

"I guess if you just go in at night to sleep it could be tolerated. But what about the daytime?" she asked.

"I'm assigned to the landscaping crew that maintains the Vandenberg base. We drive ourselves out there every morning and return in the late afternoon. It's actually a pretty good assignment."

"It's surprising that you can drive yourselves off the prison grounds."

"Only because we are very unlikely to try escaping. How are you doing Ima? You sound a little down."

"No I'm fine. Just tired that's all. I'm still having the classic ascension symptoms; fatigue, neck pain, heart burn, joint pain and I wake up at two or three in the morning. Every afternoon, I'm having to take short naps."

"Really I'm sorry that you're feeling so run down. Now I'm afraid that you have to drive back to Santa Barbara. Maybe you should rent a room at a motel and spend the night."

"No, I'll be fine. It's only an hour's drive. Besides I promised dad that I would coach him on the Internet tonight."

"He's still struggling?"

"Yes, he says that he wants to start a Facebook page and connect with old friends."

"Speaking of old friends, I saw Helga when I was at Langley.

"Oh, how is your old girlfriend?"

"She's good. She has a new boyfriend, some older guy with grown kids. You know what surprised me, well a couple of things surprised me, but one of them was that there I was talking about 2012 and the shift in consciousness. Me, can you imagine?"

"That is surprising. Were you just parroting or did it come from the heart?"

"Of course it came from the heart. I don't parrot. I've been digesting what you said, well that and other things."

"Like what other things?"

"Like, there was this kid in the county jail in Tucson and he told me that the government is spying on us, reading our emails and listening to our phone conversations, supposedly to catch terrorists and criminals like himself."

"I can believe it. Don't you remember a few years ago, when Bush was still president, there was an uproar when someone revealed that AT&T and Verizon were working with the NSA, supplying telephone records of millions of Americans. The technology to capture and analyze data has only gotten better so there's no telling what they now have on us. So yeah your fellow jailbird was probably right in thinking that his telephone and Internet communications were being compromised."

"That really sucks. The Internet was supposed to be a benefaction and now it's been weaponized to use against us."

"It's still useful, Pelon. Look how it's helping people communicate across long held prejudices like between Jews and Palestinians and it's helped democratize information and brought free education to millions.

"I don't discount that Ima. It's just that there are Machiavellian characters like Andre, using the Internet for unintended malevolent purposes."

"Well fortunately it won't be like that forever, the public is not going to stand for Orwell's 1984 becoming a reality."

We sat and talked on that foggy day for hours without a break, as easily as if we were sitting at Swami's Beach in Encinitas. She had brought sandwiches and a thermos of Pu'erh tea and we had a leisurely lunch and talked some more until visiting hours came to an end.

"Will you come next week?"

"Of course. And I'll bring you something to eat. What would you like?"

"Go to that taco place on Milpas and bring me some tacos de sesos."

"Yuk Pelon, brain tacos?"

"I like them and so does your dad so don't go judging me."

"OK, OK. I'll bring them."

We were allowed a hug and a kiss at the beginning and end of our visit and we took advantage of that opportunity both times. Having her body close to mine and tasting her lips was almost too much to bear and I considered passing on that privilege the next time she came.

I thought that the expectation of Ima's weekend visit would make weekdays seem long and arduous but I was surprised that it didn't happen. Quite the contrary I found myself continuously wondering where the time went. As usual I established a routine and in addition to reading the newspaper online and an occasional hard copy book from the library, I began an exercise regime after my job and before dinner.

My exercise program included punching and kicking the big bag to hone my martial arts skills and games of handball to increase my flexibility and lung capacity. Handball has become the game of choice for Chicanos in the joint as well as in the barrio. One only needs a ball and a wall for a game, although in the joint and in public parks, handball courts are readily available that have a front wall and two short sidewalls. It's a game that requires quickness and good hand-eye coordination, as well as ambidexterity because one has to strike the ball equally well with both left and right hands. Unlike the racquet sports that use only the one hand, handball works both sides of the body symmetrically and thus is particularly suited for martial arts training.

I had learned to play when I was at Juvi and I thought that it would be easy enough to get on the court and play a decent game. The court was twenty feet wide and about seventy feet long with a front wall and two short walls at the side that measured five feet. The object of the game was to hit the ball off the front wall in such a way as to make it impossible for the opponent to return it before it bounced more than once. Sidewalls could also be used for corner shots but the ball had to hit the front wall first. Games were often fast and strenuous.

"Hey I have the tele," I said when I saw a couple of dudes playing.

"Orale," one of the players said.

He was a short shirtless Chicano with the Virgen de Guadalupe prominently tattooed on his back as well as several other tattoos on his forearms and neck. He was serving the ball and working on his opponent's weak left hand and doing a good job of racking up points on his serve alone. But even when the other player was able to return the ball the server was quick to 'kill' the ball by placing it so low on the wall that it made another return impossible. The game ended 15 to 3.

I was up and the serve was determined by throwing the ball at the front wall from the back line to see who could place it the lowest. My throw was pathetic, hitting the wall a good two feet above the floor. My opponent's ball rolled cleanly off the lowest point of the wall. He then proceeded to surgically tear me apart with powerful serves to my left hand that even when I managed to return them, had so much backspin that they would career off my hand without even making it to the front wall. And when I did return them, he would hit them so low on the front wall that they simply died on the ground as they rolled off. The game mercifully ended 11 to 0.

I was bent over and breathing as if I had just finished a marathon race.

"Thanks for the game," my opponent said.

"That was no game ese. That was a mercy killing," I said.

"They call me Tito," he said. "You're new here?"

"Got in last week. My name's Pelon. Dude, you're a hell of a player. And I was terrible but give me a month and I'll give you a better game."

"You got it vato," he said. "See you around."

I haven't said this before because I know it's a bit silly, but I don't like to lose. And it doesn't matter what activity it is, handball, checkers, dominoes, a fight. I don't take it well when I lose at anything and I've been like this since I can remember. So I was left there by Tito with a long face and I got up from where I was sitting on the ground and walked over to the big bag and began punching the hell out of it.

"You can really punch that bag. Are you a fighter?" I heard a voice saying to me as I worked on the big bag. I stopped and turned to see who it was.

"No I don't fight if I can help it," I answered. "Matter of fact I'm here because I couldn't control myself and punched someone."

"Yeah I know what you mean young fellow. We all have something in us that needs to be controlled in one way or another. Name's Rogers, what's yours?"

"They call me Pelon. You're on that landscaping crew with me aren't you?"

"Yeah that's me all right. Best job in the camp, don't you think?"

"I prefer it. Nothing beats working with plants and flowers, especially near the ocean," I said and continued punching and kicking.

"Don't know as I would go that far, I'm more of a city person myself," Rogers said.

"Cities have their charm I suppose, but I prefer a bit more space between me and the next guy. So why are you here, Rogers?" I asked as I stopped to take a breather.

"Insider trading they say but it's…"

"It's a trumped up charge," I said finishing his sentence. He smiled and said, "Exactly."

"I hope you made a lot of money on that trade," I said and once again began punching and kicking at the bag.

"I made some but by the time I paid off fines and lawyers, hell I was in worse shape then when I started."

"They say crime doesn't pay."

"Not street crime. That's what they meant you know. They weren't talking about white collar crime cause that brings in a shitload of money."

"So why not you?" I asked. "Yours was as white collar as they get."

"Bad karma I guess, what else could it be?"

"You believe in Karma?" I asked.

"When it's convenient I do. I can't say that I was caught because I was stupid."

"Were you? Were you stupid."

"Stupid in telling my girlfriend what I had done. That bitch got herself a hefty reward out of the deal."

"That is bad karma dude," I said as I landed a thunderous kick on the big bag.

"Are you a Buddhist?" he asked me. "I mean believing in karma is a Buddhist thing."

"I don't know what I am at the moment," I answered. "So maybe."

"You're in some sort of transition I gather. That's a good place to be. I mean it's better than being a zealot about something, like some crazed Christian or Islamist."

"Yeah mostly it feels all right to be in a search mode."

Then Rogers excused himself saying that he had to attend to something before dinner. I continued with the bag, punching and kicking until my shirt was sopping wet and I was dripping with perspiration. I then did one hundred pushups and ended the workout with a hundred sit-ups. I showered and went to dinner.

Rogers became a good friend after that conversation and we often ended up working together at Vandenberg or talking politics and discussing current events.

I told Ima about him.

"He's an interesting guy, maybe your dad's age or just a bit younger but pudgy and very passionate about getting rid of the Federal Reserve and having a currency backed by gold or silver or maybe by a group of commodities. Do any of the channeled messages speak to that?"

"Not directly. The most important point to remember though is that all of our institutions are out of step with the new energies and they'll all be undergoing great transformations. The economy as we know it will change dramatically and this includes our banking system. That said, there are some messages that say that there will be five world currencies, one of them being a united Latin American currency and one of them a currency from a united Africa. I imagine one of them will be the Euro and another is the dollar. I don't know where the fifth will originate. Maybe Asia."

"No kidding. I would never have thought that African countries would come together. There's so much tribal baggage even within individual countries. Latin America however, even now I can see signs of that happening with the left-oriented leadership that has emerged."

"But look at European countries of fifty years ago, and now in spite of their present problems, have united in such a way that war amongst them has become near impossible. That's quite an achievement when one considers the many wars that have been fought on European soil. The future and the energies that support it will be about unity as opposed to separation," she said. "That's why the United States has been such a beautiful beacon for the entire world. It was created to show what was possible."

"I've never thought about it in that way but that's what's happened. I guess we'll just have to see if the prediction of those united currencies really occurs."

"Not predictions per se, more like high probabilities," she corrected.

I smiled. "I have a statement with a high probability. Exactly three months from now I'm going to make love to you."

"I know that you silly. You think I haven't been marking off the days on my calendar? And did you know that there's to be a big Summer Solstice celebration in Santa Barbara the day after your release?"

"On the twentieth?"

"They make quite a big deal of it every year. Even Dad gets into the spirit."

"Then it's a date," I said.

It was actually a little more than a month when I sought out Tito on the handball court. Since then I had learned that he was the regional handball champ and hardly anyone chose to play him as they inevitably lost. I had been practicing by myself, working on my weak left hand, even resorting to using it exclusively when I worked with hand tools at my work or handling the fork when I ate. Running around and punching the bag had greatly increased my wind and I felt that I was much better prepared this time around.

"Orale Tito. I'm ready for you dude. How about we have us a game?"

"Sounds good to me Pelon. I don't get that many challenges from these sissies around here," he said it loud enough for others to hear.

Tito won the serve and again proceeded to dominate me with his precise serves chock full of backspin. I did manage to at least stay in the game to its conclusion and even scored some points. The final score was 15 to 5.

"Not bad Pelon. You improved a whole lot dude."

"Not enough to beat you though. It looks like I need more time on the court, how about we play more often."

"I'm always ready for a game. I can meet you here right after work," he said.

"All right," I answered. "What day?"

"Tuesdays and Thursdays are good for me Pelon."

"I'll be here. I ain't going anyplace. What's your story anyway, Tito? Why are you here?"

"Just some stupid shit. I was charged with drug trafficking and given five years. I have two left, maybe less for good behavior. How about you dude?"

"Assaulting a Fed. I'll be out in a couple of months. Tell me though, were you actually trafficking drugs?"

"Hell no ese. Half the Chicano dudes and Blacks are here for the same thing. They have this bullshit mandatory sentencing to catch the big kahunas and it's the people of color that get popped. It's not right dude."

"I saw you with a woman and some kids last Sunday. Is that your family?"

"Yeah. That was my old lady and two of my sons. I have an older boy but he don't like coming up here to see me."

"They live in Lompoc?"

"No in Santa Barbara. They moved up there from East LA to make it easier to visit with me. It's been really hard ese. Man, if I could move back the clock, you know what I'm saying?"

"Definitely."

And for the next three months playing handball with Tito was my passion. Those games became the camp entertainment and for every game a small crowd gathered to watch us.

"Unbelievable," Ima said when I told her about my aversion to losing. "Does that mean that when I win at Scrabble you'll go sulk in your room?"

"Who said that I was going to lose? The probability of that happening is quite low my friend," I said. "Peruse the dictionary at every opportunity and maybe I won't beat you so badly."

"Ha, ha," she mocked. "I have better things to do with my free time."

"You have free time? Did you finish the program for the fire department?"

"I did, and it came out way better than even I thought it would. It made me realize how seductive technology is. It stealthily draws you in and before you know it, you're addicted to its power. It's little wonder that computer nerds spend countless hours on their machines. It gives them a sense of control that maybe they don't think they have in their real lives."

"And you think that non-nerds have control over their lives?"

"I know so. Actually I think that everyone has control. Everyone can exercise their will to make decisions. A particular decision may not always bring us what we truly desire but it may be the best one possible under a set of given circumstances."

"Like the one I made that landed me here," I said.

"Yeah…. Like that one. But the thing is that it's even more important to use our free will to stay positive and to have utopian dreams of a life on Earth where humanity will manifest more love and compassion for one another. We are being given the opportunity to be co-creators of the world we live in and it's a responsibility of those that are already awakened to this possibility to act accordingly."

"Do you think that I am awakened to this fact, of being positive and capable of dreaming of a more just and equitable world for everyone?" I asked.

"Of course I do. That why I stalked you."

"Aha. So you're finally admitting it? That's nice to know. I'm glad you did."

On a weekend that Ima was not visiting, my mother and stepfather showed up unannounced. I had spoken on the telephone to my mother several times and I had put her on my list of visitors but I was completely surprised when I was told that I had visitors.

"Gee Mom, what a nice surprise. Hey Jess how you doing?" I asked my stepfather.

"I'm pretty good. I guess you know I retired. What's that expression when something happens that you think has happened before?"

"You mean *déjà vu*?"

"Yes that's it, *déjà vu*. It's like when we paid you a visit at that camp you were at."

"That was a long time ago. And I hope this is the last time you have to visit me behind bars. And you Mom, how are you?"

"I'm good mijo, just older and not as good on my feet as I used to be."

"How about Grandma? What have you heard?"

"I talked to Clara last week and your grandma has been doing pretty good. She's eating and once in awhile can use her walker to spend some time outside before it gets too hot."

"Really. That doctor had it all wrong, didn't he?"

"Even death is afraid of your grandma," Jess said laughing.

"She's tough all right," I said. "Any plans to visit her?"

"No, not right now. It's such a long hot drive in summer mijo," Mom answered. "I told you we went in March. Maybe in October we'll go again."

"What do you do in here Pelon?" Jess asked me.

I explained to them my work at Vandenberg and my exercise routine. Jess was particularly interested in my handball games because he used to play when he was younger.

"Back in the 1960's I used to play on Main Street by the old brewery in Lincoln Heights," he said. "They had a court with a very long side wall and they used a ball that felt like it was made of bone and it hurt like hell when you hit it."

"No kidding? It must have left your hands badly swollen."

"Oh yeah. But I only stopped playing when I became a butcher because I couldn't grip my knives with those sore hands. Otherwise I might still be playing."

"Oh come on Jesus," my mother said, using his unabbreviated name. "With your pansa hanging over your belt you have a hard time even tying your shoes."

"If I was still playing I wouldn't have this pansa," he said. "Ain't that right Pelon?"

"It's a pretty intense workout," I said. "So you probably would be nice and trim."

We talked and kidded for a few hours and ate some sandwiches that mom had packed.

And yes, it seemed like *déjà vu*.

It was my 13th game with Tito and I had less than two weeks before my release. The games had gotten progressively closer and more heated but Tito had managed to beat me every time. The number of inmates watching the games had grown too and there were bets being taken, some for me and some against. The previous game, the 12th, had been grueling, the rallies going as many as seven or eight returns after the initial serve and leaving both of us sweating and tired. That one ended 15 to 12, not my best score but one where I nearly had him when we were tied at 12 apiece.

"Orale Tito. Did you come ready to lose?" I asked.

"No ese, I came ready to bury your ass so deep they'll need shovels to dig you out."

"In your dreams homie," I said. "Thirteen is my lucky number dude."

"Throw for serve vato, you can't beat me with talk."

I won serve for the first time ever and I felt good when I ran up three points by serving long high lobs that would land just inside the back line and then bounce far outside the court, making Tito's returns long and usually hitting at midpoint on the front wall where I easily killed them.

My fourth serve was again a long lob but Tito anticipated where it was to land and he caught it midair before it bounced and he killed it by hitting the corner, so close to the ground that it died without even a small bounce.

He also served long lobs mixed with an occasional fast corner serve that sent the ball crosscourt at an extremely sharp angle and for all practical purposes irretrievable. He ran up five points before I caught him off guard with a long tall lob when he was playing up front, anticipating a low return to the front wall.

From then on each point was fought aggressively with several returns by each one of us, many from deep outside the court and it took arm strength and stamina to keep returning the ball from that distance.

We were both exhausted at fourteen to fourteen, with Tito having earned the last point and now was about to serve. One had to win by two points so when he won the next rally that had an amazing ten returns, the game was not yet over. We were both dripping perspiration from our shirtless upper bodies and the front and back of our shorts had absorbed the sweat as it ran down. I checked on a bone bruise that had developed on my right hand just below the index finger. It was tender and painful and I knew it would hinder my game.

Tito's next serve was a low and fast cross court shot to my left that I caught by stretching and bending as low as I could possibly go but my return was weak and he easily returned it with a long lob that barely landed inside but bounced far outside the court and I had to race as fast as I could and barely managed to return my own high lob that sent him scurrying to the back. He had time to consider sending another high lob towards the back or attempting to kill it low on the front wall. He chose a corner shot off the front wall that I had to chase and again barely managing to make a weak return. He had the advantage at this point and was making me run from front to back and hoping to tire me enough to place a final death shot. He chose a lob shot and sent me running and again I made a feeble return. I sensed that he was toying with me now. Somehow he instinctively knew that it was his game to win and he made me run a few more times before he placed a powerful low shot to the front that barely trickled off the front wall. Game over 16 to 14.

After catching our breaths, we shook hands.

"Damn Tito. I was sure I had you when I scored that fourteenth point. How the hell did you ever make that shot that tied us?"

"It was a good one wasn't it? Hell I don't know. Maybe I just closed my eyes and prayed."

"That's it for me dude. You know I get out next week. I concede vato. You are the man."

"Thanks Pelon. It was good playing with you. We played some tough games. And good luck out there dude. It's a jungle you know, so stay outta trouble."

"You too Tito and if you don't mind my saying you have to stop seeing yourself as a victim of the system. Man up to your responsibility, just like you do on the court."

"Orale, that sounds good ese," he said and we knocked our right fist together and then slid our open palm on one another's in the style of the modern Chicano handshake.

On the last day before my release I said goodbye to Rogers.

"You take care Rogers. I'll send you my address as soon as I get a place. Still don't know where that will be, maybe Santa Barbara, maybe Encinitas, maybe Tucson, maybe some place I haven't even thought about. In a quantum world, anything is possible."

"There's not much quantum to this place, so you'll know where'll I'll be for the next three months."

"Definitely," I said.

Processing my release took forever. I kept thinking that at any minute someone would appear and say that I was not going anywhere but back to my assigned bungalow. But that didn't happen and by midafternoon I was holding Ima, who was crying with joy.

"How do women do that?" I asked, "Cry when they are happy? It's very strange, I think."

"We're just better equipped to release bottled up emotion. You men have to get ulcers and whatnot."

"Maybe so. Right now though, I really don't care. All I care about is that I'm free and driving back to Santa Barbara with you. God it feels GOOD," I yelled.

Ima laughed. "Yell as much as you want, Pelon."

.^.^.^.

CHAPTER XVI

It was a beautiful day to drive along the coast, the ocean calm and nary a cloud in the blue sky. The land rises from the water rather steeply in that stretch of Highway 101, yet the railroad managed to lay rails for the passenger train that goes between Los Angeles and Oakland. There wasn't much traffic on the highway and soon we were passing the town of Goleta where the University of Santa Barbara is located, just outside their namesake city. Thirty minutes later we were standing with Geoffrey outside his Montecito home.

"Welcome back Pelon," he said. "I did jail a few times back in the days and even with a bunch of my friends in the same cell it was no picnic, so I can't imagine what four months was like."

"Really it wasn't too bad. It was a minimum-security camp and nothing like a real jail, with street gangs of hardened career criminals. There it would have been much tougher."

"Well the thing is that you're out and free of that heavy burden that you were carrying around," he said.

"It feels good to be out from under it, it was really stressful."

"Well listen, I need to run some errands but I'll be back in a couple of hours and maybe we can get something to eat down at the festival. They always have good food booths down at the old courthouse plaza," Geoffrey said.

"OK Dad," Ima said.

After Geoffrey left we went inside to our bedroom and tore at one another's clothing and made enchanted love that left us spent and laughing at the torridness of it all.

"Wow! Ima it's been too long."

"Yes and I never want to be separated that long from you again," she said.

After we showered we made love again, but this time it was slow and affectionate, with lots of conversation squeezed in.

"When are we getting married Pelon?" she asked.

"Whenever you want. The only item on my agenda is to return to Tucson and see how my grandma is doing."

"You'll see Lorraine too, won't you?"

"Yeah but aren't you going with me?"

"I just bid on a job with a local Internet company called RAIN, and I think I'll need to be around here. We'll have to see what's going on with that project when it's time for you to leave."

When Geoffrey returned we all were hungry and we hurried off to the festival. We ate and then along with tens of thousands, saw an amazing dance performance on the outdoor stage, the dancers attired in elaborate and beautiful costumes. Other stage performances followed, with bands, jugglers, fire dancers and on the grounds costumed revelers of all ages, all celebrating Mother Earth and humanity's relationship with Her. And there were young people drunk and acting like young drunk people, many of them students at UCSB.

"This reminds me of a festival I attended last year when I stood next to a Hindu Goddess," I said to Ima.

"Really," she said. "Maybe you'll see her again."

"That would be really nice," I said. " I could use some of her curative powers."

"I've always liked the Summer Solstice Celebration," Geoffrey said. "It's one of the new age ceremonies with roots in every culture and so it belongs to everyone."

"Exactly," Ima said. "And I would like us to go to tomorrow's parade and be part of it."

Both Geoffrey and I agreed and the next morning we had an early breakfast and Ima excused herself to get ready for the parade while Geoffrey and I cleaned the kitchen.

"Ima tells me that you two are getting married. That makes me very happy," Geoffrey said as he washed dishes and I rinsed and stacked them for air-drying. "Have you set a date?"

"No not yet. Maybe as soon as I return from Tucson."

"Ima's not going with you?"

"No, she said she has a bid on a project with an Internet provider here in Santa Barbara."

"Well I have some money saved for this occasion so if you need it, it's available."

"Thanks Geoffrey, that's very nice of you to offer."

Ima walked in, dressed in her Hindu Goddess costume.

"Ok I'm ready," she announced. "Let's go celebrate Summer Solstice."

And she waved three of her arms as if to say let's go.

"What in the world are you wearing, Ima?" Geoffrey asked.

"I'm a Hindu Goddess and Pelon requested my presence and access to my curative powers. So here I am. Can we go now?"

We drove the short distance from Montecito to the center of town. Santa Barbara is unique in having a very strict architectural code that demands that all buildings in the downtown area be constructed in the Spanish Mission style, with thick walls that look like adobe construction and red tile roofs. And the setting is spectacular, adjacent to the ocean and the Santa Ynez Mountains rising in the opposite direction. The proximity of mountains and ocean has restricted growth and the population has spread north and south creating smaller towns such as Goleta where UCSB is located and Montecito where Geoffrey lived.

The parade was along State Street in the center of town. It was packed with people lining both sides of the street, many of them in costume, some even more outlandish than Ima's. The parade was like no other I had seen, truly New Age in many respects, many of the hundreds of floats sporting a theme of Mother Earth and indigenous cultures that once inhabited this and the surrounding regions. There were of course many bands and drumming groups and dozens of costumed men and women dancing Samba, like in Brazilian Mardi Gras.

"This is some parade," I said to Ima, who was standing next to me. Geoffrey had wandered off to have a conversation with a friend.

"It's great isn't it?" Ima said. "I feel so at home in events like this one and Halloween at the temple. What do you think is common to both of them that makes them so appealing to me?"

"Maybe because they both give free rein to people's creativity and, I don't know if this is true for you, they both have pagan origins," I answered.

"You're right. They are very pagan. Maybe that's what it is – they dig deep into our archetypal memory. They open us up to our essence, one that predates modern day religions and their restrictive, guilt-ridden interpretation of God and human nature."

"Amen," I said. "And I think that's what I felt at the rain dance ceremony with Lorraine and her grandfather—raw human cravings for rain, devoid of meteorological data or scientific reasoning.

The next day I took the train to Los Angeles and had to wait in the classic depot for my train to Tucson. Unlike my previous visit, I took time to observe it closely. The depot is designed somewhat in Mission style, lots of geometric designs in the floor tile and on walls, very high beamed ceilings with intricate designs between the beams, wooden benches and seats upholstered in leather that look like mission furniture and all of that cavernous space illuminated by beautiful hanging iron chandeliers. Outside were nicely landscaped enclosed gardens, reminiscent of Spanish/Moorish patios that I had seen in films and photographs.

I was wandering the depot and stopped to watch a film crew that had apparently rented a roped off section and were filming an action film. Actors were punching and kicking and throwing themselves on the floor. One of them was pushed and his unexpected momentum was about to land him on two girls standing to my left. Instinctively I braced myself, caught him and pivoted, releasing him back towards the fight. The move felt and looked like a man throwing the hammer in the Olympics and everyone in the crowd thought it was part of the film and they clapped appreciatively.

Moments later the director yelled cut and the small crowd of onlookers began to disperse.

"Sir," someone called as I was walking away. I turned and saw that it was I that a man was beckoning. I stopped when he began speaking.

"The director was wondering if you would be willing to allow us to include that fight scene where you caught and swung the stuntman. He thought it was great and wants to keep it in the film. Of course you would be remunerated accordingly."

"Sure I can do that," I said. "Did you want me to sign a release?"

"Yes and I have it right here," he said and withdrew a few pages from a leather portfolio and handed them to me along with a fountain pen.

"I need a few minutes to read this over. Do you mind if I sit?" I asked.

"Oh no. Please do. It's just a standard legal form that our stunt men sign. And it authorizes us to pay you at the union daily rate. It's about eight hundred dollars. Not bad for a few minutes of work."

"OK, it looks harmless enough for me to sign," I said when I finished reading the contract and I took the pen and placed my signature on a couple of the forms. I used Geoffrey's home as my mailing address.

"I know this zip code," he said, "93108 is one of the country's top ten for wealth and prestige. You're neighbors with some of Hollywood's best."

"Naw, not really. It belongs to my future father-in-law. I just don't have a permanent address right now."

"Are you between jobs, Herculano? Is that really your name?" he asked when he saw my signature.

"My legal name, but everybody calls me Pelon. And yes you could say that I'm jobless at the moment."

"Listen Pelon, my name is John Friday, and frankly what you did took great reflexes and quick thinking. You probably prevented us from having to fight off an injury lawsuit if that stuntman had landed in the crowd. I coordinate the stuntmen and I could use you in the rest of the film if you're interested."

"Good to meet you John," I said, stretching my hand out to shake his hand. "Sounds like fun but right now I'm going to Tucson to see my grandmother, so it's not a good time."

"Think about this type of work and when you get back this way, give me a call. Here's my card. You never know where Hollywood will take you. There's been several stuntmen that have turned out to be well paid actors."

"Yes I will think about it. I have always thought that I could be the Chicano Jackie Chan," I said smiling.

"Are you a martial artist Pelon?"

"I've studied martial arts for a number of years."

"Even better," he said. "Look, I have to get back to the set but give me a call, all right?"

"I will."

It was time to get our seat assignments and I went and stood in line and was soon joined by two teenage girls that were busy conversing with one another and texting at the same time. I recognized them as part of the crowd of onlookers and the ones that would have been most impacted by the stuntman had he run into us.

One of them looked up from her phone and noticing me asked, "Aren't you that stuntman?" and motioned towards the cordoned off area where the film crew was filming.

"No, I was looking, just like you."

"Well you saved our asses you know. Shit he was coming right at us. Can I take your picture? I was just texting my friend about what happened. Wait till she hears that you weren't part of the film at all."

"Yes I guess it would be okay," I answered.

"I just uploaded the video too, showing you grabbing that guy and spinning him back to the action. It was great."

"You videoed all of it?" I asked in surprise.

"Hell yes. It'll probably go viral too. My name's Sandra and my pal here is Squeaky cause she's so mousy."

"Hi Sandra, Squeaky. My name's Pelon."

Squeaky, a short shy girl of 16 or so, was dressed like her friend Sandra in tight shorts with a blouse tied at the midriff. Her dark hair was cut short in a bob and later I learned that her real name was Irene Mendez. Sandra was tallish, maybe 5'9" and the obvious leader in this duet. They were both pretty but Sandra's bravado made her the more appealing of the two.

"Where are you going, Pelon?" Sandra asked. "I hope it's San Antonio, cause that's where we're headed."

"I'm going to visit my grandmother in Tucson."

"Damn, it would have been fun to ride with you," Sandra said. "Maybe we can talk in the lounge car later, Pelon?"

"Sure that would be nice," I answered and wondered what in the world we could talk about.

We got our seat assignments and together we walked down the long corridor and up the stairs that led to the track where our train was waiting and there we parted and went to board our respective cars.

The train left at ten thirty, and by the time we were outside the city limits, probably near Redlands, I was asleep and didn't wake until we were pulling out of Maricopa, near Phoenix and two hours outside of Tucson. It was already dawn and I stayed awake until we arrived.

I used the cell telephone that Ima had given me to call her.

"Good morning Ima. I just got into Tucson. Are you up already?"

"I was lying in bed thinking."

"What about?"

"Our wedding. What do you think of getting married in Encinitas?"

"That would be fine with me. I'm sure my mother would be able to come and maybe a few old friends from Los Angeles."

"I'll make some calls then. And how was the train ride?"

"Uneventful. I slept most of the way. But I did have an interesting experience at the Union Station and next year you may be married to a movie action hero." I proceeded to tell her the story, which left her laughing at the possibility of a stuntman career.

"That's way too funny, Pelon."

"I'll tell you what's even funnier," I said and then told her the story of Sandra uploading a video of me in action. "Look for it when you get a chance," I said.

"I will, first chance I get, Pelon. Maybe you will become an action hero."

"Well I should let you get on with your day. What are you doing later?" I asked.

"I have a meeting with Timothy, the founder of RAIN, that ISP that I might do some work for. And you?"

"I'm going over to my grandmother's and at some point calling Lorraine. I'll check on you tonight or call me if you want. I have a phone now, you know."

"Yes I do know. All right have a good day love. Bye."

"Bye," I said and hung up.

I called Lorraine, hoping I would find her at her house and ask for a ride to my grandmother's.

She answered on the third ring.

"This is Pelon. Am I waking you up?"

"Hell no Pelon. Remember I have this little tit sucker and he wakes up early and hungry. He's on board right now as we speak. Where are you calling from homeboy? Are you still locked up?"

"No they cut me loose last week. I'm here in Tucson."

"Really, well get your ass over here so I can see you dude."

"So you're at home and not with Otavio?"

"Oh yeah, I've been here for over a month. I'm even back to work if you can believe it."

"Really. And how is the baby and who takes care of it?"

"Can't you come over and talk in person. My son's going to the clinic for shots in a little while, it'd be like old times."

"Where's your appointment. Maybe I can meet you there."

"It's right there on Congress, at the El Rio Clinic."

"It's eight now, what time?"

"My appointment is at nine."

"Okay I'll be there," I said, knowing that it was not far from the train station and I could walk there.

I took my time walking to the clinic, enjoying the deep blue sky of the desert and the cool morning temperature. Later I knew the summer temps would be triple digits and anyone on the streets would be staying close to anything casting shade—buildings, houses, trees, bridges, cars, etc. I arrived at the clinic and took a seat in the waiting room.

"Wow! You look like your old self, Lorraine," I said when she walked into the clinic building. She was lugging a diaper bag with one hand and her baby held in the other arm. I got up from my seat and walked toward her.

She sat her diaper bag down and we hugged for a long time.

"What's going on, Lorraine?"

"Oh same old stuff. Trying to work things out with James. I think I've just about given up on the asshole."

"I'm sorry to hear that. Last time I saw him he looked pretty enthralled to be a daddy."

"Yeah well the reality is a bit harder than the initial rush one gets at being a parent. He was here for about a month and then left, saying he was not sure that he could settle down. Meaning that he couldn't take the crying and changing shitty diapers. How about you? What's going on with Ima?"

"I'm good and so is Ima. Actually we're going to get married soon."

"Oh hell. There goes my last chance at matrimony," she said. "No seriously Pelon, I'm happy for you and Ima is very nice. Maybe you can ask her if you can take a second wife. I could be the one that bears the children."

I laughed at her suggestion, knowing that she was kidding but also hurting inside. We sat and talked. She had conversed several times with either Naomi or Esperanza so she knew much of what had taken place. What she didn't know I recounted, in particular details of my arrest and my encounter with Andre when I negotiated an end to my fugitive status, and my time spent in Lompoc. She enjoyed the story of my obsession with handball but she laughed most at what took place at the Union Station with the film crew and Sandra posting the video on the Internet.

"Damn homeboy you're going to be a media star. I have to find that video when I get to work."

Our conversation was halted when a nurse came out into the lobby and called her and the baby. Lorraine asked me to go in with them and I did. It was torturous, her son letting out bloody murder screams when he was poked and no one being able to console him until Lorraine finally stuck her nipple into his mouth.

"Well that's one experience I don't want to repeat," I said.

"Oh it wasn't that bad, Pelon. It'll be worse when I can't pacify him with my breast."

"What now?" I asked. "Are you going to the office?"

"I should. I have a ton of work. And you, what are your plans?"

"I need to go see my grandmother and I want to spend more time with you, maybe even visit your grandfather. Is that possible?"

"Definitely. I want to see you too. We'll have dinner with him."

"That sounds good. Can you drop me off in South Tucson?"

"Oh sure. It's near my childcare."

"Speaking of your child, when are you going to give him a proper name?"

"I think it's going to be soon. But there's no rush. It's not as if he needs to answer roll call."

I smiled and she smiled back.

"You look good being a mother," I said.

"Thanks," she said. "It feels great too. I can't imagine life without him."

Lorraine dropped me off at my grandmother's house, arranging to meet up at her office sometime after four.

I knocked at the door several times before Clara came to see who it was.

"Hola Pelon," she said in greeting. "Your grandma in back. You come in."

"Hi Grandma," was all I could say before I choked up and the tears flowed.

She was sitting in a wheelchair surrounded by her garden and all she could manage was a soft smile and a wave of her hand. I went over to where she sat and hugged her as best I could.

The stroke had curtailed her speech and communication was very one sided. I told her about my work on the Encinitas farm and how I met Ima and what she was like and that I was going to marry her. I described Geoffrey and his house and the beach in Santa Barbara and all about the changing colors in Cadillac Michigan and the cold snowy winter that I spent there. When I was about to tell her about my last conversation with my mother, I saw that she was tired.

When Clara appeared at the back door, I called out. "I think my grandma needs to lie down," and I wheeled her up the ramp and Clara opened the door and took over from there. I walked to my old bedroom and looked through my bookshelf for a book that I had borrowed from one of my professors and had never returned. I found it and I said goodbye to my grandmother and told her I would be back the following day.

I left the house and walked over to Rodrigo's and knocked on the door, not really expecting to see him because school was still in session. But he appeared, still dressed in pajamas.

"Hey Pelon."

"Hey Rodrigo. I was going to leave you a message with your mom. Why aren't you in school? I thought your high school was year-round?"

"It is and it's a long story. Wanna come in?"

"Yeah I want to come in. I want to hear the long story too."

He moved aside to let me enter. "We can sit here if you like. My room is pretty messy right now."

"Right now?"

"Yeah right now. You sound like my mom."

"*U yu yui*," I said. "You're a little on edge. Take it down a notch will you. I didn't come to hassle you. I was just teasing."

"Sorry. Things aren't going so great for me right now."

"So what's going on?"

"It's kind of embarrassing."

"Can't be any more embarrassing then serving time in the joint like I have."

"You've been in the joint?"

"Yep, just got out last week."

"Damn Pelon, you're an ex-con. Why did you get popped?"

"It's a long story," I said.

"Tell me your long story and I'll tell you mine," Rodrigo said.

I told him all there was to tell, with much emphasis on Andre's misuse of the government's data collection programs and my innocence. I also told him about my engagement to Ima, but he also was most impressed by the offer I received to be a stuntman.

"That's so cool Pelon, you being in movies, making lots of money. That's really awesome dude. Maybe you can teach me some of your moves?"

"Sure I can run you through some drills. But right now it's my turn to hear your long story."

"It's not really a long story like yours Pelon. Mine is really pretty short, some guys at school want to kick my ass."

"Really, why is that?"

"They think I'm some sort of geeky nerd."

"You've been a geeky sort of nerd for a long time. Why now?" I asked.

"I had one of them for a math class and I wouldn't let him copy from my paper."

"That's it? That's the reason for all your troubles?"

"Why, do you think I should have let him copy my work?"

"No, but you could have offered to help him after class, you know like tutor him."

"I suppose I could have."

"You can still do it."

"I don' know. He's pretty pissed."

"I can go with you and help you smooth things over."

"You'd do that?"

"Of course. We can go right now if you'd like, well after you put some clothes on, I mean."

"Ha ha, you're so funny baldy," Rodrigo said.

When Rodrigo was dressed and ready, we went to 6th Avenue and boarded the bus that took us into town. From there we walked the rest of the way to the high school, arriving just as the students were leaving for the day.

"Damn Pelon, we should have taken the bus here to the school. I'm all hot and sweaty."

"I thought you were used to the desert heat, homie."

"Yeah but I'm not a damn lizard," he complained. "See that group over there Pelon, that's them," he said pointing with a nod of his head.

"Well, let's go over and have you make a proposal."

"I have all sorts of butterflies in my stomach, Pelon. You sure about this?"

"Of course. Everybody wants peace dude. It's just a matter of finding some agreements."

"And if you can't find those agreements?" Rodrigo asked. "What then?"

"Well then you have no choice but to fight, or run away and perhaps be forever taunted."

"Is that what happened to you? You ran away?"

"Sort of. My situation had a couple of layers of complexity to it. Initially running away was fighting and later fighting was running away."

"Whaaat?" Rodrigo asked.

I explained to Rodrigo what I meant by telling him that when I was being arrested by the Border Patrol, I thought about resisting.

"I could have kicked their ass and run away again, leaving them handcuffed to each other. But I went ahead and let them take me in. It was time to let go, to surrender to the events and allow them to unfold as they were meant to unfold."

"So maybe I should run away."

"I don't think so," I said. "You'd be running away out of fear, not because you are resisting some evil. There's a difference and you just have to be honest with yourself and examine your motives."

"Sometimes it's okay to run away though. Like when you're sure that staying may get you killed."

"That's true and you are the only one that can judge that level of danger. In this situation with me backing your play, the danger of you getting killed is quite low. But I think that a pure pacifist would say that one should never fight, no matter what the circumstances. So if you are a pure of heart pacifist go ahead and take a beating."

"What do you mean, pure of heart?"

"Well like Christ. He was pure of heart, loved everyone and everything and could never hurt anyone. That's why he could advocate turning the other cheek. Make sense?"

"That's crazy, Pelon. Nobody can turn the other cheek."

"Very few people can but there have been a few, Cesar Chavez, for one. Are you with me?"

"Yeah. I don't think I'm pure of heart. If I could kick their ass I would."

"Well that's honest. That came from the heart. So what do you want to do, Rodrigo?"

"I guess we can talk, see what he has to say."

"What's his name anyway?"

"Willy Espinoza."

We walked over to where a group of five boys were standing and they straightened up in anticipation of trouble when they saw Rodrigo and me approaching. I held up my hand in a gesture of peace.

"We just want to talk and see if we can avoid any trouble. That sound okay with you?"

One of the boys shrugged as if to say, 'let's hear it'.

I looked over at Rodrigo, letting him know that it was his play.

"I just want to say that I couldn't help Willy and maybe get caught for cheating but I should have told him, you know, that I could help him after school if he wants. That's it. That's all I want to say."

"Well what I got to say," Willy said, "is that you're a chicken shit lambion that wouldn't help a vato when he was down."

"Are you planning to go on to college Willy?" I asked the boy that Rodrigo had faced when he was talking.

"Thinking about it," he replied.

"That's good, real good," I said. "Here's the thing Willy, to get help on an exam is just for that day. But what you need and what Rodrigo is offering you, is a better understanding of math that will get you through all future exams. It's like that story about a hungry man. You give him a fish and he eats that day but if you teach him to fish, he eats for the rest of his life. Comprendes mendes?"

Willy nodded that he understood.

"And," I said. "I think Rodrigo would be a good resource for you to have. Out there in the world it's all about making good connections, developing a network of people that can give you a hand when you need it. And I think that you would also be a good resource for Rodrigo. You know many things that he doesn't. So it's not a one-sided kind of arrangement. There'll come a time that he may have to call on you. How's that sound?"

"I'll think about it," Willy said.

Two of the boys were off to the side whispering among themselves.

" 'Sup?" Willy asked them.

One of the boys that were whispering answered. "He's the dude on the video," motioning to me with a tilt of his head.

"What video?" Willy asked.

"The one I showed you this morning."

Willy studied me momentarily. "Yeah it is. You're the dude at the train depot. That was a cool move, dude." He smiled.

It was good from that point on. We talked about martial arts and about school and lousy teachers and what college was like. Rodrigo and I left feeling good about the way things had turned out.

This time we did take the bus back to the bus terminal.

"That was solid, Pelon. I owe you one. Will you be around for awhile?"

"No, I leave tomorrow, but I'll be texting you."

When we reached the terminal Rodrigo took a bus back to his house and I boarded a different one to the Congressman's office to meet up with Lorraine.

I sent her a text message on my new cell phone.

"on way 2 ur office. there in 20. Pelon"

She answered a little later. "good."

When I arrived, Lorraine was already waiting for me and we left quickly to pick up her son at the daycare.

"Have to get there before five or they charge me extra," she said.

"Are you on a tight budget? Doesn't White Elk send you money?"

"He does. He's been good about that and about calling to see how the baby is. Still I have to watch my money more carefully. Trying to put some away for a rainy day."

We picked up her son and decided that I would drive while she fed him.

"We are going to your grandfather's, no?"

"Yes, he said he would put some carne asada on the grill for us."

"What else?" I asked. "I didn't eat lunch and I'm starving."

"I'll make some rice and you can make a salad. He always has tortillas too," she said.

The drive to the reservation was as beautiful as always and I had to ask Lorraine why she wasn't living on it.

"Last time you said that you son was going to be born and raised a T.O. What changed? He's stuck all day in a childcare center."

"I know and I hate the way things are. I think they are about to change though."

"Really," I said. "Tell me more."

"The reason I've been saving money, not just now but even before my pregnancy is so that I can stop working and move back in with my grandfather."

"That's a great plan, Lorraine. You'll be a full time mother."

"Not only that, I mean being with him full time will be great, but I also want to get more serious about my spiritual duties. I had a powerful dream recently that I think is telling me to move in that direction."

"Can you tell me about it?" I asked.

"Sure and you're probably the only one I can tell, other than my grandfather. In this dream I was standing in front of a group of native women, some were dressed in beaded buckskins and others in colorful skirts and blouses, some even had beautiful shawls that they had wrapped around themselves. It was a large group and they were standing in two lines across from one another, forming a passage that I knew I was to walk through. The women were smiling and they had extremely happy contented faces and I too felt happy and content as I walked between them. When I emerged from the passage, a very beautiful woman came to me and placed an embroidered woolen mantle on my shoulders and led me away to a cave where I was seated and made to understand that I was to receive secret esoteric instruction. That was the end of the dream, although I know that it was just the beginning of my training."

"Wow," I said when I saw that she had finished her account. Maybe it was the sunset casting a golden light, but Lorraine looked radiantly beautiful in that moment, while she held her baby in her arms and he suckled at her breast.

She began humming what she later told me was a lullaby that she had learned from her grandmother and she stopped when she saw that her baby had fallen asleep. She put away her breast and sighed.

"Life is good, Pelon."

"Yep," I said, "Life is good."

"By the way I saw that video of you, it's had almost seventy thousand hits. You're a big star, homeboy."

"Yeah, you can tell everybody that you knew me when."

Otavio was out front watering some potted plants when we arrived.

"Howdy," he called out.

"Hi Otavio," I answered. "How you doing?"

"Doing real good. And you?"

"Me too." I answered. "I came to see my grandmother, and Lorraine and her baby, of course."

"That boy is something, no? I'm surprised he's asleep. He's always eating, that kid."

"How's the woodworking, Otavio?"

313

"Pretty good. I sold a table to a fellow that came around last week. Said he'd pick it up later but so far he hasn't come by. What about you? Lorraine told me that they locked you up for awhile."

"Just got out last week. I don't really know what I'll be doing just yet. I don't want to go back to Washington. Maybe I'll set up an office somewhere and practice law."

"In Tucson?"

"No, California I think."

"He's going into movies Grandfather. He's going to be one of those kick ass action heroes and he going to marry Ima, the girl that came for Christmas."

"She's kidding about the movies but I am getting married," I said.

"Congratulations Pelon," he said and began shaking my hand in earnest.

We sat down to eat and little was said until the baby woke up and Lorraine had to get up to attend to him.

"I need to tell you Otavio that I appreciate everything that you told me, you know about the trouble I was to undergo and about having to experience all that was happening to me. It was a great learning. So thank you."

"I don't think I did very much but thank you for saying it," he said.

"And also the sweat lodge, that was a great experience," I said. "Have you been having them regularly?"

"Oh sure. I have them pretty often," he answered.

"The time I came, there seemed to be quite a few that were not Native American."

"About half the group are always Anglos wanting to be part of something. So the sweat is one way for them to do this."

"Don't Native Americans object to non-Native people attending?"

"Sure, but I don't," he answered. "We are all brothers and sisters and we need to help each other honor the

Creator and live a balanced life. We are like the branches of a giant tree and the Creator is the trunk. People believe different things, some are Christians, some are Jews, some believe in Buddha, some in Mohammed, and some are like me, Native Americans. We live as different branches but the Creator, the trunk, gives us life and we can honor and respect everyone else. The sad thing is that right now, very few Anglo rituals and traditions help people understand that we are like the tree of life and instead they help to divide people."

"Absolutely. That's why I think that non-native people need to develop their own traditions, their own rituals, ones that come from their own cultural experience."

I told Otavio about the Halloween and the Summer Solstice events that I attended and how those two pagan celebrations seemed to resonate so strongly with contemporary times.

"I hear truth in your words Pelon."

Lorraine returned with the baby and we finished dinner and while Otavio rocked his grandson to sleep, Lorraine and I cleaned the kitchen.

"Can I crash at your place tonight Lorraine?"

"Sure, there's a fold out bed in the front room. I don't think it's a good idea for you to sleep with me," she answered.

"Agreed," I said. "It's strange that we have this really strong bond and yet we have never made love. But it seems to work to our advantage because we can continue to have a lifelong friendship without lying to anyone."

"That's one way of looking at it," she answered and continued cleaning counters.

I almost asked her if she thought there was another way of looking at our situation but I realized that there was and I didn't pursue it any further.

It was late in the evening when I drove us back to the city. Lorraine went to sleep with the baby in her arms.

There was no traffic for many miles and I was to the point of being mesmerized by the constancy of the darkness and the unfolding double yellow line that divided the two-lane highway. I began reviewing the day in order to stay awake.

I was surprised at how frail my grandmother had looked earlier that morning and how I had left her feeling that she was at the end of her days. I thought about her dramatic personality transformation after my mother had discovered her betrayal of my father. I wondered if, gradually or overnight, she had become the sweet and caring person who had eagerly provided a home for me when I came out of the juvi camp. This led me to thinking about the camp and the events that led to my arrest, about Rebecca and Segunda and my first fight with Puma. Then I thought about my second fight with Puma and then about what I told Rodrigo about turning the other cheek and about Christians and how they selectively chose what to embrace, very few embracing the turning of the other cheek and I smiled at that and I knew that The New Testament had layers of meaning and that each person could burrow down to the meaning that was appropriate to their level of understanding and development and that not everyone could turn the other cheek or give up their coat as well when someone took their cloak. I made a mental note to talk with Ima about this insight about The New Testament and I thought some more about Ima and this led me to think about the last evening we spent together and about Summer Solstice and about creating new ceremonies and then I remembered the temple and their chants and that singing opens the heart and how Aunt Marie also quietly chanted. I was about to think about Helga when I heard Lorraine.

"Where are we, Pelon?"

"We've just entered the city limits. We're almost there."

We arrived and I carried the diaper bag and opened the door. Lorraine went into the bedroom and put her baby in his crib and then gave me some linen for the foldout bed.

"Goodnight Pelon, I'm dead on my feet. I'll see you in the morning. I need to be up by six thirty. You okay with that?"

"No problem."

Lorraine shut the bedroom door and I went into the living room to prepare my bed and to call Ima.

"Hi, it's me," I said when she answered. "You're not in bed are you?"

"No, Dad and I are sitting outside talking. How was your day?"

"It went fine," I said. "I saw my grandmother and I'll go see her again tomorrow. She doesn't look that strong but it is what it is. I also spent time with Lorraine and her cute baby. We had dinner with her grandfather and I'm staying with her tonight. No spooning though, in case you were going to ask."

"I wasn't. But I'm glad you told me."

"How was your day Ima? Did you get the contract?"

"Yes I did. I was just telling Dad. RAIN's been around a long time so Dad knows their work."

"How is your dad?"

"He's good. He's here entertaining me with some old stories and smoking his cannabis cigarettes."

"Your dad is one of a kind. I have lots to tell you but I'll save it for when I get back."

"When's that?"

"I'll take the train tomorrow night and it'll get me into Los Angeles at five thirty in the morning and the train to Santa Barbara leaves at nine so I should be there before noon.

"OK Pelon. I miss you. Be safe."

"I miss you too. Goodnight."

The next day Lorraine woke me from a sound sleep. I was dreaming that my mother and I were walking through a shallow stream, our feet splashing water with every step. It was night and she was leading the way, pulling a red children's wagon loaded with food for a picnic that we were to have. The trees and bushes were alive with an other-worldly luminous glow and I was happy and content.

"Good morning Lorraine," I said. "You're moving pretty fast. Are you late?"

"No, this is the way I move so I won't be. Can you watch the baby while I shower?"

"Of course. Where is the little guy?"

"He's on my bed, sucking his toes."

I showered after she was dressed and had started making breakfast. We ate quickly and she told me that I could drop her off and keep the car.

"You won't need it?"

"No, I'm in the office all day."

"All right. Can I buy you lunch?"

"Sure come by at noon. We'll go to Anita's market and grab something there."

"Sounds good," I said.

My day was uneventful. I spent the morning with my grandmother, telling her about my recent travels and describing the people that I had met. I told her about Lorraine and her baby and how the father was being a jerk and that I was leaving on the train that evening. She had tears when I said goodbye and I left with tears in my eyes as well.

I drove to the Congressman's office for Lorraine and we went to Anita's and I ordered a chile relleno burro and she ordered a burro with machaca and egg.

"What are you doing this afternoon?" she asked when we were seated and eating our food.

"I'm just kicking back. I think I'll go to the University for a swim and then I want to drop in on one of my psychology professors and return a book that I borrowed and never returned. My train leaves at eight so I'll probably just hang out at the U until then. You should probably keep your car and just drop me off when we finish here."

"I won't see you later then?"

"Probably not. By the time you get off from work and pick up the baby, it'll be close to the time I need to be at the train station."

"You're right. It would be rushed. It's been too short a visit Pelon. When are you coming back?"

"Soon, I promise. My grandmother doesn't look very strong so I want to see her again before she passes. Any idea as to when you might quit working and move back to your grandfather's place?"

"Maybe as soon as next month. I want to give the Congressman enough time to find a replacement. It feels really good to be doing this Pelon. It's a different feeling to be so decisive. I feel strong and empowered, as if my will can accomplish anything."

"Wow! I'm sure that is a good feeling. I'm very happy for you. The Tohono O'Odham are lucky to have you."

We finished our lunch and she drove me to my Alma Mater. She parked and we both got out of the car and gave one another a long, heartfelt hug. We didn't say anything further and she got back into the car and drove off. I was very sad as I began walking.

The University was established in 1891 during the time that Arizona was a Territory. Back then, the residents of Tucson were vying with Phoenix for the real prize: the Insane Asylum, which had more jobs and money involved. Initially the residents of Tucson didn't appreciate the University much, but of course this attitude changed and this story is a favorite of professors and students. It's a nice looking campus. Most of the old buildings were constructed in red brick and new buildings continue with this look. Summer session was in progress and I encountered some students on campus, but very few by comparison to the regular school year, as I walked to my professor's office.

I was asked to come in when I knocked on his door, and I was greeted warmly when he saw me.

"Pelon. How are you? Let me give you a hug."

"Hi Dr. Shamas. Believe it or not, I'm bringing your book that I borrowed and had forgotten to return."

"Well, it's a good thing you did. I think I can still call off the book police who were looking for you," he said and laughed. "Did you ever read it?"

"Some, not all. But I was thinking of some of your ideas about play being a spiritual practice."

"It's all about having fun, Pelon. In India play and laughter are an integral part of spiritual development. So why are you now thinking about this? As I recall it didn't seem that interesting to you when you were in my classes."

"I guess I've changed."

"Did you have some life-altering experiences?" he asked with a big smile.

"A few," I answered. "I've had an interesting time since I received my Law Degree. Do you have time to talk?"

"I have a class that starts in ten minutes but after, I'm free for the rest of the afternoon. Can you come back?"

"Yeah as a matter of fact. Originally I was going for a swim before coming here but I thought I better check with you first. So now I can swim and come back. How long is your class?"

"A couple of hours before I can get back to the office. Will that work?"

"Sure. I'll see you back here."

The Olympic-size pool and the clear blue water reflecting an even bluer sky was very inviting and I immediately dove in and surrendered to the water's embrace. While in school I used to swim almost every day except on those rare exceptionally cold winter days.

There were twenty or so students in the pool, a mixed group of women and men, and I studied them after I had swum a few laps. Almost all were young and tattooed. There was one young mother with two children, but even she had a tattoo on one of her ankles. I also had a tattoo, one that a homeboy in juvi had inked on my arm below the shoulder. It was something that I had seen in a martial arts book and it showed a tree within the familiar yin yang circle, the branches and the roots symmetrical in size and shape situated above and below the curving centerline. It looked like a prison tattoo and I was never too keen on showing it, but since my conversation with Otavio I had a renewed respect and appreciation for my tat, knowing that now I could explain what he had envisioned: the branches representing all of the various religious and spiritual traditions, the trunk representing the Creator, His roots extending and holding firmly the entire world. Before Otavio's explanation whenever I had been asked what it was I would stumble and merely say that it was the Tree of Life. Hell now I could probably talk for an hour about its meaning. I laughed at myself.

I was lying in the shade when a ball rolled towards me and stopping it with my foot I saw that its owner was one of the young boys that was with the woman with the ankle tattoo. She was engaged in a conversation with a man and didn't notice or didn't care that her son was with me, a stranger. The boy had intentionally rolled it to me as a way of inviting me to play with him. He was about six and the other boy was about eight.

"Want to play?" he asked.

"Does your mother know you are asking a stranger to play with you?"

"No, she doesn't care. She's talking with her boyfriend."

"What game did you want to play?"

"You bounce the ball to me and I catch it and then I bounce it back to you."

"OK but let's stay in the shade," I said.

I stood up and began bouncing the ball back and forth to my young new friend. His brother came over and asked if he could play and soon the three of us were bouncing the ball.

A short while later the mother came and grabbed both boys by the hand and pulled them back to where she was sitting, without bothering to say anything to me. They did though.

I swam more laps, rested in the shade again and left after two hours to meet with my professor.

He had me jump right into my tale without any formalities and I told it slowly and in great detail, knowing that he would appreciate such a recounting. He asked few questions and let me unfold the story as it happened, but was particularly intrigued by Aunt Marie's India experience as he had also had a similar experience and he promised to tell me about it later.

It was late by the time I finished, the sun low in the horizon. I had talked for a couple of hours nearly nonstop.

"That was some journey you took," he said. "But it's not finished is it?"

"Not by a long shot," I answered.

"I think I have a piece that you might find of interest and want to add."

"Really, what is that?" I asked.

"I started something called Global Chant that I think qualifies as a new age ceremony. There are maybe a hundred or so people that get together once a week to chant spiritual songs that literally come from all over the world. We have songs that are Sufi, Hindu, Native American, Jewish, Christian of course, Buddhist, Islamic, Hawaiian, and a few others. It's a great way to embrace the world and all its spiritual traditions."

"It sounds like something I should experience, but my train leaves at eight tonight. Maybe when I come back next time."

"It must be meant to happen because we meet today at six here on campus at the Newman Center. You should come if you're really interested."

"Synchronicity, huh?" I asked.

"Absolutely."

That night as the train rocked and squeaked, pelted by rain from a powerful thunderstorm, there were chants from Global Chant running inside my head, songs that spoke of Mother Earth, of flowing ocean waves, of forgiveness, of God's everlasting peace, of Divine Mother, of the need to be like hollow bamboo and allow love to shine through. And I kept reliving that evening, recalling that some of those chants were in English but that many were in their original language and that I had difficulty in pronouncing the words.

And I remembered that there were instruments that accompanied the chanting: drums from many parts of the world, a violin, a didgeridoo, an electric bass, several guitars, tambourines, cymbals, bells and assorted gourds and rattles. And there were some people that danced, some that sat quietly in prayer, and some that chanted every song with strong voices, hitting the hard-to-reach keys. It was all great fun, and at the end we chanted OM three times, gathered in a large circle, and one at a time gave our name. There was hugging afterwards but I didn't stay long for that part, as I had to walk to the train station, lest I miss my train.

Hours later my excitement was finally overtaken by sleep, and I didn't awake until I heard the conductor announce that Los Angeles was the next and last stop and that everyone should gather their belongings.

I was still groggy from sleep and not until I had walked through the long tunnel to the seating area did I realize that the Tucson train was two hours late in arriving and that my Santa Barbara train was about ready to leave. I had to double back and board.

I had a window seat and looked out as the train bound for Santa Barbara left the station, marveling at the capacity of humanity to create and live amidst such ugliness. This view is not the view of California that one sees during the Rose parade or the Rose Bowl that takes place in affluent Pasadena neighborhoods. No, this train ride through Los Angeles proper and through the valley, gives passengers a different perspective, the tracks seemingly running down back alleys and side streets that one never sees when traveling by car. Train passengers see the underbelly of this very large metropolitan area; fenced off industrial facilities and factories, their yards strewn with material for their work, lumber, metal and plastic containers of every size and shape conceivable, discarded vehicles, stacks of metal parts for outdated industrial machinery and every flat surface vandalized with graffiti. One also sees the back yards of residential dwellings, poor homes mostly, for what person of wealth would live adjacent to railroad tracks.

I was glad when the train reached Oxnard, where one could begin to see the ocean in the distance slowly becoming a panoramic view of the blue Pacific.

When the train reached the City of Ventura, which stretches along the coast somewhat like Santa Barbara, only larger and less attractive with its mishmash of box-like buildings, I called Ima and told her that I would arrive in thirty minutes.

I saw Ima waiting as soon as I stepped off the train and we walked towards one another, hugged with one arm and began walking to Geoffrey's car.

324

"I'm glad you're back, Pelon. It feels as if we have cleared pending affairs and are ready to get on with our life together."

"I feel that too. But I'm on looser ground, not really sure what I need to do next, or where."

"But we can stay here with Dad for awhile, can't we? I did land that consulting job and it's at least a couple of months of work. I would hate to be apart again or to have to commute."

"No, no more being apart. If Geoffrey can put up with us, I don't feel any pressure to jump into anything right away."

"You know Dad loves having us here. He must have been very lonely all those years I have been away."

"I would miss you too my Hindu Goddess."

"You're just saying that to bed me, like that night on Halloween."

"Naw, actually I was thinking of practicing abstinence for a while. You know, to get me into the spiritual frame of mind of 2012."

"Oh really. Well I'll have you know that everything being said about sex is that it's good for us and that demonizing sex is old energy at work. There's a lot of that going on, people with old energy refusing to let go. It's happening in politics, in banking, in education. People don't want to let go of the familiar, especially when it's their bread and butter."

"I was just kidding. You don't have to convince me that sex is good, but I'm glad the stigma is being done away with."

"So what interesting experiences did you have in Tucson?" she asked.

"Well let me see," I said, and thought about my trip and what I could say to Ima. "There are three or four things that I wanted to share with you. One is about Lorraine."

"What about Lorraine? Is she getting married to that James fellow?"

"I don't think so. And she seems to be fine with it and has totally embraced being a mother."

"That's positive."

"Yeah it is. The other thing is that she has decided to quit her job, move back to the reservation, and prepare herself to become a medicine woman."

"Gosh that seems like a big change," Ima said.

"It's huge. But she's very determined, so I don't see that she'll have any problems."

"What's her baby like?"

"Small and fat and with a lot of black hair on his head. He's very cute too."

"Do you want to have some cute babies with me, Pelon?"

"Hell yes. Barefoot and pregnant is how we like our women," I said laughing.

"Mexicans liking their women barefoot and pregnant reminds me to tell you, that my dad arranged for a doctor friend of his to inseminate Sara. She and Miguel are now expecting."

"Really? Wow! That's good news. I bet Miguel is really happy. Thanks for doing that Ima. You're very special."

"Sorry, I didn't mean to pull you off on a tangent. Finish telling me about your trip."

"I think I mentioned that my grandmother looks very weak and weary. I don't think she'll be around much longer. It was a big shock to see her that way."

"It's good that you went to see her."

"Yes, it was." I paused to think of my grandmother and offered a quick silent prayer. "Death is strange, Ima. I remember putting down our dog when I was about seven. One minute he was with us, wiggling on the vet's table and the next he was gone. In a flash he was no more."

"I think so too," she said. "I think about Dad and how much he has slowed down. I wonder how much longer he'll be with us."

"In my head I believe in reincarnation and that really there is no death, but my heart hurts when I think of my grandmother dying," I commented.

"I feel the same about my father. I know it's no great consolation to pass this on, but for what it's worth, they say that the energy that was a loved one never ceases to exist. That when we leave our own body, those we loved will be waiting on the other side of the veil to greet us."

"Doesn't the soul of the deceased reincarnate?"

"Yes but the essence of that soul's other incarnations remains as an energy. I think it is like a living holographic image."

"That is a comforting thought. I like it," I said, "although I hope not to put it to the test anytime soon."

"Pelon! Of course you're not," Ima said emphatically.

"I was just kidding. Are you in a hurry to get back to your dad's?"

"No not really. Do you want me to stop someplace?"

"Can we go to Shoreline Park and take in the ocean?"

"Sure. Did you miss the water?"

"I did. And Tucson was very hot. It'll be nice to feel the ocean breeze."

We drove up the hill and parked the car and walked across the grassy area to an empty bench, situated along the cliff that overlooked the ocean.

"This is magnificent, Ima," I said, looking at the vast Pacific Ocean below and in front of us as far as the eye could see, its white tipped waves breaking on the undulating shore below, going north and disappearing behind the cliffs at the UCSB campus. "What is it about the ocean that leaves me so tranquil and contemplative?" I asked.

"It does it for me also," Ima said.

We didn't talk for a good while. Finally she said, "I saw the video of you at the train station. It was amazing. Are you thinking about pursuing a career as a stuntman?"

"I'm not planning on it. But I haven't ruled it out. Might be fun. Would you mind?"

"Not if you have a passion for that kind of action. You ought to do something that gives you joy," she answered.

"It is about following the heart isn't it? This reminds me that I have to tell you about a gathering I attended, something one of my professors started. I really think that it is the sort of New Age gathering that will help create this new world that you tell me is emerging."

.#.#.#.

EPILOGUE

Time seemed different in 2012. Mostly it seemed to go too quickly for me and everyone else, the days, weeks, and months flying by, leaving us constantly questioning what day of the week it was, or if we were really already at midyear, etc. We all wondered what was causing such an aberration, I especially, since I always found enough time to accomplish my tasks. How is that possible I would ask, that time seems to be moving faster than normal and yet I had time to do whatever needed doing?

Ima said that our concept of time, our thinking that it was linear was a characteristic only found in the 3rd dimension and that in the higher dimension we were moving into, there was no past or future, that all that existed was the present, the now. Therefore in the now there was plenty of time, seemingly time expanded to afford us whatever we needed. Naturally I scratched my head as it was difficult for me to wrap my mind around the concept. That was not the only concept difficult to comprehend. There were others. One of those was that there are multiple universes and that in all probability we exist somewhere else. This was a statement by scientists, unknowingly affirming what Ima had read in various channeled messages. The example given by scientists is one that utilizes a deck of cards that are shuffled and dealt to the players. The exact hand that a given player receives in all probability will be obtained again if the deck is shuffled and dealt an infinite number of times. Perhaps that exact hand will be dealt a number of times not just twice. Therefore scientists conclude that in our infinite universe a similar condition exists and that in all probability there are other universes and that everyone exists somewhere else, maybe in many other places. Wow! I thought, another me. That can't be!

Or how about the concept of entanglement where sub-atomic particles that at one time interacted physically and were then separated, will both show reactions if only one of them is manipulated. And this sort of entanglement occurs even when the particles are separated by great distances. How is that possible? I asked Ima. She said that physics and other sciences in our third dimensional Earth are unique to our planet and that in the more prevalent higher dimensions, the laws of physics and other sciences can be quite different. As we, and our planet Earth, move into a higher dimension our scientists will begin to make further discoveries that will bring more clarity and understanding.

But for me the most difficult idea to understand is that of energy—energy radiating from the galactic center, energy radiating from the heavenly bodies, energy that becomes part of the Planet Earth's grid, energy that becomes part of humanity. And according to Ima, humanity's consciousness is key to the energy that is available. She used Plutonium as a metaphor for a person's consciousness, so that just as that element radiates energy so does a person give off energy in accordance with a person's development. And as humanity continues to evolve, the collective consciousness is grounding the energy that is creating a new world based on love and compassion.

Thus it was with many expectations that I, and many millions of people, anxiously awaited the end of 2012 and entry into the new era. To say that it was the greatest and the most palpable letdown would be the understatement of the new millennium.

We sailed past the end without so much as a hiccup. The hair on the back of my neck didn't stand on end, I didn't see flashing lights, there weren't any sightings of

UFO's or of extraterrestrials, no mass disappearances of cult members, no sinkholes that swallowed millions, no second coming of Christ to take his brethren into heaven, no fiery chariots in the sky with ascended New Agers, no volcanoes or tsunamis tearing apart cities and towns.

Hell, there was nothing at all, nada, zilch.

Ima said that humanity and our Earth had transitioned successfully and that from that moment on changes would begin to manifest, perhaps at first imperceptibly to the great majority, as is the growth of a seed buried within fertile soil obscured until suddenly it erupts and reaches for the light of the sun. I guess we'll just have to see how things develop in 2013 and beyond. Will we be able to collectively create a more just and equitable world, a world without war and hardship?

What was very perceptible in 2013 was the transparency of the government's surveillance apparatus when Edward Snowden released the documentation that he had stolen.

Andre was one of the first casualties of that transparency and he was taken to task and lost his position for the use of the powers of his office to intimidate and coerce various individuals for what appeared to be totally unrelated to government business. Under questioning by a Senate Committee he pleaded the Fifth Amendment to much of the questioning and he came out looking like the nefarious individual that he was.

The NRDC increased their efforts to expose bribery among elected officials once Andre was out of the way. They had already gathered evidence from other sources on several elected officials but once the threat of Andre was removed they released the documentation Esperanza obtained from Randolph Hamilton's office. Even Congressman Jimmy was caught in that web and he never returned to Washington.

My friends Robert, Esperanza, Naomi and Farley all continue working in Washington and Ima and I see them occasionally there or here on the West Coast. Helga married her beau Rufus McGuire and we exchange Christmas cards. Ima and I baptized Miguel and Sara's boy, whom they named Geoffrey, but you would think that Geoffrey was the godfather the way he spoils the child. Ima and I live with her dad, an arrangement that for now seems more than satisfactory.

I end this at this time, as I am due on the set in twenty minutes to shoot a violent fight scene. And yes, I do find there is joy in that.

.#.#.#.

ABOUT THE AUTHOR

Antonio Solis Gomez was born in El Paso, Texas but moved to East Los Angeles when he was nine. He graduated from East Los Angeles Community College and from Cal State Los Angeles.

He worked as a social worker for several nonprofit agencies and was one of the founders of the Chicano literary magazine <u>Con Safos: Reflections of Life in the Barrio</u>. Later he moved to Tucson, Arizona and received a Masters in Library Science from the University of Arizona. He worked as a librarian until he retired from the Kellogg Foundation. He now lives in Tucson with his wife Margaret.